ESCAPING
YUGOSLAVIA

Printed in Australia

Cover and internal design by Shawline Publishing Group Pty Ltd

First printing: July 2024

Shawline Publishing Group Pty Ltd

www.shawlinepublishing.com.au

Paperback ISBN 978-1-9231-7124-4

eBook ISBN 978-1-9231-7136-7

Hardback ISBN 978-1-9231-7148-0

Distributed by Shawline Distribution and Lightning Source Global

Shawline Publishing Group acknowledges the traditional owners of the land and pays respects to Elders, past, present and future.

A catalogue record for this work is available from the National Library of Australia

ESCAPING
YUGOSLAVIA

LEONARD KOPILAS

To my father, Rajko Kopilas, who did what was necessary to create a better life.

CHAPTER 1

Raj would always remember the strange men.

The harrowing incident happened one freezing winter's night in 1946 when Raj was just six years of age. It would remain one of his earliest and most unpleasant memories and, after the initial shock wore off, would shape his view of the world for the rest of his life. The visit from these uninvited guests created a phantom in the young man's mind that filtered his decisions from that day on and Raj never forgot and never forgave.

Dinner was simple that night, as it was most of the time. The last of the slaughtered pig from a week earlier sat thinly sliced atop a wooden platter, a pinkish-brown deliciousness that emanated heat and steam, filling Raj's nostrils with a simple joy. It was indeed a treat, with the rest of the swine's flesh to be cured or smoked as refrigeration was unaffordable at that time. The soup that accompanied it was thick and salty, laden with boiled carrots, potatoes and onions. Hard, dark bread was a staple in the household; the satiating carbohydrate was cheap and plentiful and made his mother's hands tough and dry from the years of kneading.

The aroma of dinner was exacerbated by an empty stomach and a freezing winter. Neither Raj nor his siblings had left the home that particular day. The bite of cold in the Balkan Mountains was severe, especially for a child of six years. The freezing cold was just as great a risk to children as was the falling snow, with sudden and rapid storms that could trap the most experienced woodsman in a dreaded maze of perpetual white as visibility just vanished. The winter winds at such a high altitude were also extremely hazardous, breaking branches and felling trees as the tremendous force of air pushed the deadly freeze into every corner of their world. The snow had fallen hard for the past few days and, if it wasn't for the brave men of the village, communication between the farmers would cease to exist. As it was, leaving the house would only be risked for absolute necessities, while leaving the town would be undeniably foolhardy.

But still the men came.

Prayers were said before the first bite. The fire that baked the bread kept the home warm too, and the family's two cats showed their appreciation by sleeping spread out on the warm stone in front of the roaring flame. A few well-placed candles helped brighten the room as well, illuminating the meals before them as shadows danced against the old, stone walls. Raj focused on his plate as he unconsciously mumbled his thanks to the heavenly hosts. His mouth salivated and fingers itched for dinner to begin.

'Amen.'

The final blessed word was a relief. Raj ignored the cutlery, which allowed him a split-second start toward the food and a larger initial portion than his slower siblings. For his age, his technique was flawless, dipping his bread into the broth before him with one hand while grabbing a cutlet of meat from the platter with the other. The din was wordless now, with only the primal crackle of fire and consumption of food, filling the air.

'Slow down, Raj.' His father broke the silence. 'No one will steal it off your plate.'

As if spurred on by those words, his older brother Vlad reached over to take a piece of meat from under his nose.

'Vlad,' Raj's mother snapped, offering a well-worn look that posed more of a threat than mere words ever could.

Raj kept eating, chewing faster to fit more in while his jaw started to tire from the incessant, rapid movement. His brothers and sisters must have been starving too, as they spoke no words and chewed vigorously themselves.

'Mirko.' Raj's mother looked at his father. 'Did you put Chomp in the barn?'

'Sure did,' answered his father. 'Why?'

'He's barking at something out there.' His mother had keen ears.

In unison, everyone suddenly stopped chewing and listened.

'So he is.' Raj wasn't sure if his father sounded surprised at the dog barking in this weather or that his mother could actually hear it through the din. 'What could be out there now?'

'Could just be a rat,' offered his mother then returned to her meal. 'Even rodents need shelter in this weather.'

Raj stopped his feasting to take a drink. A little sip of water was all he needed to keep the food moving and clear his mouth for the next round. His eldest brother Krizan burped aloud, which drew the ire of his father.

'If you want to be a pig,' his father scolded, 'you can eat outside in the pen, if you like.'

'Beg pardon,' whispered Kriz, embarrassed.

Raj's dad, Mirko, was a well-respected man in the village to whom many came to seek counsel. Mirko had a great respect for tradition, both patriotic and religious, often telling stories to the children that were passed down through the generations. But, as he taught Raj often, good manners were beyond mere tradition; they were an intrinsic virtue and a sign of class that transcended social status or educational pedigree.

'You might want to check on him, dear,' suggested Raj's mother, worried about their pet dog Chomp. 'He hasn't stopped barking.'

'I'll just finish this...' But Mirko's voice was cut off by a loud rap at the door.

'God almighty, who could be out there now?' His mother sounded genuinely surprised.

'I'll get it,' insisted Mila, Raj's youngest sister. She jumped off her stool and was ever ready for a social event.

Raj kept eating, as did the other two boys. Manda, the eldest sister and most cautious in the family, put her spoon down and stared in anticipation at the door.

'Wait, Mila,' her father warned. 'I'll get it.'

So Mila stopped in her tracks, looking a little disappointed. Another knock cracked at the door; this time louder than the first.

'Hold on,' Mirko yelled.

'Brother,' came a distant voice from beyond the door, 'we can't hold for much longer, it's freezing out here.'

'Who is it?' asked Mirko, purposefully slowing his gait. 'Who's out there?'

'Brother.' The strange voice pleaded this time, a little louder, thumping at the door now. 'By the grace of God, please let us in.'

'Gather the children, Kata.' Mirko's voice turned hard, with an edge that demanded respect. He grabbed a walking stick resting near the front door. With the stick now in play, both cats instantly decided they were warm enough before silently darting from the scene.

'Come to me, kids,' Raj's mother immediately called.

The children had already stopped eating, mystified by the exchange at the front door. They scampered around the table and sat beside their mother. Kata grabbed her youngest offspring closest to her; Mila nestled in her lap and Raj snuggled as close as he could before reaching to the table for another slice of crusty bread.

'Brother, please.'

Mirko cautiously lifted the timber bar that held the door in place, but before he could pull the door toward himself the outsider pushed hard and barged his way in.

'What's wrong with you?' the stranger asked brusquely, almost shouting, as he looked down at Mirko who lay on his back after taking the surprise hit from the door. 'A brother could freeze out there.' The man coolly smiled, taking off his fur-woven head cover and shaking snow all over Raj's father. There was no warmth to this stranger's charm, and his actions did nothing to assuage the family's trepidation.

'Does Tata have another brother?' Raj stopped chewing and enquired to no one in particular.

Raj had a large immediate family, and an even larger cohort of cousins, uncles and aunties, but he had never seen this brother before. The only familiarity the strange man showed came from the smell he had brought with him. Raj knew that smell; his father called it the devil's brew, or Rakija, and cautioned all his children against acquiring the taste.

'No,' Raj's mother replied, 'this man is no...'

'As usual the children show us the way,' the strange man interjected lightly, 'after all, we are all brothers in this lovely land, all comrades working to the same goal.'

'You're no brother of mine,' cursed Mirko, but as he tried to rise to his feet the stranger slapped him across the top of the head with his snow-covered hat, sprinkling a slurry around the rising man, then the stranger kicked Raj's father in the chest, forcing him back to the floor.

'Now, now, Miki,' the man mocked. He reached down and grabbed the thin walking stick that lay across the floor. 'Is this how you welcome *all* of your guests?'

The cold was now filling the room from the doorway left ajar and Chomp's incessant bark was heard far more clearly through the opening. A couple of candles had become extinguished adding both a touch of darkness and further suspense to the space. Raj and his siblings huddled closer to their mother and watched uncomfortably as the shadow of the stranger danced across the room.

'Slavek, shut that dog up!' Another man peered through the door and grunted an indistinguishable answer before disappearing.

'What do you want?' asked Raj's mother.

'Oh, my lovely sister, Kata.' The man's smile exuded a dark sarcasm; in fact, his intimate knowledge of everyone's identity only heightened the tension in the room. 'We want what everyone wants.' He raised Mirko's cane and pointed around the room as he spoke. 'A warm fire, a fine meal and a safe home.'

'You could start by closing the door,' Kata spat back, her intuition overruling any logic required to ease the situation. 'The poor kids will freeze.'

The strange man made his way to the table, ignoring Raj's mother completely. As he approached, he reached beneath his coat and drew a broad hunting knife. Mirko leapt to his feet as Kata hugged the children closer.

'Petar!' commanded the stranger and a third man suddenly entered the domain, a long-barrelled rifle in his hands, pointed directly at Raj's father. 'You should stay down, Miki.'

'Leave my family alone.' Mirko's ire began to show, but he made no further move toward the antagonist. 'What do you fucking want, anyway?'

'Do you hear this, Petar?' the man smiled at his gun-slinging colleague, then shook his head. 'No one listens anymore. I just told you what I want, Miki, but you seem to be hard of hearing.' And with those words, he quickly turned and smashed the butt of his knife into Mirko's forehead. Raj's father stumbled back to the floor, his hands holding his face, which only partially stopped the crimson flow from smearing the floor.

'Tata!' Raj cried, tears streaming down his face. Mila, too, was in tears.

'Is Tata alright?' whispered Manda to their sobbing mother.

The older boys breathed heavily, but their mother gripped them tighter as to avoid them acting foolishly. Their hearts were pounding and sweat glistened across everyone's face. The temperature grew considerably warmer even with the door open and the freezing mountain winds circulating. The distant dog bark accelerated both in tempo and volume only heightening the fear and confusion in that little stone room.

The stranger turned his attention back to the table and nonchalantly flipped his bloody knife around. With a stab he gorged a large piece of pork from a plate then ever so slowly slid it off his glistening blade with his tongue and teeth, not once taking his eyes off Raj's mother.

'How often do you eat meat, Kata?' asked the man, chewing purposefully with his mouth open, meat juice flowing onto his stubbly chin, his left foot now casually resting next to the plates on the dinner table.

'Take your feet off the table, please?' Raj's mother held back her tears, but the disdain in her tone was ever clear.

'If you joined the Party' – the man totally ignored her once again – 'you would enjoy it daily!'

'You're godless,' Mirko interjected, 'and drunk.' He still bled but seemed to have retained his composure slightly as he began rising to his feet yet again. 'You and all yours are godless. No soul. Not even the devil would waste his time in your precious Party.'

'You have a hard time taking orders, Miki.' The stranger smiled, tapping the walking stick in a sign of frustration.

'We fought your kind for years,' Mirko proudly announced. 'If all you're doing here is looking for members, you can fuck off right now.'

'Oh, Mirko the wise!' The stranger didn't seem to be leaving in a hurry. 'It seems to me you're still fighting.' The man appeared a little more irritated with Mirko's insolence. He continued chewing but more aggressively than before.

'Has no one told you?' the man spoke faster now and turned to face Raj's father. 'You lost! The war has been over for years. Your God and Jesus were defeated. Your Hitler and Himmler were smashed. Your generals and priests were slaughtered.' A sinister laugh followed the man's gaze as he turned to the crucifix hanging above the fireplace.

'Go on.' He seemed to enjoy pointing with Mirko's stick, particularly at the holy symbol. 'Say your useless prayers.'

He threw Mirko's walking stick into the fire as he walked across the chamber and violently tore the wooden cross off the wall, throwing it at Mirko before spitting a chunk of masticated pork at his feet. As his final insult, he stood with his back to the crackling fire before stretching both arms wide in an emulation of the crucifixion of Christ, his shadow now ominously spreading even further across the small room, almost enveloping everyone beneath it. The sinister stranger then looked at the ceiling and took a deep breath before making an announcement. 'Welcome to Yugoslavia!'

Mirko was on his feet now, with crucifix in hand. A blood smeared forehead enhanced the anger in his eyes. His body looked tense and his breath moved fast. Petar was still pointing the barrel at Mirko's head, but his hands were now trembling and he had taken an inadvertent step backward; the threat was clearly over and a violent reality was emerging. Even the menacing stranger, who sarcastically chewed everyone's ear off moments earlier, stood silent and focused, with his arms back at his side and knees slightly bent, ready to pounce with blade still in hand. The youngest two children, Raj and Mila, were openly crying now, with their mother Kata still holding tight as silent tears also ran down her cheeks.

Bang.

The distant shot rang from the outside cold; its echo was quickly swallowed by the wind. The dog's continual bark now fell silent; the beast's final act relieved all the tension in the room.

'Mama?' Krizan asked. 'What was that?'

'Hush now,' their mother consoled, 'everything will be alright.' But her tears told a different tale, as did the quiver in her voice.

'What have you done?' Raj's father turned from stoic to inquisitive, an authentic surprise overtook him as he suddenly ignored the intruders and walked to the door.

As a final strategy, the leading stranger pulled out a small pistol and aimed it coldly toward Mirko's head.

'Keep walking.' The strange man was confident once again. 'We can finish our conversation outside. You might just meet your God tonight.'

The tension arose once more. The execution of the family dog was devastating, but now the threat had reached a new level.

'No, no, no,' Raj's mother cried, raising her voice at every word.

'Mama?' questioned little Mila.

'No, no.' The matriarch seemed lost to her children.

'Mama?' This time Raj looked to his mother.

'No... no...' The men had left Kata and her children to themselves.

The wind gathered momentum and blasted an icy breath into the room forcing the remaining candles to dance violently before extinguishing their tiny flames. The hearth still burned, but the fire's roar no longer held sway in that room; the flame was now forced to submit to the wind's domination. The diminishing fire reflected perfectly the hopelessness engulfing the young family.

'Mama, where are they taking Tata?' Vlad asked in a tone that was not eager to hear a truthful answer.

'We should go to him,' offered Krizan, the eldest sibling. 'We can help.'

'No, no, no.' Their mother tried to grip all five children at once and raised her tone after hearing her son's idea, but her arms were nowhere near wide enough, and just as her husband's fate seemed out of her hands, so was the control of her eldest children.

'We've got to do something, Mama,' Krizan desperately suggested.

'What are you going to do?' Kata answered meekly, her voice losing its earlier assured authority.

'Grab a knife, Vlad,' Kriz ordered. 'You too, Manda.' He got up and slipped away from the table.

'Me?' Manda sounded shocked. 'A knife? What? Do I need to, Mama?'

'Do I need a knife too, Kriz?' asked little Raj, confused by the ordeal.

'Don't be silly,' Mila told her younger brother. 'Only the older kids can carry knives. I'll get mine ready, Kriz.'

'No, you won't,' Kriz commanded. 'Stay with Mum. You too, Manda. Come on, Vlad.'

'Are you sure?' asked Vlad.

Krizan didn't offer an answer and both boys made their way toward the doorway and into the cold and dark of the outside world. A step away from breaching the threshold and a familiar, but louder, sound was once again heard...

Bang.

A few moments later Mirko came stumbling into the house, snow covering his head and blood pouring out of his left arm. The Communists only injured him, but the same couldn't be said for the family dog. Kata and the older children rushed about getting all that was required to tend to her husbands' wound while Raj and his youngest sister sat with their father and hugged him while crying.

'It's okay, kids.' The injured patriarch tried to comfort the little ones. 'I'll be fine. It's just a scratch.'

'Why would those bad men do this?' asked Mila, sniffling between words.

'I don't know, child,' answered Mirko, giving her a kiss on the forehead. 'But I do know in this country now most people do things for one of two reasons: they are either hungry or they are greedy.'

CHAPTER 2

School began the same way every day; a devoted pledge to the united nations, which were amalgamated into the southern European state known as Yugoslavia. The words were full of loyalist rhetoric and sprinkled with disdain for any opposing system of belief, political or otherwise. The fertile lands were praised and the natural beauty of the terrain was also heavily mentioned. The history of the area was not so revered, as the country was still quite young and, apart from years of tension between the current political bedfellows, there really was no combined history to speak of.

The bravery and strength of the people were celebrated and finally, the leaders were extolled. The students had to be heard loudly and clearly praising the new nation lest they experience the corporal punishment met to those foolhardy enough to rebel. But a strong voice was not enough. A proud posture, straight and true, had to also accompany the sounds. Shoulders were back, chests were out and chins were up as the children belted out the morning oath. Furthermore, all the students' eyes had to be wide open and beaming toward the framed photographs hanging on each and every classroom wall: Karl Marx, Vladimir Lenin, Joseph Stalin and Marshall Tito. The future might see these figures as the four horsemen of the Apocalypse, but to the children staring up at the images, they were four old men who saved the combined Slavic nations from the grip of the evil capitalist empire.

The indoctrination began from the first grade. The Communist Party knew the youngsters were the future and they also knew many of the children's parents did not share the same political enthusiasm as the ruling class. So, apart from the morning pledge, students were separated into groups that either belonged to the Party or didn't. The mash of cultures and languages that formed the country were generally overlooked in the classroom, but the political affiliations were of utmost importance. Keeping pressure on the family at home could be coaxed from within if the children were taught right. Beliefs about God and dialect, righteousness and history, even philosophy and morality, were all malleable in children of primary school age. So, the students were hammered in every possible lesson with the virtues of the Party, in the hope they would grow up and see the folly of their parents' ways.

This meant very little to Raj when he first began school. The words repeated every morning were vacuous to a child of six years, but after the cane lashed his legs a couple of times for being too softly spoken during the ritual pledge, he at least learned the importance of the volume and appearance required. By his fourth year, and with the help of his brothers, he had a far greater sense of what was really going on. Raj grew up fast and had learned his place in the order of the institution.

His brothers were older and had now moved on; Kriz was in the preliminary stages with the clergy, while Vlad was farming full-time with the family. Raj's sisters were not allowed at school, as only Communist girls had the right to become educated. Now, at ten years of age and in his fourth elementary year, and alone in the school system, Raj knew the ropes quite well. He understood that the communist families had better stationary, and better clothing, and better desks, and better chairs, and better... well, everything. He also learned that openly questioning the logic behind such protocols only ended up with more lashings.

'Raj!' his teacher yelled at him.

Raj was staring out through the window, looking at the old bus passing through the town beyond the school grounds. Every day, just before lunchtime, the large, slow diesel engine could be heard chugging through the town's centre. By bus, Raj imagined it would take no time at all from his home, but since local bus rides were only for Party members, the trip was a particularly exhaustive hour by foot. Raj traversed along the ridge of a small hill for half an hour before making his way down a well-worn track. He then navigated over an area of mud flats that remained relatively dry through the spring and summer months, before moving downhill once more, passing through a valley that eventually became the small town of Siroki Brijeg.

Unfortunately, State School No 1275 was on the other side of the town, so it took even longer before he reached his scholarly destination.

The travel during winter was far less appealing. The freezing wind and pelting rain were all part of the daily journey when the cold season was in control. The mud flats turned to bogs, which meant a longer journey to a bridge further away, and if it snowed heavily then school would often be missed. Grades one to four were free and a compulsory requirement by the state, and the education department would visit the homes of absentees, regardless of the weather. After the fourth grade, non-Party members would have to pay a fee if they wanted their children to be further educated.

'Raj!' his teacher yelled again, but Raj was oblivious.

His head was spinning into foreign lands and strange customs that he only ever witnessed from the pictures in the specifically approved books that were allowed at school. His older brother had stolen several books from the library over the years and Raj loved looking at the pictures of the different places and cultures of the world. Eventually, as his reading improved, Raj would learn the names of famous cities, landmarks and histories that were featured in those books. He would learn about strange and beautiful beasts that were indigenous to these foreign lands, and he would see how different people looked and dressed around the globe. Now, every day when the old bus rambled past, Raj's thoughts drifted to imaginary places that he might one day see for himself. He wondered where from, or where to, were those mysterious bus travellers moving, and how long would it be before he too, was travelling far away from this place.

Smack.

The thump shook him out of his day dream as Mrs Ivanovic angrily splintered her ruler on Raj's desk.

'You need to wake up, sir,' the elderly teacher sharply stated. 'In more ways than one.'

All the students had to address the male teachers as 'sir' and the female teachers as 'madam'. Mrs Ivanovic ensured this was remembered by calling all the male students 'sir' as well.

'Yes, sir,' Raj playfully replied. The entire class murmured with a suppressed laughter lest they too faced the wrath of the old lady, although the smiles on each child's face could hardly contain the level of entertainment just experienced.

'Is that the way it is, *sir?*' she smirked confidently at Raj before casually looking around the class, silencing the children with her deadly gaze.

'Perhaps it's time for a visit to Colonel Raspic, *sir*. Would anyone else like to join him?'

Raj thought it was impossible for the room to get any quieter, but at the mere mention of the colonel's name, the silence almost turned into a vacuum. All the students immediately faced forward and looked down at their desks, busying themselves with their schoolwork, or at least making it appear so.

'I didn't think so.' Mrs Ivanovic sounded pleased. 'So I guess it's just you... *sir*.'

Raj took a deep breath. Over the years he had been to visit the principal on occasion for smaller offences. The punishment was usually a few lashings across the palms, or the buttocks, acting as a sturdy reminder of the transgressions every time he later used his hand or sat on a chair. Rarely would a student even make it into the colonel's office; the punishments were met in his secretary's foyer with little discussion or elaboration. But now, in his final year, the old man seemed far stricter.

The colonel also seemed to have taken a greater liking to alcohol. The drink not only heightened the redness of his face but also the ire in his temperament. All the rambunctious children agreed; the punishments that were merely punitive in the early years had now become darker for the old man, almost entertaining. He was particularly tough on those children whose families were not members of the Communist Party. Parents could do little to stop it, as the powers that be ruled with an iron fist, and the only way the abuse would stop was if the students acted accordingly, or the family signed up to the Party.

According to Raj's father, Colonel Vlatko Raspic was most likely less educated than Raj, but due to his political persuasions, and war time atrocities, and the fact he owned the property that housed the school buildings, he seemed the perfect candidate to be put in charge of an elementary school. Even the military status of 'colonel' was dubious, and a subject definitely not discussed in front of the man. Raj's dad had little respect for the Raspic family, or any so-called patriot that changed sides during the Second World War.

'Keep your head down,' Mirko would say to his sons, 'and remember why you are going to school.'

Raj was getting nervous as he walked down the hall. He turned toward the toilets when his chaperone interrupted him.

'Where are you going?' Luka Nikilic was a little older than Raj, and everyone knew him as the teachers arse kisser. 'Straight to the colonel is what Mrs Ivanovic said.'

'I got to take a piss, Luka.' Raj tried to sound cool, but his mind was nervously racing to buy time to find a possible way out of the predicament.

Running from the school would most certainly lead to a worse punishment later, and he might have to endure his father's wrath as well. There were only a few months left of the school year, Raj quickly ascertained, so if he did run, then maybe his father would let him remain home to work on the farm, although, the communists might then send out a search party, which would bring the entire family into the spotlight. Running was clearly not the answer, but as Raj opened the toilet door, he had an idea.

'What? You want to watch?' Raj looked disgustedly at Luka.

'No,' the boy answered, embarrassed. 'I was just...'

'What am I going to do?' asked Raj, with a pretence of disbelief. 'You think I'm going to break through the windows?'

'Okay, okay.' Luka stopped at the door. 'Just hurry up.'

Raj placed his hopes in two things; the colonel's tendency to focus on the students buttocks when delivering excessive beatings and a plentiful supply of Communist Party approved toilet paper. The smell in the lavatory was worse than usual and Raj tried to ignore it as he quickly moved to the first cubicle and reached for the dispenser – nothing. The second cubicle was the same and Raj's cheeks started to clench. The final cubicle must have had far less use and Raj could see why; a giant floating turd swam atop the brown toilet water and the smell emanating from it was putrid. Raj held his breath and kept his eyes focused on the dispenser as he started to pull out the small paper squares. He worked quickly as he knew Luka would eventually come in to check on him, such was the boy's disposition; a natural sticky nose and tattle-tale. Three toilet paper squares were carefully stuffed in between his underpants and his trousers. He shook his legs a little to see if there were any issues with movement or noise. Everything felt fine, if a little uncomfortable, but comfort was not high on Raj's list of priorities. He desperately needed some kind of insulation between the leather strap and his bottom.

'You done in there?' Luka's voice called from outside the restroom.

'One second,' answered Raj. 'Just washing up.'

Raj grabbed six more squares and pushed them tight into his pants. He wasn't sure if it would work, but he was sure more layers would be better than fewer. Besides, this paper was cheap and nasty and it could quite well become even thinner on the walk to the principal's office. The restroom door started to open as Raj sucked in some disgusting toilet air, lifted his pants unnaturally high, up near his naval, then tied the rope he used as a belt, before exhaling. He then dropped his loose-fitting shirt over his trousers and hoped no one noticed how exposed his ankles now were.

'You're a pervert!' Raj purposefully walked toward Luka, who had made his way into the bathroom. 'Just had to have a look, didn't you?'

'Hurry up,' was all Luka could manage to say, inadvertently looking around the room for any evidence of shenanigans.

'Since you're in here' – Raj passed Luka through the open doorway – 'there is something definitely worth reporting in that last cubicle.'

Raj knew Luka couldn't help himself. The older boy would just have to take a peek into the booth. Raj waited patiently outside the toilet for Luka to appear.

'You're disgusting.' Luka didn't sound pleased as he stormed out and toward the principal's office.

'What do you mean?' Raj tried to hold back his laughter. 'I think it's important that the principal knows exactly what's going on in the cubicles of the toilets, don't you?'

The older boy made no sound and just kept walking.

Raj had resigned himself to his fate. He relaxed on the walk toward whatever punishment awaited and the simple prank he played on Luka earlier was enough to keep him smiling. Before long, they reached Colonel Raspic's office. They made their way into the small foyer chamber where the principal's secretary busily typed away on her machine. It was a dark area, with one window high above the secretary's position, which allowed a little light to pass onto her table to help enlighten her administrative duties better. The floor, as in the whole school, was covered in matt grey linoleum and the walls were decorated with an off-white wallpaper, devoid of any pattern except for the bubbling and tearing areas that had escaped the grip of the adhesive.

'Do you have an appointment, Luka?' Miss Inga Evgelin was a calm, petite lady, who wore large, round spectacles most of the time and was rarely seen dressed in any colour other than brown. She didn't bother looking up from her menial duties.

'Mrs Ivanovic sent us,' Luka responded seriously.

Now Miss Evgelin did look up from her typewriter and down her nose at Raj.

'You again?' she asked rhetorically.

Raj didn't bother responding. He knew now that any smart quiff could only lead to a worse punishment. Besides, Raj had studied sex education earlier in the year, and rumour had it that Colonel Raspic was studying Miss Evgelin behind the colonel's wife's back. What made matters worse was the fact the colonel's wife was also teaching at the same school. It was a messy situation that inspired whispers and innuendo around the school and within the community. The colonel had a soft spot for his secretary and Raj knew better than to stir that particular hornet's nest.

'Sit down and the colonel will be back shortly.' Miss Evgelin went back to work as the two boys took a seat on a cracked black leather couch, placed on the wall opposite the secretary's desk. The wall to the right of Miss Evgelin's position was adorned with a large portrait of Marshall Tito, Yugoslavia's founder and current leader. His eyes looked forward, so they followed the onlooker from every angle within the room. In the picture, a wreath surrounded the military man's head, adding an air of divinity to the shot, reminding Raj of scenes from books about Ancient Rome.

'I don't need you here, Luka,' offered Raj, after Marshall Tito's gaze had taken its toll. 'I'm fine by myself.'

'Mrs Ivanovic said to deliver you to the principal.' Luka was stoic in his response, his gaze still locked onto the glorious leader.

'Which you have,' countered Raj.

'Do you *see* a principal?' mocked Luka, his eyes leaving the portrait and pretending to look around the small antechamber.

'You will both see the principal if you don't keep quiet!' inserted Miss Evgelin, ever so calmly.

'See me for what?' a brusque voice interjected from the hallway; the footsteps that accompanied the booming voice only became stronger, as did the smell.

A mix of body odour, cigarette smoke and alcohol suddenly, and profusely, infused the atmosphere of that small lobby. Even the size of the room shrunk as the big man entered, making it not only smelly, but crowded too. As relaxed as Raj seemed to be, he still tightened his grip on the sofa's armrest as the colonel made his entrance. The only presence that could usurp the principal at that moment was the picture of Tito on the wall.

'Nikilic' - the colonel didn't seem to notice Raj - 'why is this pig farmer's son sitting next to you?'

'Mrs Ivanovic sent us.' Luka looked more nervous than Raj.

'Well,' the colonel ordered, 'on your feet, Krizic.'

The colonel hardly ever called the students by their first names, and Raj responded quickly, rising off the couch. The smell of the man became even stronger now that Raj was standing closer.

'What brings you here, boy?'

'I wasn't concentrating in class, sir,' Raj answered.

'Do you think I'm a fucking idiot, Krizic?' The colonel spat a little as he spoke, and Raj fought with himself to keep his hand from rising and wiping the drop of spittle that now sat just above his left eyebrow.

'No, sir,' said Raj, as respectfully as he could.

'Nikilic' - the colonel turned back to Luka, who still sat on the couch - 'why is this goat-herd in my office?'

'He was disrespecting the flag, sir.' Raj was shocked at the lie but knew better than accuse the older boy. 'He also said detrimental things about Tito and the teachers, especially Mrs Ivanovic.' A little smile crept into the corners of Luka's mouth as the colonel looked venomously at Raj.

'Is there anything else, Nikilic?' the colonel glared as he asked the question.

'No, sir,' answered Luka, proudly.

'Well, there was that other thing,' Raj surprisingly interjected, albeit with the most modest voice he could muster. He was incredulous within, though, so he decided to throw caution to the wind. The colonel straightened up and turned back to Luka.

'Well, Nikilic, are you keeping something from me?' the colonel's tone grew impatient.

'There's nothing else, sir,' Luka's smile suddenly disappeared and now the older boy seemed perplexed at Raj's new position in the conversation, 'What are you talking about, Raj?'

'Remember?' Raj showed his most innocent look, eyes wide and head tilted slightly forward. He now confidently wiped his brow from the colonel's spit. 'Back at the toilet, in the last cubicle.'

'Enough from you, Krizic.' The colonel raised his voice again. 'Out with it, Nikilic, what is going on at the toilet?'

'Nothing, sir,' Luka pleaded. All his confidence seemed to dissipate. 'I swear.'

The colonel's eyes darted from an innocent looking Raj to a petrified Luka, clearly trying to ascertain the truth behind the boys' words. The tension in the little room was growing as the two students avoided eye contact with their principal while at the same time shooting each other subtle death-stares. Just as the colonel took a deep breath to begin to speak again, the phone rang. A loud ringing reverberated around the chamber cutting the silence and easing the tension.

'Colonel Raspic's office,' Miss Evgelin answered. 'Yes, he is.' She coolly handed the large sky-blue receiver to the colonel. 'It's your wife.'

'Get inside my office, Krizic,' the colonel commanded while grabbing the phone, 'and you can go wait for me by the toilet, Nikilic!'

Raj proceeded into the colonel's office satisfied with the result. It was an empty victory though, as he was sure the wrath of the colonel would be just as dire regardless of Luka's fate, but it still felt good to give it back to the lying scum for elaborating on Mrs Ivanovic's initial punishment.

The colonel's office was far larger and better illuminated than Miss Evgelin's diminutive foyer. A dark brown wooden panelling rose from the grey linoleum floor, reaching half way up the walls to encase the rectangular room. Square windows crossed with thin timber frames and white, sheer laced curtains created a sense of openness to the left of the entry, while the wall on the right had a couple of glass cabinets in front of it adorned with even more pictures of Tito, Stalin and other unknown military men. Large bookshelves covered the wall behind the colonel's broad oaken desk, which was kept very clean with surprisingly little paperwork on show. A blue phone and an empty ashtray were all that sat neatly atop the colonel's desk. A couple of chairs and some filing cabinets filled the room and, for the most part, its appearance seemed typical for a primary school principal's office.

But Raj's love of books made him notice little inconsistencies; for instance, there were few books on the shelves. Rather they were adorned with military paraphernalia and personal bric-a-brac. The desk had no lamp on it, which would not be typical for either an academic or a head administrator and there were no diplomas or tertiary accolades on show anywhere on the walls.

As Raj stood there, he suddenly noticed the silence that encompassed that moment. He turned to look back through the opening to see where the colonel was and, to his surprise, everyone had gone. In his reverie, Raj missed the grand exit made by the rest of the group. Even Miss Evgelin was gone. He stepped cautiously back into the foyer and peeped around. Still no one was to be seen. *Perhaps the colonel's wife had harkened him to her. Or poor Luka was explaining the importance of the floating turd in cubicle three of the latrine.* Perhaps this was Raj's chance to casually slip out into the hall and return to his class unviolated by the colonel's rage.

'Vlatko?' A voice came from the hall, followed by the sounds of women's heels gradually becoming louder.

Raj only knew one person who called the principal by his first name at the school.

'Where is Vlatko?' The colonel's wife, casually leaning on the door jamb, a long grey skirt covered her legs and a knitted purple cardigan, clipped by three large buttons, loosely fell over her torso hiding a lacy white shirt beneath. She wore large, black circular rimmed glasses and had very long hair that was tied back very tightly.

'I don't know,' Raj genuinely responded, then his cheeky side took hold. 'He was here a second ago, told me to wait in the office, then he and Miss Evgelin just' – he paused for effect – 'disappeared.' He wasn't lying, nor was he telling the whole truth. He thought that if he was to face the fury of the colonel, then the colonel could at least face the fury of his wife.

'But I just called.' Now Mrs Raspic straightened up and looked irritated. 'Bloody fool.'

Raj just stood, staring at her innocently, pretending to be oblivious to the colonel's wife's increasingly reddening cheeks.

'What are you doing here, anyway?' she asked, attempting to keep her poise as her voice lowered in tone and she tugged and straightened her cardigan.

'He is in trouble.' The answer came from the colonel's lover. Miss Evgelin mysteriously appeared and stood behind Mrs Raspic at the doorway, respectfully awaiting an opening.

'Inga.' Mrs Raspic sounded as surprised as Raj was as she addressed the other woman. 'I didn't see you there. Where is my husband?' she asked the diminutive secretary.

'I don't know, Jelena,' answered Miss Evgelin, slipping through the smallest opening made by the colonel's wife and making her way back behind her desk. 'I just went to the toilet.'

'What do you mean you don't know?' insisted Mrs Raspic. 'You *are* his secretary, aren't you? I imagine there is not much you don't know about my husband.'

Inga Evgelin ignored the larger lady as she sat down and began fastidiously typing. Mrs Raspic looked at the younger secretary, then at Raj, and then shook her head before turning to leave.

'There you are, darling.' The colonel reappeared just in time. 'I just had to check something at the toilets.'

'I'm sure you did.' Mrs Raspic glared back at the secretary. 'Seems like the toilet is a popular place today.'

'What?' the colonel feigned interest but strode past everyone, determinedly heading straight to his desk. He sat down, took a deep breath, then pulled open a drawer and removed a bottle and glass and poured the clear liquid before emptying the contents down his throat. He sat back, let his shoulders drop and his earlier tension disappeared.

'That will fix everything,' Mrs Raspic sarcastically remarked as she had made her way past Raj to stand between the boy and the man drinking at the desk.

'Nothing is broken, darling,' countered the colonel, pouring another drink, 'so nothing needs fixing.'

'Then what were you doing at the toilet?' Mrs Raspic was persistent.

The colonel paused and looked at his wife, a large grin appearing on his face.

'Investigating a giant shit.' The colonel laughed out loud then drained the next glass.

He offered his wife a cigarette before lighting one himself. The couple stood there smoking and discussing some aspect of the curriculum while Raj took a tentative step toward the exit. Perhaps they had forgotten about him.

'Krizic!' the colonel yelled. 'Go outside and pick the slimmest branch from the purple plum tree in the yard, around half a metre long' – he took a long drag from his cigarette – 'and bring it to me.'

Now the colonel's wife turned and looked at Raj with a soft compassion in her eyes.

'Vlatko.' Her voice turned gentle. 'Must you?'

'This boy needs to learn, Jelena.' The colonel hadn't forgotten. He took another swig before continuing. 'That fear is a form of respect.'

The colonel's broad smile was the last thing Raj saw before grudgingly leaving to locate the instrument of his own upcoming torture.

CHAPTER 3

Raj was now in his fifteenth year and had been making the journey to the greater family fields in Blidinje with his father and brothers for a few seasons. Land was abundant and the generations that had earlier sought higher ground fleeing the Ottoman oppression, eventually returned when the Islamic conquests of the Balkans came to an end. As time marched on and bloodlines spread, siblings and cousins moved far and wide, but many still returned to the distant communal grasslands at the base of the mountains every spring, with sheep, cows and goats in need of fattening for the winter ahead. The highlands were used predominantly during the warmer seasons for grazing as weather conditions this high inland during winter were extreme for man and beast alike.

It was just Vlad and Raj on this journey, as Kriz was in town and their father had maintenance issues around the home. If they left at the break of day they would make it by sundown and they planned to stay for the whole summer season this year. Raj was looking forward to it because he usually caught up with whichever cousins were coming up too. It was also far cooler up there in the summer months and there was an icy lake that melted just enough for bathing.

The preparation was always the same: food, water, clothes and tools were prepared the night prior. And just as importantly was salt. The magic white granule that flavoured mankind's food also kept the larger animals from some kind of bestial insanity. That was how Raj understood it. Why or how it worked was a mystery chalked up to historic folklore and social acceptance. Before dawn Vlad packed the horse while Raj attended to the sheep, herding them under the careful watch of Mugo, the family hound and, as the first ray of light broke the dark sky, the two brothers began their hike.

There was one make-shift dirt road the communists had 'built' during the war several years earlier, but no one in Raj's village had a car, let alone knew how to drive one, and the distance added by foot, just to use a smoother trail, was not worth the time lost. The closer trek was unforgiving; steep rocky paths and muddy tracks that, although well-worn, still made for tough going in handed down shoes and grey morning light. Being older, Vlad got to ride atop the horse as Raj and the animals kept a slow pace, lest the horse's shoes cracked or a sheep got left behind. The winter was over according to the calendar, but the chill mountain wind still blew, making the slow trudge cold and dreary, at least till the morning light rose well-above the tree line and wrapped the world in a touch of energising warmth.

By nightfall they arrived safe and sound but were not the first to arrive for the season. Animals were already settled around the grasslands, dogs barked and light and smoke appeared from the many barns that littered the grand area. Raj and Vlad quickly fenced off their own livestock before finding their way into an empty barn closest to them. They fed the horse and the dog, then settled down for a makeshift dinner of bread and cheese before retiring for a well-earned sleep.

The brothers awoke at the crack of dawn and headed out to assess the herd and landscape. The morning sunshine sparkled across the fields that day. Grounds that hid their natural secrets under a frozen white blanket just a few weeks ago, now revealed their true glory; meadows of swaying grasslands became exposed once more as the winter snow melted away. Christmas ferns of the darkest green surrounded the plains, their pointed spines acting as a natural boundary that clearly defined the end of the farmlands and the beginning of the mountainsides. As was found throughout the Balkans, grey and white stones of all shapes and sizes interspersed the land, and it was no different here, but the highland sunlight made the myriad of rocks appear softer and somehow more welcoming.

At their peaks, the distant mountains still held snow, as they did all year round; acting as a striking reminder that nature's cycle would eventually turn again. But for now, and for the next few months, the birds would sing their sweetest songs and tend fussily about their nests while the smaller critters would rustle below and hunt and scavenge for their own survival. Larger, more dangerous beasts were also known to pass through these areas; awakened bears and roaming wolf packs were no strangers across the southern European wilderness and would usually travel wherever they pleased. Amongst the natural world the dedicated farmers respectfully toiled their lands in preparation for a promising yield, always accompanied by man's best friend and most zealous of alarms.

But Raj's dog was playful on this morning and found neighbouring dogs to play with almost immediately. The hounds chased smaller creatures, and each other, through tall grasses on the outskirts of the family farm, assuring all who worked those fields of the safety in that moment. The pack horses too, were relaxed and grazed casually, only annoyed by the pesky insects that magically appeared the instant the season turned towards the slightest warmth.

The farm animals started feeding at the crack of dawn. They were easily left to their own devices and had plenty of wild grass to gorge on. Sheep and cows covered the plains as others from different villages had made the journey a day or two before. Vlad tended their horse near a large communal barn while Raj made his way to the lake to wash his face from the overnight grit. His feet were still sore and he just wanted to relax on the first day of the sojourn and stretch out on a log near the water's banks, away from animals and humans and any kind of responsibility. He would be here for a month or two, with plenty of chores to complete, so there was no hurry in getting started.

'Yo!' A distant cry caught Raj's attention, just as he crossed the dirt track. 'Raj!' He turned to see a rider in the distance calling out and galloping toward him.

'Bero!' Raj called back to his older cousin. He waved his hand in the air and kept walking toward the lake. In no time Bero had caught up to him and leapt off his horse.

'What brings you up here all alone?' inquired the elder boy, breathing heavily and still holding the reins, suddenly looking serious. 'Don't you know there are wolves surrounding us as we speak?'

Raj kept his cool and noticed a small movement in the corner of his older cousin's mouth. He turned and feigned a scan of the distant woods buying him some time for a counter rouse.

'Yeah, the dog was going crazy on the way here.' Raj played along. 'I would have come by this commie road, but I reckon they cut us off near Black Rock Ridge.'

Now Bero looked a little more perplexed. He also checked the surroundings and even looked to the sky.

'There is also a bear up to the north, near St Mary's Chapel.' Raj had him worried now as he could see Bero's grip tighten around his steed's strap. 'And Pete swears there's a family of boars wrecking everything in their way along the path from Kupres.'

'Boars?' Bero had an unfortunate encounter with the family pig when he was just five and, ever since, the entire clan constantly reminded him of it.

'Yeah, I know, so far south.' Then just as if the universe approved of the joke, Raj belted out a voluminous fart that felt like it ripped his pants. 'And a dragon was spotted flying straight out of my arse!'

And with that, both boys hit the dewy grass in fits of immature laughter, scaring both the horse and a couple of nearby crows that leapt to the air to get away from any potential danger.

'You idiot!' Bero was first to sit up. 'Look what you did.'

'You started it,' Raj replied, noticing how wet his back and legs were after sitting up from the soggy grass.

The boys grabbed each other's hands and levered each other straight up into a standing position and turned their backs toward the sun.

'How have you been, Raj?' asked Bero. 'I haven't seen you in years!'

'All good, Bero,' answered Raj, 'and I'm not here alone. Vlad is back near the barn.'

'Vlad?' Bero looked toward the barn. 'He actually made an effort this year!'

Both boys cracked up laughing again.

'Shouldn't you be in school or something?' Bero asked. 'I remember you always liked your books.'

Raj made his way to the lake and bent over with his hands cupped. He splashed his face a couple of times and Bero brought his horse closer for a drink.

'You know how it is, Bero.' Raj stood up, rubbing the back of his wet neck wistfully. 'There's only so much to go around.'

'Krizan?' asked Bero.

'Yeah,' answered Raj solemnly. 'Dad could only afford one of us to go any further. And he is the oldest. Plus, it seems he had a calling.'

'I know.' Bero looked defeated. 'Fuckin' commies.'

'Yeah,' added Raj. 'Fuckin' commies.'

'Who's fucking commies?' interrupted Vlad upon his arrival, with a broad smile, proud of his comic timing.

'Vlad!' Bero turned to the older brother. 'You sorry excuse for a lazy shit. What are you doing here?'

'Hunting for pigs.' Vlad was joking, but the smile on his face was diminishing quickly.

'Don't be so sensitive, Vlad,' Bero added, who was older than both the brothers. 'I just haven't seen you up here since... well, never!'

Bero and Raj were in tears again, at the expense of Vlad, who smiled sarcastically and walked a few steps around them toward the lake.

'Where is Kriz now?' asked Bero, 'how long does it take to become a priest?'

'Who knows,' answered Vlad acerbically. 'Maybe he is becoming a bishop?'

'Shut up, Vlad,' interjected Raj, 'you're just jealous!'

Vlad walked over to his younger brother and shoved him to the ground, but before he could jump on to Raj, Bero stepped in and pulled Vlad away.

'Whoa!' Bero seemed genuinely surprised. 'You're brothers, what are you doing?'

'Little shit!' Vlad shook off his older cousin and returned to the water hole.

'You okay?' Bero reached down to Raj and helped him up.

'Yeah,' answered Raj. 'I'll be fine. Like I said, Vlad is just jealous.'

'Every penny went toward him,' Vlad shouted out. 'Every meagre penny.' He pointed to his feet, showing off his torn, wet boots. 'We haven't got a fucking pair of new shoes between us, yet he gets to mingle with the priests and brothers around the country. Fuck him as much as the fucking commies!'

'Bero doesn't need to hear this, Vlad,' said Raj sheepishly, feeling embarrassed.

'Why not?' asked Vlad with a superficial smile. 'It's all about the family isn't it? Sharing is caring, isn't it it?'

'Sorry, Bero.' Raj offered the apology, sounding far more mature than his older sibling, but he knew Vlad was not about to give up.

'Bero knows,' Vlad continued. 'Everyone knows. It's not just us. Why all our parents didn't join the Party and give us a better life is beyond me!'

'Don't be an idiot,' argued Raj.

A splattering motor cut off the quarrel. No one in the entire town owned a vehicle, so when the sounds of an engine echoed within ear shot everyone knew the government must be somehow involved. Bero's horse trotted in placed, huffing and puffing nervously at the morning air as the older boy regained the reins. Mugo barked in the distance and, after a short whistle from Raj, started racing toward the boys.

'This can't be good,' expressed Bero, moving slowly away from the water hole and toward the crude road that cut across the field, acting like a shield for his younger cousins.

'What would they want this far north?' asked Raj.

'They want what they always want, Raj,' answered Bero regretfully. 'They want what is ours to become theirs.'

'Here's your chance, Vlad,' joked Raj.

'Chance? At what?' Vlad sounded suspicious.

'You can join the commies here.' Raj was teasing. 'And I'll let Dad know when I get home.'

'Fuck off!' Vlad spat back.

The truck approached ever so slowly. The moment felt like an eternity as the panting Mugo had enough time to race over, receive a scratch behind the ears from all three boys, have a sniff around Bero's horse before taking a drink at the lake. Eventually, an old, large Mercedes-Benz semi-trailer chugged its way towards the boys. It looked to be an ex-army transport, with larger wheels than a standard road vehicle and slimmer window panes all around the leading compartment. It had clearly seen better days. The cabin's camouflage green had visibly lost its power of concealment, with a fading patina, cracked glass and rusted spots covering the front of the truck. Years had passed since this particular vehicle would have blended into these surroundings. A black soot steadily flowed from the exhaust above the cabin, smoking high through the mountain air, accompanied by a stench of diesel and a spitting sound that at one time boomed, and at another coughed, ensuring anyone who couldn't see the smoke would still be well aware of the old truck's presence. A torn, black canopy flailed atop its long box trailer, adding a touch of comedy to the sad state the vehicle was really in.

Raj saw two men in the cabin and three hanging off the closest side of the trailer. As the truck finally stopped before them, three more men appeared from behind the truck. All the strangers were armed with various rifles or pistols, although none were pointed directly at the boys. Still, a mysterious tension between the groups rose steadily the closer the strange men approached.

'Look.' Bero half-turned toward his cousins. 'It's the moustache crew!'

Raj smiled unintentionally as he noticed all the men had hair above their top lips. The trend had been sweeping the region as even his older brother, Krizan, was trying to break through the facial hair fluff that separated the men from the boys.

'Where is your dad?' asked a large man, ignoring the moustache jibe. He held a rifle across his left shoulder with one hand and used his right hand to calmly light a cigarette.

'Our parents are back at home, these are our grazing fields...' started Bero before being cut off by the smoking leader.

'*Your* grazing fields?' He coolly puffed out a perfect blue grey smoke ring that caught all three boys' attention as it drifted up and spread wide before thinning and vanishing. As if to add to any sense of vulnerability that the outnumbered teens might have felt, the smoking stranger shifted his rifle to his right shoulder and grinned broadly at the boys.

'Leave the youngsters alone.' An older voice called from beyond the truck. 'They hold no sway here.'

'Dane.' The smoking man turned his back to the boys. 'Is that you, you feckless old bastard?'

The old farmer came into view from around the truck. He, too, was smoking. But more importantly, he was also carrying a firearm. Raj felt a sense of relief now the moustache crew no longer paid attention to the boys. But that changed quickly when he saw the rifle in the old man's hands.

'Feckless?' Dane answered. 'That's a big word for an imbecile like you, isn't it, Bruno?'

'I'd rather be a rich idiot than a poor wise man, Dane,' answered the ring leader.

The men around Bruno straightened up as the insults flew, but Bruno just spat, remaining relaxed and in control. He turned to his men and gave orders in a dialect that Raj was not totally familiar with. The men returned to the back of the truck and released their hounds. They then grabbed their tools before hurrying off across the fields.

Raj was perplexed. The men looked like they had a real purpose now, busying themselves at a specific job. Then he realised what was going on.

'They can't do this.' He had snuck up behind Bero. 'It's not right!' he whispered.

'You going to stop them?' asked Bero quietly.

The men were gathering as many animals as they could harness. Mostly sheep as they were the slowest and smallest of the beasts. Some cows were also caught, but the bulls and horses were all left on the pasture. Mugo was excitedly running around in circles as Raj did the best he could to keep the dog from bolting across the field. Other hounds barked in the distance as farmers around the field threw their hands in the air at the actions of the gun wielding enforcers.

'Control your dog. Or I will!' commanded Bruno without even looking at the boys.

'Yes, sir,' Raj answered automatically, pulling tighter on Mugo's leash and forcing him down to his belly, adding a guilt induced scratch behind the ears.

'What I don't get' - Vlad confidently strode up to Bruno - 'is if you guys are so smart, why travel all the way up here for a few sheep? Why don't you just force the townspeople to bring them to you?' Vlad smiled, cocksure in his delivery.

'Ignore him, Bruno,' Dane quickly interjected. 'He is a dim-witted boy, barely able to tie his shoes. Most things that come from his mouth are likened to cow dung.'

'That's a nice way to say "he's a fucking idiot", Dane,' laughed Bruno, looking at a confused Vlad. 'But he may have some merit in his point. I might take it up with my superiors. That way I won't have to waste my time with all this bullshit small talk.'

'Fuck you, Dane.' Vlad stormed off toward the big shed, his face red with embarrassment. 'Fuck you all.' He shook his head, muttering something else to himself as he walked away.

'Fucking idiot,' Raj whispered, drawing an ironic smile from Bero.

'Are you taking them all?' Dane asked after a very long duration of uncomfortable silence had passed. Bruno was clearly a chain smoker, puffing on yet another cigarette while confidently watching the unfolding robbery all around him.

'It's tax time, Dane.' Bruno rested his rifle beside his leg before undoing his pants and pissing in front of the old man. 'You know how it is.'

'I know how it is becoming,' answered Dane, then turned and slowly walked away.

'Don't worry, boys.' Bruno twisted his head back to the two remaining youngsters, still releasing a steady stream away from them. His voice was garbled as he talked through the cigarette, smoke pouring from his mouth and steam rising from his urine, both hands occupied with relieving himself. 'We'll leave a few of your beasts behind. Keep them breeding; it gives us something to come back for next time.' He winked and raised his zip.

And with that, he spat his cigarette out, raised two piss-drenched fingers to his mouth and gave a long whistle. His men and their dogs began making their way back to the truck with beasts in tow. Crude roped nooses were fastened tight around the necks of the larger and slower animals. The ropes were knotted together so many beasts could be delivered by one man. The sheep came first though, quickly and easily with the help of the dogs. Cursing could be heard from across the fields as helpless hard-working farmers were being ravaged by the people who were supposed to be there to protect them – the government.

'This is bullshit,' Bero defiantly stated.

'Sorry?' Bruno turned fully this time, genuinely interested in what the young man had to say.

'You heard me.' Bero wasn't backing down.

Bruno turned and pointed his gun at Bero. Raj's heart skipped a beat as he took an inadvertent step back, holding fast to Mugo who had risen to follow the boy.

'Sorry' – Bruno took a step toward Bero – 'I'm a little hard of hearing. Please repeat that.'

'Never mind.' Bero was tense as he answered, taking a little step back himself. His horse was also uncomfortable dancing from leg to leg as it shuffled backward with Bero.

'No, no,' insisted Bruno, now pointing the gun toward Bero's feet. 'I'm sure I heard you say something.' He took a break for a moment, cocking his head to one side before continuing. 'Something about volunteering?'

'What?' Raj exclaimed without any self-control.

'You too, eh?' Bruno looked past Bero, catching the younger boy's eye. 'So be it. Dejan, bring those sheep over here,' Bruno shouted to one of his conspirators. 'Our young comrades have offered their services herding our animals onto the truck.'

Dejan promptly dragged twelve head of sheep to Bero and flung his end of the rope at the young man. 'Don't let them get away.'

Raj could see the rage growing on Bero's face and was afraid that something tragic was about to unfold so he released Mugo and ran toward the rope. With a quick swoop he grabbed the end of the thick cord and whistled back to his dog. Mugo knew that whistle and it could only mean one thing – sheep-herding time.

'That's the spirit!' laughed Bruno. 'We'll make you a fine comrade one day.'

The words cut into Raj. His father had vehemently, and publicly, denounced the Communist Party for not only stealing off the townsfolk, but for also disavowing the right to any spiritual faith and for reducing a once proud people into greedy sycophants or starving beggars. Raj's clan lived sparingly off the land and that was the only thing that allowed them to maintain a semblance of autonomy at the time. All his years, Raj was taught to hate and fight this dictatorial system, yet here he was helping the hand that dealt them so much pain. But he knew that Bero was close to tipping and needed to assuage the situation before his cousin lost more than just some farm stock.

'Ilijah,' cried Bruno. 'Bring them over here.'

Ilijah brought another group of sheep toward them, while Bruno gently took the reins off Bero to commandeer his horse.

'Now, listen well,' Bruno began between clenched teeth. 'You would be better to shut your mouth in my presence from now on or I'll lock you in the back with the animals next time.'

'Just do what he says, Bero,' Raj called out while leading the sheep under his supervision up the ramp at the back of the truck.

'Yes, Bero.' Bruno seemed to enjoy knowing the young upstarts name now, his tone becoming lighter as he spoke. 'Play along and we will let you continue to tend to *our* fields, in peace.'

Bero begrudgingly released his horse into the moustached leader's care. Without looking back, he moved toward Ilijah and grabbed the end of his rope and dragged the herd of sheep toward Raj at the back of the truck.

'It's not worth it,' Raj whispered when Bero was in ear shot.

'I don't give a fuck!' Bero aggressively whispered back. 'They can have the fucking sheep, but there's no way that partisan is taking my fucking horse!'

'What can we do?' asked Raj as he moved to make way for Bero's herd.

'I'll get him back,' Bero defiantly whispered.

'Hurry up back there.' A call was heard and two loud slaps against the trucks canopy followed.

The two boys hushed their banter and quickly finished tethering the livestock to the various metal poles and cages affixed to the inside the truck's carriage. Other men followed with sheep, cattle and Bero's steed, and before the sun had moved too far into the afternoon sky, the party faithful were aboard their old Mercedes and slowly rolling off into the distance.

The dust had settled, the diesel engines song died and the black smoke cleared as Raj and Bero sat near the lake. The scene was peaceful once more as if nothing untoward had occurred this day. However, both boys felt ashamed and demoralised as they looked across the field, feeling a little more to blame than the other remaining villagers. Some farmers were already packing their things to begin their premature departure home. Even Mugo the hound sat pensively near Raj, apparently just as sadly defeated as his master.

'Well, well, well,' called Vlad as he returned, trotting toward the dejected duo upon horseback this time. 'How are my communist friends feeling now?'

'Fuck off, Vlad,' Raj quietly answered, but Bero kept to himself.

'It looked like you guys really helped the cause.' Vlad was beaming with pride. 'You know, helping them load the truck and all that.'

'Shut up,' Raj grumbled a little louder, not wanting to even look at his brother.

'Commie jokes don't seem to be so funny now, do they?' Vlad aggressively persisted.

'You're a dickhead.' Raj finally raised his voice.

'It's okay, Raj.' A gloomy Bero spoke. 'He's right. If we can't take a joke after we give it, then we have no integrity.'

'See?' Vlad agreed. 'Comrade Bero understands.' He couldn't help himself and burst out laughing at the last jibe.

'Besides,' added Bero coolly, 'Vlad is about to give me his horse to pursue the motherfuckers.'

'Huh?' Vlad stopped laughing. 'What?'

Raj laughed this time. Mugo's ears pricked up too and Bero was smiling once again.

'You're going to give me your horse,' Bero repeated confidently, looking up at the horse. 'Don't worry, the horse won't miss you.'

'You're not taking my horse!' Any sense of humour previously enjoyed by Raj's older brother was now lost. 'How will I get home?'

'You can walk,' answered Bero. 'Just like Raj.'

'You're crazy, Bero,' Raj interjected, feeling a nervousness growing in the pit of his stomach.

'I don't care,' Bero answered. 'And I can't go home without my horse. It's just not right.'

'Of course it's not right,' Raj agreed. 'But what are you going to do? How many of them were there? And God only knows how many more might be waiting?'

'I'm not giving you my horse.' Vlad spoke louder.

'Then you might as well come too, Vlad.' Bero smiled.

'What?' Vlad sounded surprised. 'Why do you need me?'

'I don't,' answered Bero, rising from the ground. 'In fact, I reckon you might just get in the way.' He patted down the legs of his trousers casually, flicking off bits of grass that had attached to the fibres of his clothing.

'In the way?' Vlad was now definitely insulted.

'Yeah.' Bero remained calm. 'I'm not sure if you will crack under pressure.'

'I can keep my head,' Vlad insisted. 'You'll see.'

'Plus, you really put your foot in it back there,' Bero reminded Vlad. 'This whole thing could easily be seen as your fault.'

'Fuck off.' Vlad was angry. 'They would have taken the animals anyway.'

'Sorry, Vlad.' Bero quickly apologised, looking sullen. 'That was too far. You're right; they came for the animals, whether you were here or not.'

'What's the plan?' asked Vlad after a moment of contemplative silence, looking now sympathetically at his older cousin.

'This is crazy.' Raj was worried. 'If they catch you, they can make you disappear.'

'Wake up, Raj' – Bero raised his tone – 'and look around. We are already invisible.'

CHAPTER 4

According to the law, every male born in the Socialist Federal Republic of Yugoslavia must complete three years of military training after their twentieth birthday; two years in the army, and one year in the navy. A punitive law, Raj thought, particularly now that he was at the requisite age. But moreover, he felt confused by the idea that he might have to stand shoulder to shoulder with someone who could have easily been an enemy only a generation earlier, or even worse, a potential foe at any time in the future. There was no hot war to speak of in Europe at the time, but the history of the region was long and bloody and the new establishment was yet to be proven an absolute success.

On the surface, Yugoslavia seemed well maintained, but the mix of southern Slavic cultures was not blending well at the grassroots level. Heated clashes were occurring at work places, school grounds and sporting fields throughout the federation. Rather than growing closer as the history of the Second World War grew more distant, the tensions between the peoples were clearly becoming ever greater as time moved on.

The political pressures were clear; the patriots wanted independence. A Croatia for Croatians, a Serbia for Serbians, a Macedonia for Macedonians etc. The old guard, who fought and bled, maintained their rebellion in protests both clandestine and overt. Those who fled the new nation continued the fight from afar in the form of underground media publications and boisterous street protests. The age of television helped the cause, allowing viewers worldwide to see and hear the stories behind the iron curtain; stories which the capitalist empires were more than willing to perpetuate. But independence might as well have been the only thing that all the nationalists agreed upon, because once borderlines were mentioned, a new level of division quickly became apparent.

Of course, there were spiritual tensions too. Communist Party members were not allowed to partake in any faith or religious observances. If Party members were seen to enter a place of worship, they would be stripped of their membership and be considered anathema to the Yugoslav cause. So, the large Catholic, Orthodox and Muslim regions within the country all shared a common cause far beyond this mortal world. The communists were fighting this widespread faith by not only indoctrinating the young children through the education system, but by far more nefarious means too. Priests were disappearing, mosques were being torn down and crosses were removed from atop old churches. Jewish communities were extremely concerned as the Second World War was not yet a generation passed and the communist regimes were already behaving in the same way as the fascists did only a few years earlier.

Raj was unsettled at home. The future seemed filled with a destiny that had little to do with his personal aspirations and more to do with some grand political game being played by the rich and powerful. But what personal aspirations did he actually have? He loved the land: toiling the fields, tending the livestock and maintaining the homestead were quite enjoyable. The air was fresh and the food was delicious and a life lived on the fertile land would comfortably suffice. But his was not the only mouth to feed and a bad season or two could make life dangerously uncomfortable. Besides, traditionally, the eldest male inherited the family fields and Raj was far back on that particular list. He knew that any chance of working his own farm was extremely slim because non-Party members were not allowed to attain newly released land. Even if he could be a farmer, the tax rates were ballooning every year as livestock and agriculture were taken more often and in greater quantity. The future for farming might not be as sustainable as it was before the war.

Education was something that Raj often fantasised about too; reading and studying different topics always interested him and he thought getting work had to be easier with a good education. He also saw the toll farming took on his father as the years passed. There would be no way Raj's parents could maintain the land on their own, in their later years. The physical demand, that working the land required, wasn't the same as a career behind a desk in a comfortable office, and so the years may be kinder to the folk with a good education. But that academic dream was even more difficult to obtain without communist membership, as studying required money, influence and support.

Raj's older siblings were following their own paths. His sisters had no real say in matters: marriage, children and homemaking were the clear choice for any aspiring farm girl in a village such as theirs. Raj was sure the girls secretly hoped to wed an eldest son and takeover the in-laws' fields. To the delight of his parents, Raj's oldest brother, Krizan, had continued to pursue a life with the church and moved to a seminary a couple of years earlier. Raj didn't really see himself as a man of the cloth, but also suspected Kriz of ulterior motives. Vlad, however, was a drifter. He did as little work as possible and took as much as anyone was willing to give. But not even he could escape a few years in the army. He was already half way through his military training and sent sporadic letters home exalting the martial experience, cheering for the day his younger brother signed up. It was common knowledge that all correspondence from the military was vetted to maintain order among both the soldiers and civilians, so any mail received was taken with a grain of salt and did little more than affirm that Vlad was still alive.

Raj was sure of one thing – money. He knew that without the dinars, dollars, sterling or marks, any dream would remain just that – a dream. Work was scarce in Yugoslavia; there were rudimentary mines scattered around the land, but the work for non-communists was extremely labour intensive and the pay was a pittance, with a wage that really only covered food and board. Raj was not afraid of physical work but hauling rocks and ore from the ground was not only heavy, but dirty and dangerous, and deserved a befitting salary. But, like most careers in the communist system, any higher paying wages required membership to the Party, which left a large swathe of the population broke and hungry or broken and still hungry.

Many of the young men from the town were already evading the draft by fleeing to neighbouring countries with democratic leanings and stronger, growing economies. This came at a great risk to both themselves and their families. If caught, those who took flight from Yugoslavia faced prison and a permanent record, and their families also became greater focal points for the authorities. But if dissidents managed to escape, there was little the government could do, except watch border lines and track incoming packages.

As much as mail was scrutinised throughout the land, not all correspondence could be filtered. Local mail and parcels were far less suspicious in the eyes of the paranoid government, particularly if it was exclusively civilian. Vlad wasn't the only brother to post mail. Krizan also sent letters home from all over the country as he moved often with the clergy. He was either trying to help the poor in remote places or was evading persecution from the long and brutal arm of the atheist law. The last letter Kriz sent came from a seminary in the coastal town of Split. That part of the world had a great reputation for tourism due to its gorgeous beaches, surrounding views and moderate climate. It also had a rich history with the Roman Catholic Church, a history that was being eroded under the current regime. Raj had never been quite that far west, but had travelled close on occasion, mainly for distributing dried tobacco to any black market wholesalers that managed to still remain in business.

Krizan's letter left Raj with no doubt about his elder brother's intentions; he was fleeing the country. It held clues in the wording that seemed to affirm the finality of his departure, which was bittersweet for Raj's family as they would miss him dearly, but at the same time they were happy for him to escape the communist oppression and find freedom to live as he pleased. Historically, the church was well known for aiding in the migration of Catholic refugees, but those operations were becoming more difficult as the nation states of Europe settled their borders and tightened security against people smuggling.

Amidst the mixed emotions Raj felt for his big brother's escape, there was a definite sense of inspiration. Kriz always had time for his youngest brother and, unlike Vlad, he was not so condescending. When Raj would fall, Kriz would lend a hand, whereas Vlad would laugh. If Raj had an idea, Kriz would counsel, whereas Vlad would scorn. Krizan's move away from home and apparent flight to freedom was extremely motivating for Raj. And so he hatched a plan.

The last letter had a postal address located on the fringes of Split. Raj looked up the address in an old atlas he had stolen from school many years earlier and saw no mention of a church or friary of any kind at that location. In fact, the nearest holy house was at least a mile away. This piqued his interest furthermore. He knew the authorities would never sanction a new church built at that locale and, as it was an old area with no specific historical significance, the address had to be some sort of residential dwelling designed simply for common folk to inhabit. Raj had a clear destination to aim for and a chance not only to dodge the bothersome military draft but also to once more see his dear elder brother. He just had to hope that Krizan was waiting and willing to help him.

'What are you looking at there?' asked Tomo, a local friend Raj had known from school, who was passing by one fine Saturday morning a month into the season of spring. The air was warm and the breeze was gentle and Raj was so lost in his thoughts he didn't even notice his friend's arrival.

'Just a map of the coast.' Raj was staring at the atlas yet again, a nervous tension built up inside him every time he looked at the page. He was working up the courage to let his parents know of his plans, but kept going over the details in his mind just to be sure.

'You planning a trip?' inquired Tomo, peering over the front edge of the atlas without waiting for an answer. 'Split, eh? It would be nice to get away from the cold around here.'

Tomo was nosy but innocent enough, Raj thought, as he lifted the book for a little privacy. Raj wasn't yet ready to share his plan with his parents and so definitely would not be sharing it with his friends.

'Maybe a holiday?' Tomo stepped back, throwing a nod and wink, and giving his friend some space.

'Yeah.' Raj looked back at the map, trying to act cool. 'Maybe.'

'Well.' Tomo stretched both arms wide and let out a great yawn. 'If you need company, let me know. I got my letter the other day and I don't want to serve these fucking commies for three years either, but a holiday on the beach does sound nice!'

With that, Tomo respectfully turned and made his way off toward town. A letter addressed to Raj would be arriving soon too and he would have to open up to his parents. But Tomo's visit also made Raj realise just how obvious his actions were. If Tomo could see through him in an instant, then his parents probably already knew of his ideas, too. Then a fear struck him – who else knew? He would often look at the map while relaxing around the farm and had been doing so for well over a year, and villagers in the area walked freely through one another's properties all the time, taking short cuts and stopping by spontaneously to say hello and share coffee. There were no real strangers in this part of the world and families had been dealing with each other both socially and financially in the same way for generations. With fields this vast and roads so poor, short cuts were appreciated whenever they were available and gates were rarely locked. How many people saw Raj perusing his maps without him even being aware of their presence?

The cold war had changed one thing among the locals: trust. Earlier generations would have been far more open to political discussions and public commentaries. Social gatherings would be full of drunken experts extolling the virtues of the left or the right and scuffles would often break out in public places over which policy was better for the future of the people. But since the communist regime took hold, everybody held their tongues a lot more and double checked to see they weren't being watched or overhead whenever they might be doing something unsolicited.

There was many an occasion where false accusations prevailed to the detriment of the innocent party, quite often associated with bitter family feuds. Words could often be taken out of context if half a conversation was overheard, and second-hand testimony was more than enough for a requisition to question time in a private jail cell. It was also difficult knowing if a neighbour might have joined the Communist Party surreptitiously and was now spying on the community that only a day earlier was trusting and open with them.

'Dad.' Raj approached his father, his stomach in knots and a light sweat starting on his brow. 'I want to talk to you about something.'

'By the look on your face,' Mirko answered as he milled cobs of corn at a rudimentary iron machine, run like a bicycle with blades that sliced vertically along the sides of the vegetable, 'I'd say it was serious.' He stopped milling and stepped off the seated contraption.

'It is,' Raj agreed.

'And from the amount of time you have been studying that atlas' – Mirko smiled gently at his youngest child – 'I'd say you have been giving it some thought.'

'I have.' Raj felt relief now that his father clearly knew of his plans, but also embarrassment at how poor his stealth skills really were. He would have to be far more focused and cunning if he was to survive his intended adventures. 'I want to get out before they draft me.'

Mirko's face changed in an instant, which caught Raj unawares.

'Actually, son,' Mirko started, 'there was something we needed to talk to you about too.'

Raj's emotions were swinging back and forth, now he was genuinely surprised by his father's tone.

'Your letter came yesterday, Raj.' Mirko now spoke directly. 'We wanted to let you enjoy your weekend before giving you the news.'

'How long do I have?' asked Raj, a little shocked by how good his parents were at keeping their secret.

'You have a week to get organised,' Mirko informed him, 'and by next weekend they are expecting you at the barracks outside Mostar.'

Raj's mind started to race. He had hoped to get going as soon as possible, but this news was forcing his hand. He realised it was a good chance to really commit to the move, but also wondered if he had thought every possibility through. Although travel times, routes and provisions required were easy enough to organise, the real challenge would be what awaited him at the border. And which border? Italy and Austria were the most commonly whispered names in Raj's social circle. Many of his friends had siblings that had fled; some more successfully than others. Heading east through Hungary or Romania seemed as stupid as jumping out of the frying pan and into the fire. And Greece to the south was rumoured to have plenty of its own domestic issues. Besides, a western catholic nation would always be more welcoming than an Orthodox counterpart. Or so Raj thought.

A pang of regret entered his heart at that moment. As he stood looking at his ageing father, Raj became acutely aware this next week might just be the final time he would ever see his parents again.

'Relax yourself, Raj,' Mirko interjected.

'I'm relaxed.' Raj spoke quickly and came across as offended without meaning to.

'You are far from relaxed, young man.' His father smiled again. 'Your breathing is shallow, your eyes are darting around, and you are so unsettled I'd swear you needed to take a piss.' Mirko laughed out loud. 'How will you get past border patrol if you can't even get past me?'

That last statement unsettled Raj even more. The words "border patrol" really put the matter at hand into context. He would be up against professionally trained agents, both from home and abroad, who probably had years of experience, possibly had military training and definitely carried guns. To shoot an illegal alien or political dissident would be the easiest thing to get away with, Raj thought, and most likely, well within the law of the land. Language was another barrier, he just realised; who will Raj call for help if no one understands his tongue?

'You're stressing again, Raj.' Mirko broke Raj's despondent reverie once more.

'I don't know if I'm ready, Dad,' Raj admitted. 'There is so much to plan and new things are popping into my head as we speak.'

'You will never be ready,' Mirko suggested. 'No one man can think of everything.'

'You're right!' Raj's mind raced to Tomo's offer. 'I don't think I can do this alone.'

'Now, now.' Mirko lowered his voice. 'Don't be hasty. If you want to get out of Yugoslavia, you need to be very careful who you trust and who you tell.'

'You're right, Dad,' Raj said nonchalantly, but his mind was on the task ahead and he was no longer really paying heed to his father's advice. Raj felt more assured if he had someone to share the experience with, but knew Tomo was off toward town, so would wait for later that evening before approaching him with his idea.

'What's your plan?' Raj's dad asked.

'I'm thinking Italy,' Raj answered. 'Past the Blidinje fields, over the mountains, go the long way north-west toward the coasts. A few of the boys reckon they are accepting newcomers and there is work all around.'

'They reckon?' Mirko's face grimaced as he spoke. 'You are going to base your plans on what a few of "the boys" reckon?'

Raj looked perplexed.

'How many of these "boys" have made the trip?' asked Mirko.

'Well...' Raj thought deeply. 'None.'

'And that's your source of information?' Mirko laughed. 'You might as well go and enlist today.'

Raj felt a little sour after his father put him in his place. He looked down at his feet and flicked a kernel of corn away as he thought about his prospects.

'Head to Germany,' Mirko offered, breaking the silence. 'As soon as you can. Via the old empire or through Italy. But either way head to Germany.'

'Germany?' Raj questioned. 'I don't know, Dad, they might still be rebuilding after the war.'

'Exactly,' Mirko answered. 'Where better to find work than a nation that is rebuilding.'

'Italy is rebuilding too,' Raj countered.

'The Italians are lazy.' Raj's dad didn't hold back. 'All the southern states are. Siestas and parties, drunken buffoonery and every kind of indulgence. You will never find a purpose there because that is where the world goes to holiday.'

'Sounds like a fun place,' Raj joked, but his father wasn't smiling.

'You also have to be careful with their underworld,' Mirko added, almost ignoring Raj's attempted humour. 'You don't want to get mixed in with that mob. They're deadly serious.'

'I think you're being overly dramatic.' Raj was now sure his father was exaggerating. 'You've never even been to Italy.'

'How do you know where I have and haven't been?' Mirko countered abruptly.

With that, they both made their way to the kitchen for a bite of lunch. Raj's mum, Kata, made the call and they all knew the last one into the kitchen might just be the hungriest leaving later. Kata was preparing some goat's cheese and buttered wholemeal bread, while a stew was already on the fire slowly simmering for dinner later that night, infusing the air with an aroma that whet the appetite of any passer-by.

'You told him!' was the first thing Kata said when she saw Mirko's face. 'Why?'

'He is looking to leave,' Mirko said solemnly. 'So I didn't see the point to wait anymore.'

'Oh.' Raj's mother's eyes opened wide as tears appeared and then she stopped what she was doing. 'My dear baby.' She rushed to Raj and gave him a tight hug and kissed him plumb on the cheek.

'I'm not a baby, Mum.' Raj squeezed back and felt his emotions well up again. For all his bravado, he still loved a cuddle from his mother.

'You will always be my baby, Raj,' Kata said unashamedly without letting go. 'And I've lost the other boys. I don't know if I can lose you too.'

'You haven't lost Vlad, Mum,' Raj reminded her. 'he'll be back in a year or so.'

'I think Vlad has been lost for a while.' Raj's mother ironically smiled as she eventually released her youngest and went back to her kitchen bench to serve lunch to her family.

Meanwhile, Mirko had fetched the official letter from the federal government and handed it to his son. Raj put a piece of cheese in his mouth as he re-opened the envelope.

'Isn't it a crime to open other people's mail?' Raj joked as he reached for another piece of cheese. Kata and Mirko looked at each other and shared an unspoken moment.

'I saw that.' Raj made certain they knew he was aware of their secrets now too.

'What's going on?' Mila asked as she and Manda entered the room for lunch. Mugo came not long after, waving his tail profusely, excited by any activity held in the kitchen.

'I'm off to serve my beloved country,' announced Raj, waving the letter in one hand while stuffing a large piece of bread into his mouth.

'We thought you were going to run away.' Manda smiled at her little brother as she said the words. 'You know, with the whole atlas obsession.'

Raj stopped chewing and looked around at his giggling family. Did the whole world know of his plans?

'He should go tonight,' Mirko said coolly, looking at Raj's mother then at Mugo, before throwing a piece of cheese out the doorway which the dog was delighted to fetch.

'So soon?' Kata's tears welled up again as she stared at Raj, her eyes attempting to imprint the image in front of them for posterity.

'We can help pack,' Mila offered, taking a glass of milk to her lips. 'I hear Greece is the place to be at this time of year.'

'Greece?' Raj's mother lifted her hands in the sign of the cross.

Everyone suddenly spoke on top of each other with ideas and counter-ideas about where to go, and when to go, and what to pack and what to expect.

'Hang on!' Raj shouted to interrupt them, now feeling quite abandoned in a room full of family. 'Do you think I could have something to say about this?'

'Go on, then.' Raj's father encouraged his youngest son and the whole room fell into a moment of silence as suddenly, Raj became lost for words.

'I'm going to ask Tomo to come with me,' was the best that Raj could conjure. And the silence was broken with an instant disapproving chatter shared around by the rest of his family and that, once again, excluded him.

'Tomo?' asked Manda to no one in particular. 'You mean, Pero's brother?'

'Try to talk him out of that, Mirko.' Kata was pleading with her husband, acting as if her youngest son was no longer present.

'I wouldn't trust Pero as far as I could throw him,' Raj heard Mila through the din. 'You remember Jemima's wedding? Disgusting!'

Mugo had returned and was whelping lightly to join in the spirit of the moment.

'Okay, okay.' Mirko tried to calm the situation. He looked at Raj when the voices fell silent. 'Why Tomo?'

'I've known Tomo since school.' Raj had nothing to hide. 'And I saw him this morning...'

'Were you reading the atlas?' inquired Mila, smiling broadly in sarcastic delight.

'Yes.' Raj could feel his face blushing. 'But he has the letter too, and made it clear that he was ready to leave. And it would be much easier with another by my side.'

'He has the letter?' asked Mirko strangely.

'Yes, that's what he said.'

'He is older than you, isn't he?' asked Raj's mother.

'I think so, but we were in the same class.'

'He got rejected last year.' Mirko looked at his wife. 'A heart condition, they say.'

'Yes, I heard,' Kata concurred. 'Born with it, his mother tells me. They didn't even know until his service papers beckoned. He failed the medical. But that was over a year ago.'

Raj's ears pricked up at the news. Tomo hadn't mentioned anything regarding his heart condition. 'He said he got his papers the other day.'

'Interesting,' Mirko said. 'Maybe the Soviets have developed new drugs.'

'I don't know.' Raj felt as if he was in an inquisition. 'But if the army will take him, then he might want to come with me.'

'But is he telling the truth?' Mirko asked. 'If he is anything like the rest of his clan...'

'It's my life and my choice.' Raj interrupted his dad with a raised tone and clear ire in his voice.

'Yes, Raj,' Mirko counselled, 'but the Drembanovics are loose cannons, hardly trustworthy for returning farming tools let alone fleeing the country.'

'Plus,' Mila sardonically added, 'Pero is disgusting.'

'I'm not taking fucking Pero!' Raj blurted out, now feeling frustrated that this plot he had been so carefully germinating for over a year had somehow been hijacked by his family, picked at and torn to pieces and was now open to further debate and ridicule.

'Okay, okay, that's enough for now.' Raj's mum changed the subject.

'Finish eating and outside all of you. Calm down and get back to the chores that need tending. I'm sure Raj has figured this out. He is a smart boy.'

Raj left the kitchen instantly, both frustrated and hungry. The half-eaten bread and cheese left behind on his plate was a testament to the importance he placed on his upcoming days and the irritability his family could so easily bestow upon him. "Smart boy" were the trailing words his mother used and they stuck in Raj's mind for the rest of that afternoon. Up until that conversation, Raj thought he was the only one who knew of his plan. He thought Italy was a good idea based on the advice of friends just as young and naïve as he was. And he even thought that months would pass before any official summoning would arrive for military service.

The more he thought about it, the less smart he seemed to be, and the more dangerous this grand endeavour was becoming. Flee the country? Outsmart the law? Make a better future? Maybe he was just kidding himself and putting everyone at risk for a selfish dream. He held the Yugoslav Military document in his hand and read and re-read it. What chance did he really have in his pursuit? The more he despaired on these thoughts, the more confidence he lost in his beliefs. Even relying on Krizan's assistance seemed like a stupid thing to do now. How would an elder brother, on the other side of the country, whom he hadn't seen for years, be able to help him when clearly Kriz hadn't escaped the country himself, yet? There was not much left for it, so Raj decided that in the morning he would make his way toward Mostar and sign up; the sooner he began his tour of duty the sooner it would be over and he could then think about forging a brighter future for himself.

'If you want to ask Tomo to go along, he is waiting outside.' His father had entered the stable in the late afternoon as Raj was tidying up the tool area and spoke in a gentle voice as he addressed his son.

'What?' Raj was not sure if he had heard correctly. A few hours had passed since lunch and he had no contact with the rest of the family since their kitchen fracas, which gave him plenty of time to brood and wallow in his self-defeat.

'Tomo is outside,' Mirko repeated. 'I saw him passing as I was cutting the grass and called for him to wait.'

'Wait for what?' Raj was still holding on to his earlier rejection as he turned back to continue sorting the larger tools. 'I'm not going anywhere anymore.'

'Don't be foolish, Raj,' Mirko counselled with a raised voice. 'And for God's sake, grow a thicker skin. This is the time you want to have holes discovered in your plan and by the people you love, not later when it could cost you more dearly.'

Raj thought a moment and knew, yet again, his father was right. The jibes about the atlas, the move to Italy and his choice of fellowship all hurt his pride, but they were shallow insults that were tainted with loving humour; the kind of humour that Raj's family had shared their whole lives. Perhaps Raj was just too sensitive regarding this particular topic and far more scared about the whole upcoming ordeal than he was willing to admit.

'You think it is a good idea?' He dropped his guard slightly as he questioned his father.

'Bringing Tomo? No. I would ask someone – anyone else, but that might prove even riskier with the schedule.' His father hadn't changed his position on that topic. 'But leaving this God-forsaken place is the best thing you could do, son. And if you find a way, get your mother and me out of here before we die of old age.'

'I promise I will, Dad.' It was the first time Raj sensed his father's vulnerability over his station in life, and if there was a way out for all of them, he would do his best to find it.

'For heaven's sake,' Mirko added, grabbing Raj firmly by the arms, 'wherever you go, whether its Germany or Italy, plead for political asylum. Tell them you are being persecuted. Don't just go looking for work. As much as these nations are rebuilding, there are precarious covenants across the continent about migration, and the communists don't want their able-bodied men building capitalist cities while the eastern bloc gets left behind.'

'Political asylum?' Raj's question was as much angled toward the enlightenment of his own expedition as it was a surprise to the depth of his father's understanding of European politics.

'Yes,' Mirko affirmed, 'political asylum. Not economic asylum.'

Raj strode out into the dusk light and the evening air that had become markedly cooler. The smell of fresh cut grass permeated the scene, only masked now and again by the occasional whiff of dinner floating from the kitchen openings, or dung from the animal enclosures. He knew he would miss this place. He would miss the magic of the evening sights, smells and sounds; he would miss his mother's cooking and his father's lessons. And just as Mugo ran up for a pat, he knew he would miss the hound too. He grew up with that dog and felt that he was as much part of the family as any human.

'Raj,' called Tomo from just beyond the horseless cart parked near an opening at the top of the property.

'Tomo,' answered Raj, his stomach beginning its well-known journey into nervousness.

'Over here.' Tomo raised his hand and walked toward Raj. The darkness was coming fast as Tomo appeared more and more like a silhouette on that well-worn stony path. 'Mirko said you were looking for me.'

Raj swallowed deeply before speaking, the weight of destiny suddenly perching on his shoulders, while an increasing excitement once again flowed through his veins.

'You alone?' He looked past Tomo for dramatic effect, not that he could really see much in that light.

'Yeah,' Tomo sounded intrigued. 'What's up?'

'You still want to go on that holiday?'

CHAPTER 5

Split was a beautiful coastal city with a rich and diverse history. It was a summer haven for rich tourists from all over the world and a particular favourite for the European aristocracy. Over its long history it rivalled some of the best French and Spanish locations for summer recreation, but now offered a little more privacy, so to speak, hidden behind the iron curtain. A history as long and bloody as any in the Yugoslavian Federation, the Dalmatian peninsula surrounding Split had experienced domination and independence. It had been annexed and liberated, and had been named and re-named multiple times for over two thousand years. The Greeks were believed to have founded the town prior to the birth of Christianity, while the Italian city states fought over the area with both the Austrians and French many years later. Split was a flourishing economic capital well before the Second World War brought raging violence to its shore. It served both axis and allied powers well as a strategic naval fort, offering easy access to the theatres of war in both southern Europe and northern Africa via the Mediterranean Sea, and was hotly contested for just such a reason.

Split was flush with people after the war. The Dalmatian coast was a fishing paradise and it was said the Dalmatians had sea water in their blood. Seafood caught off the coast of Split was some of the best found in homes and restaurants throughout the land. Yugoslavian ship-building was also centred in Split, and so workers came by the thousands for maritime jobs, both military and commercial. This had a flow on effect to every satellite industry that played a supporting role, from hospitality to real estate. The ancient city was also the main seaport for the federation. With years of infrastructure and experience already in place, the new nation could handle all that the global economy could send across the oceans. This city was experiencing a peaceful and mercantile renaissance, abundant and under strict communist control, with the Dalmatians enjoying the new stability after changing hands so many times during the war. A railway was also in development to connect the western coast to greater Yugoslavia, allowing quicker transport of goods and people throughout the land and into the greater continent.

Raj and Tomo had entered the city in the false dawn light on a Saturday morning. They had been travelling for a few days and Raj kept them at a brisk pace as he was quite paranoid about their adventure. Tomo was far more relaxed, nonchalantly so, Raj sometimes thought. Both men knew there was nothing illegal about a couple of travellers seeing the country, but Raj was still worried lest any tongues wagged back home regarding their departure. They initially used the annual pilgrimage to the Blidinje grasslands, as a cover on the first leg of their journey. The beasts were all comfortably grazing and under the watchful eyes of uncles and cousins, so the two young men slipped through the forest and headed west toward Imotski. Tomo had some family in the border town, so they rested there for a night and stocked up on some food before catching an overnight bus headed for Split. To be safe, Raj insisted they hop off just outside of the municipality and make the remainder of their journey by foot. The duo was thankful for the lovely weather they had, but their feet were still very sore as they strode lightly downhill and toward the centre of the old town.

'Ooh,' said Tomo, 'that smell...' and he sniffed in the air whilst smiling.

'Yeah.' Raj looked at the bakery they were passing. A light could be seen around the edges of the glass façade where the blinds within couldn't completely cover the windows. 'Can't be too long before they open for business.'

'How much money you got?' Tomo asked.

'Enough to get to Italy,' Raj answered. 'Unless I eat at every bakery and restaurant we pass.'

Tomo laughed. 'I'm not sure I can pass by that smell and not eat something.'

'It's your money, Tomo,' Raj stated seriously, stopping at a stone bench two stores away from the bakery. 'You can spend it how you please. But as soon as that morning light brightens, we'll need to keep moving.'

'Sure.' Tomo sullenly reached into his pack. Rummaging around, he pulled out a bottle of Rakija: the local Bosnian moonshine. The glass bottle could have easily been mistaken for water as its contents were clear and it had no wrap-around stickers advertising a product. The only thing that made it conspicuous was the golden bottle top branded by red Cyrillic lettering for a Soviet children's tomato drink.

'You want a nip?' he asked.

'A bit early for me,' Raj declined. Tomo's relatives insisted that both men take a bottle each on their adventure. Raj tried to resist, especially since he couldn't understand how nearly a litre of the clear rocket fuel, that took up half his rucksack, could possibly help them on their journey, but Tomo's uncle would not budge and Raj didn't want to escalate the argument.

Tomo happily took a swig then capped the bottle before pulling out an apple and taking a crunchy bite.

'That's a better idea.' Raj copied his friend and both men sat quietly enjoying the smell of the bakery and the taste of their apples. Seeing his friend taking a stiff drink at the crack of dawn perplexed Raj. Was Tomo's heart condition true, or simply another ruse to get out of military service? Raj was hoping Tomo would broach the topic but there was no mention of it yet and Raj didn't want to speculate on his friend's personal matters.

'Pretend its homemade apple pie,' Tomo suggested and Raj smiled as the morning sunlight got just that little brighter.

Whether it was the permeating sea air or the rhythmic sound of crashing waves against the surrounding rocky shore in the distance, both young men's appetites had grown considerably since entering the town. The fresh smells of the early bake houses didn't really help their cause so when they finished their fruit they made their way toward the coast, and closer to the docks and fishery areas. The white and beige stone that enveloped the city was ever so slowly coming to light. Narrow pathways between ancient buildings were still shrouded in darkness and could easily have caused the two journeymen to become lost, so they stayed on broader roads and just kept descending slowly. As the sunlight grew stronger, the sea grew more visible between all the winding pavements. Once closer to the ocean, the smell in the air hitting their noses was far better for two hungry fellows who couldn't really afford a baker's delight, as the fishermen who had been out overnight were already filleting their catch, cleaning their gear and preparing for the day shift. Salty sea, bloodied guts and body odour destroyed any appetite the two travellers might have had.

'Stinks like hell around here.' Tomo held his nose and looked disgusted. 'How long before we catch up with Krizan?'

The question made Raj nervous. Although Raj specifically told Tomo his older brother's guidance was not guaranteed, Tomo still held tight to the belief that Kriz would spirit them away and make the journey to Italy quick and painless. Raj wasn't expecting so much, he knew their destiny was in their own hands, but just hoped Kriz might have some tricks up his sleeve to help them hurry along.

'I think it's still a bit early.' Raj looked at the sky without breaking his step. 'Maybe just before lunch.'

Raj's plan was to mill around central Split for a few hours then move back west toward the edge of the town and find the address of Krizan's last correspondence.

'Why don't we just go now?' Tomo insisted.

'Because if Kriz isn't there,' Raj answered, 'I don't want to be one of two weirdos who rocks up to a stranger's place at dawn asking for someone who doesn't live there.'

'If he doesn't live there, then what does it matter if we show up at midday or dawn?' Tomo countered.

'At midday, we could just be a couple of lost brothers,' Raj offered. 'But at the crack of dawn we look like criminals trying to catch our victims by surprise.'

'You think criminals don't work in the afternoon?' Tomo laughed. 'You haven't met Luka, my cousin in Zagreb.'

'Please Tomo,' Raj pleaded honestly. 'Bear with me, I'm trying to minimise our exposure.'

With that, they kept walking away from the commercial fishery area until they stumbled upon a wide boardwalk, which narrowed, then turned into a long pier, protruding well into the water. The sea air was even stronger here as the young men stopped on the old, grey timber decking and looked out across the Adriatic. The sea was littered with vessels that bobbed up and down with the gentle sway of the ocean's tide, as rods and lines hung over the edges of the fishing craft attended to by salty mariners who busily maintained their chances for a catch of the day.

Further up the coast, larger boats were anchored, with clear indications of a booming ferrying industry. The boys looked upon the promenade that fed onto the boardwalk and saw the beginnings of the daily hustle as shopkeepers slowly opened for the day's business. As the hour passed, the low morning sun had lifted further and now gently blanketed the city streets, cutting swathes of light and shade through narrow pathways, also illuminating the orange and red terracotta roofs that were so commonly found throughout coastal southern Europe. The sound of motors moving vehicles was also gaining volume around the town, particularly the high pitch revolutions of motorcycles, followed by the howling of pet dogs and screeching of wild birds, in a typical chorus found in most old European towns at this time.

'We should get some breakfast.' Raj changed his tune as he looked at the movement of people on the street.

'What?' Tomo appeared to feign hearing loss. 'Did I hear correctly?'

'It's more suspicious for us to loiter around here than it is to sit somewhere and have a coffee.' Raj's mind was always working, trying to stay a step ahead of any possible danger.

'And God knows we got time...' Tomo added as he confidently strode toward a small cafe that had just opened its doors. A young waitress attended to the tables just outside the store, wiping chairs and placing ash trays. She greeted the two young men with a cordial smile.

'Good morning, gents,' she said, 'what can I get for you?'

'Anything you like,' Tomo's eyes beamed intrusively at the sight of the girl and his slimy answer made her smile shrink just a little.

'A couple of Turkish blacks,' Raj respectfully interjected, 'and maybe a broom to sweep my friend's jaw off the floor.'

The remark seemed to go straight over Tomo's head as Cupid's arrow had clearly shot him through the heart and turned his wits to jelly. The waitress smiled at the joke but looked relieved to get back into the store with the knowledge that at least one of her morning customers had a semblance of social grace.

'Put it back in your pants, Tomo,' Raj insisted, his tone lowered but still quite forceful.

'Relax.' Tomo didn't seem to care as he casually took his seat on the wrought iron chair and stretched his arms behind his head. 'It's just social banter, and it's expected.'

At that point Raj's father's words started echoing in his mind. Was Tomo a good choice for this escapade? Did he have the ability to keep cool under pressure? The travel through Bosnia was one thing, but Dalmatia was a very different place. Firstly, the customs on the coast were different, with a far calmer social environment. Bosnia was well known for hot-headed, moonshine-induced spats at the drop of a hat. Dalmatia was far more refined, with discussions preferred rather than arguments. Conversely, being far more agrarian, Bosnians needed patience in their farming and produce development, whereas the coastal towns of Yugoslavia were becoming more urban and thus day to day life moved at a quicker pace. The dialects were different too, with Italian influences very clearly heard in the language on the coast while Arabic and Persian words had influenced the languages to the east.

'Just be careful, is all I'm saying,' Raj advised his friend. 'We don't want any uninvited attention. We are just passing through.'

'Lighten up, Raj,' Tomo responded. 'We'll be fine. In the city there is so much going on that we will just blend in. Nothing to worry about.'

'Good morning.' A man's voice interjected their conversation. 'I don't mean to interrupt, but...'

Raj jumped a little at the surprising sound before turning to look up at a tall, slim stranger dressed flamboyantly, standing right behind him. He wore pressed sky-blue pants, accompanied by a collared orange shirt under a double-breasted green blazer. His shoes were of a black and white chequered design, polished and clean while his spotted grey hair was slicked back and groomed to perfection. A pencil thin moustache sat above his thin lips which held a cigarette in place that was not yet ablaze.

'...Do you mind?' He leant forward gracefully yet creepily; his words seemed unnaturally elongated.

'Rudolf,' the waitress had returned and placed a tray at the table, 'stop harassing the customers.' She reached into her pocket and produced a gas lighter that sparked the man's cigarette.

'Much obliged, Maria,' he tilted his head to the waitress before placing a yellow fedora on it, that he had been holding behind his back, 'what brings you young bucks to such a fine establishment as this?'

'On our way north,' Tomo offered freely, not taking his eyes off Maria.

'We are just passing through,' Raj cut in, 'is what my friend means. On our way to my friend's cousins wedding in Zagreb.'

'Zagreb?' Rudolph took another puff. 'You boys going the long way around, eh?'

'What?' Raj looked surprised.

'Enough, Rudi,' Maria interjected, her tone a little more demanding this time. 'If these lads wanted to talk with you they would have offered you a seat. Now order something or get lost!'

'I like a lady that takes charge.' Tomo couldn't keep the grin from beaming across his face.

Rudolf smiled thinly and bowed his head yet again. A bellow of smoke passed over Raj and Tomo's table before the creepy stranger ambled slowly past, keeping his eye on the seated patrons to the last possible moment.

'Strange guy, dressed like a tropical bird,' Raj said to himself as he watched Rudolf meander down the promenade and back toward town.

'You don't know the half of it,' Maria revealed.

'Thanks,' Raj said as she removed the coffees from the tray and moved back toward the store.

'What do you mean?' Tomo quickly pressed before Maria had a chance to open the cafe door.

She stopped and looked suspiciously at Tomo. 'Is there anything else I can help you with? Some breakfast perhaps?'

'Coffee is good for now, thanks,' Raj interjected, allowing Maria to escape Tomo's awkward glare by disappearing into the cafe.

'I think she likes me,' Tomo stated confidently, still grinning from ear to ear.

'Yeah.' Raj shook his head. 'So much she probably poisoned your coffee.'

'What do you mean?' Tomo looked confused, staring into his cup.

'Never mind.' Raj changed the topic. 'We should make a move sooner rather than later.' He took a sip from his cup, then blew across the top to help cool it faster.

'Really?' Tomo teased, lighting a cigarette of his own. 'I'm starting to enjoy it here.'

'I didn't like the look of that guy.' Raj was referring to the smoking stranger, Rudolf, as he twirled the cup in his hands.

'You're too paranoid, Raj. You're taking the fun out of this.'

'It's not going to be fun if we get thrown in a fucking gulag!' Raj respected Tomo's notion of enjoying the trip, but he also felt that his friend took it a little too far.

'Gulag?' Tomo sounded surprised. 'You've been talking to the old men in the village for too long. The war scrambled their brains. Gulags are in Russia. My brother reckons worst we'll get is a slap on the wrist.'

'Your brother?' Raj knew of Tomo's brother's reputation and knew many of the words that came out of his mouth were far from trustworthy.

'Yeah,' Tomo added. 'He's tried to get out three times.'

Raj kept his frustration within as the logic of taking advice on a subject from someone who had failed multiple times at that subject was apparently lost on Tomo, and so explaining it would have just infuriated Raj all the more.

'How far did he get?' Raj asked, scratching at the overgrown stubble under his chin while being curiously amused.

'He made it to Romania,' Tomo announced proudly.

'Romania? Why Romania?' The amusement Raj felt was turning slightly sour as he questioned his friend.

'He was going toward Germany.' Tomo took a long drag on his smoke before raising his coffee to his lips.

Raj left the conversation there. Questions arose in his mind regarding Tomo's family's intelligence; did they know how to read a map? Had they any idea of the political and social climate in their neighbouring lands? Were they retarded? All these quickly ceased when it dawned on Raj that Tomo was his first and only choice for the trip. Perhaps Raj's own intelligence should be the subject of questioning because Raj did no responsible vetting beforehand, no checks into Tomo's past and no due diligence into the Drembanovic family.

Sure, they went to school together for a few years, but that was a long time ago and even then, Raj would hardly call them best of friends. Raj's father warned about the trustworthiness of Tomo's family in regard to lending farming tools, but nothing more insidious was mentioned. And apart from seeing each other in passing because of their geographic locales, they rarely socialised with each other. Raj's paranoia arose in that moment as he calmly looked across the table, his eyes just above the rim of his cup, slyly gazing at the young man sitting opposite him. Tomo was peering at the shopfront in the hope that the waitress would return, all the while Raj's mind spun into a questioning vortex of accusations and disillusion. At the forefront of the words dancing in his mind – could Tomo be a spy?

Of course, Raj firmly believed Tomo was no espionage master. The only spies Raj knew of were simple informants so low in the pecking order that quite often they would tell lies just to be noticed by their masters. Raj had also never heard of such an elaborate ruse as this; to follow a mark around the country simply to inform on them, was something Raj began to doubt, particularly as no radical officials or organised establishments were involved in their meagre plans. Most informants would sell their flimsy tales even if they only became aware of the knowledge via the grapevine, in the hope of collecting a few quick dollars from their handlers before moving on with their day to day lives. Tomo had plenty of time to offer Raj up to the authorities, but up to that point had not, nor was he exhibiting any overly curious interest in the future of their plans. If anything, Tomo was quite languid in their movement, which was not really beneficial in making a quick buck.

'Maybe we should go.' Raj surrendered to his current situation albeit with a new-found suspicion toward his companion.

'I haven't finished my coffee yet,' scowled Tomo before his eyes changed focus and his face lit up again. 'Besides, it looks like things are hotting up around here.'

Raj turned around and saw three young women pull up chairs at a table just behind them and start chatting while diving into their handbags.

'Looks like the waitress has some competition.' Raj's sarcasm seemed lost on his wide-eyed friend.

'She sure does.' Tomo abruptly straightened up in his chair, smiling broadly. 'Morning ladies!' He raised his coffee to the girls and added a sleazy wink. The young ladies, who looked no older than Raj, just giggled amongst themselves.

Raj ignored the banter and looked around the promenade. He noticed just how many people were now out and about and it settled him a little to see the world revolving at its own pace, ignorant of the two young men just sitting and enjoying a coffee on a Saturday morning. He checked his old fob watch, a parting gift from his father and a family heirloom of sorts, the hands showed 9.25. They had been circling Split for a few hours that morning and had settled at the cafe for at least forty-five minutes. Raj noticed a shoe store across the street and thought about his feet for the first time since they stopped walking. The pulsating pain from the excursion through south western Bosnia with poor footwear had finally eased a little, allowing him some reprieve. Once he was working and making good coin, he thought, the first thing he would do is buy new shoes.

Suddenly, Tomo stood up and walked toward the table hosting the flirting young ladies. Without looking down, he covertly pinched Raj on the shoulder as he passed, which sent mixed messages. Was he encouraging Raj to join him, or was he simply boasting of his magnetic prowess? Either way Raj was not interested. In Raj's opinion, the less people he, and Tomo, spoke to on this trip, the better. Unfortunately, Tomo didn't quite subscribe to the same ideal and would start up a conversation with nearly anyone. Raj knew that a slip of the tongue to a stranger, even a pretty one, could lead both men toward a very different destination.

'If you like, I can get you a glass of ice?' Maria broke Raj's reverie.

'Ice?' Raj questioned the waitress. 'Why would I want ice?'

'So you can sit there sucking on it like a tight-arse while keeping your dinars in your pocket.' The cheeky waitress made a good point, both from the cafe owner's point of view and, inadvertently, from Raj's.

'What's good for breakfast?' Raj suddenly asked, now becoming aware that a man sitting at a cafe for nearly an hour with an empty cup in front of him could be viewed with suspicion.

'The Burek is excellent.' The waitress smiled and held a pen and pad at the ready.

'Burek it is then,' Raj agreed, ordering the cheesy, meaty pastry. 'And another coffee too, please.'

Raj knew the trip would cost and was hoping he would have enough to cover any travel, food and bribery required along the way. He really didn't want to spend any more time and money in Split but knew he had to maintain flexibility on the journey, and if that meant spending a few coins to fit into the cafe scene, then that's what he would have to do. As much as he would have liked to, Raj was sure that pulling out a day-old piece of rye bread from his worn out rucksack might not be construed as fitting in. Besides, the journey still had a way to go, and if things did go wrong, there would be no point having a full purse while sitting in a jail cell.

The Burek was served simply, steaming hot at this time of morning, with a dollop of cold sour cream to the side. It really was fresh and delicious. The smell alone made Raj realise how hungry he actually was as he quickly shovelled the first piece of crusty pastry into his mouth.

'Slow down,' Maria suggested, smiling as she returned with Raj's coffee. 'If you want to sit out here and enjoy the scenery, then take your time.' She winked as she turned on her heels and made way to the next table where an elderly couple had just assumed their Saturday morning position on the promenade.

Raj took heed from her kind words, but then wondered if she was giving advice based on any other evidence. Was Tomo shooting off his mouth to the girls at the other table? He turned casually and slowed his chewing, but the morning din was effervescent by now, and nothing clear could be made out from Tomo's discussion.

'You look stressed.' This time Maria quickly sat down in the chair Tomo had abandoned, crossing her legs before lighting up a smoke.

Raj looked dumfounded at his new female colleague. Rarely did he talk to any girls outside his family, let alone have them drop in and strike up the conversation.

'I'm fine,' was the best Raj could muster, still chewing his delicious breakfast.

'Your eyes are darting all over the place. You needed me to remind you to order food at a fucking cafe.' She took a big drag of her cigarette. 'And you keep turning your head to listen in on your sleazy friend's chatter. Yeah, sure you're fine.'

She sounded like his father, Raj thought, easily spotting out flaws in both his demeanour and, by extension, his plan. He took a deep breath and relaxed back into his chair.

'That's better.' Maria smiled. 'You see? You weren't even seated comfortably!'

'What do you want?' Raj was becoming frustrated with her attitude, so he cut to the chase.

'I'm just an old friend that is having her break at a cafe on the promenade.' She butted out her cigarette, a puff of blue grey smoke wisped above the table. 'Break's over.' And with that she got up and went back to work.

'Wait,' Raj commanded, his level of discomfort arose measurably in that moment. 'I mean, can you please wait? I feel like I'm missing something here.' Raj released his vulnerability, feeling that only his honesty might allow her to open up some more.

Maria didn't sit down again but reached over to Raj and casually pretended to straighten his collar. 'You think you're the first Herceg to enter Split on his way to Italy?'

Bosnia-Hercegovina was the state that, for centuries, lay under the rule of the Ottoman Empire. With such a long time as rulers, many Christians switched faiths to make life easier for their families, leaving a large Muslim population sharing the state with a minority of Christians. Bosnian was the more common name for the Muslim cohort, whereas the Hercegovacs were generally seen as Catholics.

'How do you know where I'm from?' asked Raj, puzzled by her reference.

'Jesus.' She sounded more sympathetic than annoyed. 'Next time you travel, take the cross off your neck, idiot.' She smiled gently and pulled away from Raj, then added, 'And invest in some better clothing. The closest farm is miles away.'

Raj stopped chewing from shock. What could he say? His stomach felt queasy all of a sudden, but he wasn't about to spit the remnants of his breakfast back on his plate.

'You look pale,' Maria said. 'You okay?'

With a great effort, Raj swallowed and pushed his plate to the centre of the table. 'I just lost my appetite, that's all,' he answered. 'I'll be fine.'

'Maybe take it easy on the Turkish coffee, too.' The waitress smiled cheekily then darted back toward the cafe entrance.

Raj felt ashamed. Here, a street wise girl, with no greater rank than waitress, could tell which part of the world Raj was coming from, what he did for a living and what his eventual future plans were. He subconsciously fingered the small, silver cross beneath his collar, which immediately returned his thoughts to his mother and the glistening tears in her eyes as she fastened this parting gift around his neck. It, and the old fob watch, were the only two trinkets he took with him on the trip. Raj then looked down at his clothes, then around at others sitting on the strip. The elderly couple were dressed impeccably; the old man even wore a royal blue ascot beneath his pressed white collar, while his lady was adorned in sparkling jewellery around both her neck and fingers. Raj then turned fully to look at the girls in Tomo's company. They wore darker colours, with leggings, skirts and blouses that hugged tightly, but revealed little, yet looked clean and classy. Their jewellery was worn over their clothing, highlighting the silver and gold sparkle against the dark hues of their fashion. One of the ladies was applying lipstick with the help of a small, hand-held mirror, ensuring her intended look was being maintained.

'Time to go, Tomo.' Raj had seen and heard enough. He and Tomo looked like filthy hobos escaping from a garbage infested prison when compared to the refined populace that now mulled around the promenade. During the pre-dawn hours, their look really had no effect, as the dark made everyone look more or less the same, particularly among the fishmongers. But the morning light was shining brightly now, and its beam was nowhere near strong enough to polish the two homeless vagabonds that were accosting the fine citizens of this worldly metropolis. Raj's paranoid musings beheld police and militia of all sorts descending violently upon the cafe, ridding these clean, coastal streets of such vermin as himself and Tomo.

'Relax.' Tomo turned and smiled, showing his coffee stained teeth while trying to keep cool in front of the girls.

'Fuck your "relax".' Raj cursed forcefully yet quietly, struggling to keep the spit in his mouth. He looked at his tired, journey worn friend with new found pity, as the girls around Tomo's table childishly giggled amongst themselves.

'What happened?' asked Tomo, standing up from his chair, looking concerned at Raj's changed behaviour.

'We've been made, Tomo,' Raj whispered, sounding as serious as he could. 'Say goodbye to your lady friends. It's time to go.'

Raj walked into the cafe and noticed town maps for sale on the counter. He knew finding Kriz's place might be hard without a map, so he grabbed one and settled their account. Maria graciously accepted the money and asked innocently, 'You leaving already?'

'Yes,' Raj answered curtly, placing the change in his pocket.

'Well.' Maria coyly smiled. 'Enjoy the rest of your holiday. And keep a look out for those bright birds.'

Raj walked quickly out of the cafe a little confused by Maria's parting words. He strode straight past Tomo and made his way down the promenade without waiting for his friend. As far as Raj was concerned, the further away from Split they got, the safer they became. Tomo had to run just to catch up.

'What's the hurry?' Tomo was still trying to catch his breath as he asked the question.

'We've been fools,' Raj answered tersely, his mood not lifting at all and while they marched through the town, he subtly removed the crucifix from his neck and placed it in his pocket with his watch.

'That's a bit harsh, don't you think?' Tomo said. 'I thought we blended in nicely.'

'But you also think going through Romania is the best path to Germany!' Raj was becoming frustrated, and caught himself before he released a broader, vitriolic barrage against his naïve companion.

'What's Romania got to do with anything?' Tomo innocently inquired.

'Never mind.' Raj didn't want to make a scene but also felt a little sorry for his dim-witted friend.

'Look, Raj.' Tomo pointed toward a corner across from the street they walked on. 'There's that guy, from before, the one that's dressed like a bird. What was his name again?'

A bolt of nervous energy shot up Raj's spine as he looked across to see Rudolf talking to a man in front of a corner store. Both men smoked and casually looked around at the people passing by. Rudolf's height and bright attire was hard to miss, but the man with him was shorter, broad and stocky, dressed plainly in black, with shoulder arching stirrups keeping his pants from falling, while high laced, black boots kept his pants from dragging. Just as Raj was about to look away he made eye contact with Rudolf, who then leant over to his shorter companion while only slightly moving his lips, the man in black turned in the direction of Raj and Tomo across the street.

'Trouble is his name,' Raj belatedly answered, thinking of the waitress' last words while purposefully stepping just a little faster.

'What's going on Raj?' Tomo was starting to sound frustrated himself, skipping a step to keep up again.

'I'll explain later,' Raj said. 'But for now, let's make some distance between us and that bright bird.'

So uphill they went, via back alleys and narrow avenues while trying to avoid main thoroughfares. The morning sun was high and beating down on the town as the afternoon heat approached. Shadows were thinner and gave far less cover than earlier, but the sunlight now allowed the two men to see the distance far better. A few times they found dead ends due to their haste and had to pull out the town map to find their bearings. Often, main streets were there only choice, and after passing Rudolf earlier, Raj noticed many more men scattered around town dressed in black, complete with stirrups and boots, usually congregating in groups of three or four on busier street corners.

Finally, after about half an hour of consistent walking, they made their way to the address Raj remembered on the envelope. A long road awaited them, paved and cemented, complete with drainage and sidewalks, and wide enough for a horse and cart to pass side by side. The broad street cut a straight line for half a mile and housed many dwellings, styled differently throughout the centuries, and stretched as far as the eye could see. Like most buildings in Split, Kriz's particular lodging was a conjoined townhouse that was rendered in beige cement, with small windows adorned by wooden shutters that closed toward the centre. It looked to be three stories from the outside and Raj spied a balustrade on the edge of the roof, and a window at the foot of the building, hinting at a sub-floor. A large red door faced the two men as they stopped at the bottom of the three concrete stairs that led up to the entrance.

'You sure this is it?' asked Tomo.

'Yep, this must be it,' answered Raj. 'Can you see the small faded crosses on the walls?' The render had faintly discoloured to a lighter shade at three distinct places on the facade.

'Yeah... you're right.' Tomo finally saw the residue of the holy symbols once Raj had pointed them out.

'The commos must have pulled down the crosses.' Raj's nerves settled after seeing the sign, but still tentatively stepped up toward the front door.

'Can I help you?' a short, olive-skinned woman, black of hair with wide, dark rimmed spectacles answered through the slimmest opening. Her brown eyes looked larger than normal because her glasses were so thick they exhibited a greenish hue at the edges. Even with just those few words, Raj could tell her accent was quite different from many of the other people they heard talking on the streets, but Raj felt no threat from her, only curiosity.

'Good morning, madam, I am here to see my brother,' Raj respectfully replied. Tomo kept on the footpath, not venturing up the steps as yet.

'And who is your brother?' the little lady inquired, opening the door slightly wider.

'Sorry.' Raj just realised his error. 'His name is Krizan. This is the last address I have for him.'

'Krizan?' The lady repeated the word, her eyes leaving Raj's, looking past him toward Tomo, and for the first time she seemed a little frightened by the strangers at her door. 'I don't know any Krizan.'

'Krizan Krizic?' Raj raised his voice accidentally forcing his point, desperate for a different answer. Perhaps if she heard is surname then she would have a better recollection?

'Keep your voice down, foolish child, I'm not deaf.' The woman still seemed quite calm, but she looked to be losing patience with Raj, closing the large, red door ever so slightly as she spoke.

'Krizan Krizic?' Raj said quietly, becoming forlorn now the conversation wasn't going as planned.

'Krizic?' the woman replied innocently. 'I have never heard of him. Good day to you.' She quickly closed the door in Raj's face and left the young man staring blankly at another dead end, but this time his heart sank and no map could help him get around the giant obstacle in his way.

'Krizan Krizic,' he whispered to himself, as the first tear of the journey slowly rolled down his cheek.

CHAPTER 6

The two friends sat quietly next to each other on the bottom step in front of the townhouse where Kriz was supposed to be. Raj held his head in his hands as he leant over and stared between his feet. His eyes had dried and his emotions had settled only slightly, but still a myriad of questions kept racing through his mind. At the centre of his turmoil was a genuine concern for his brother's safety. If the letter was sent from this location, but Kriz was not here, then either the authorities had caught up with him, or were hot on his heels. The old lady at the door acted mysteriously and certainly changed her demeanour when Raj mentioned his family's last name. She also had a strange accent that really wasn't native to Split, or any part of the Croatian state, at least that Raj knew of. Every couple of minutes he raised his head and turned in hope, looking at the building behind him, trying to catch sight of the slightest movement at a window, but, just like his brother's whereabouts, there was nothing there. He touched the cross in his pocket as he thought of home as well as wondering what the next step in his journey would be.

Even the ever-exuberant Tomo was lost for words. Raj's companion was strangely pensive and had said nothing since they sat down. In fact, it might have been the first time on the whole trip that Tomo was speechless. After all the times Raj wished his friend to keep quiet, right now would have been a great time for Tomo to say a few words. But he knew Tomo had high hopes in Kriz and, in many ways, he was more disappointed than Raj.

'What now?' asked Tomo quietly, as if he had read Raj's mind.

'Two options,' Raj revealed after a moment. 'Go forward, or go back.'

'Go back?' Tomo seemed uncertain of Raj's meaning.

'We've done nothing illegal as yet.' Raj looked up and elaborated.

'If we go home now, we are just a couple of Hercegs on an adventure to Split.'

'I'm not going home, Raj,' Tomo spoke seriously. 'You had a plan. You said Kriz wasn't essential and we shouldn't rely on him. You said we shouldn't rely on anybody but ourselves. You said there is something better waiting for us beyond the border. Remember?'

'I remember, Tomo,' Raj replied quietly, looking down at his feet again. 'But I'm just worried now.'

'About what?' asked Tomo, sounding frustrated.

'About Kriz, mostly. Also about my parents,' added Raj. 'They think we are all together moving toward liberty. I need to get them a message. I also need to find out if they may have heard anything.'

'Your brother will be fine.' Tomo rose from his seat and stretched. He faced Raj and kept one foot on the stairs and the other on the street. 'If he got this far, and is almost ordained, then the church will protect him. They are clever with their investments.'

'Tell that to the eleven priests at Medugorije.' Raj reminded Tomo of the clerical slaughter throughout Hercegovina.

'Nah, not your bother, Raj.' Tomo looked back at the house and stated confidently. 'This old bitch was hiding something. Did you see how cold she grew after hearing your surname?'

A spark arose in Raj at that moment. 'Yeah, I saw that. I wasn't sure; I thought maybe it was just me.'

'She doesn't trust us,' Tomo added. 'She sure doesn't trust your surname.'

Raj thought about it before responding. 'But surely Kriz would have let her know?'

'Let her know what?' Tomo asked. 'That he was trying to get out? That his brother was trying to get out? Why would he tell her anything? Did he even know you we were coming?'

A few people walked past, silencing the two friends and allowing Raj to ponder Tomo's questions for a longer moment.

'No,' Raj answered solemnly. 'He had no idea I was coming. There was no time. Plus, communications like that can be dangerous.'

'Then this woman could just as easily be protecting him.'

'Maybe.' Raj paused at the thought, feeling a little confused.

'Well.' Tomo moved onto the pavement properly, with a little skip in his step. 'There you have it. Kriz had no reason to hang out here. For all we know, he could have gone the day after he sent you the mail. Hell, he might have even put a fake address on his post. He clearly couldn't have told this woman about you, so questioning her would be pointless either way.'

Raj mulled that over in his head. If Kriz wasn't expecting him, then Tomo was right, there would be no reason for keeping him here. If the church was moving him about as they had previously, then he would be at the whim of the prefect and would have to obey the rules like the rest of the clergy. They gambled to find Kriz and it hadn't paid off. *So what?* Raj thought, *Kriz isn't the be all and end all.* They got this far without him and could go on further just as easily. A confidence began growing in Raj yet again and just as he was about to rise...

'Have you noticed a lot of black clad, angry-looking militia types lurking throughout the city?' Tomo inquired, his gaze turned toward the far end of the road.

'Yeah, all over the place.' Raj looked at his friend. 'Why?'

'I think there might be four coming our way,' Tomo replied.

'Are they coming for us, or just our way?' asked Raj, moving his head to see past Tomo.

'They are quite far but looks like one just raised his hand toward me,' Tomo said. 'He is smiling... I think.'

'Maybe it's time to go?' Raj stood up and casually walked back the way they came and away from the four black shirted men.

They kept a good pace without making it look like they were avoiding anyone in particular. But once they turned a corner, they moved even quicker, then they turned a couple more corners to throw off their would-be pursuers even further. Unfortunately, the two men were now lost and didn't want to stop to unfold the map. They chose to follow a straight road, quite busy with pedestrians, which gently curved, before reaching an intersection that was closed to traffic. They were at an open social precinct, not dissimilar to the promenade near the shore, but far smaller, with six asphalt streets that fed into it from all sides. Dining tables were stuffed into the central area, where dozens of residents sat enjoying their midday feasts. There was a claustrophobic and frenzied feeling to the place, it was packed with people as waiting staff lifted trays above their heads and quickly skirted between tables and chairs just to service the hungry lunchtime crowd.

Large, beige umbrellas dotted the pavement, casting shade from the sun, while the tables were covered by thin, white table covers, creating an artificial canopy between the boutique shops and cafes that encircled the town square. A gentle sea breeze cooled the area nicely and pushed at the edges of the canopy, helping waft the copious amounts of cigarette smoke around the tables, adding a further feeling of movement to the overall scene. On the periphery, window shoppers shared the cover of shop verandas with buskers and hustlers of all kind, as chatting, music and laughter permeated the area. The din was loud and breathless and a perfect cover for two men avoiding notice.

'Are they still behind us?' asked Raj, having to slow down as they made their way through the Saturday crowd.

'I don't see them.' Tomo followed closely. 'But we have some distance.'

'Are you sure they were coming for us?' Raj looked back now too, but could not see them.

'I'm not,' Tomo replied. 'But I didn't really want to find out.'

Raj spied a couple leaving a table located just off the middle of the outdoor mall and made his way straight to it. He apologised as he bumped and knocked other seated patrons in his attempt to secure a seat, and once seated, he lowered his body deep into the timber chair. The shade, provided by the umbrella right next to them, was a relief from the sun, and Raj hoped the thick, wooden shaft might help conceal them a little more too. He could barely see past the other customers and tried to keep one eye on the road from where they just came. Tomo joined him and quickly lit up a cigarette as soon as he sat down.

'Tell me you have a plan, Raj?' Tomo kept looking back from whence they came too, his demeanour not as relaxed at as it had been earlier in the trip, even though he was now sitting down and enjoying a smoke.

'This time *you* should relax,' offered Raj, 'I have my eye on the road, and they haven't appeared.'

'Okay, okay.' Tomo settled in his chair.

'I *have* been thinking about it,' Raj continued, 'and I think by sea might be the fastest way to go.'

'Shit.' Tomo sounded and looked really surprised. His voice rose in pitch while he cocked his head at a strange angle. 'You want to cross the Adriatic?'

'No... what?' Raj was taken aback as he hadn't contemplated anything nearly as dangerous as that. 'You insane? I have heard horror stories about that crossing. I meant straight up the coast. Remember the commercial ferries near the docks? We can see where they land up north. Pula, or Rijeka... wherever. It might save us time and get us away from this black shirt brigade.'

Raj looked again to where they entered the area and saw the four pursuers staring over the scene before them with a glaring intensity.

'Can I get you a drink?' A waiter suddenly appeared, dressed properly in a clean, white shirt and pressed black pants. His left hand gripped a notepad and a white cloth was neatly draped over the arm, while his right hand held a pencil at the ready. He bent over slightly and had to talk quite loudly just to be heard, but was courteous and professional in his attitude.

'No thanks,' Raj replied, then he saw a couple of menus tucked under the waiter's arm. 'But what's good for lunch?'

The waiter promptly passed two menus to his new customers and briefly explained the specials for the day. He then cleared their table, leaving only an empty glass ashtray and a box of serviettes.

'I'll give you a moment,' he said and left the two men some time to peruse the menu.

'You buying lunch?' Tomo asked quizzically.

'No.' Raj smiled, lifting the menu in front of his face and adding to his cover. 'Just buying time.'

Tomo followed his friend's lead and covered his face too. 'Ferry, eh?' he asked.

'I think it's our best bet,' added Raj.

'Do they go straight to Italy?' Tomo sounded interested and lowered his menu from excitement.

'Keep the page up, Tomo,' Raj reminded his friend. 'I'm not sure where it stops. I'm not sure what time it leaves, or even how much it costs, but my gut tells me to check it out.'

'Are you gentlemen ready to order?' The waiter had returned rather quickly with pencil and pad at the ready once again, eager to take the two new customers' money.

'Give us another minute.' Raj pretended to be reading the page, then glanced up to see the waiter roll his eyes before leaving. Raj looked further out to the street and noticed a few more black shirts around the precinct. He turned to look around behind Tomo, and even more black shirted toughs were meandering on the outskirts. 'We may have a problem, Tomo.'

'What is it?' asked his friend.

'Just casually look around.' Raj indicated with a small wave of his menu. 'Please tell me I'm being paranoid again, because it seems we are being circled by these fuckers.'

Tomo did as Raj suggested and agreed. 'There is definitely more of them here now than when we first arrived.'

'They can't be all here for us.' Raj leant forward to change his viewing angles. 'I mean, we haven't done anything wrong!'

'Maybe it was that old witch, back at the house,' Tomo suggested. 'Maybe she is udba.'

'Udba? That old bird?' Raj knew the Yugoslavian Secret Police could get to anyone, but that little old lady might be a bit of a stretch.

'Sure,' Tomo was confident. 'Why not?'

'Maybe it was the girls you were flirting with earlier,' Raj countered. 'Do you remember opening your mouth about anything?'

'Fuck off!' Tomo took offence at Raj's accusation. 'Maybe you were giving the waitress some info, in the hope you could give her something else later? I saw you two talking. She was even touching you at one point.'

'Jealous?' Raj smiled.

'You're just paranoid, my friend.' Tomo smiled back, relaxing once again in his chair and then just as quickly tensing up again. 'It's got to be your brother!'

'Now you can fuck off,' replied Raj calmly. 'What's Kriz got to do with it?'

'Think about it: we rock up to a strange house, where a strange woman awaits and has a pleasant enough conversation with you. Your last name gets mentioned and "bang", all of a sudden there are some kind of paramilitary thugs after us.' Tomo was puffing his cigarette more quickly now and staring into space. 'It has to be it.'

'Are the gentlemen ready to order?' The waiter promptly returned for a third time, sounding curter than on his first two sorties.

'Jesus.' Tomo raised his voice as he glared at the waiter. 'Give us a fucking minute, would you?'

The waiter turned in a huff once more and slid through the congested eatery to get away from the two men. Raj looked at the menu quickly, before his eyes followed the waiter back to the cafe from whence he came.

'You said it yourself,' Tomo continued, 'we've done nothing wrong.

Maybe your brother has been up to something and now we are embroiled!'

'Not good, Tomo.' Raj's heart skipped a beat, his eyes sticking to the waiter.

'I know it's not good.' Tomo was oblivious. 'He's your brother and all, but he should have been more careful.'

'Not that.' Raj nodded discreetly in the direction of the waiter. 'Look...'

'Shit!' Tomo now understood the severity of Raj's words. The waiter was chatting to a black shirted man and pointing toward the two unwilling patrons refusing to order meals during the lunch time rush.

'We need to move,' Raj insisted but didn't get up.

'Where can we go?' Tomo looked around. 'It seems there is even more of them now!'

'Shit, shit, shit...' The whispered expletive was all Raj could manage in the heat of the moment; his mind went blank and his heart pounded through his chest as he looked around at the crowded area. He took a deep breath, settled himself a little and scanned the scene; a clear exit was not apparent, and even if he found one, a fast escape was never going to happen through this kind of congestion. They had to stay low and use stealth, of that Raj was sure, but with so many tables, chairs and umbrellas side by side, getting to the outskirts would be impossible without standing up tall and sliding between the other consumers. Maybe they could hide behind someone else who was leaving, but when Raj looked around, all he saw was people moving into the dining area. He did, however, see the black shirted man raising his hand to his colleagues around the precinct, gesturing for them to close in.

A light sweat broke out atop Raj's brow, as the reality of the situation also began closing in. So far from Italy, so far from home, yet the two young men had not really reached any particularly important goal on their journey. The quest to find Krizan ended in failure and the rest of the journey looked to be headed the same way. Raj dejectedly turned his attention to the excuses he would make; details of their journey, schedules and routes, and how the two paupers from the farms of Bosnia planned to pay for it all. As he pondered the possible conversation he would have with some low-ranking communist official, a waft of alcohol cut across his nostrils, jolting him out of his reverie.

'What are you doing?' He watched Tomo take out his home-made brew and dab some on the corners of the menu, on the napkin box and on the table liner in front of them. He then pulled out a few soaked napkins and threw them under the feet and across the tables of other diners.

'Grab a couple more.' Tomo indicated to Raj. 'Spread 'em out.'

'Oi!' A call was heard from across the way. 'What are you fucking doing?'

'Sorry,' Tomo called out without even looking at the plaintiff, then quietly turned to Raj. 'This is going to hurt.'

Raj was perplexed as he watched Tomo drop beneath their table. Raj casually tilted his head to catch a glimpse of his friend using a napkin to wipe Rakija on every leg of every chair, table and table liner within arm's reach. He then threw the napkin away and raised his hand to Raj.

'Quickly, give me another,' he said, prompting Raj to follow his order.

As Tomo rose from the floor, he wrapped a soaked napkin around the umbrella shaft and slid it up towards the canopy, ensuring the entire wooden pole was covered in the potent home-brew. By now the closest patrons to the two desperate men were shifting uncomfortably in their chairs, trying to slide over as far as possible and avoid eye contact with the crazy guy that was crawling on the floor while wiping the furniture.

'Salute!' Tomo cried, his hair was a mess and his raised hands and blue shirt were filthy, which played right into the part of an insane man at a social gathering. He took an overly dramatic swig from the bottle, then sprayed a little of the alcohol over the tables and umbrellas closest to them, as if drinking champagne in his own private celebration.

Raj was feeling less and less impressed, as were the other patrons who did not appreciate the buffoonery on display and started to rise and leave the vicinity.

'Do you have a better idea?' Tomo whispered, looking down at Raj's unimpressed demeanour.

'At the moment' - Raj sighed within the defeated response - 'no.' For once Raj surrendered and had to let Tomo take the lead, which made him even more nervous.

'What do you think these table cloths are made from?' Tomo's smile helped portray his sinister plan.

'You're not serious, are you?' Raj looked at his friend, who was quickly stuffing a napkin into his quarter full bottle of Rakija.

'Let's go!' he ordered Raj, as he lit the bottom of the table cloth where he had earlier been sitting. 'I'll leave the cocktail for later.'

Rather than smoulder lightly before catching ablaze, the alcohol on the table cloth burst into a quick, bright flame, racing toward the upper side, forcing Raj to jump out of his chair and push the table away. Tomo had to move his hand away quickly as, even he was surprised by the speed of the flame.

Noticing the fire, the other patrons were quickly rising from their chairs too and moving toward the safety of the outskirts. Cries of *Fire* and *Help* were immediately heard alongside smashing glass and breaking porcelain as the turbulence expanded. Raj was caught between some customers and Tomo, when a large whooshing sound was heard. He looked back and saw the umbrella ablaze; its canopy looked like a flaming tree, shooting red and orange plumes into the sky and across to other umbrellas. What followed was a thick, black smoke that stunk of a kind of chemical that Raj had never smelled before.

'So much for stealth,' Raj said to himself, caught in the crowd while trying helplessly to accelerate his movement and catch up to his friend. Tomo must have lit the Molotov cocktail just then, because to Raj's right a smash was heard on the ground followed by a new fire under another table. Gasps of shock cut through the melee as everyone suddenly veered to the left.

Raj put his hands to his mouth because the acrid stench from the flames was now being pushed around by the gentle breeze that had earlier been so pleasant. Black smoke was wafting freely around the public square, made all the worse by the large outdoor umbrellas that trapped the smoke under their canopies, which was then pushed laterally, making the footpaths beneath the shop verandas uncomfortable and far from safe. Vision became diminished and the people were in a frenzied panic now; screaming, cursing and coughing were accompanied by pushing, falling and crying as the instinct for survival took hold. All the while, the fire gained momentum, catching onto the next table, and then the next table, putting the entire area under a serious threat. Within moments, hoses and buckets of water came from all sides to help extinguish the blaze before it spread to the dwellings that surrounded the area. The people fleeing the middle kept their heads down, held their hands over their mouths and wrestled through the spaces between the flaming tables.

Raj struggled to follow Tomo. The amount of movement and noise was both inundating and deafening. He had to squint to see anything through the haze, which in turn caused tears in his eyes which blinded him once again. At the outer edge, a myriad of people mulled around; some sitting and coughing, others tending to them while still more tried to help stop the flames from spreading to the buildings. Shop entrances, windows and walls were populated by the throng as sirens could be heard in the distance. Raj began to cough a little more as he strode along the street, catching glimpses of Tomo's dirty blue shirt here and there.

Eventually, he lost his friend and just stopped. He coughed a couple more times, rubbed at his eyes and made his way toward a concreted wall space between a closed, wooden door and a shop front window that housed mortified onlookers. The haze of smoke was not too bad here as the breeze seemed to be blowing in the other direction, which allowed Raj to clear his eyes and search once again for his companion. The roof protruding from the shops above Raj's head was quite high as well, meaning most of the smoke had room to rise above all the suffering patrons' heads. Raj tried to catch his breath and survey the situation. Tomo was nowhere to be seen and the two men had made no contingency plan if they ever had the misfortune of becoming divided.

Suddenly, a hand grabbed Raj's shoulder and yanked him through the doorway that was closed only a moment before.

'You good?' Tomo asked.

'You're fucking crazy,' answered Raj, with wide eyes and in shock. 'I thought you were... Oh, fuck me.'

'Take it easy,' laughed Tomo, an apparent pride beaming from his face.

'You know the fucking mess you made out there?' Raj wasn't laughing. 'You could've killed somebody!'

'Maybe.' Tomo didn't disagree. 'But the black shirts aren't catching me. They can burn in hell for all I care.'

It was the first time on their trip that Raj saw such darkness in his companion.

'They're not all black shirts out there.' Raj then surrendered and dropped down to the floor to take a seat.

'We should move.' Tomo glanced around the small room.

'Where are we?' Raj looked around too, his eyes adjusting to the light and his lungs clear of any serious damage.

'Looks like a store of some kind.' Tomo sounded just as confused as Raj. 'I just pushed on a few doors, and this one, surprisingly, opened.'

Raj reached up, flicked the handle and locked the door. 'I don't want any more surprises.'

Within the square room there were cardboard boxes stacked unevenly multiple levels high against three of the walls. Some rudimentary timber shelving lined the back wall, containing more boxes and small, plastic buckets. The place had a generally dirty feeling about it, with a musty smell permeating the space, mixed with dusty and damp old cardboard and laced with a hint of stagnant air and untreated timber. A high set window, between the entrance and the ceiling, rectangular and thin, allowed some light into the room, but not enough to clearly highlight what was through the opened doorway past the shelving at the end of the space.

Raj rose to his feet and followed Tomo.

'It's dark back here,' Tomo said, walking slowly.

'I'd ask you to light a fire,' Raj joked, 'but after what just happened, you probably shouldn't even own a lighter.'

Tomo laughed, then pulled out his lighter and flicked on the flame. They found themselves in a long, slim corridor, with a high ceiling that arched above them. The plaster was discoloured from age and flaking badly in many places, leaving dust and crumble all over the timber floor. They passed two doors to their left as they made their way to a third entrance at the end of the hallway.

'Be my guest.' Tomo moved over allowing Raj to pass.

'Why me,' asked Raj, 'when you're the one with the deadly weapon in his hands?'

'Because it's your turn.' Tomo remained with his back steadfastly pressed against the corridor's wall.

Raj pushed slowly down on the handle and as quietly as he could to pry the door only slightly ajar. He cautiously peeked into the room before opening the door fully.

'It's empty.' Raj waved Tomo to follow him. 'Someone's bedroom, by the look of it.'

The room was a bright change as sunshine poured in through the thin, lace blinds in front of a large window on the far wall. Another door was tucked into the corner, located at a right angle to the window, on the same wall that followed from the hallway. A single, steel framed bed was an unmade mess and sat against the wall between the doors, while a desk with paperwork and stationary scattered across it was on the opposite wall, next to a free standing, double door wardrobe.

'Fuckin' commies.' Tomo pointed to a picture of Tito on the wall above the desk as they made their way toward the back door.

'Look.' Raj stopped at a large window and moved the curtains slightly. 'There's a small street directly behind us, doesn't look busy either.'

'That's good.' Tomo had his ear to the corner door by now. 'Because there's plenty of noise coming from behind this door.'

'Check the wardrobe,' Raj ordered.

'Why?' Tomo asked.

'Because if people recognise us,' Raj insisted, 'we're fucked.'

They saw a couple of winter coats and plenty of white shirts and black pants. The two men quickly threw on the crisp, white shirts before heading toward their escape.

Raj was first to slip behind the curtains and unlock the window. It was a sliding style of opening without any screen to protect from insects. He pushed one foot over and leapt a small distance to the cobbled street below. Tomo quickly followed, and both men found themselves in a service alley that tended to the logistics of the stores that faced the town square, and to the buildings on the other side. The two men quickly and casually turned right and walked toward the end of the alley, buttoning and tucking their shirts in as they went. Steel rubbish bins lined the old, paved street on both sides with cardboard boxes stacked next to them and scraps of food lying freely around the ground. Flies were buzzing around in the spring warmth, feasting on the plethora of available scraps while a few alley cats looked cautiously at Raj and Tomo before disappearing silently beneath a building. The smell of garbage was easily covered by the ongoing smoke still floating through the air, but the haze was not as bad with the buildings as a barrier. As the two men approached an intersection, the street noise became louder exponentially and the congestion they had left moments earlier was upon them once again. Sirens were blazing by now and a couple of vehicles were also parked just ahead, which meant the black shirts were no longer the only trouble Raj and Tomo faced.

'What now?' Tomo asked as both men slowed.

'Grab a box and cover your face.' Raj leant over and picked up a couple of flat, rectangular cartons that looked to have housed vegetables at one stage, he propped them onto his shoulder with his right acting as support. 'For all purposes, we are just a couple of waiters tending to our errands.'

No one noticed as the two men walked quickly by the wailing ambulances and police cars and directly through the crowd. They headed away from the ruckus toward the relative quietude of the next district. Once they had put enough distance between themselves and the mess they made at the town square, Raj pulled out his map and took a seat at an undercover bus stop.

'We need to circle around' – Raj pointed to the map – 'and get to those ferries before it gets too late.'

'Too late for what?' asked Tomo.

Raj looked to the heavens. 'It's going to get dark in a couple of hours, and I don't want to spend a single night in this town.'

'Fair enough,' Tomo agreed.

'On the positive side' – Raj stood up and pointed to the empty street around them – 'your earlier shenanigans seemed to have caused the entire town to move toward the fire.'

'Hey.' Tomo had just noticed how quiet the street was. 'You're right.'

'At least the black shirted men won't be bothering us,' Raj added before pressing on.

CHAPTER 7

'These prices are expensive!' Raj exclaimed as he looked at the rusting steel tablet fixed against the outside wall of a small fishing shop at the beach end of the promenade.

'Shit,' Tomo added, 'and look at the times.'

'Yeah.' Raj noticed that too. 'We are either too early, or way too late. It means the travel time up the coast must be ridiculous.'

'We'd get there quicker by bus!' Tomo calculated.

They stepped back from the shop and looked up and down the coast. There was plenty of action still going on. Fishing boats were still bobbing up and down, trawlers were setting off and returning and multitudes of people now milled around as the sun continued its slow movement toward the western horizon. There were more beachgoers now too; towels and beach lounges were laid across the pebbles by the shore and a few swimmers even splashed around in the beautiful blue sea. On the other side of the shore, the large ferries were all gone, but beyond their mooring positions were plenty of smaller boats still docked and waiting in the marina.

'There has to be another way.' Raj scratched his head.

'Another way for what?' A familiar voice snuck up from behind and entered their conversation.

'Oh God.' Raj wasn't impressed. 'Not you again.'

Maria, the waitress, stood in front of the two men with a smile beaming across her face. She lit up a smoke then offered the boys one each.

'Why so sad?' Maria asked, puffing away with a flirtatious look in her eye. 'Even your friend doesn't seem as interested to see me as he was this morning.'

'We don't need this shit right now.' Raj turned and looked to other side of the bay, still hoping an idea would come to him. 'Shouldn't you be at work?'

'My shift is done for today,' she answered before continuing to probe. 'But what are you doing back here? I thought I'd never see you again.'

'We need to get out of Split,' Tomo said. 'Our plans didn't work out too well.'

'Ah.' Maria lifted her head, blowing a perfect smoke ring at Raj. 'Not as smart as you think you are.'

'Some things are hard to foresee,' Raj stated irritably, waving the smoke away. 'Like all those black shirted fucks.' He looked around to make his point even more dramatic but could see no black shirts on the beach.

'You encountered the militia?' Maria's expression now changed to one of surprise. 'And they let you go already?'

'We didn't let them get too close.' Tomo smiled, but his eyes betrayed his mouth, and the grin didn't last long.

'Who are they?' Raj turned to Maria, who obviously knew details about the group.

'They are communist heroes,' she began, 'or at least that's the way they sell themselves. Most are children of the partisans; some are ex-soldiers, others are off-duty police and some are just rejects from the armed forces; they're the most dangerous ones.'

'And what is their business?' Tomo inquired.

'They help keep the streets safe from criminals and activists,' Maria added sarcastically. 'Unfortunately, no one keeps us safe from them. If you see them, keep your distance. They are real trouble.'

'Why did you help us before?' Raj tried a different approach, cutting the small talk. 'You know, with the guy dressed like a bird?'

'You mean Rudolf? He is slimy and sells secrets, and you boys are green and Catholic.' She reached deep down at the front of her shirt, between her breasts, and pulled out a long necklace with a small silver cross at its end. 'Not everyone here blindly follows Belgrade.' She quickly returned her hidden jewellery back into her shirt, then smiled at the men. 'Besides, I felt sorry for you.'

'Do you *still* feel sorry for us?' asked Raj, wondering if their last hope of escaping this town was the helpful Catholic waitress standing before them.

Maria raised her eyebrows and cocked her head, then dropped the smouldering butt before stamping it out on the ground beneath her feet.

'What do you need?' She seemed cautious in her tone.

'We can't go back through the streets.' Raj opened up and talked faster. 'Too much shit went down today for that. We either need a place to hide and crash for a day or two, or a trip up the water, away from roads.'

'You don't ask for much.' Maria laughed. 'But I can't keep you at my place. My parents would freak out. My dad would do worse things to you than the militia. Besides, I don't even know your names?'

'I'm Raj.' He introduced himself. 'And this is Tomo.'

'Well, Raj and Tomo, let's go to the bar.' Maria turned and strode away. 'I might know someone.'

They strode down the promenade on the opposite side of Maria's cafe. Raj wondered why they would go to a bar except to drink, and neither he nor Tomo were in a partying mood. There were still plenty of people on the streets, though, with cafes and restaurants serving food and drink to all the socialites who were in the mood for some Saturday afternoon entertainment.

'People live like kings here,' Tomo announced excitedly as they kept walking.

'Do you know how to tell the difference between the communists and the rest?' Maria asked without breaking her stride.

'No,' answered Tomo.

'Neither can I,' she answered. 'So be very careful.'

The two men followed Maria when she turned right down a side street with small buildings on both sides that ran parallel to the shore. It was more a narrow lane than really a street, and was quite long, covered with rough blue stone and had bags and boxes of rubbish and materials spread everywhere. The longer they walked, the dirtier the laneway looked and the more dangerous the area appeared. From the mishmashes of timber and sheet metal covering some of the buildings, it seemed the street simply served as a maintenance access point, leaving the more attractive parts of the buildings on the opposing sides.

Suddenly Maria turned. 'Wait here, please.'

Raj and Tomo could hear the racket form the perpetual workings of the docks in the distance and could smell the sea salt in the air, but the buildings surrounding them covered any view of the sea and the garbage on the street cut through the smell of the ocean. No other people were around on the little lane, which made Raj feel both secure and unnerved at the same time.

'At least there are no black shirts around,' Raj said to break the silence, but Tomo didn't respond.

'Okay.' Maria returned shortly after. 'Follow me.'

They followed Maria into a small, wooden shack via a thin concrete path that was overgrown with weeds and grass to the point where the very cement would soon disappear. They passed a burly man, with a shaved head and tattoos on his muscular upper arms hardly hidden by his tight, black t-shirt. He sat at a high stool and had a beer in the same hand that held a cigarette, watching the trio enter the building and giving Maria the slightest nod as she passed. Inside, a short, dark corridor gave way to a much larger room, with a curved bar to the right, some tables and chairs were ahead of them and a small billiard table stood to the left. There were a few patrons loitering around: some at the bar, one played pool alone and a couple shared a table in the middle of the shadowy room. It was a smoky, dark atmosphere, with a few red and white lights illuminating the space, helped by some windows at the front end of the room. Fast, energetic music was being played on the radio, in a language Raj didn't comprehend and a style he had never heard before.

'Rock and roll!' Tomo exclaimed a little loudly, smiling at Raj.

'Keep cool.' Maria turned and looked venomously at Tomo.

Raj threw his friend a look to help settle him and Tomo heeded the unsaid advice and relaxed in his stride and in his comments. They followed Maria to the bar where a tall, blonde headed fellow was cleaning beer glasses by hand. Raj and Tomo instinctively kept their distance while Maria had a quick word before the bartender walked around the bar and opened a door that was hardly visible in the darkness of the room.

'Just wait,' Maria insisted.

'What is this place?' Raj whispered.

'This place is safe,' Maria looked around. 'For now. Do you have money?'

'Money? For what?' Tomo cut in, a little too loud once again.

'Geez.' Maria's head snapped back before she looked at Raj. 'Was he your first choice?'

Raj smiled ironically. 'What are we doing here, Maria?'

The mysterious door opened yet again and this time a tall, grey haired man followed the barkeep into the common room.

'Maria.' He opened his arms wide as he approached.

'Hello, uncle.' She turned and stepped towards him, greeting the big man with a loving cuddle then whispered a few words in his ear before turning back toward her new friends. 'Uncle, this is Raj and Tomo. Raj and Tomo, this is Captain Lutko Maltokovic, my uncle.'

The old man had bright blue pupils within large yellowish eyeballs, surrounded by years of fine cracks and lines stretching from his weathered forehead to his smiling mouth. He had a thin, grey beard, hardly perceptible when he first entered the room, and he also had one gold tooth that sparkled as he smiled. He wore a white shirt in desperate need of ironing while gold necklaces, gold rings and a fine-looking watch also adorned his person. He seemed to have a refined demeanour but stunk of alcohol the closer he got, stumbling slightly as he approached.

'Greetings, gentlemen.' The captain firmly shook both men's hands.

'Nice to meet you,' Raj humbly said, still unsure of what was going on.

'Maria says you be looking for a quiet passage up north, aye?' The captain got straight to business.

'We are,' Raj answered cautiously.

'Seventy dinars.' The captain was nobody's fool and pulled out a long cigar as the negotiations began abruptly.

'Shit.' Tomo spoke quickly to Raj. 'that's nearly as much as the ferries.'

'Except the ferry will ask for papers, too,' Maria interjected this time. 'He could charge even more.'

'Leave the negotiations to the men, aye.' The captain was condescending. He then turned back to Raj. 'I love women, but sometimes they be too quick to talk.'

Tomo then moved even closer to Raj and whispered in desperation, 'That might be all I have, Raj.'

Raj felt his friend's grief because fifty dinars was Raj's family's life savings and Raj's father gave it all to his son a few days ago. Raj also wasn't sure what to make of the old man; he bought time by slowly rummaging through his bag pretending to look for his wallet as he really pondered his next move in the negotiations. Suddenly, the captain pulled him up.

'What have you got in that flagon there, aye?' he asked Raj. 'Doesn't look like any tomato juice I've seen before.'

'This?' Raj held up the glass bottle, wondering how keen the captain's eyesight must be to have figured out the small label on the bottle top so quickly. 'Just some travelling brew, from back home.' He put it back and kept searching for his leather purse.

'That bottle is Soviet.' Captain Maltokovic looked at Maria with concern. 'You boys commies? I thought I was finished fighting commies and now you bring me this?'

'They're not commies, uncle,' Maria interjected.

'Where exactly did you say you came from, aye?' The captain's cigar was alight now and creating a thick smoke as the old seaman dragged multiple times in quick succession at the burning leaf, trying to catch a stronger flame to the cigar's end.

Raj was about to start counting dinars, but the question surprised him and he threw a look at Tomo and then Maria, uncertain again of where this particular conversation was heading.

'I didn't say where I am from,' was Raj's initial response. 'But it's definitely not Russia!'

'It's okay,' Maria ensured him. 'You can trust him.' She waved her hand in front of her face. 'Even if you can't see him through this God-forsaken smoke.'

'You know I love my cigars, Maria.' The captain puffed again and smiled proudly, his gold tooth the only thing visible for a second through the brownish-grey smoke wafting before his face.

'Hercegovina,' quickly added Raj. 'North-west of Mostar.'

'Well, well, aye.' Captain Maltokovic licked his lips, then looked at his cigar. 'Some of the finest tobacco in the world is grown in your parts, son. And some of the finest hooch too, aye.' His attention returned to Raj's knapsack as his tone eased. 'Would you be kind enough to tell me whether it be plum or grape?'

'This one is grape.' Raj could see the old man knew his alcohol. 'The aftermath of the wine season. A little sweet, not too hot in the aftertaste and would put hair on virgin's chest.'

'Ha!' The captain liked the sound of Raj's answer. 'And would you by any chance have any more, aye?' The old sea dog seemed to have forgotten about the money and was excitedly transfixed on the drink.

Raj looked at Tomo then again at the captain.

'We *did*,' he confessed, taking the bottle out once more very slowly. 'But it is so good we couldn't help ourselves.' If the captain was a full-blown alcoholic, then Raj thought they could use it to their advantage.

'It has been too long since I have tried the proper stuff, too many days at sea, or up north with the nancy-boys that drink that swill they call alcohol.' The captain seemed lost in a memory, his blue eyes never leaving the bottle as his dramatic story took hold. 'You land lubbers know how to make the good shit but my legs are made for the sea, so I don't get inland as often as I used to.' He took another drag and no one interrupted his monologue. 'I'm sick of cheap wine, too. And beer just makes me piss, aye,' he laughed out loud, 'can you imagine how much fun taking a piss is on a rocking boat in the dead of night?'

'Well, it seems we might be able to help each other,' Raj hinted carefully.

'Aye?' Raj had the captain's attention as he casually flipped the bottle and caught it by the neck, the golden bottle top resting in Raj's hands and its pressed glass base now pointed toward the old sea dog as an offering of sorts.

'We can give ten dinars when we arrive in Rijeka.' Raj started purposefully low to give him some room to move.

'Ten dinars?' Tomo sounded a little shocked, 'do we know what we are actually getting for that kind of coin?'

'And' – he looked at Tomo with a poker face, then back at the captain – 'since you are a connoisseur of fine liquor, perhaps you could take this bottle off our hands now, as a down-payment?'

'Thirty,' Captain Maltokovic replied. 'And the bottle.'

'Twenty.'

'Deal!' the captain wasted no time in any further negotiations and stuck out his hand to seal the deal. Raj kicked himself for not starting even lower in price.

'And my payment?' Maria surprised everyone in the circle.

'Your payment is the love of your uncle.' The old man smiled at his niece and gave her an uncomfortable hug with one hand holding his cigar and the other gripping his prized new bottle of moonshine. 'And send greetings to my brother, the worthless git.'

Captain Maltokovic gave the girl a kiss on each cheek and turned back toward the door he had originally entered from, before suddenly stopping and turning to ask in a very serious tone, 'No shenanigans. You need to be open and up front. I don't want to find out I'm in deep shit when it's already up to my neck. You two aren't in any kind of trouble?'

'No.' Raj looked innocently at Tomo, trying to keep his cool under the interrogative question. 'Just passing by.'

'Pier 35, the Red Seagull, half an hour, if you be late, the deals off and

I keep the hooch, aye.' He waved the bottle in the air and disappeared into the next room with only a trail of brownish grey smoke as proof he had been there at all.

'Let's go.' Maria didn't wait for a response from the men and just moved back the way they came.

'What's the hurry?' Raj skipped a couple of steps to keep up. 'I thought you said this place was safe?'

'It's safe enough from the commies,' Maria elaborated. 'But if my dad finds out I've been here, he's going to kill me.'

'But that was your uncle, you said?' Raj was a little bewildered as all three companions squinted, returning into the light of day at the back of the seedy bar.

'My dad and his brother, the captain, haven't spoken to each other for nearly ten years.' Maria turned right at the laneway and continued back toward the promenade.

'Sorry to hear.' Raj spoke after a respectful moment, then all three kept silent as they headed toward the marina.

'Now.' Maria stopped well short of the laneway intersecting back to the promenade. 'I'm leaving you here.' She smiled at the two young men, leant over and kissed both of them on the cheeks. 'And I hope I never see you again, Raj and Tomo from Hercegovina.'

Raj and Tomo found their way to the piers of Split's large private harbour, north along the shore and past the vacant ferry ports. Every few metres, timber landings jutted from the main shoreline deck and ran straight into the Adriatic, like the wet, grey fingers of a strange wooden hand that rested atop the water, acting as walkways for the seafarers to get to and from the land to their ships. Yachts, trawlers and dinghies of all shapes and sizes were moored here, and anchored further out into the bay, but there were still many vacant spaces as the day was long, the sea was wide, and the boating enthusiasts were out on the water enjoying their skill in the bright sunshine of the afternoon.

As they strode down pier 35, Raj kept hoping the next boat was theirs. It seemed the further from the ferry port they walked, the worse the condition of the anchored crafts around them. Sure, there were still some larger vessels awaiting cast off, but the condition of the boats was far from pleasing to the two land-lovers about to set sail for the first time. Some fishermen were returning while others were preparing to leave, but overall it was a quiet place that added a little to the general feeling of neglect.

'Rent must be cheap out here,' Raj joked, as he pointed to a mid-sized fishing trawler that had old, dried paint peeling off its stern and port bow, and rust spots riddling the side of the second storey cabin.

'Or the commies don't want the world to see this part of their spectacular shore,' rebuffed Tomo. 'This doesn't fill me with confidence, Raj.'

'Nor me,' Raj answered. 'Let's hope the captain's boat is in better condition than some of these rust buckets.'

'Ahoy!' a familiar voice cried out in the distance.

Raj looked to the end of the pier and saw the captain surrounded by a few men moving goods onto a large yacht via a notched plank used as a makeshift gangway.

'Is this it?' Raj asked as he looked up at the boat, trying to sound inquisitive without being condescending. The closer they got, the stronger the smell of diesel became, cutting through the salty air along with the sound of the boat's engine sputtering in a low gear.

'That it be.' Captain Lutko Maltokovic smiled proudly and looked the part as he now wore a blue skipper's hat complete with gold embroidery on the visor. 'Got it off a Turk. I couldn't tell you how many thousands of nautical miles she has served me and never let me down, aye.'

'Hurry up, Malto,' one of the men on board said with a heavy accent. He was topless, showing a very dark tan with serious tattooing on his muscular torso and arms. 'We should make move.'

'That's Skorzi.' The captain introduced the man, who nodded back as a form of acknowledgement. 'He is Slovak, and my first mate. Anything you need, ask him. Just don't fuck with Skorzi, aye.'

'I don't know about this,' Tomo whispered nervously to Raj.

'You okay?' asked Raj, concerned about Tomo's secretive heart issue.

'I'm good. Just nervous.'

'We'll be fine,' Raj said. 'Unless you have a better idea?'

Raj was last up the plank, after the captain and Tomo had already boarded the large vessel from the port side. The Red Seagull was a thirty-foot gulet yacht, propelled by twin masted sails, that were furled at the moment, and augmented by a sputtering and smoking diesel engine.

Raj had never been out to sea before, nor had any experience with marine vessels, but it was quite clear to his inexperienced eyes that the Red Seagull needed work. In its glory days, the boat might have stood proudly in any marina, but at this stage of its existence, serious upgrades were needed to renovate the old schooner. It had two levels that Raj could see; a cabin and cockpit, and some levels below that were only apparent from the large hatch open near the aft. The timber decking needed polishing and was beginning to split in places, the anchor chain was turning orange from rust and the small, circular windows to the floor level cabins were all void of glass. Above the middle cabin was an assortment of antennae reaching up to a modest Yugoslavian flag hoisted at full mast. Raj counted six others on the deck, all men, and all busying themselves with bits and pieces in preparation to set sail, without any desire to introduce themselves to the two young greenhorns that had just entered their maritime world.

'Throw that plank onboard, aye.' The captain turned to Raj, pointing at two rusted metal clasps screwed into the hull just below the taffrail. 'And fasten it there.'

Raj looked over the edge and realised just how high he was from ground level from his new perspective. He then dragged the long timber board onto the deck and slipped it gently into the clasps that were not as tightly screwed as they originally looked. Tomo was already moving bags on the starboard side while the captain's voice was heard booming around the deck, barking orders and pointing at sections of the craft that needed tending.

'You can leave your bags with Mal,' Captain Maltokovic pointed to a sailor rising from the hatch.

'If it's okay,' Raj argued, 'I'd rather keep them close.'

'It's not okay,' the captain ordered sternly. 'It's all hands on deck.'

Raj grabbed his and Tomo's packs and made his way slowly over to the hatch. Mal snatched them off him and disappeared immediately. Raj tried to sneak a look into the hull but all he saw was a shadowy darkness that was interrupted by the barking commands of an unforgiving captain.

'Now join your friend and take those bags into the utility cabin there,' the captain again instructed Raj, pointing the way and smiling. 'And watch your head.'

The amount of rigging about the vessel was mind boggling; lines of rope and wire, taut and loose, vertical and horizontal, decorated the craft like a spider's web. Raj cautiously approached a few duffle bags beneath the boom, ducking to grab them and then heaving to lift them due to the weight within.

'Jesus Christ!' Raj had carried heavy objects on the farm, and was confident in his strength, but these large black, cloth bags were so heavy he would have to carry one at a time. 'What have you got in here?' he shouted as he bent his knees and walked toward the cabin.

'Never you mind what we be carrying,' Captain Maltokovic answered, then brusquely added, 'You didn't pay to ask questions!'

'I should be charging *you* for this,' Raj joked to the captain who was moving up toward the cockpit on the second deck amidships.

'Did you think you could travel with me without lending a hand?' the captain called down to Raj as he lit a cigar. 'This isn't a fucking holiday, aye!'

'So much for a nice cruise up the Adriatic,' Tomo said as he passed Raj near the cabin entry, after dropping a duffle bag off himself.

'As long as there are no black shirts on board,' Raj retorted honestly, 'I'll manage the weight.'

'Too right,' Tomo agreed.

Raj placed the bag on top of a crate in the corner and looked around the cabin. He was amazed at the amount of cargo the ship had on board. There were crates on top of crates, and bags of different varieties sitting on top of the boxes. The hull must have held even more as it would have been larger and Raj did see men moving goods into it earlier. But bags and boxes weren't the only thing found in this cargo hold; a wide hatch was open at the far end of the utility room and noises could be heard coming from below. Raj snuck a peek over the edge where a small set of stairs descended into a timber area that glowed with a yellowish light.

'You sticking your nose where it doesn't belong again?' laughed Tomo, carrying another bag into the room.

Raj leapt out of his skin a little at the surprise.

'You scared the shit out of me!' he said to his friend, then punched Tomo in the arm on the way out.

'Cast off, Skorzi. The seas are calling!' Captain Maltokovic shouted. The yacht's motor roared and all hands were on deck finalising preparation as the Red Seagull's long journey northward got underway.

CHAPTER 8

The Dalmatian coast was a spectacular site to behold, particularly from the water. In the distance to the east, giant mountains began their journey from inland Croatia and eventually divided into long rocky ranges that either slowly descended toward the Adriatic coast, or kept cutting the land into giant segments, before suddenly turning into great cliff faces that dropped straight into the ocean. The shoreline was a mix between lush coastal bushes, cave speckled rock or stone covered beach. Prime real estate was strewn atop the miles of cliffs, with views that encompassed many of the splendid islands throughout the Adriatic.

Unfortunately, most of the coastal residencies were clearly still tarnished by the ravages of World War Two: bullet riddled walls, exposed interiors and collapsing roof structures were visible far too often on once majestic homes that were now abandoned and in desperate need of repair. Down below, pristine beaches were another drawcard for people to this part of the world. Most beaches were simply small alcoves cut between the mammoth crags; the shorelines here were covered with tiny pebbles and dotted the western Yugoslavian coast, creating some of the finest swimming places on earth. Deep waters were found relatively close to the land on this mountainous coast, and a few steps into the water at any Croatian beach and swimmers would find themselves suddenly neck deep in the cool, turquoise sea.

The depth of the Adriatic Sea allowed aquatic vessels to pass relatively close to the seashore, but the archipelago of larger islands still forced most cruisers out wider and closer to Italian waters. Raj estimated the travel time saved was a few hours but didn't really care as long as they were off the ancient streets of Split and far from the mess they left behind. They were now well on their way toward Rijeka which was the third largest city in Croatia and the most northern port where the Red

Seagull would dock. The captain said they would arrive shortly before midnight, which worried Raj a little, but not as much as staying behind.

After the initial bouts of vomiting, Raj and Tomo eventually found their sea legs and were placed on cooking duties hence forth. Both young men passed through the cabin and went down to the small galley to accompany the cook, Miro, who only entrusted them with menial tasks like cutting vegetables and fetching ingredients. No one seemed to have a last name on the ship, and no one was forthright in conversation, except for the captain, who was busy at the helm ensuring a safe journey.

'I get a strange sense, here,' Raj whispered, as he diced onions for a fish broth that was already starting to boil.

'Yeah,' Tomo concurred. 'Onions do it to me too; taste delicious fried, but stink like hell raw.'

'No.' Raj rolled his watering eyes. 'Not that. I mean this ship. Something odd, I can't put my finger on it.'

'Yeah,' Tomo said as he chopped celery, 'but we are odd too. So, it's a perfect fit.'

'I suppose,' Raj pondered. 'But look at the amount of food here in the galley!'

'So what?' Tomo didn't even look up. 'We got to eat.'

'We have a three- or four-hour journey, no more.' Raj tried to draw Tomo's attention to the copious amounts of produce neatly stacked and packed into every possible nook and cranny. 'The ship is running a small crew. I'm no sailor, but I reckon this would be enough for days at sea.'

'Who cares?' Tomo answered nonchalantly. 'They might continue onward after Rijeka. Does it matter?''

'I suppose you're right.' Raj got back to chopping onions. 'If they don't ask us about our travels, then what right do we have to ask about theirs?'

'Too right!' Tomo agreed, busily chopping away.

'Still.' Raj just couldn't let it go. 'Keep your wits about you, and trust none of these pirates.'

'Pirates?' Then Tomo did stop slicing. 'You think so?'

'Or smugglers.' Raj wasn't sure himself. 'Just don't talk too much to anybody, okay?'

'That won't be hard.' Tomo laughed. 'I haven't heard a word from anyone except the cook!'

'Back to work!' barked Miro the cook, who seemed a little slow in the intelligence department but handled a kitchen blade with aplomb.

the Seagull's. Raj quickly grabbed as many dishes off the table as he could and beckoned to Tomo to do the same. Raj moved quick to clear the table, dropping all the wooden plates and steel cutlery into a giant bucket full of soapy water and more dirty dishes.

'Jesus,' Tomo quipped. 'I've never seen someone in such a hurry to do the dishes.'

Raj wiped his hands then looked at Tomo and put his finger to his lips, he then moved silently toward the steps at the galley's entry. He climbed the five steep stairs and reached for the hatch. As quietly as he could, he slightly lifted the small door in the ceiling and peered through into the utility cabin full of duffle bags and timber boxes. Raj was glad the light was left off in the cabin because the darkness of the evening would work in his favour.

'What do you see?' asked Tomo in an excited voice, standing at the base of the stairs and once again talking a little too loudly for Raj's liking.

'Keep it down.' Raj didn't take his eyes off the small crack as he kept opening the hatch wider. 'Turn off that light,' he added and as soon as Tomo flicked the switch in the galley Raj opened the door fully and silently crept through.

Raj looked back as Tomo followed him up the narrow steps. 'Keep that hatch open, we might need to move quick.'

'Sure thing,' Tomo whispered back.

Raj kept his head down and squatted as he moved all the way next to the closed door of the utility cabin. He made himself comfortable under the broken window to the left side of the door. Tomo joined him but sat on the right and both men stayed silent, their backs to the wall, listening carefully to the crew on deck beyond the small cargo hold. The motor Raj heard earlier had stopped and a large flood light suddenly illuminated the deck, and much of the cabin, making the Red Seagull's lighting seem paltry in comparison.

'Ahoy!' Raj heard the captain's voice call out in a jovial tone.

'Salute,' another voice replied sternly, still on board the incoming vessel. 'Prepare to be boarded.'

'The Red Seagull welcomes all sailors.' Captain Maltokovic was putting it on thick, Raj thought, but he dared not to look over the sill to see what was going on.

'That's very kind of you.' The voice became louder and the thuds of multiple footfalls followed the increase in volume. 'It's been a while since I've searched such a... *fine* vessel.'

The sarcasm in the voice of the newcomer was punctuated by a short burst of muffled laughter accompanying the insult. Raj wasn't sure who was onboard, but he had never heard anyone make a peep regarding the Seagull while they sailed. The crew held a quiet reverence for the yacht and the captain, who held absolute authority on board, but, with a smart quip, this confident stranger had just usurped it within a moment aboard.

'Admittedly' – the captain played along – 'she has seen better days, aye. But the war was rough and the fascists hammered her. We pulled through and are trying to make some coin to rebuild her.'

A silence ensued after the captain played the political card. Raj was surprised to hear the captain had been affiliated with the partisans during the war, particularly since he admonished Raj regarding communists in the bar earlier. Maria wore a Catholic cross, albeit hidden under her garments, so Raj had automatically thought the captain must have been on the Croat side. But with the discussion he was overhearing, he was no longer sure.

'You fought the Nazis?' asked the commanding voice of the stranger.

'Indeed,' answered Captain Maltokovic. His men all murmured in agreement. 'On this very ship. We still keep the flag hoisted' – he paused for a moment, dropping his tone – 'we lost many good partisans. Just ask Commander Damir Vreskolac. Speaking of which, he is usually patrolling this time of night. Where is my old friend?'

'I know Damir,' the stranger acknowledged. 'He is busy tonight.'

'Really?' The captain sounded surprised. 'He is a fine man, and an excellent sailor. I just hope the tides be kind to him and his wife, Veselka.'

Raj could hear how shrewd the old captain really was; dropping names and political affiliations in an attempt to gauge the newcomer's level of influence while potentially creating a new ally on the Adriatic Sea.

'I'm sure everything is fine with the commander,' the voice stated, now sounding a little less authoritative and a little more respectful.

'I'm sure he is fine, too,' Captain Maltokovic concurred, dismissing the earlier topic easily while at the same time subtly taking over the conversation. 'But I'm not sure if you know of the Commander's agreement with the Seagull?'

'Agreement?' The voice now sounded a touch perplexed.

'He's got him,' Raj whispered to Tomo.

'Huh?' Tomo's face was hidden in the shadows, but his tone was one of confusion.

'Yes.' The captain's voice now took on a new volume, only slightly louder but enough to wrestle back his dominance. 'A gentlemen's agreement, of sorts.'

'The commander hasn't mentioned anything to me, or to headquarters.' The visiting man was now clearly unsure of the sway held by the smooth-talking captain before him.

'It's no great deal.' Captain Maltokovic now tried to assuage the newcomer's concerns. 'Call it a personal tariff, shall we? It is done all over the Adriatic. I'm sure you have multiple clients. We usually avoid the freight chargers at the docks by paying in advance. You understand? A small boat, such as the Seagull, can be held up indefinitely with paperwork and red tape by those filthy land lubbers, aye. This way, we get our business done out here and everyone benefits.'

'Interesting.' By the tone in his voice, the newcomer knew of the implications of such a deal. 'I can trust you have no contraband, captain?'

'Please, my friends call me Malto.' The captain continued playing his game. 'And, no, no contraband. Everything is above board, so to speak, with appropriate documents, but...' The captain's voice trailed off for a moment and footsteps were heard instead of conversation. Raj was becoming ever so tempted to take a sneak peek through the window above his head, but the captain's voice cut the silence again. '...I have a special gift tonight.'

'Gift?' The newcomer now sounded far friendlier.

'Yes, I was going to save it for Damir because I know how much he loves a nip after dinner, aye.' The captain was returning from across deck and abruptly changed the subject. 'Sorry, I didn't catch your name, sir?'

'I am Lieutenant Sergo Mihalj,' the man answered proudly, 'of the third naval fleet.'

'Wonderful to meet you, Lieutenant,' the captain announced. 'I say, you think you could pass this on to the commander?'

'What do you think he is giving this guy, Raj?' Tomo whispered.

'I don't know, but I'm about to find out,' answered Raj as he dared rise a little in the darkness of the cabin. Fortunately, the visiting naval vessel cast its blinding spotlight from the starboard side causing any shadows to fall across the deck. The Seagull's weaker illumination came from up high, directly above the cabin, allowing Raj to avoid any direct penetrating light into the little room in which he hid, which meant his shadow wouldn't appear suddenly on the far wall and alert those on deck. It did allow for a fantastic view of the actions on board, though.

The lieutenant was a short man, Raj spied, probably the shortest out there, but he was built with a solid frame and his naval attire looked to be bursting at the seams. There were four others with him, all dressed in military camouflage, with balaclavas over their heads and machine guns in their hands. The deck was full of idle sailors but they seemed calm as the two leaders talked diplomatically while everyone else simply watched. Raj moved a little closer to the window's opening, quietly shifting a duffle bag to conceal himself all the more, while he snooped on the scene.

'What are they doing?' Tomo hissed, not chancing a peek.

'Of course,' the lieutenant answered.

'It's a very good drop,' the captain explained. 'Made from the finest grapes. The aftermath of the wine season, I believe. A little sweet, not too hot in the aftertaste, and would put hair on a virgin's chest.'

'Bastard!' Raj murmured. 'That was my fucking line.'

'Is he giving him what I think?' Tomo asked, managing to still keep his voice down.

The lieutenant turned the bottle in his hands, looking for a brand, but only found the golden bottle top with Russian markings.

'Looks like no tomato juice I've ever seen before.' The young lieutenant laughed. 'Is it Soviet?'

'Yes,' the captain lied and then lit up a cigar. 'From a connection of mine near the Black Sea.' He offered the lieutenant a smoke, who graciously accepted.

The atmosphere on deck was becoming lighter as the smoke was becoming thicker. The lieutenant's henchmen even took off their masks and lit up cigarettes themselves while some of the Seagull's crew returned to duties around the deck. The lieutenant even called for the lights to be dimmed, as they were blinding the Seagull's crew who stared toward the starboard side.

'I don't mind a drop myself, Malto,' Lieutenant Mihalj stated between drags on the cigar.

'Well, in that case,' Captain Maltokovic added, 'you keep it. The commander will understand. I'll try to get him another next time I'm out that way.'

'You sure?' the lieutenant asked surprisingly.

'You've earned it tonight, aye.'

Raj could see the golden bottle top from the old tomato juice brand and a broad smile across the lieutenant's face.

'It's your uncle's hooch.' Raj looked at Tomo then looked back, 'That's what the captain's giving... plus a white envelope.'

'Let me see.' Tomo hopped to his feet and moved to Raj, accidently kicking a wooden crate in the manoeuvre.

'What was that?' the lieutenant asked, looking directly at Raj who ducked as he heard the sound.

'Probably just some rats,' Captain Maltokovic replied. 'Miro, can you have a look if any *rats* might be lurking in the cabin.'

Raj kept moving and quickly crawled his way back to the hatch and down into the galley.

'My uncle's fucking hooch.' Tomo laughed once both men were safely downstairs. 'Who would've thought?'

Raj was feeling confused about the captain and everything that had been going on since they met. 'Who would've thought what?'

'That my uncle's moonshine would save us not once, but twice on this trip.' Tomo laughed out loud at the thought.

Raj understood the humour but knew that building an escape plan based on trading Bosnian moonshine would never work out in the end, besides, they were all out now, so they had no more of the magic drink to persuade any future negotiations that might arise.

'Yes, it sure is funny.' Raj even faked a smile. 'Now let's get back to these dishes before Miro returns and uses us as his ingredients.'

CHAPTER 9

Rijeka came into view shortly after the lieutenant and his cronies sped off into the darkness of the Adriatic night. The sails of the Seagull were unfurled now as the tide and breeze were sweeping everything toward the shore. With the engine cut and midnight approaching, a calming silence settled upon all those on board. Raj and Tomo stood quietly near the bow of the yacht with nothing left to do in the galley and nothing entrusted to them on the deck, so they watched the flickering lights in the distance of an old town that neither of them had seen before.

Not all the flashing lights were land based though, as the closer they got to the port, the more the traffic increased in the bay. From smaller fishing craft to larger oil tanks, the bay was clearly another strong hub for Yugoslavian industry and recreation. The Red Seagull increasingly sailed north-east now that the Croat islands were behind them, avoiding any potentially larger vessels through the deepest part of the Kvarner gulf and steering away from the main port at the centre of Rijeka's bay.

'How long you reckon before we get to shore?' Raj asked Tomo.

'I reckon within the hour,' Tomo answered.

'Can't wait to get off this thing,' Raj added, having had not only enough of the constant motion beneath his feet, but of the silver-tongued captain who Raj no longer trusted at all.

'You sick of us already, aye?' Captain Maltokovic snuck up on the two, just as a new motor sounded in the dark distance.

'You want us below deck again?' Raj asked the captain as the engine sound became slightly louder. This time though, there was no depth to its din; the power of this motor would not compare to the naval vessel accosting the Seagull earlier.

'Skorzi, ease up,' the captain shouted, followed by his first mate shouting orders from up on high to the crew behind amidships as they moved to furl the sails once again. 'No, these are friendlies,' Captain Maltokovic indicated.

'You have friends?' Raj remarked sarcastically.

'Everyone is my friend.' The captain smiled.

'The way you were fighting during the war, I thought everyone was your enemy.' Raj didn't hold back, feeling played by the sly old sea dog.

'The war was shit for everyone,' the captain stated, 'except for those who be really behind it.'

'And who was that?' Raj didn't want to play word games. 'The Partisans? The Ustase? Nazis? Commies?'

'I don't follow, aye?' Captain Maltokovic questioned Raj and then looked at Tomo for an answer that wasn't forthcoming.

'We heard your discussion earlier.' Raj came clean. 'And saw your gift. Where was it from again? That's right, the Black Sea. Soviet, I believe.'

'Oh.' Now the captain smiled. 'So there *were* rats in the cabin, aye.'

A dinghy came into view, but still had a while to go as it was travelling leeward and cutting against the tide from the starboard side. A second motor was then heard but coming from a different direction than the first.

'Yeah,' Raj opened up. 'You are fighting Nazis when talking to Commies, and fighting Commies when talking to Catholics – so much for being "open and up front".'

'Take it easy, Raj,' Tomo interrupted.

'Listen to your friend, Raj.' The captain called him by his first name. 'You are still green to the ways of the world. I told you I'd get you to Rijeka and here we are. Have I not kept my side of the bargain?'

'I hate hypocrites,' Raj spat back, wondering now if these dinghies were coming to take himself and Tomo away.

'Hypocrite? Ha!' Captain Maltokovic laughed out loud. 'You can talk! There seems to have been an incident in Split earlier today, where a couple of idiots started a blaze. Caused a lot of damage. You wouldn't know anything about that, would you?'

Raj could feel his face burning even in the cool hours of the night, so he looked away from the captain and back to where the first dinghy approached. Then a third motor could be heard as the first dinghy got even closer. Now the smaller motors created a chorus from all sides that enveloped the Red Seagull and quickly disrupted the earlier quietude.

'Don't lecture me, son.' The captain raised his tone as his posture swivelled toward the incoming craft. 'My niece likes you and she is the closest thing I have to a family, aye, so she got you onto this trip. But trust me when I say that I don't answer to you, or to any of these fucking scoundrels, because they don't pay the bills. The Red Seagull does and, as long as she is mine, then mine are the rules to follow.'

'How can I trust scoundrels or turncoats,' Raj asked bluntly, 'when you seem to swap sides like the changing of the tide?'

'I don't trust you either. In fact, at the moment, there is less trust in the world than there is faith, so it's not just a condition aboard this particular ship,' Captain Maltokovic replied cynically, then looked over the edge of the hull to see how far the dinghy was. 'Listen.' He cooled his tone. 'There's no hard feelings, aye, you seem like good boys who are looking for a better life. In many ways we are very much alike.'

'Sure, sure,' Raj agreed sarcastically, not buying Captain Maltokovic's reasoning.

'You want to know which side I'm on, is that it?' The captain must have sensed Raj's continual mistrust. 'I'm on *my* side, because *my* side is the only side that gives a shit about *me*.'

'That's just selfish,' Raj argued. 'Many of our people died for their country; died with honour and for a great cause.'

'Dead is dead, aye.' The captain's eyes softened as if finding a new compassion toward the ignorant greenhorns and, before he continued, he did the sign of the cross in respect to those who passed away. 'Tell me, would you rather have a dead father in a free land, or a living one in an occupied territory?'

The question took Raj aback. The captain was a shifty scoundrel, of that Raj was sure, but the question he posed was an issue Raj kept trying to push to the back of his mind. Family always came first, but with so much distrust against the Yugoslavian regime, the political struggles of the region easily blinded people into taking their families for granted. Raj knew the answer to the captain's question; of course he would rather live under occupation and see his father alive and well. But now he was the one leaving his family behind and, to all effects, would find freedom without a family to share it with. Perhaps the captain was right; Raj was just as selfish and just as guilty of hypocrisy as anyone aboard this ship.

'How do I know these boats are not coming for us?' Raj pointed to the speed boat now only moments away, trying to change the topic and relieve his guilt.

'They are!' laughed the captain in surprise. His voice was still strong but far more playful. 'You've got one more job, aye, then our business is complete.'

'What job?' Tomo asked.

'Sidelights, Skorzi!'

With the last command, Skorzi killed the main lights atop the helm and only left a red spotlight for the upcoming endeavour. Captain Maltokovic was already headed aft, not waiting for the two youngsters.

Raj and Tomo made their way to the main deck and saw a procession of bags and boxes being moved hand to hand from below deck, up and over, until the last of the crew handling the goods, threw it over the side. The movement was efficient and quick, and all done in semi-darkness beneath the weak red spotlight to avoid unnecessary attention. Raj made his way across the deck, checking out the operation a little more closely.

Out in the water, the runabouts had two-man teams; one to pilot and the other to catch the goods. Even though the Red Seagull had its masts down, the large schooner was still moving swiftly with the tide, so the smaller powerboats had to maintain the same speed as the yacht for the scheme to work. Raj could see the wild spray off their bows as they wrestled both the current and the Seagull's wake, splashing up and down in the water as the soaked smugglers held on for their lives while trying to do the job at hand.

These small craft might not have had the power of the earlier visiting naval boat, but they did have weight on their side. By now, the first dinghy was already racing away and the second was nearly full. Four or five bags were all that could be carried by the runabouts, but Raj wasn't sure if that was a power to weight issue, or if it simply spread the risk, because the second boat zoomed off in a different direction than the first. Just as the crew aboard the Red Seagull worked as one unit, the small vessels taking delivery did the same. Within two minutes four dinghies had come, loaded up and then were gone.

'Keep it clean,' the captain yelled. 'If you drop one, it comes off your share, aye!'

'What have they got to do with us?' asked Raj, who was wet from the ocean spray and was having to speak louder among the commotion.

'Nearly done. Skorzi, let's speed her up, aye,' Captain Maltokovic screamed to his first mate at the helm who threw his silhouetted thumb up and hit the ignition button. The spluttering engine of the yacht kicked in making the noise on deck even more annoying. The captain stepped toward the stern to check the motor after some black smoke coughed out into the night time air.

'Well, captain.' Raj followed the man. 'What have they got to do with us?'

'Those bags, in the cabin.' The captain was in a hurry, striding back past Raj on the wet deck with the surest footing on the yacht. 'You two. Let's go.'

Tomo was closest to the cabin and went in. Soon Raj was at the doorway grabbing bags and passing them on to another sailor before they made their way down the chain and were eventually launched overboard. Within a minute the small room was close to empty.

'Duffle bags only. Boxes are for another drop.' The captain was behind the crew keeping a keen eye on the goods and the timing of the operation. 'Times up, let's move.'

Raj had worked up quite a sweat in that minute of intense labour, pushing even harder at the very end to assuage the captain. He was thankful for the sea spray now as he stepped toward the middle of the deck to cool off from the fervour.

'So.' He looked at the captain yet again, who was looking at his watch. 'Any more?'

'Only two,' answered the captain, who then indicated to Skorzi to bring back the main lights.

One more dinghy approached, but Raj saw no bags held by any of the crew. One of the sailors responsible for hurling the bags so accurately, now stepped aside leaving the hull exposed. Raj and Tomo looked around, a little dumfounded by everyone's sudden statuesque demeanour. The organised hustle, shown only a moment earlier, turned quickly into a juxtaposition of human calm, set against the continual movement of the boats, the sea and the roaring motors.

'Which two?' Raj called out, looking around nervously, not sure if he wanted to hear the answer.

'The last dinghy is for you two,' the captain announced, opening his hand to the starboard side with tentative encouragement.

'What do you mean?' Tomo yelled out as he made his way toward the edge. 'How is that for "us two"?'

'You are going to stop the boat, aren't you?' Raj inquired.

'Sorry, boys,' the captain revealed. 'No time to stop. This is how it's always been done.'

'At least slow down,' Tomo pleaded.

'Can't do it.' Captain Maltokovic wasn't giving an inch. 'If we stop, or slow down, then we are all sitting ducks out here. We are already way too close to town for my liking.'

Raj's heart was pounding so hard that his throat felt like it was bursting. The pit of his stomach was also churning at the prospect of what was to come. Memories of his parents and siblings, of his home and the family fields, and even of his pets came flooding to him in an instant. He remembered his school days and the books that his elder brother had stolen for him. He remembered the day he left and the argument he had with his family, and how his loving father settled the matter with a wise word and a tranquil manner.

'You said you'd take us to Rijeka?' Raj screamed, hoping the tears in his eyes were disguised by the sea spray as the boats moved a little faster. 'You're a fucking liar, *aye*.'

'The Seagull isn't exactly welcome in Rijeka.' Now the captain gripped Raj around the shoulders and moved with him toward Tomo, speaking as evenly as he could among the noise. 'So we circumvent the port. Don't worry, we do this all the time.'

'Don't fucking worry?' Tomo yelled, his head turning toward the captain and back to the dinghy multiple times. 'Don't fucking worry? That's easy for you to fucking say!'

'If you want to make it to Rijeka, you need to jump. Now!' Captain Maltokovic urged the two frightened greenhorns, subtly manoeuvring them even closer to the precipice. 'Trust me, I got you this far, my man will get you the rest of the way.'

'And where are you going?' Raj reached desperately, hoping for another port of call that might work out just as well as Rijeka.

'We are heading back.' The captain looked Raj straight in the eye, 'You can do this!'

'Bullshit,' Raj cursed. 'You have so many supplies on this ship you could be headed to America.'

'You can do this.'

'Take us with you?' Raj asked and demanded in the same breath, turning more and more desperate, clutching the captain's tunic with both hands. 'We'll work, we'll cook, we'll clean...'

'Where we are going, you are not welcome,' the captain answered, shaking his head to his men who had now made a move to protect their leader as Raj grabbed hold of the old man's shirt. 'Now let go. You can do this.'

Raj released the captain then crossed himself, said a prayer and grabbed the crucifix from his pocket, gave it a kiss and wrapped it around his neck once more. Miro, the cook, then walked by, holding the two men's rucksacks and, without a word, threw them down into the dinghy.

'What the fuck?' Tomo yelled looking over the starboard side again. 'That was our stuff!'

'Fuck!' Raj cried, knowing their money, food and clothes were all in those bags. He took a cautious step toward the edge, holding the taffrail that circled the interior of the hull.

'You sure, Raj?' Tomo looked more scared than ever before.

'What choice do we have, Tomo?' Raj replied, trying to keep a calm tone. 'We can't go back. And thanks to the captain, all of our shit is now down on that dinghy.'

'Let's go, boys,' the captain insisted once more.

'Fuck you.' Tomo turned angrily to the man who made certain promises but delivered vague results. 'Fuck all of you!'

But the hardened crew showed sympathy toward the youngsters, allowing for Tomo's frustration, without adding lewd comments or sardonic remarks. They still remained quite close, though, insuring that the night went according to the captain's plan. Raj and Tomo looked at each other, sharing a silent moment of acceptance and fear, surrendering to the fate that brought them to this point of their journey.

Raj grabbed onto the wet gunwale with both hands then raised his right foot up to use as a lever off the taffrail. He hoisted himself but decided against standing upright, rather taking a crouching position, with both hands between his bent legs still holding on firmly to the edge of the hull. He swayed dangerously on the precipice, but hung on, finding a point of balance before trying to take in the scene. Below, the dark, rushing water transfixed his attention, adding a hypnotising vertigo to the nausea he was already experiencing. As the Red Seagull bobbed up and down, splashed water to and fro, and cut through the sea with ease, Raj's mind went blank and his stomach retched from the motion, suddenly hurling his earlier dinner all over the Adriatic Sea.

'Oi!' a voice shouted from below. 'Take it easy, man.'

The unhappy pilot from the final dinghy was trying to bring the smaller boat in as close as possible to make the leap easier but swerved back when Raj vomited, avoiding a disgusting yellow spray all over his head and craft. Raj hardly noticed the boat but did hear the man's voice which helped wake him from his reverie. The pilot tried once more, but Raj wasn't prepared to look down again so he closed his eyes.

'I don't think I can do this,' he said softly to himself, taking a deep, salty breath. Just then he felt a hand on his back. It must have been Tomo, Raj thought, offering support as he balanced unsteadily on the edge of the slippery hull.

'You can do this,' the voice of Captain Maltokovic whispered in Raj's ear, as the gentle touch suddenly tensed up and shoved forward.

The world began to spin upside down in that instant, forcing Raj to open his eyes. He suddenly saw the approaching dinghy from the top of his sight, seemingly above him. His hands kept grabbing for something solid but only felt air. In a moment that felt like an epoch, the young man reached the boat below and his hands finally felt the timber he was looking for, smashing his right hand against a seat across the hull and his mid-thighs against the edge. His feet dipped into the ocean for a moment, but then his body slipped backward immersing his legs into the sea; the wet cold shocking him into awareness and the instinctual response for safety. He grabbed for anything he could but all he felt slipped away while he kept sliding into the water. Suddenly, a hand grabbed his shirt near the shoulders and dragged him aboard.

'You okay?' the pilot asked.

The runabout was tossing the two men all over the place and it took Raj a moment to realise he wasn't totally safe just yet. The pain across his legs was intense, his hand was a little sore, but the rest of his body felt fine, albeit drenched. Still, if it wasn't for the pilot, he would have been thrown overboard when they hit the next wave.

'Grab the rope,' the pilot yelled out, turning toward the Seagull again.

Raj was still a little dazed and held onto the flying dinghy for dear life. The Red Seagull looked enormous from this vantage point, as the hull of the yacht approached quickly, its shadow killing the light that shone down from above its helm.

'Now,' the pilot yelled again, but Raj was still unsure what the man was talking about.

'What?' The sea was smashing the two men and the small boat felt much, much faster than the larger one. Raj wondered what the pilot was talking about as he already held onto the rope within the dinghy.

'I already have the rope,' he revealed.

'No.' The pilot's mind was clearly far more occupied than his passengers. 'Over there.' The man behind the wheel pointed to the yacht but quickly returned his free hand as they hit another wave.

'What?' Raj was confused as his body rose in the boat then hammered back into his seat a second after the craft hit the water.

'There.' The pilot let one hand go of the wheel for a longer time. 'Off the cleat.'

'That rope?' asked Raj, pointing to the Seagull's freewall upon which he could barely make out a thin line descending vertically into the water.

'Yes.' The pilot returned his hand, sounding frustrated. 'That fucking rope.'

'Why?' Raj was unsure of the procedure, but he had just been launched from a yacht that was speeding through the sea, so he felt he had a right to question any other moves that were required in the open water.

'You can reach a hand up to your friend,' the pilot answered. 'It helps guide me as well.'

Raj wondered how often this group of sailors actually had transported people this way. The cargo being flung across the sea was one thing, but if this pilot needed Raj's guiding hand, then perhaps this wasn't the career he was best suited to. *Still*, Raj thought, *I would have much preferred a guiding hand from below earlier, than a shove in the back.*

On the next round, Raj waited for the last possible moment before letting his hands free of the dinghy and reached over and grabbed hard at the thin rope that ran down most of the length of the Seagull's outer hull. As the waves hit, Raj's backside rose off the dinghy's seat again, and the pain in his right hand came to life. The rope was taut near the hull, only having a little movement, which allowed for a closer merge between the boats, but also made Raj's knuckles scrape against the rough, salty hull, cutting his skin while stinging it at the same time.

Raj looked up and saw Tomo peering over the edge, still not brave enough to stand on the gunwale. As the wake of the yacht pounded them, Raj released the line and lurched forward, smashing his face against the Seagull's wall. He bounced back into the dinghy, so the pilot revved the motor, leaned to starboard before turning back to port, screaming, 'Again!'

Raj grabbed at the rope once more and got a hold again, but this time stood up a little in the runabout, crouching in the hope his knees could act as a kind of suspension against the current. His thighs were sore, his right hand throbbed and his knuckles were raw, but he was determined to hold on this time. He now only hoped Tomo was feeling just as courageous. Raj looked up and saw his friend scuffling with one of the Seagull's men. As their heads came in and out of view at the top of the hull, Raj struggled to both hold on and keep a clear view above him. He tried to reach a hand up toward his friend but thought better of it as his balance was far from secure.

'Come on!' he cried to his friend, looking up just as another head appeared and pushed the greenhorn over the edge.

With a scream of terror, Tomo crashed on top of Raj who had to let go of the rope now to help break his friend's fall. With the dinghy so close, Tomo made a clean landing in the middle of the craft, but still hit Raj across the shoulders which actually helped keep them both on the boat. The entire dinghy then leapt in the air as it bounced from Tomo's impact, making all the men onboard airborne for a scary moment before falling back again, violently hitting the water.

'You good?' the pilot cried as he turned the runabout toward the coast without waiting for a reply.

Raj gathered his thoughts and ignored the pain that he now felt in most parts of his body. He was wet and dirty, his thighs ached, his hands were bleeding and his face throbbed. With all the action going on, his adrenaline had not abated in the slightest, so he quickly moved some of the cushions around in order to get comfortable. He sat down next to Tomo who was cold, in shock and speechless. Raj wrapped a comforting arm around his friend's shoulders in an attempt to console him, all the while looking disgustingly toward the Red Seagull, and seeing the silhouette of one Captain Maltokovic, who stood on deck, puffing away on a freshly cut cigar, waving courteously to the two greenhorns who had just been pushed off his ship while an Italian flag was being slowly hoisted in preparation for the Seagull's next adventure.

'You guys... are fucking crazy!' the excited pilot yelled above the motor, which now was at full throttle, racing into the Kvarner Gulf with little more than a pen light at its bow to lead the way.

'Yeah,' Raj answered meekly, hardly able to his own voice. Tomo was yet to say anything.

'When Malto said... you guys would jump...' The pilot had to keep stopping mid-sentence due to the speed of the boat and the larger waves that crashed against the hull, lifting the boat and taking his attention away. 'I said... no fucking way.'

'Yeah.' Raj kept it brief. He was tired, and the adrenaline suddenly began subsiding quite quickly, beside which, he was in no mood to scream above the motor, water and wind just to be heard. He looked at Tomo again, with concern, but didn't want to bring up his health situation. Raj thought if his friend survived that jump across the water, then his heart condition couldn't be too bad.

'I had to double check... if I heard right,' the pilot continued, unconcerned that the conversation was mostly one way. '...Fucking crazy.'

He circled his temple with one finger as he turned his smiling face at Raj; he then pulled the throttle back all the way, slowing the engine right down until it turned off. He flicked the headlight off too and hopped out of his chair then quickly pulled out a couple of oars that lay between Raj and Tomo, on either side of the keelson.

'What are you doing?' Raj asked, suddenly becoming awake again.

'No problem,' the pilot said. 'Windward is much easier. We should be there soon enough.'

He turned to face the stern, placed the two levers in their respective oarlocks and began to heave.

'Why did you power down?' asked Raj, perplexed by the pilot who now sat directly in front him, face to face, rhythmically moving forward and back, rowing to shore.

A few more minutes passed until the boat had a good enough momentum that it made rowing much easier for the man.

'It's too loud,' the pilot continue. 'And I was told you wanted discretion, no?'

Just then the radio engaged and a familiar voice was heard. 'Goby Six, Goby Six, this is Seagull One, come in, over.' The voice sounded very familiar.

'Is that Maltokovic?' Raj's ears pricked up, as did Tomo's, who sat upright for the first time since they boarded the smaller craft. As if concerned about their reaction, the pilot just kept pulling the oars, ignoring the radio.

'Goby Six, Goby Six, this is Seagull one, come in, over,' the voice called out again, although this time there was a little more interference in the broadcast.

'I'll kill that fucker,' Tomo was incensed. 'Should never have gotten onto that fucking boat.'

'Shouldn't you get that?' Raj asked.

'I'll call him later, we need to move now,' the pilot said dismissively.

'Allow me.' Raj purposefully stood up and made his way carefully past the pilot and sat at the helm. He had never used a radio before, so fumbled around a little at first before it became unhooked from beneath the steering wheel. He could see one main button on it, so he pressed it and responded, 'Seagull One, this is Goby Six, we hear you... over.'

'Tell him, if I see him again, I'll fucking kill him.' Tomo was seriously angry and the darkness Raj had witnessed in his friend earlier seemed to rear its ugly head once more. '*I'll fucking kill you!*' he shouted, but Raj had released the speak button, so no communication was heard.

'Easy,' the pilot answered first, sounding concerned. 'Why do you want to kill Malto? He is a good man.'

'Goby Six, are the packages safe, over?'

'Motherfucker!' Tomo ignored the pilot. 'We are just packages for him.'

'Packages are fine,' Raj responded, 'but if we see you again, we'll be throwing you over board.'

'Is that you Raj? Over.' The captain was breaking up more and more the further they travelled.

'Yeah.'

'All in one piece? Over.' The captain gave a slight chuckle, leaving his side of the broadcast open until his laughter ceased.

'Barely.'

Raj wasn't sure why he had picked up the radio now. He was ready to unleash a barrage of insults against the old sea dog in the hope of somehow regaining a semblance of dignity. But as the conversation began, he remained quite civil with the captain; he felt tired and defeated, and couldn't wait for the whole damn affair just to be over so his feet could feel solid ground beneath them once again. Then something the pilot had said earlier jolted Raj.

'Can I ask you something, captain?' Raj began, thinking about his question while holding radio silence. 'How many times have you had men jump from one boat to another? You said you have done it many times, but your pilot seems to disagree, over.'

The pilot kept quiet, a feeling of angst emanating from him. He kept rowing the boat as the radio remained silent for a few moments, before the captain finally responded, 'That was the first time, over.'

'Lying till the very end, you motherfucker.'

Raj was happier now that he rubbed the captain's nose in it, albeit way too late.

'I said I'd get you to Rijeka,' the captain finished up forcefully, sounding a little frustrated through the static. 'That's what you paid for, that's what you got. Over and out.'

Raj put the radio down and his mind started ticking over once more. All three men sat speechless for a moment until Tomo just couldn't handle it anymore.

'Something's got you startled, Raj. Come on, out with it.'

'Did you pay the captain, Tomo?'

'No.' The question settled Tomo. 'Did you?'

'No,' answered Raj. 'He never asked. I thought we'd pay when we arrived. I thought that was the agreement.'

Raj hopped over an oar, rocking the boat uncomfortably before sitting in front of the pilot once more.

'What's your name, sailor?'

'I'm Zlatko.' The pilot stopped rowing and nervously shook Raj's hand.

'My name is Raj.'

'We are not giving you a fucking cent,' Tomo piped up again, refusing to grab the pilot's hand.

'Are you expected to take payment, Zlatko? From us?' Raj questioned sternly.

'No, no.' Zlatko returned to his menial task, sounding a little concerned. 'Malto always pays us.'

'Okay.' Raj looked at Tomo worriedly. 'Check your bag.'

Tomo grabbed his gear and after a moment shouted, 'Fucking prick!'

'Easy, friend,' Zlatko warned. 'We are near the coast, not too much noise now, please.'

'Fuck off!' Tomo cursed. 'Mine's gone, Raj.'

'All of it?' asked Raj with his own purse in hand.

'The notes.' Tomo lifted his hand and shook his purse, the jingling sound was proof enough. 'He left the coins.'

'Mine too,' Raj agreed, dejectedly shaking his head and taking in a deep, frustrated breath. 'It seems Captain Maltokovic was a step ahead of us all the way.'

CHAPTER 10

'Out you get,' Zlatko called to his two passengers after he jumped out of the boat with rope in hand, pulling the dinghy closer to the small pier. 'Quickly now.'

Raj grabbed his pack and followed Tomo off the starboard side and onto the rough, timber decking. Zlatko tied the craft to a pillar and then made his way quickly toward the beach. The three men's landing was the only real disturbance to the gentle splashing of waves in the clear and quiet night. Rijeka's centre was still a few miles away, so the hustle of the large city wasn't evident at that distance, even if its illumination shone like a welcoming beacon in the distance. The stars sparkled in the night time sky and provided most of the light on the beachhead, and although some ambient light could be seen from the outskirts of town, much of it was up high and blocked by the mountainous walls that faced the trio as they came ashore.

The cliffs ahead were pock marked with cave entrances large and small, stretching before them both vertically and horizontally. Dark holes on dark walls on a dark night made for perfect hiding places, Raj thought, and he couldn't wait to take cover and finally rest both his mind and his body. After reaching the beach's end, Zlatko turned and moved laterally, following the base of the cliff where the only foliage on the beach acted as a token border between the mountains and the shore. With so many holes to choose from, Raj felt a little frustrated that their new leader kept moving past cave after cave, each step on the rocky ground more and more fatiguing, and after a while, he began to wonder if Zlatko was going to use the caves at all.

'Raj.' Tomo kept his voice down as he stopped and turned to his friend. 'Why are we even following this fucker?'

'You got a better idea?' Raj stopped too, but saw Zlatko finally entering a cave no more than fifteen metres ahead of them.

'I don't know about this.' Tomo sounded worried. 'I'm not great at small, dark places. And God knows what's in these fucking holes.'

'We'll be fine.' Raj tried to reassure his friend, but wasn't convinced himself.

'That's what you said before I got thrown off the fucking yacht!' Tomo certainly wasn't letting go of the whole seaborne adventure and Raj noticed his friend's tone becoming more and more accusatory. 'In fact, that's what you said before we even got onto the fucking boat.' He took a small step toward the water and kicked a pebble that sat atop other, larger stones.

'Piss off.' Raj tried to keep his own voice down, but wouldn't let Tomo vent upon him. 'Are you blaming me for something here? I don't remember holding a gun to your fucking head. And in case you forgot, I got thrown off the fucking yacht too!'

'Yeah, yeah,' Tomo said dismissively, dropping his tone and looking at the stones beneath his feet. 'I know, I know.'

'I asked before and I'll ask again,' Raj inquired. 'You got a better idea?'

Tomo paced up and back a couple of steps before picking up a stone and throwing it angrily into the sea. 'We could just ditch this clown and make our way off this beach and into town.'

'You have a map?' Raj asked.

'I'm sure we can find one,' Tomo added.

'You have money for a map?'

'We could steal one.'

'Okay, I need to think about it,' Raj concluded. He felt too tired for verbal jousting and was in no condition to begin a new sortie in a strange town. 'But I'm not going anywhere until I get a rest. I need to relax a bit and get used to the ground beneath my feet. Ten, fifteen minutes, I don't know, but I can't think clearly just yet.'

'You boys coming?' Zlatko called from within the cave, where a small light could be seen reflecting off the stones on the floor at the cave's entrance.

'Fair enough,' Tomo said tersely, moving closer to Raj to illustrate his point. 'But mark my words: I'm not just going to follow you blindly from now.'

'Don't follow me at all, if you like.'

The cave was wide enough for five men to sit side by side. Raj looked to find where it ended but the darkness seemed to go on forever. It was high, too, and Raj stood and stretched his arms to the ceiling comfortably without coming close to touching the rock. The light Zlatko used was an old war lamp; it smelled of gasoline and was adjustable regarding its brightness. The lamp looked to be a permanent fixture as Raj didn't see Zlatko carry it in, but apart from that, the cave was empty.

'Come in, come in.' Zlatko moved aside and let the two Hercegs sit in deeper within the fissure.

'What's back there?' Tomo asked warily before sitting down.

'I'm not sure,' answered Zlatko. 'It's a new one. I haven't been all the way to the end yet. You can have a look if you like and let me know.'

'Smart arse.' Tomo's mood wasn't easing.

'What's your friend's problem?' Zlatko asked Raj.

'Never mind him, he's just tired,' Raj said, throwing Tomo a dirty look. 'What do you mean this is "a new one"?'

'We have to change all the time.' Zlatko pulled out a bottle for a drink. 'Never in the same one, and never too long. Actually, I think I have been here before. Some say they lead all over the place, but I stick to the edge, its closer to the sea.'

Raj sat on a large, flat rock and took off his shoes to dry. Everything felt damp and clammy ever since they left Split. 'Any chance of a fire?'

'No fire. It can be seen a mile away. Even this light is a little risky, but my position should cover it and we won't be here too long.'

'How long?' Tomo asked, sitting down himself now.

'Depends,' Zlatko pulled out some dried fish, which smelled unpleasant to Raj. 'What's your plan?'

'Rest,' was Raj's immediate response as he folded his rucksack over itself as a makeshift pillow and put his head on it.

'I wouldn't sleep here,' suggested Zlatko. 'If the police find you then you'll end up sleeping in prison. Maybe for a while.'

'I just need a few minutes rest, that's all.'

'Princess needs her rest,' Tomo remarked, suddenly finding his sense of humour, albeit underpinned by a dark timbre.

'So.' Zlatko kept chewing. 'What's the plan? Where are you headed? I know you have little money, and probably little connections. So, tell me, maybe I can help.'

'Like your precious captain helped?' Tomo still didn't trust the situation.

'You need to grow some fucking balls, friend.' Zlatko suddenly toughened up, raised his voice and looked directly at Tomo. 'What did you think? You were on a Riviera cruise and would be handed caviar and wine as part of the fucking deal? As much as Malto is an old brigand, he got you this far and entrusted me to see you safely out of Rijeka. You might not see it, but I think he likes you.'

'Fuck me,' Tomo retorted. 'If this is how he treats those he likes, what does he do to his enemies?'

Raj kept his eye on Tomo throughout the exchange, preparing for a fight to break out. But Tomo seemed surprised by Zlatko's change in demeanour. Raj took the moment of silence to look closer at Zlatko. The smuggler was clearly older than his two passengers, and was thin and muscular, wiry almost, with some small scarring across his face, poorly hidden by a thin beard that looked closer to a three-day growth than a permanent fixture.

'You want to move through Yugoslavia undetected? Then you'll get thrown off cars, trains and boats. Just be thankful you weren't in a fucking plane!'

'Fuck off,' was all that Tomo could muster, but his voice lacked the venom to really insult their new guide. He reminded Raj of a small dog that was resentfully putting its tail between its legs.

'Heh, if I fuck off, you'll be in jail within an hour.' Zlatko was showing his true colours and was in no way intimidated by Tomo's earlier gruff attitude. 'Believe me, Rijeka isn't Split. Those black shirts that patrol the old town are pussies. Here, there are far more partisans and far more military. And much, much more money. They can probably already smell you coming.'

This immediately caught Raj's attention, so he asked, 'What do you recommend?'

'Where are you headed?' asked Zlatko again.

'Italy.'

Zlatko checked his watch.

'Okay, in about half an hour, a train will come through, not far from here. At Sisak-Pecine. Last train to Slovenia. You need to get on that locomotive or you will be partying with the commies on a Saturday night.'

'Then what?' Raj asked.

'Jump off at Pivka. Then head west. If you don't get lost in the forest, you should find the border within an hour. Maybe longer.'

Tomo still looked a little sour but said nothing.

'Hey.' Zlatko eased up a little. 'I'm on your side. If I can help you get the fuck out of here, I will. What Malto did to you was tough, I know. But trust me. I'll get you to that train station, but after that, you're on your own.'

'How long do we have?' Raj asked again.

'I hope you're feeling rested.'

'Tomo.' Raj approached his friend after they both got up. 'Are we good?'

'Sure, sure,' Tomo responded and Raj sensed that Zlatko's earlier barrage schooled and humbled Tomo quite considerably. 'But remember what I said before.'

Raj ignored him.

'What about the dinghy?' he asked Zlatko who had killed the light and was already walking out of the cave.

'Not my problem.' Zlatko didn't stop as he talked. 'Not my boat.'

The trio kept moving northward, following the cliffs, and after five minutes or so, a break in the mountain appeared. It was a short-cut, with a steep, man-made path of well-worn, flat rocks stepping upward toward the sky, accompanied by wooden hand rails placed at strategic spots where the ascent was particularly precarious. The three men moved in single file up the mountain, carefully watching their long steps in the dark of night. Within ten minutes they reached the top, where they found the thin path continued through thick brush and short trees scattering along a very large plateau. Raj took a moment and turned around to appreciate the view across the Adriatic one last time.

They walked past the tree line and into a rough car park, laid with crushed rock that had been dug up by heavy vehicles leaving pot holes and divots everywhere. Around the gravel, a greater community park lay, complete with steel playground and cemented seating areas. There was a solitary, yellow street light at the entry to the car park, atop a high post that weakly illuminated a wide area. It was positioned at the end of a longer road that Raj thought must lead from a highway or public street of some kind. The three men avoided the light and made their way quickly across the flat grass until they hit another wall of trees.

'Through that industrial area.' Zlatko breathed heavily as he pointed across a long, quiet road that ran parallel to the cliff and fed into the park. 'Then a few houses, then the train. I hope we have time.'

The trio waited for a solitary car to pass before they ran across the two-lane road and into an empty plot with overgrown grass and thistles. They were always ascending, not overtly, but still constantly. The horizon was obscured by both the night and the buildings around them, but Raj could feel it in his legs and knew of the mountainous regions north of the city through his studies of the country's geography. Dogs barked in the back ground, bringing Raj out of his reverie with an immediate gratitude for the timber fencing surrounding them in that moment. They stopped at the fence at the end of the land and peered over. Raj saw a car park, with two small cars parked next to a long, double storey factory that had windows running the entire length of the building. The sign on the side of the building read *Torpedo* and two lights on the second floor were illuminated.

'Someone's in,' Tomo announced the obvious.

'Extra quiet, now,' Zlatko stated, and leapt the fence with consummate ease.

They made their way as close to the building as possible, hugging the shadows and almost running in silence. A new smell entered Raj's nostrils just then; an unpleasant and unnatural odour that made the air feel thick. They quickly crossed another small road, leapt another shorter fence and made their way to the back of a smaller brick building which seemed unoccupied. They stopped at Zlatko's behest to take stock of their position, catch their breath and plot their next move. Suddenly, a deep, growling boom echoed around the industrial suburb as a security dog started barking angrily from the neighbouring building.

'That's got to be a big fucking dog,' Raj said, startled, but thankful for the break in their movement and the safety of their location.

'Yeah,' Zlatko concurred as a second dog created a chorus, from a few factories down the road, the reverb around the concrete structures amplified the noise quite considerably. 'The sound is good cover, as long as we don't hang around long.'

Zlatko jumped the next fence without even checking. It was then that it dawned on Raj that the smuggler knew this route quite well and had run it so often that the timing of the animals was probably part of his itinerary. Raj and Tomo followed blindly, both literarily and figuratively; they had no idea where they were going and the lighting in the industrial area was extremely poor. However, by the look of the unexpected street lighting at the end of the next driveway, the industrial area was finally coming to an end and the domestic area would soon emerge.

They waited for two small vehicles to pass before crossing a well-lit, wide road which they followed north before turning right up a poorly lit street that had run down cement and timber houses on both sides. Another left turn before another right and the zig-zagging seemed over as they finally walked straight up this final dark street for a few minutes. The suburb seemed neglected with nature strips unkempt as were most of the yards, overgrown weeds and short, haggard trees grew wildly all about. No lights could be seen in the windows and no sound could be heard from within the homes. There were no cars parked in the street and no other people were anywhere to be found.

'This is a ghost town,' Raj said as they still walked at a brisk pace out in the open. 'There was more life in the factories we passed.'

'The factories are the reason for the ghosts.' Zlatko sounded very cryptic.

'What does that mean?' Tomo asked.

'There was an accident. At a chemical factory not far from here. It spooked everyone,' Zlatko explained.

'I smelled something disgusting before.' Raj remembered. 'Was that it?'

'No,' Zlatko elaborated. 'The accident was odourless.'

'Is it safe?' Tomo asked.

'I don't hang around long enough to find out,' Zlatko answered.

As tired and sore as Raj was feeling, those words inspired him to dig a little deeper and get through this next stage of their travels. He tried to keep his mind on the train ride ahead. He imagined the firm footing, cushioned seating and stunning views. He saw himself snoozing in quiet comfort while the train moved quickly through the night. Raj had never been on a train before, so all he had was his imagination, but he was sure that anything had to be better than the journey made over the sea.

'Okay.' Zlatko stopped once more. 'We have time for a smoke.'

They had traversed the abandoned street and found themselves on the corner at an intersection where the sounds of everyday life began again. A couple of cars chugged past and one motorcycle flew through the area, but no one paid any attention to the three smoking men.

'Just over this road.' Zlatko pointed casually. 'You'll start seeing more people. After you cross, turn right and you'll see a small walking bridge.' He checked his watch, as did Raj.

'What time does the train stop?' asked Raj.

'We have plenty of time.'

'So?' Raj was a little bewildered as to why they stopped. 'What are we doing here?'

'Time isn't the issue,' Zlatko explained. 'Timing is.'

'Timing?' Tomo seemed to be just as confused as Raj.

'To the right of the small bridge the stairs take you down to the platform,' Zlatko detailed. 'But you can't get on at the station.'

'Why not?' Raj asked.

'Because there are inspectors everywhere. Especially at this time of night. And on a Saturday night. There are lots of idiots out partying and it's a great time for scores to be settled and quotas to be made by the commies. They will want to see tickets, but you guys haven't got the money for tickets. Which means they will then want to see personal documents, which I'm sure you don't have either.'

'Shit,' Tomo said. 'Why didn't you tell us this before?'

'I'm telling you now.'

'How's that supposed to help?' asked Tomo again, with an agitation returning to his voice once more.

'It helps because you are not on the train yet.'

As if on cue, a small car drove past with a young, drunk man protruding out of the front passenger window. He held a glass bottle in one outstretched hand while proudly singing along to the vehicle's blaring radio. In fact, the car was full of singers, all stuffed into the back seat and screaming the words with joyous abandon. The sound was upbeat and in a foreign language that reminded Raj of the music he had heard at the bar in Split.

'Rock and roll?' Raj tried to remember correctly.

'Yes,' Zlatko stated. 'It will rock you to prison and roll you for a few hundred dinars.'

'Really?' Raj thought the smuggler was exaggerating. 'But it's only music.'

'It's a threat, is what it is,' Zlatko pointed out. 'Western imperialist propaganda is the official line. And I'm not counting the liquor out on the street.'

'So what are we supposed to do?' asked Raj, getting back on track after the partying car had moved along.

'To the left of the bridge there is another set of stairs. These are smaller, more hidden and used to access the lines for servicing and such. You'll have to jump a small fence. No big deal. Once you're on, avoid the uniforms, they carry guns.'

'Shit.' Raj was concerned. 'How many uniforms are on the train usually?'

'That can change,' Zlatko responded, just as the sound of a train was heard. A loud horn blared across the suburb followed by a high-pitched squeal of steel against steel as the driver hit the brakes early enough to stop the locomotive in time. 'Time to go boys. Good luck!'

'You not coming?' Tomo asked.

'No, I've had just about enough of your company.'

Then the smuggler turned back into the lifeless street and within a moment disappeared silently into the darkness leaving the two smoking journeymen to their own devices.

The train was getting louder, even as the squealing brakes had eased. Raj led the way, and, just as Zlatko promised, a small walking bridge appeared at the end of a cul-de-sac that acted as a car park and entry way to the station at Sisak-Pecine. Here, the yellow street lights were brighter, illuminated up high at four points around the public area. There were three small cars parked and a few people making their way quickly toward the station's ramp.

Raj and Tomo slowed down as they entered the car park and waited for the area to be clear before committing to their next move. Again, just as Zlatko said, a small stairway was found behind some overgrown bush just to the left of the bridge. Raj went first, moving aside the foliage and stepping past the public pavement. He moved slowly to allow his eyes to adjust to the new environment, which was darker due to the bushes on their left and the shadow cast by the bridge to their right.

'Watch your step,' Raj alerted Tomo. 'It's quite steep.'

The flat, concrete steps were rough under foot which allowed for a better grip, but they were quite narrow and had no handrails to help with the short descent. Within a minute, the two men landed on a short ramp that jutted to the left, parallel to the train tracks that now lay a few metres before them. There was no fence to jump, as Zlatko had warned them of, but there was a small service light that shone from beneath the bridge's substructure, with enough glare to illuminate the tracks and immediate surrounds. Raj welcomed the light but quickly realised it was a double-edged sword; allowing others to see them just as clearly as they would see the train.

The tracks continued for miles, curving to the right and beyond sight after passing another bridge in the distance. The man-made valley was cleverly cut into the earth and allowed the train to avoid traffic congestion and keep a stricter schedule for travellers. The twenty-foot retaining walls looked to be hardwood sleepers pressed between large rocks that dropped from the street above. Thin, black electric lines criss-crossed the air at street level driving thousands of volts to power down the locomotive without the need for steam, coal and manual labour.

'We should head away from the bridge,' Raj counselled his friend.

'Yeah, too much light for my liking,' Tomo agreed.

They jumped off the concrete riser and onto the crushed rock that staged the tracks and surrounds. Raj felt his sore feet immediately as he took a few steps away from the bridge and couldn't wait for the train to come past. A small red light turned green around half a mile down the line followed by the great horn of the locomotive announcing the beginning of the next phase of its journey up the Croatian coast.

'Ready?' Raj asked.

'I don't know,' answered Tomo nervously, and Raj felt the exact same trepidation.

The two men found a shadowy corner where the tracks began to curve slightly away from them. They stepped into the dark, keeping their backs tight against the retaining wall, and waited. The tracks suddenly became slightly more illuminated and the sound of the train gained volume. Squeaks and cracks from turning wheels and straining joints boomed through the valley as the locomotive moved. Beneath the foot bridge the front of the train could now be seen. The leading carriage moved slowly, with the lights still on in the cockpit, and Raj could clearly see the train driver, complete with uniform and captain's hat. Two bright headlights beamed across the area directly ahead of the locomotive and Raj just hoped the curve in the track would help keep the rays of light away from them.

'Which carriage?' asked Tomo.

'I don't know.' Raj never actually gave it much thought. 'How many are there?'

'I don't know.'

'Well aren't we fucking prepared!' Raj laughed out loud.

'Maybe the last carrier will be the best?' Tomo offered.

'Sure,' Raj concurred, as the second carriage now passed under the bridge. He quickly tightened the rope that held his wet rucksack over his shoulders. By the time the third carriage passed under the bridge the train was picking up speed. The fourth car could now be seen under the bridge light as the train driver passed the two men with the blue, white and red Yugoslav Railways inscription clearly labelled across all the cars. The thrusting sound of the long, steel behemoth started to find a quicker rhythm, and before Raj knew it, a fifth carriage emerged. Then a sixth. By this time the train had gained a considerable speed and soon would be too quick to catch.

'We might have a problem.' Tomo realised the dilemma ahead.

'No shit.' Raj made his move. 'Let's go!'

The two men ran toward the locomotive at full sprint, the fear of finding themselves stranded in Rijeka for the night inspiring them into motion. No longer caring about the number of cars being pulled, Raj saw a gap between the fifth and sixth carriage and headed for it, having to turn the angle of his run to the left in order to keep up. As he got within touching distance he sensed the train pulling ahead ever so slightly, his mind was torn; should he dig deep to keep up or fall back to catch the next car? He decided to push on, feeling his legs burning every step of the way, and the sound of crunching rocks beneath his sore feet becoming covered by the din of the turning metal wheels that were now only half a metre away. He no longer saw or heard Tomo either, and only hoped that his friend could find the speed required to board the moving cars too.

Raj knew once his momentum matched that of the train, he would only have a small window of time to make his move. He looked to the gap between the carriers; he could see the furthest carriage had handle grips running vertically from the top of the train to waist height when standing at the rear door. A small podium jutted out beneath the entry way and some thin, iron railing acted as framework beneath the platform to support or safeguard the underside of the carriage. He couldn't make out how the train cars were connected; all he knew was they were very close to each other. He supposed all carriages had the same build and his hopes were justified as his left hand reached blindly around the corner of the car closest to him and felt a cold, steel rod protruding from the flat metal chassis. The train then lifted into yet another gear and Raj's feet gave way under him, forcing him to jump a couple of times or scrape his knees all over the moving ground. He jumped once, twice, and then on the third landing pushed his legs even faster, all the while holding firmly onto that metal pole with straining ligaments from his shoulder blade to his wrist. His face and torso were now up against the carriage, but he was not letting go. The fourth jump was more of a leap up to the small railing that protruded at the foot of the carriage. He used his left arm to pull while his feet pushed as best as they could at that speed. The thin railing was at a perfect location for his feet and gave him enough time to bring his right hand around and secure his grip.

Raj caught his breath for a moment, then suddenly felt the bumps of the track for the first time and grabbed a little tighter. Before moving on, he looked down the outside length towards the rear of the carriage and saw no signs of Tomo. If his friend made it, they would meet inside; if not, then Raj was officially alone. He swung his left foot toward the platform and then his whole body came over. The door to the carriage had a square window that looked straight through into a small antechamber, then through to another door with a smaller window, effectively allowing a view through the entirety of the train. He reached for the door and the lever clicked beneath his hand and opened inward. The antechamber was no more than half a meter long with just enough room for the door to swing and allow Raj in. Some steel compartments were built into the walls to the left and right, but they were all locked. The second door led to the main part of the carriage which had dim lighting within and was sparsely populated.

Raj's dilemma now was one of detection; how could he enter the carriage with the least amount of exposure? Just then the train moved under a bridge, or through a tunnel, as darkness engulfed the outside world. Some kind of electrical impedance must have occurred because the light in the train flickered on and off as the train sped on. Raj took his chance and darted into the cabin and found the closest seat to the door, facing to the rear of the train. In moments, the light inside returned to full illumination as soon as the outside structure had passed, and Raj looked around casually to see if anyone was staring inappropriately toward him.

He took a deep breath when he realised the coast was clear. Everyone else on the carriage was minding their own business: reading papers, books and magazines. A younger couple who sat across the aisle to his left talked privately with each other while an older lady behind them was passing time by knitting with giant needles and plenty of yarn. Raj yawned wide as he peered out of the carriage window and saw very little in the dark of night apart from his own haggard reflection in the window. He knew he needed sleep but now was fully aware of just how badly he also needed to bath and shave.

CHAPTER 11

Rijeka was a bustling town on par with any of the major cities throughout Yugoslavia. Its geography positioned it at a pivotal point for connecting southern Europe, being a hub of activity socially, politically and economically. Rijeka's long record traced back to the Dalmatian coastal province under the auspices of the Roman Empire. As kingdoms rose and fell throughout history, Rijeka played an integral part at the northern point of the Adriatic with maritime trade at the core of the city's strength and appeal. Croatia held sway over Rijeka for a time, as did the Holy Roman Empire. The Venetians and Turks fought over its custody, and even Napoleon understood its strategic value. The Hungarians felt its importance so keenly that they issued a governor that reported directly to Budapest, giving Rijeka a sense of autonomy within the empire and allowing it to flourish with international trade.

Rijeka expanded greatly in the latter years of the nineteenth century under the Austro-Hungarian Empire. The population exploded as the city grew into a modern metropolis drawing bright minds and strong hands to bring new ideas into life. The empire's naval academy was established in Rijeka and the first ever torpedo was trialled at the institute. Urbanisation was at the forefront of the leaders' minds and world-famous cities, such as Vienna, inspired drastic changes.

Many old sections of the town were destroyed in order to make way for new designs and buildings, including a grand theatre to rival those famous opera houses throughout Europe. Water and sewerage lines were also modernised to keep up with growth. Coupled with the emerging electrical grid, the town was able to construct a railway that linked to Hungary, allowing fast travel throughout much of the continent on a single train. Oil was discovered too and a refinery was built to accommodate the growth in energy and transport industries, particularly the combustion engine.

Power continued changing hands during the early twentieth century: Italians, Croats and Germans all held sway at some point until the end of World War Two, when Yugoslavia took control and held onto it with a firm grip. Many Italians were purged during this time, forced back to mainland Italy in an attempt to ensure no further claims were made based on ethnic majority. It also sent a clear message regarding the ideological separation that existed between the southern nations of Europe.

Rijeka was heavily bombarded during the war, and so the first thing needed was a rebuilding campaign, sparked by manufacturing industries around heavy machinery, oil refinery and shipbuilding. A decade after the war, Rijeka was booming as the black crude from beneath the city poured into engines that were built in the city, helping craft goods designed and assembled by the people of the city.

Raj looked out of the window of his carriage and saw specks of artificial light rushing toward him. The big city soon enveloped the train line as the locomotive rose above the man-made valley that it had traversed for the last few kilometres. The speed of the carriage seemed to increase now the train was at street level, because the surroundings gave Raj a point of reference to the movement.

The noise was greater and the line seemed rougher, making the train creak and groan with every little move it made. The locomotive was yet to make a stop, but Raj knew it was only a matter of time before they arrived at Rijeka's central station. Within moments the city closed in even more around the train. Straight steel poles topped with yellow lights dotted bitumen roads and concrete pavements that ran parallel to the train, while other roads intersected and ran off in different directions, highlighted by green and red traffic lights that aided the many cars, motorbikes and buses to move carefully through the city's streets. Pedestrians also scurried along on the clear Saturday night adding a slower counterpoint to the movement of the surrounding vehicles. Some of the buildings were the tallest Raj had seen, with lights on sporadic floors all the way up to the top. In fact, there seemed to be lights everywhere, so much so that Raj could no longer see his reflection in the carriage's window because of the illumination from the outside.

Next stop, Rijeka station.

The announcement brought Raj back from his reverie. He surveyed the carriage and saw many of the travellers looking around as if they too had been daydreaming. He tried to see further down the line, but the train's trajectory was quite straight which didn't allow him a better view through the window. He rose and walked toward the back of the car, his thighs and feet immediately responding with a rekindled sense of tire, but he soon stopped when he saw a map of the railway system printed on a board next to the sliding door. He placed his finger on the thin black line and traced it along until he hit a red spot: Rijeka. He then continued the trace to Pivka in Slovenia. It showed six more stops after the next one, but they were well spaced apart and Raj knew he had plenty of time still ahead in his journey.

Raj's mind then turned to Tomo; he wondered about his travelling companion and hoped he was safe. He continued moving toward the rear of the carriage in the hope that Tomo might be on the next car, when the train suddenly eased off its pace and a myriad of new lights assaulted Raj's eyes. The station had been entered and it looked like daylight had dawned upon the town once more. Raj's carriage passed waiting travellers on the bright platform as it continued to slow while most of the seated patrons within rose to their feet. Raj decided to wait near the door feigning an egress but all he really wanted to do was pop his head out to quickly see the station and maybe even catch a glimpse of Tomo just in case his friend was also searching for him.

A young man, around Raj's age, walked up just as the train stopped and pulled the sliding door to the side. With that one action both doors slid open and the commuters began to exit. Raj stuck his head out and scanned the scene the best he could. The smell of oil, sea and body odour was the first thing to assault his senses as a gust a wind pushed the station's smells into the cart. There was no evidence of Tomo anywhere, although with the number of commuters moving around, it would be easier to miss him. People of all shapes and sizes mulled about on the dirty, grey tarmac; some descending into a sub floor, others standing in groups, while a few solitary travellers frantically ran along the platform.

Black and white boards against one wall had information about train times and a giant map of the greater Rijeka region was painted on a far wall. Two telephone booths were occupied in the distance, situated next to a small and overstocked newspaper stand where a few men mulled about smoking and chewing on snacks. Raj was genuinely excited because he had never been to a metropolitan train station, so he took it all in as quickly as he could. The noise was another surprise; the din was constant, overtaken only by the next train arriving or a screaming voice trying to reach a familiar ear across the crowd.

Before the train began to move once more, a voice called 'all aboard' and a shrill bell rang very loudly. The man behind the sounds was a warden, dressed in dark blue, complete with official badges and uniform hat. He began at the rear and slid each door closed before ringing the bell again and making the call. Raj still had a few moments before the warden reached him, so he took another quick look up and down the outside length of the train but still could not see Tomo. However, he did notice two uniformed officers entering the train's forward compartment. Raj quickly took a mental note of the number of carriages ahead of him before turning away from the door.

'Shit,' he mumbled to himself and his heart began to pulse faster.

Raj quickly made his way to the rear of the carriage. He now knew there were three more cars behind him, and five more to the fore, which bought him some time before the inspectors reached him. But what to do now? He had no ticket, nor any documents and he wasn't going to get off the train as he didn't know what awaited him on the platform. Besides, Zlatko said this was the last train to Slovenia, so this ride carried all Raj's hope at that particular moment.

The train began to move but Raj remained standing. The other travellers shimmied in their seats in an attempt to find a more comfortable position for the journey ahead. There were a few more people aboard now, and the noise was a little louder, but there were still plenty of seats available and no one paid Raj any real attention as he reached for the back door. The handle moved easily and he quickly entered the utility compartment. It was the same design as on the other side; a small, dark booth with lockable cabinets on all sides built right into the metal walls with windows in both internal and external doors. Raj nervously looked back from where he just came for any signs of the inspectors but saw nothing, so he kept moving and crossed the outside platform that linked the carriers.

The next two carriages were more of the same; daydreaming commuters wrapped in their own thoughts, or in books, or each other, so much so that they hardly glanced at the stranger that walked by. There were fewer travellers on each car until Raj arrived at the very last carriage which had only two passengers; an older couple who sat next to each other, quietly sleeping the journey away. By their side was a small, golden haired dog that yelped lightly as Raj entered the cabin.

'Stop that.' The lady berated the dog as the couple awoke, startled.

'Sorry about that.' The gentleman apologetically addressed Raj, then taking a deep breath before continuing. 'At our age it's good to have a guard dog.'

'He looks ferocious.' Raj joined the sarcasm as the dog was hardly an ankle biter, yet did awake the couple on Raj's entry.

'Hulo looks after us; don't you, boy?' The lady reached down by her feet and scratched her pet lovingly behind the ear. The dog looked up adoringly before sitting down directly on the woman's left foot.

'I hope Hulo has a ticket,' Raj added as he walked past. 'I saw a couple of inspectors jumping on at the station.'

The couple gave no response as Raj made his way to the very last possible seat; he turned and sat facing forward then gazed up the aisle toward the door to the utility room from whence he just came. He now knew Tomo was gone; left behind in Rijeka to a fate all on his own. There was nothing Raj could do to help his friend; he just prayed Tomo was healthy and hadn't injured himself during their plight to board the moving train.

The inspectors would arrive shortly, of that he was certain, but how he would deal with them was still the mystifying part. He reached surreptitiously to the back door, the final utility cabin on the train, but this door's handle failed to budge so the option of hiding out in the back was gone. Hanging off the outside door was suicide as the train was now moving at a rapid speed. It seemed Raj's only recourse was to lie about losing his ticket which was with his paperwork, including his identity papers. Then when the train stopped, and the doors opened he would have to run and hope his legs would carry him away from the authorities.

Raj breathed deeply but just couldn't relax and constantly looked to the other end of the carriage. The outside world had once again returned to a relative darkness now that the station was behind them, as was the centre of the city. The train ascended as it pushed on, into the hills on the outskirts of Rijeka and onward toward Slovenia, well into continental Europe. Occasionally, Raj looked through the windows, but his eyes invariably darted back to the ominous door at the front of the carriage. Hulo, the mutt, looked back at Raj a few times, as if sensing the unease emanating from the young man.

The train had travelled for at least fifteen minutes before Raj finally heard the outside cabin door open and saw a head appear through the window into the carriage's utility room. Now there was no escape. The moment had arrived and was punctuated by a light sweat that broke upon Raj's brow and across his palms. His imagination took an even firmer hold as a thousand possible scenarios played out in his mind: from the extremes of prison time, to the joys of an impossible escape. Over and over the thoughts raced in his mind, accompanied by an increase in the rate and depth of his heart beat, both moving at such a volume that when a mysterious hand tugged at his right sleeve he nearly jumped out of his seat.

'Shit!'

'Ssh,' the voice called quietly.

'Tomo?' Raj was shocked and spoke louder than he intended.

'Don't you know the meaning of "ssh"?'

Tomo was hiding in the rear utility cabin all along and opened it to quickly let his friend in. Raj silently made his way into the dark space and crouched beneath the door's window to avoid the elderly passengers, and inspectors, noticing him.

'How did you get in here?' Raj was full of questions. 'I checked before. It was locked.'

'It wasn't locked.' Tomo smiled looking up at the handle. 'I was just holding the lever. I didn't know who was trying to get in.'

'Have you been hiding out here the whole time?' Raj asked, glad to see his friend.

'No, I got on a couple of carriages ahead.'

'I was scared for you, Tomo,' Raj opened up. 'I thought you never made it. I came to the rear to find you, but I ran out of carriages to check. Thank God you made it.'

'I heard the door opening at the front and thought for sure it was some kind of inspection team. So, I snuck in here when the older couple passed out.'

'You were a bit early, but you were right,' Raj revealed. 'The inspectors are here now.'

Just then the small dog barked. Raj felt the tiny room shrinking around him. Both men crouched down beneath the window and Tomo continued to hold firmly onto the handle.

'Last time we were hiding beneath a window and eavesdropping, we ended up getting thrown off a ship,' Tomo whispered.

'I remember,' Raj responded grimly.

The dog's bark took on a new dynamic in the moments that followed. The voices within the cabin quickly rose in volume, which pushed the pooch's bark to new extremes again. Before a minute passed, the ruckus from within the carriage became loud, aggressive and quite menacing. Raj made out a few words, but the steel door insulated the carriage very well, and the noise of the moving train was also louder in the utility room, so the two stowaways really couldn't glean much simply from the aggressive conversation in the main carriage.

'I'm going to take a quick look,' said Tomo, still holding the handle.

'Alright,' Raj replied.

'Shit.' Tomo ducked back down.

'What is it?'

'Take a look,' Tomo suggested. 'Don't worry, they won't see you.'

Raj popped his head up and was horrified. An inspector sat on the floor of the aisle, his leg bleeding profusely. His comrade stood protectively in front of him, with a pistol in his hand pointed down at the little dog that barked extremely aggressively up at the gun wielding superintendent. The old man held the dog's reins and pulled back to keep him at bay while his wife added to the furore by shouting some kind of profanities at the inspectors.

'That's a fucking mess.' Raj returned to his hiding position out of view.

'Yeah,' Tomo began, 'good for us, but...' then a gun shot rang out cutting him off abruptly.

'It just became a bigger mess,' Raj whispered in shock.

'Shit,' was all Tomo could offer.

Raj then lifted his head again, this time with even more caution. The dog laid limp and bleeding on the floor while the woman wept over the body. The woman's husband was also hunched over with a hand on her shoulder. The injured inspector still sat on the floor while his partner started wrapping some cloth around the wounded leg. Suddenly the train slowed and the two hideaways looked at each other.

'Next station?' asked Tomo.

'I think so.' Raj thought back to the map fixed against the carriage wall. 'Five more stations after this one, if I remember correctly.'

'This is about to turn into a nightmare.'

Raj reached for the back-door handle but it wouldn't budge.

'I tried that when I came in,' Tomo said. 'I think it's the only locked door on this fucking train.'

The train swayed, creaked and jolted even more as its velocity slowed. The light in the main carriage turned off and on a few times as the current must have hit some kind of turbulence. Both men sat firm in the dim light of the small cabin so as not to be thrown around. As the train kept slowing, Raj looked around desperately for salvation. He quickly tried opening all the small cabinets, but none were unlocked.

'Tried that too,' Tomo stated nonchalantly.

'Well, if you've got some new fucking ideas, now would be the time to share them.' Raj became frustrated once more and it dawned on him in that moment that he might not have missed Tomo as much as he previously thought.

'I think we should wait and see what pans out,' Tomo suggested, still sitting with his gripping hand stretched up unmoved from his position on the floor. 'I don't think we have much choice at the moment.'

Raj reluctantly accepted his friend's capitulation as there really was nothing left to do. So, he sat once more beneath the door's window and waiting silently for the locomotive to make a full stop. It took a few more minutes before the movement completely ceased, but once it did, the cabin with the injured inspector sparked into life.

Both Raj and Tomo stuck their heads up to see a swarm of uniformed authorities enter the carriage and take hold of the two elderly passengers, and the two visibly shaken attendants, and the carcass of the dead pet between them. The woman swung her hands wildly at the policemen as they tried to control her, while the man was already in handcuffs, looking forlorn as he was led away. He turned his head toward the rear door and Raj was certain he caught the man's eye. Finally, a cleaning crew entered; gloved hands and masked faces spraying a concoction of chemicals across the car before scrubbing clean any evidence of wrongdoing that had occurred.

Within ten minutes the scene had changed from one of carnage to one of normality and, as the train began the next leg of its journey, the final carriage was left unoccupied but for Raj and Tomo, who moved from their darkened hiding place to enjoy their hygienic new environment.

The two men sat in silence for a long while, firstly staring at the brown stains on the linoleum train floor, then vacuously through the windows into the darkness of the outside world. Raj found the monotony of the train's movement quite relaxing and his complacency grew as did the distance between stations. Fatigue quickly enveloped him and so he closed his eyes just for a moment.

'Where are we?' Tomo's voice disturbed the locomotive's din.

'I don't know.' Raj struggled to open his dry eyes. 'Have we hit a station yet?'

'Ha.' Tomo laughed. 'We've past three. You slept right through them.'

'Three?' Raj was a little surprised. 'No way!'

'Yes way.'

Raj immediately awoke at the shocking news and blinked his dry eyes a couple of times before rubbing at them with the back of his hand. He wasn't sure if he should believe his friend until he saw a strange, middle-aged man sitting at the far end of the carriage who wasn't there only a few moments earlier. Raj rose in confusion and moved toward the central doorway, stretching and yawning as he walked. He looked at the map before realising how pointless it was without a reference.

'What was the last station we passed?' he called to Tomo.

'I don't know.' Tomo laughed. 'I think I fell asleep too.'

'Shit,' Raj mumbled to himself.

'Next stop is Pivka.' The stranger at the far end looked up from his newspaper and chimed in.

'Thank you, sir.' Raj breathed a sigh of relief and made his way back to Tomo. 'For a moment I thought we were on our way to Austria.'

'Austria?' Tomo questioned.

'Never mind.' Raj relaxed in his seat and focused on keeping his eyes open.

Minutes passed before the locomotive stopped at a tiny station with one concrete platform, one small, orange light and one entry. A small wooden sign just beneath the solitary light read 'Pivka' and Raj and Tomo remained the only travellers standing on the platform as the train departed into the night.

'We made it this far.' Raj broke the silence as the two men descended a few steps to move onto the street. 'I think the hardest part might be behind us.'

Tomo remained silent as they walked down a dark, narrow road and toward the only visible civic lighting near the train station. The fresh country air reminded Raj of home and his thoughts immediately returned to his parents and siblings; particularly his eldest brother,

Krizan. As he walked, he wondered once more where his brother could be and whether they would see each other ever again.

'Are we sure about this?' Tomo broke the reverie.

'What?'

'Walking straight into town in the middle of the night?'

Raj was surprised at Tomo's paranoia.

'You're right, doesn't seem like the brightest idea, does it?'

The two pulled off the road and tried to look around. Raj remembered the map of the country side as best he could; he used the train tracks as a reference and worked out which way was west and hence the most direct route to Italy.

'This way,' he announced and turned into some grassland and away from the tracks.

'You sure?' Tomo was not quite sold on the idea but followed anyway.

'Yeah, I reckon we might run into a farm and somewhere to try and catch some sleep. I can't go on like this for much longer.' Raj knew that walking into the town was a rookie mistake brought on simply by fatigue. Falling asleep on the train was also another clear sign that slumber was required now far more than speed. 'Just watch out for snakes.'

They hadn't needed to walk too long before coming across a low-lying timber fence that seemed to stretch far into the darkness on either side. Once over the boundary, the grass was far shorter and large silhouettes dotted the landscape ahead of them. They had clearly entered a large property with a spread of dwellings dotted randomly all about the land. In the distance, Raj saw a couple of lights he assumed were atop the farmer's domicile, but they were simply specks across the field and quite a way from any possible chance of revealing the two illegal entrants.

Barking dogs cut the silence just as Raj and Tomo found their way to the door of an old wooden barn. They immediately stopped their movements and waited for the canines to settle. The dogs, too, were at a distance, but the animals could easily work themselves into a fervour thus drawing their master's attention. Fortunately, the dogs settled, and the door was unlocked, so the two men quietly slipped inside and checked their lodgings.

Visibility was difficult inside the shelter, but there were enough cracks in the walls to illuminate a large pile of straw that sat right in the middle of the chamber. Without a further word, the two men took their positions on each side of the bale and laid their heads down to sleep. Raj said a quick prayer of gratitude before closing his eyes and finally getting the rest he deserved after surviving quite possibly the most difficult day of his young life.

CHAPTER 12

The rooster's distant cries were enough to rouse Raj at the crack of dawn. He blinked quickly before feeling the shock of awaking in a strange and dangerous environment. He rolled out of the hay and stood up in a defensive pose as if an attack was imminent. When he remembered where he was, he took a moment to compose himself and checked his timepiece. The old fob watch had stopped at exactly 2.37am. He wound it several times but to no avail; the family heirloom would no longer help Raj on his travels. A profound sadness hit him in that instant; it was another sign that his connection to home was becoming more and more fragile. Tomo still snored comfortably though, ignorant of his friend's personal despair.

'Get up, Tomo,' Raj called, without raising his voice too far.

Tomo kept snoring and only moved subconsciously to turn in the hay. The rooster called again.

'Tomo,' Raj insisted, just a bit louder this time. He looked around the barn now with a far clearer sight. The morning sun had started to peek over the horizon outside and the light poked through every crack and crevice of the old stable walls. Yellow and brown was the dominant theme, with timber, hay and particles of dust the only items occupying the structure apart from the two hideaways.

'Tomo.' Raj reached over this time and shook his friend on the shoulder.

'What?' a bleary-eyed Tomo answered.

Just then, the sounds of dogs accompanied the rooster's crow. At first a single excited bark, then two more, then another two more simultaneously.

'The dogs are coming!' Raj whispered in his friend's ear.

Tomo's eyes widened as reality took an immediate hold. He sprung clumsily from the hay and reached straight for his pack before replying, 'How long have we got?'

'I thought that might get you up.' Raj laughed quietly as he reached for his own pack. 'But in all seriousness, if the dogs are barking, it means the farmer is up and the day is beginning. We need to move. Now!'

The two men snuck slowly through the same east-facing door they entered the night before. Raj looked up first and saw a clear bluish black sky, cloudless and empty save for a few remaining stars twinkling and holding on to the last possible moment of night. There was no wind and the stillness in the air helped carry all sounds from near and far. The dogs barked again, but this time the sound was a touch closer.

'We should head for those trees,' suggested Tomo, pointing to a bushy area along the fence line that enveloped the farm.

'Good idea,' Raj agreed then ran straight for the trees.

The two men lay down and took cover in the thick underbrush before checking their surrounds. The area seemed to be the forerunner of a larger, thicker copse of trees and shrubs that ran deep into one side of the farm, following the old timber fence the two men hurdled the night before. The trees were an excellent and welcome cover for the men, but Raj also thought the farmer enjoyed the wind break and natural border supplied by the large strip of foliage. Beyond the bush, the farm was now exposed by daylight and Raj could clearly see the expanse before them. Past the farm and well into the distance, mountains rose out of a large forest that sprang up well past the open field before them.

'There's no chance we can make it out there,' Raj stated as much to himself as to his comrade.

'You're right,' Tomo concurred just as the dogs barked once more, 'and I don't want to know what kind of dogs are out there.'

'Or what kind of gun the farmer keeps.'

With that, Raj turned and made his way deeper into the woods. After a while, the dogs barking became more distant and the men stopped to rest.

'I figure these trees follow the fence all the way around.' Raj picked up a stick and provided a rudimentary drawing in the loose earth at their feet. 'If we follow it, we should find a spot where we can leave the farm unnoticed and find our way to the border.'

'Sounds good,' Tomo replied. 'But it's getting a bit thick in here.'

'It shouldn't last.' Raj looked around. 'From memory, I think there is a state forest between us and the Italians, so we should find it a bit easier soon enough.'

They kept an even pace for the next half hour and tried to stay as far away from the farmer's land as they could. The bristles and thorns made them pay as, the nicks and cuts delivered, forced both men to grab walking sticks to help clear and avoid unnecessary injury. At times they forayed onto the grass as the going was too tight in the woods, but they were never noticed by any one from the farm.

'It seems to be getting easier.' Raj stopped after another hour or so. 'The trees have thinned out.'

'And they're getting taller.'

'Oak trees,' Raj revealed. 'We might have left the farm.'

'But there was no fence?' Tomo inquired.

'I don't know.' Raj looked around. 'Maybe they didn't bother putting one up. Maybe they didn't bother fixing the old one. I don't know.'

'I suppose there wouldn't be too many bandits coming this way,' Tomo said.

'I don't think *that* fence would have stopped many bandits, Tomo.' Raj was kind with his tone before deflecting his friend's embarrassment. 'Regardless of borders and fences, bears would be the bigger threat out here. And wolves.'

The two men took a seat on a fallen log and rested their legs while inspecting the cuts upon their hands and arms.

'That's a nice one.' Raj pointed to his left hand, near the wrist, where a small trickle of blood made its way from a thin wound. 'Stings too.'

'This one ripped my shirt.' Tomo turned slightly to show Raj a tear just beneath his right arm pit.

'That Rakija would have come in handy for these wounds,' Raj offered, still looking at his cut.

'I could sure use a drink as well.' Tomo laughed, easing the mood in the woods.

'So could I.' Raj chuckled as well before getting up and dusting himself off. A crack sounded, not too far from the men, which shattered their minor revelry.

'What was that?' Tomo stood too, looking concerned.

'I don't know, but I think we should keep moving.'

The two men kept an even pace for a couple of hours once more. They knew they were well clear of the farm now, but Raj started to worry. Since they departed the farmer's woods and entered the state forest, he had no sense of direction. He had heard of stories where travellers became forever lost on their journeys through the wilderness and dehydration became a real concern.

'I'd kill for some water.' Raj kept walking this time, now also worried that nightfall might sneak up on them and pose yet unforeseen threats.

'Same here,' Tomo added in a dry, parched voice.

'Keep your eyes and ears focused,' Raj indicated. 'If you see, or hear, a stream, we should make way toward it.'

Another hour or so passed and the sun was now high in the clear, blue sky above them. The shade from the broad oaks and tall ferns was welcome and, although the spring air was warm, the forest provided plenty of shade to keep the men cool. Raj trudged on, leading the way. He knew the sun set in the west so followed that direction roughly and hoped they would find some kind of landmark soon.

'Feels like we've been marching for hours.' Tomo spoke the first words in a long while. 'Maybe we should have joined the Yugo army?'

'My watch broke,' Raj answered sombrely, 'but I reckon we are close to lunch time.'

'Shall we stop?'

'Sure.' Raj was feeling exhausted yet again as both men sat to eat.

'What's on the menu?' asked Tomo cheekily.

'Let me see.' Raj joined the joke, pretending to scrimmage around his sack for food. 'Hard bread, hard cheese and hard prosciutto. And you?'

'Why, that's the exact menu that I've got too.' Tomo laughed. 'You have fantastic taste, my old friend.'

'I'd love to eat a meal with a spoon again.' Raj missed his mother's cooking.

'Same here,' Tomo agreed before taking a big bite of bread.

The buoyancy deflated within Raj soon after he realised just how much food remained.

'Thank God we stocked up at Imotski,' Raj stated melancholically. 'But I still think we should eat lightly in case we are out here longer than planned.'

Tomo's mouth was too full to answer so he agreed by nodding and wrapped the remainder of his meat as he ate. They chewed the rest of their meagre meal in hungry silence before rising once more.

'You know where you're going, Raj?' asked Tomo.

'Honestly, no.' Raj wasn't about to hide the fact. 'But if we follow the sun then we have to hit Italy at some time.'

They continued their quest through the beautiful forest that bordered north western Yugoslavia with north eastern Italy. The beauty soon began to sour as the more time passed and the more Raj started questioning his sanity. He was sure they had passed the same tree not too long ago so he stopped and pulled out his knife and began carving a cross into the bark as a precaution.

'What are you doing?'

'I'm scared we're lost, Tomo,' announced Raj. 'It feels like I'm going in circles.'

'I'm pretty sure we're not.' But Tomo also sounded uncertain.

'I'm scared we might never get out of here,' Raj confessed. 'It's been a few hours and with no guide I'm starting to get worried.'

'We'll be alright.' Tomo tried to assuage his friend. 'You got us this far. Imagine if I were leading?'

Raj appreciated Tomo's attempt at changing his mood, but he didn't really feel any different. So he continued digging into the bark with the blade so as even a blind man could spot the mark. Tomo stood silently watching him when a sound ruffled some bushes not too far ahead of them.

'Did you hear that?' asked Raj, looking worriedly at Tomo amid fears he was probably now hearing things too.

'Yeah.' Tomo took a few slow steps toward the sound. 'Straight ahead, to my ears.'

'And close, too,' added Raj.

They moved quietly and took cover behind another tree and waited. After a few moments, a deer appeared from behind a bush, a doe specifically, chewing vociferously on some leafy greens and unaware of the two humans hiding just ahead of her.

'Maybe we will eat like kings tonight?' Tomo whispered.

And those words were enough for the animal to stop eating and look up before turning and bolting through the woods to the right of the two men. Raj quickly took off in pursuit. His feet were sore, but he knew the deer provided a great sign of the territory ahead of them.

'What?' was all Tomo managed before trailing after his friend.

'There was no way I could have kept up,' Raj admitted once both men stopped, and the deer was far gone.

'So why chase it?' Tomo was puffing.

'Because those creatures rarely stray too far from open pastures and running water,' Raj confided, 'and I was hoping she might lead us to either.'

'So why was she lurking in the woods?'

'Maybe there are wolves in the area?' Raj offered.

'Great,' Tomo sounded frustrated. 'We'll find water... only to be mauled by wolves!'

'Relax,' Raj reassured. 'If wolves were hunting us we would be dead already.'

The two men stepped around a wide thicket of dark green vegetation that rested behind a few wild olive trees. To their amazement, a large opening could be seen through the trees ahead of them. They moved slowly toward the grassland, but something felt strange to Raj, so he motioned to Tomo to slow down and keep quiet. They crouched among the longer grass and noticed a few large boulders spread out before them, so they took cover behind one rock and looked around.

'I don't see anyone,' Tomo began in a whisper.

'Nor do I.' Raj kept his eyes peeled. 'But these rocks don't look natural here.'

'No,' Tomo agreed. 'It reminds me of home.'

'I think this is the border.' Raj was putting the pieces together. 'The rocks form a line. Can you see if there are rocks on the other side?'

Tomo stood for an instant then ducked. 'Yes. Same as these.'

'I think the grass between acts as the crossing. The cut through the forest looks manmade.'

'There'll be patrols, then,' Tomo added.

'Yes. Maybe we should follow the line behind the bushes until we are sure it's clear?'

'Good idea.'

The two men traversed at a safe distance but saw no movement along the open zone. After ten or so minutes, they decided to make a move and ran as fast as they could across the grass land. Sunlight glistened on their smiling faces as they entered the plain at full pace. A group of deer grazing gently on the wild grasses before them took a few steps away from the running men. To Raj's right, the forest curved around, continuously rising into the distant mountains that led to central Europe. To Raj's left, the field sloped gently, mostly wild grass, with some smaller shrubs scattered around. But a glance each way was all Raj could take, at least until they made it across to the safety of Italian soil.

'You were right,' Tomo proclaimed once they stopped and found cover.

'About what?' Raj was catching his breath.

Tomo smiled and pointed to the deer that remained unperturbed on the grass.

Raj smiled back. 'Just lucky.'

'Maybe our angels are watching over us,' Tomo added.

'Perhaps.'

'This forest is stunning,' Tomo announced, taking in the picturesque scene before them while also taking in a deep breath. 'But if I'm honest, after seeing these rocks, I miss all the white stone scattered around our home.'

'Yeah, me too.'

'Which way?' Tomo asked after a few moments.

'I think we head down.' Raj pointed to the opening and it's gentle slope. 'I think if soldiers are patrolling this area, then the chance that they are coming from down the hill are greater than from up on high. But we need to be extra careful now.'

'We sure do.'

'Both sides will have patrols. And God knows what kind of deals they do with each other out here. If we tread carefully, maybe our angels might bring us luck again.'

'I won't argue with the angels.' Tomo crossed himself, as did Raj before making their way down the hilly forest.

The two men kept a small distance from the border but not too far as to get lost within the woods. After thirty minutes or so, it was made official, as an old steel sign was posted on the open grass that read *Italo-Yugoslav Border.*

'Would you look at that?' Raj stated, as both men stood staring at the sign from a safe distance within the woods.

'We made it,' Tomo said. 'We actually made it.'

It was not long after that the two men found a small stream running deeper into the western woods. Raj was first to hear the sound and, on further investigation, the water provided plenty to drink and to fill their containers.

'Angels,' Tomo murmured excitedly, but Raj was too busy drinking to answer.

'What are you smiling at?' Raj looked up at his companion from a crouching position with a wet face and a water-logged belly.

'We made it.' Tomo suddenly laughed, releasing all of his pent-up excitement. He skipped around Raj before giving him a kiss on the top of the head. 'I can't believe we actually made it.'

'Alright, alright.' Raj wiped his face. 'We haven't made shit until we get through these woods. Hurry up and grab your pack and let's get moving before it gets dark.'

'I'm telling you' - Tomo quickly returned for his things - 'our angels are watching us. I can feel it.'

The two men pushed on, but this time every step felt lighter, confident and energised with a regained purpose. They moved deeper into the forest, leaping over rocks and jumping fallen logs to help them move quicker toward their destination. Raj felt a new drive and a freedom he could never remember having before in his young life. They were officially outside of Yugoslavia and free from the dogmatic political apartheid that strangled anyone who wouldn't bow to the suppressive party. The feeling of excitement had also returned as the adventure now moved to a different phase; no longer needing to escape, but to enter and find acceptance.

After a short while, Raj stopped and looked around. He hadn't noticed the subtle changes going on around him until that moment.

'What's wrong?' asked Tomo, looking around now as well.

'Do you see it?' Raj returned with his own question.

'See what?'

'Can you smell it?' Raj smiled and took a deep breath.

'Did you fart?' smiled Tomo then took a big whiff himself and suddenly smiled very broadly.

'Yeah, you can smell it now.'

'The sea.' Tomo was delighted. 'It smells like Dalmatia.'

'Look at how the trees are getting shorter with more shrubs around,' Raj pointed out. 'And the amount of stones now under our feet. More larger rocks around too.'

'We must be really close,' added Tomo excitedly.

'If my memory serves me well, we should be close to the northern point of the Adriatic,' Raj added eagerly and started moving once more. 'There should be a big town nearby.'

The sun was losing its grip on the day as the two escapees stopped at the edge of the tree line and walked up onto the top of a rocky precipice. The large forest trees were truly gone by now and a different majesty lay before them – the Adriatic Sea. The small pebbles were white and grey and were still mixed with grass under their feet but the further the hill descended, the more stones appeared. Raj had seen the ocean more times in the last two days than in his entire life, but this felt extra special because the vantage point was on foreign land. In the distance, the two men could see a large town sitting on the beach, beckoning them onward with white walls reaching toward the orange terra-cotta roofing that hid beneath it a new labyrinth of ancient streets.

'Is that the one?' asked Tomo.

'I believe that is Trieste.'

'I told you,' Tomo added.

'What?' Raj was perplexed.

'Angels.'

CHAPTER 13

Trieste had a similar history to most towns on the Adriatic coast. In many ways it had even more favourable conditions than its southern counterparts; a temperate climate that didn't suffer from excessive heat due to its more northern location, calmer tides, as it was further from the Mediterranean, and a closer locale for travellers around central Europe. But vacations and tourism were not the cities only claim to fame. In Roman times, Trieste's location acted as a pivotal point on the road between east and west and it quickly established itself as an important trading hub in the Empire. In fact, many believe the name of the city translates to marketplace.

Of course, drawing crowds with money and wares will also draw attention from foreign powers, both malevolent and benign. The Byzantium Empire used Trieste as a military outpost to help keep it under Eastern Christian rule, and as Western Rome was a shadow of its former self, eventually the Ostrogoths, Lombards and Franks swept through and all fought for control of the coastal town at one time or other. During the middle ages, Venice held sway over Trieste for a period, before a self-imposed submission to the Austro-Hungarian Empire brought nearly a century of peace and autonomy.

Ever the rival of Venice, Trieste began to suffer during this time from a loss in trade and, eventually, the Venetians regained enough political power to squeeze the town into an even smaller footprint, before smashing it again with armed force. The French then took hold of Trieste for several years during Napoleon's reign, but as dynasties rose and fell, the Hapsburgs once again reclaimed the town and kept it within the Austro-Hungarian Empire until World War One

The rise of European Nationalism at the start of the twentieth century exacerbated tensions in Trieste. Multicultural as it was, Trieste had been annexed to Italy who swung further to the right politically, leaving Slavs, Germans, Austrians and Jews in a town controlled by Italians and surrounded by political tension. The tension eventually exploded with World War Two creating a direct conflict between Yugoslavia and Italy, both of whom recognised Trieste's strategic importance. Allied forces liberated the town from Yugoslavian Communist occupiers and at the end of the war the town, and greater coastal region, were divided into two zones – the south went to Yugoslavia, the north went to the Allied Military Government. It took another ten years of Cold War intrigue before the majority of Trieste was once again handed completely to Italy in order to ensure another region was safely away from the clutches of Communism.

The evening sun had dropped quickly as Raj and Tomo carefully made their way down the rocky precipice toward the old town. Scattered wooden shacks and small farms eventually became closer and smaller until the pastoral scenes from a few hours ago were enveloped by a modern suburbia with modest brick homes and light industrial areas. Now that the two men were at sea level, the sun-drenched beach disappeared from view too, the salty smell still persisted though, but was now mixed with the scent of oil and diesel as they walked the tarmac paths through the outer streets of Trieste.

Another hour passed before the sun was completely gone and the town's minimal streetlights flared just enough for Raj and Tomo to read the street signs.

'San Sabba,' Raj read. 'Ever heard of it?'

'No.' Tomo shrugged. 'But I'm tired, and thirsty, and just need a rest.'

Their water had run out just as they entered Trieste and were now both quite parched.

'Yeah,' Raj agreed tentatively. 'I just don't know how safe this place is.'

'I think you can relax now.' Tomo laughed as they kept walking. 'We are in Italy. No communists here.'

Raj wasn't so sure but said nothing and just kept pace with his confident friend. The two men quickly came to a three-way junction in the suburb called San Sabba. Two of the three streets looked to be leading into complete darkness, but the third looked promising. Up ahead, the public lighting grew in ambience and some larger structures sat in the distance. A few cars could be heard beeping their horns and a din rose subtly from that general direction. Without another word both men stepped instinctively toward the light.

'Shall we stop for a drink?' Tomo whispered.

'Do you know how to order in Italian?' asked Raj.

Without answering, both men kept walking past the first inn they saw as mostly young townsfolk excitedly entered the building, allowing the sound of merriment inside to burst out onto the street for the briefest moment through the opening entry.

'Sure could use a drink.' Tomo looked back and licked his lips.

'My nose tells me you should probably look for a bath before a bar.' Raj smiled to himself.

'Yeah.' Tomo sniffed at his underarm before wincing. 'You're not wrong.'

Both men laughed and kept walking deeper into the city. Raj felt a sense of greater freedom in that moment. Even his laughter felt lighter, unburdened by any possibility of saying the wrong thing in front of the wrong person. In Trieste, there was no evil eye watching their every move, no vile neighbour who sold secrets and no black shirted communists lurking behind every corner. The smell of the sea, the wind off the beach and an Italian tone now surrounded them and, for a moment, Raj allowed his cares to melt away. As the day all but disappeared, lampposts and shop windows artificially illuminated the street until the stars in the night sky no longer appeared clearly visible. All sorts of people walked around the town and Raj was pleasantly surprised to hear the many Slavic dialects being freely used.

'I think we chose well,' Raj admitted proudly, his confidence grew but he still kept his voice subdued. They were now surrounded by many more people and Raj thought they might just be close to the town centre.

'You're right,' Tomo agreed.

'What?' Raj was a bit surprised. 'Why do you say that?'

Tomo pointed to a large, white tavern sitting on the corner at the end of the street before them. A large, glass panelled door hung invitingly right at the intersection of the road, and the three stories above showed signs of life with lights shining out from behind the drapes that covered most of the windows.

'Looks expensive,' Raj spoke as he thought.

'Can you see what it's called?' Tomo asked with a smile.

Raj looked closer, and then smiled too. 'The Travelling Slovene.'

'Close enough for me.' Tomo made his way toward the building.

Slovenia was a state within Yugoslavia with a long and proud history. Although the dialect was not exactly the same as the Bosnians, the language was easily understandable, and the customs were very similar to the Catholic side of the Yugoslavian nation.

'You remember the plan?' Raj had to skip a few steps to keep up with his excited friend.

'This is the easy part.' Tomo laughed, not holding back his volume whatsoever.

'Just let me do the talking.' Raj always felt a little uneasy when Tomo rushed ahead like this.

As night truly fell across the town, Raj and Tomo entered the dwelling. The small ante-chamber was dimly lit, with wooden floors and bevelled wooden panelling rising a quarter of the way up the walls. A couple of large paintings decorated the entry, depicting pastoral scenes that reminded Raj of home. Traditional Croatian music could be heard above the light chatter of the public enjoying their social evening within the establishment. The smell of home permeated Raj's nose, with meat, gravy and the herbs used in many Croat dishes, wafting throughout the large, dining hall. More and more the scene and smell lured Raj's focus away from the moment and back to his much-loved homeland.

'How many tonight?' a Slovene voice cut through the din.

Raj jumped a little from the shock, as before him a younger chap stood attentively, holding a pen and pad and dressed in black and white attire.

'Oh,' Raj mustered. 'We just want a drink, if that's possible?'

'This way, sir.' The waiter led the two young travellers through the dining area toward a bar in a long room toward the back of the building. The firm timber floor was dark, and the tables and chairs were wooden as well. Both Yugoslav and Italian flags accompanied the continued pastoral art across the walls. Beach scenes were also painted, offering the patron a reminder of the old land while celebrating the new.

'I'm starving,' Tomo whispered as they sat at the polished wooden bar. 'Why didn't you take a table?'

'Did you see the prices?' Raj asked, looking at the myriad of bottles placed on the wall before them.

'No.'

'Nor did I,' Raj revealed. 'So let's get a drink and take it from there. You won't die of starvation.'

The barman was sharply dressed in black and white as well, and addressed his two new customers in what Raj thought had to be Italian.

'Croat?' Raj inquired.

'What will it be?' The barman smiled, easing the slight tension that arose between the trio.

'Whiskey, please.' Raj tried to sound casual, but the barman paused, his eyes looked over both men cautiously before grabbing a bottle and two glasses from somewhere beneath the bar.

'Ice?'

'Sure.'

'You boys not from around here?' The barman kept chatting in Croatian as he poured the brown liquid.

'No,' Tomo answered confidently, taking hold of the glass. 'We came directly from Slovenia.'

Raj suddenly became nervous as the barman grinned.

'Oh, yeah? Which part of Slovenia?' he asked Tomo.

Tomo slowly sipped his drink and looked at Raj. And Raj then knew that Tomo had no idea about Slovenia.

'We made our way to Italy,' Raj interjected. 'Looking for work. It's pretty slow back home and we heard the Italians are hiring. Maybe you could help us?'

The distraction seemed to work as the barman put the bottle back and started to remove dishes from the sink and wipe them with a towel.

'Work?' the barman asked. 'What kind of work?'

Just then a loud voice cut across the room.

'Why can't you?' I don't fucking get it!' a man yelled in a Serbian accent from the corner.

Raj turned and saw a group of men sitting down at a table trying to silence a younger male who stood up and was doing the shouting.

'Hey,' the barman cried as he moved away from Raj and Tomo. 'Let's keep it down over there.'

'Grab your drink,' Raj whispered and moved to a table away from the bar.

'What are you doing?' whispered Tomo. 'That wasn't the plan.'

'Neither was declaring your Slovenian citizenship,' Raj responded.

'I was working an angle.'

'The "get thrown back into Yugoslavia" angle?' Raj laughed, but Tomo had no smile on his face. 'Look, I don't know that barman any more than I know anyone in this place. We have to make sure.'

'Fuck you,' the same young man that had cried out earlier yelled. 'I'm not shutting up. You promised!'

'Take it easy...' was all Raj heard in response from an older gentleman who remained seated but offered his hand to the standing patron.

Then, in one action, the younger man pulled his arm away from his companion before returning it and swiping across the tabletop. Glasses, plates and ashtrays went flying as the sitting men ducked for cover.

'Dejan!' cried the barman as a fight ensued.

Within moments a burly man, well over six foot in height, broad of shoulder and clad all in black came loping in and headed straight for the corner fracas. Behind him, the barman followed to give a hand. Then a third man joined, just as the melee settled down.

'What the hell's going on here, Petar?' the third man asked.

'Nothing, Simon,' the guest named Petar answered. 'We are sorry. Everybody' - the stranger looked around the room and spoke louder - 'we are very sorry. It won't happen again.'

'I know,' the third man insisted, then looked at the security guard. 'Dejan, escort these men from my premises.'

'That's the guy,' Raj said to Tomo, nodding to the man known as Simon. 'He's the boss.'

Raj watched the security brute follow the five men from the room and then noticed Simon and the barman start cleaning the mess in the corner. Tomo pushed his chair back to get up, but Raj grabbed his arm and forced him to wait. The volume in the room settled and the barman made his way back to the bar to serve a new patron when Raj finally rose and moved toward the owner.

'Is it Simon?' Raj tentatively pressed as he closed in, his breath a little shallow and his heartbeat racing.

'Yes, who is asking?' Simon turned from his duties.

'Ahh,' Raj began, 'my name is Raj. And this is Tomo.'

'Nice to meet you, Raj and Tomo.' Simon was polite enough, but Raj could see caution behind the man's eyes.

Raj composed himself, took a deep breath and began to open his mouth when Tomo rudely interjected.

'We are political refugees,' Tomo almost shouted at the man, 'from the Communist state of Yugoslavia.'

Simon's eyes rolled.

'Not this shit again,' he murmured, and any caution Raj saw a moment earlier, quickly disappeared.

'We seek asylum in Italy,' Tomo continued to announce, 'and demand to be taken to the appropriate authorities.'

Simon turned and continued wiping down the table, ignoring the two strangers that were standing foolishly behind him.

After a few awkward moments Tomo began again, only slightly louder this time. 'I said, we are political...'

'I heard what you said.' Simon turned back quickly. 'Half of Italy heard what you said.'

'So, can you take us to the police or something?' Tomo asked.

'Sit down.' Simon offered the two a seat at the table that had just been cleaned. 'And have a drink.'

'With all due respect, sir.' Raj tried to be polite as possible. 'We are not really here to drink.'

'And I'm not really here to service every fucking dim-witted moron that escapes that shit hole across the border.' Simon took a few steps toward the bar. 'It's like I've got a sign on my back or something.'

Raj looked at Tomo hesitantly, unaware of the tavern owner's implications.

'If you want my help, sit down, have a drink, let me finish my work, and I'll get back to you when I'm good and ready.'

With those words, Simon disappeared beyond the bar, leaving nothing for Raj and Tomo to do but order another drink and sit and patiently wait for their probable saviour to return.

A few hours passed and the two travellers ate and drank their fill. The crowds had come and gone for the evening, but Raj and Tomo sat in relative silence awaiting the next uncertain phase of their journey.

'You know this guy might be full of shit,' Tomo suggested as the barman began stacking chairs on top of tables at the far end of the empty room.

'He could be,' Raj reluctantly admitted. 'What do you want to do?'

But Tomo continued to sit in silence offering no answer to their dilemma. Raj was tired, and he realised the dejection on his friend's silent face was probably a mirror of his own.

'Barman,' Raj called. 'Is Simon nearby?'

'You've asked me that six times already,' the worker responded a little frustratingly, without stopping his closing bell duties.

'You two!' A deep, heavily accented voice suddenly boomed from a door way behind the bar.

Raj looked to see the burly security guard Dejan waving his fingers their way.

'Us?' Tomo responded.

'Yeah, let's go.'

Raj leapt to his feet and made his way behind the bar and through a service door built right between the shelves on the back wall.

'Finally,' Tomo murmured, as he followed closely behind.

They walked swiftly through a dimly lit, narrow corridor which had boxes, bottles and crates of all sizes stacked up at different intervals along the way. Above the stockpiles were found clip boards and creased pages offering a semblance of order to the messy hallway. Raj felt he had entered an artery of the Travelling Slovene and was making his way rapidly to the heart of the establishment. They passed a doorway where a young woman was milling over paperwork behind a desk. Two other men, dressed in filthy overalls and black work boots, passed them by carrying timber crates on their shoulders that jingled as the glass bottles within gently touched each other at every step.

'Here,' Dejan announced and returned the way they came.

Raj and Tomo entered a small office where Simon sat behind a desk, this time with glasses on, reading from a sheet of paper. He didn't look up straight away, so Raj remained standing.

'So,' Simon began, putting the sheet down and taking his glasses off, 'just out of curiosity, between the two of you, how many years of schooling have you had?'

Raj looked at Tomo, who seemed just as perplexed by the question.

'Eight, I think,' Raj responded a little warily.

Simon took a moment and stretched in his seat.

'What's this got to do with anything?' Tomo's fatigue was making him edgy, so Raj placed a hand on his friend's shoulder to calm him down.

'So, four grades each?'

'Yes, sir.'

'So, neither of you are worldly scholars?' Simon added, with a wry smile.

'No, sir.' Raj looked again at Tomo.

'And I imagine neither of you have high ranking diplomats in the family?'

'No, we don't.'

'So how the fuck do you two clowns know about the asylum laws of Italy?' Simon asked with a little more emphasis in his tone.

Raj waited a moment and contemplated lying to the man, but thought against it before responding. 'My brother got word to me a while ago, about the United Nations conventions.'

'Ha.' Simon burst out in what sounded like genuine laughter. 'It's funny to hear farm boys such as you quote United Nations conventions. Jesus, you haven't finished primary school and you are talking about the UN.'

Raj and Tomo stood silently for another moment as Simon seemed caught in a reverie.

'Still,' the tavern master continued, 'what needs, must. And who am I to go against the United Nations. God knows these commies are causing enough shit in the world; the least I can do is help. Grab a seat and I'll pour us a drink.'

The three men sat around Simon's desk with stiff drinks in hand and began to chat.

'Your brother, you say?' Simon began.

'Yes,' Raj answered excitedly. 'Krizan Krizic.'

'Can't say I have heard of him, but not all that come through this town, come through this inn.' Simon emptied his glass and poured another one for himself.

'He said that Italy had to take us in if we were political refugees,' Raj continued.

'And he is right.' Simon looked directly into Raj's eyes. 'But you're not political refugees. Are you?'

'We most certainly are!' Tomo insisted.

'Well, not directly,' Simon expounded. 'You are economic refugees, on paper at least. The commies will pay you; just enough to keep you alive, but not a penny more. But if you told that to the Ministry of Immigration, they would throw you back in a heartbeat. You need to be careful,' his eyes glazed over momentarily as he took a deep breath, 'and I need to be careful too.'

'What do you have to worry about?' Raj inquired, taking a sip of the plum moonshine.

'This is not my first time around the ride, young man,' Simon pronounced. 'I have helped others like you before. And I know we are not that far away from prying Communist eyes. That's why I kept you waiting so long. I had to make sure you didn't have a keeper with you; or had someone tailing you. If word gets out that I am funnelling rebels through my tavern, I am going to have both sides of the border putting pressure on me.'

'So why would you help us?' Raj asked.

Simon took a deep breath and shifted in his seat. 'Someone once helped me, and I'd like to pass it on. Besides, I'm not a fan of those commie dogs. They did brutal things to my old town not that long ago and I still have family over there that I'm trying to bring over.'

'So, what now?' asked Tomo.

'Now.' Simon stood, yawned and stretched. 'We get some sleep. You guys can share a room upstairs. Tonight is free. Tomorrow we will visit a friend of mine. Hopefully he can help you out.'

'And if he can't?' asked Raj.

'Then you are on your own.'

CHAPTER 14

Raj had slept very well that night. In fact, he was sure it was the best night's sleep he had ever had. The room was a modest, two bed dwelling with a small kitchen and bathroom on opposite sides of the entry way. There was no radio or television in the sparse quarter and the furniture simply consisted of two bedside drawers and two stools tucked under the kitchenette's short bench. The carpet was old and stained, the paint had cracks and blemishes and the once white curtains were now slightly yellow and torn. And apart from the smell, Raj thought it was as close to comfort as he had come in the last few days.

The early morning light barely poked through the two windows, but Raj was already awake and thinking. He was mulling over last night's conversation with the manager of the inn and his mind could not help but wonder back to the salty captain of the Red Seagull. Raj hoped he wouldn't be getting thrown out of another boat for trusting an elder stranger once more. Tomo continued to snore softly, so Raj lifted his pillow and threw it at his friend.

'What the...?' Tomo barely lifted his head.

'Rise and shine,' Raj announced as he rose to sit on the edge of his mattress.

'What time is it?'

'I just told you,' Raj mocked. 'Time to rise and shine.'

And with that, he made his way to the bathroom to freshen up for the day ahead.

Once clean, Raj felt rejuvenated to his core. His muscles were still tired, and he still felt quite sore, but his mind was clear and he found little else to dwell on apart from the upcoming actions for the day. The past was suddenly gone, and even his missing brother's whereabouts could wait until the situation at hand was resolved. He was in Italy. He was safe. He had made a promising contact and things were looking good once more.

'Why are you so proud?' Tomo was still lying in bed, but fully awake now.

'I slept well,' Raj responded modestly. 'And I'm excited to see what the day brings.'

Suddenly there was a knock at the door and a voice beyond called, 'You awake in there?' then knocked once again. Raj recognised Simon's voice and opened the door to their benefactor.

'You boys have a good sleep?' asked Simon from the doorway, then continued talking before anyone had the time to answer. 'Good. Now get packed. Our business is best done in the early hours. I'll meet you on the street.'

The town was quiet with few people wandering the streets so early in the morning. The sun had risen by now, but was still so low in the eastern sky that the whitewashed buildings surrounding the men, still cast long, dark shadows that made the dawn seem to move in slow motion. Raj noticed how different the town felt without the hustle and bustle from the previous evening. He was glad he could soak up the cool atmosphere without having to look over his shoulder in fear. Still, he was not that naïve to get too comfortable; after all, there was a reason they were treading quietly at an untimely hour.

'This way,' Simon whispered while looking at his watch. 'Quickly.'

He turned around a corner and into a street that ran east toward the sun. A few glimpses of light between buildings and several bright lines across their path indicated that the day was growing in strength.

'What's the hurry?' Tomo asked from the rear.

'He'll be finished his shift soon,' answered Simon. 'We don't want to miss him.'

Simon had not given any sign of their destination but just kept moving at a brisk pace. Raj was beginning to contemplate Captain Maltokovic once more when they saw a man standing in the distance while lighting a cigarette. As they slowed, Raj looked closer to see the smoking man dressed in a dark uniform of some kind, complete with hat, buckles and holster. He immediately slowed down even more, allowing Simon to move a few feet ahead. A shiver ran down Raj's spine as he moved his arm out to halt Tomo behind him.

'I'm not sure about this, Tomo.' Raj spoke softly.

Tomo seemed ignorant to the fact before them, but then the penny dropped as he caught up and simply said, 'Shit.'

As if sensing the men's distress, Simon turned and stepped back toward them. 'Come on you two. Now is not the time for cold feet.'

Raj took a reluctant step forward and cautiously asked, 'Who is this guy?'

'Your best chance.'

'Are you going to dilly-dally all morning, Slovene?' the smoking man asked in broken Croatian.

'Apologies.' Simon sounded quite deferential toward the man. 'This is Raj and Tomo. The two we spoke about. They are in need of some assistance.'

Raj and Tomo stepped a little closer to get a clearer view of the man. He was broad of shoulder and a head taller than Raj. His dark blue uniform had a white sash running across from his left shoulder to his right hip, where a holster was fastened to a white belt around his waist with a large, black pistol being held securely in place.

'This is Senior Sergeant Frederico Falzone.' Simon turned to the boys. 'And he can help in ways I can't.'

'Pish-posh, Simon,' the sergeant blurted. 'We can save the introductions for later. I don't want to stand out here any longer than I need. You are either coming or not.' With that, he turned and made his way down a smaller street that ran off the main thoroughfare. They had no alternative but to follow.

As the sun grew stronger with each moment passing, Raj looked up at the sign on the building before them. It read Trieste Polizi. Raj had no real understanding of Italian, but he knew the purpose of that particular building and he also knew that standing in front of it for a while would draw unwanted attention.

'Are we following this guy?' asked Tomo.

Raj paused before answering with his own question. 'What are our options?'

Both Raj and Tomo then stood in silence for a moment, contemplating their next move as the sergeant walked away.

'Come on, boys,' Simon pushed. 'If we lose him, you won't get this chance again!'

'Oh well,' Raj surrendered. 'We got this far. Let's see where this takes us.'

The three men quickly caught up to the sergeant and walked briskly toward a slim, three-storey townhouse. The rows of houses down this street all looked the same to Raj; white stone facades with one large rectangular window per floor and shared boundary walls joining the properties to make them appear as one long house curving with the road. There were no courtyards to speak of and the only thing that segregated the properties were the three steps off the footpath that led to the front door of each home. Raj was also surprised at the amount of concrete surrounding them. Having grown up on a farm, he was used to seeing foliage everywhere he looked. But here, not one leaf, nor stone, nor bark was present, only grey and white surfaces wherever he laid his eyes.

'Quickly.' Simon stopped at the foot of the stairs. 'Follow the sergeant inside.'

'After you,' Raj offered.

'This is where we part ways.'

'What?' Raj became a little more anxious again. 'Why?'

'I can do no more for you.' Simon bowed slightly as his right hand pointed up the steps.

'Thanks for all your help,' Raj said genuinely as he passed the publican and followed Sergeant Falzone into a dark passageway within the strange new townhouse. Raj and Tomo found themselves in a large kitchen toward the back of the home. The motif was black and white, and Raj was impressed with the simplicity of the style.

'This is my wife, Yovanka.' Sergeant Falzone introduced a buxom woman who stood in the corner stirring vociferously with a wooden spoon through a white and pasty mixture in an oversized bowl. She turned a little and smiled at the foreigners without missing a rotation; her face, hands and apron speckled with flour.

'Are you hungry, boys?' Yovanka spoke in a Slavic tongue, but it was not the same accent as the sergeant, or of Simon the Hotelier.

'Starving.' Tomo made himself at home. 'What's for breakfast?'

Yovanka looked to the ceiling and laughed aloud while stirring, filling the room with a wonderment Raj hadn't heard in a while.

'Forgive my friend.' Raj saw that Sergeant Falzone's expression didn't share his wife's mirth. 'We are just passing by.'

'Pish, posh,' Yovanka countered forcefully, never missing a stir. 'If I came into your home, your mother wouldn't let me leave with an empty belly. It would be a disgrace!'

Raj was a little speechless at the woman's insistence, partly because she was right, but partly because it seemed she just might be the boss of this household. Raj turned to the sergeant as if to certify Yovanka's demands but the strong matriarch cut in. 'Ohhhh, don't look at him, Freddy is all bark and no bite.' Yovanka laughed again and looked lovingly at her husband. 'My Freddy-weddy.'

The two exchanged a private glance and Raj looked away, a little uncomfortably. Tomo had already made his way to the rectangular table past the sergeant and sat down in anticipation of breakfast. Raj surrendered, quickly followed Tomo and avoided eye contact between the lovebirds.

'Go get changed, Freddy.' Yovanka turned back to the bench. 'And after pancakes we will see what we can do for these boys.'

Raj's ears pricked up at the last statement. It seems he was right after all; Yovanka was indeed the leading force in this conspiracy.

'If you don't mind me asking,' Raj inquired, 'where are you from, Yovanka?'

'My family is originally from Macedonia,' Yovanka replied as she poured the first batch on the hotplate and the sizzle and smell filled the air. 'My mother fled ten years ago, after the Communists took my father.'

'Where did they take him?' asked Tomo, blissfully unaware.

Yovanka simply smiled at the young man. 'My sister and I found love here and never looked back.'

'Is your mother still here?' asked Raj.

'No,' she answered solemnly. 'She got ill shortly after we arrived. They were some hard times. She passed a few years back. Cancer or something. I don't think the doctors really know what it was. But I think she died of a broken heart.'

'I'm sorry to hear,' Raj responded.

'Mama,' a little voice called from the hallway, breaking the glum mood in the kitchen.

'Dearest.' Yovanka's mood changed immediately. 'Come in here.'

'No.'

Raj looked toward the hallway opening and saw half a face peering shyly into the room.

'Are you hungry?' Yovanka asked, flipping a pancake in mid-air effortlessly.

'Yes,' the little voice answered softly.

'Then come and get ready, the pancakes will be done soon.'

'No,' the little voice responded, bringing a smile to all the adult faces in the kitchen.

'Do you still like pancakes?' asked Yovanka playfully.

'Yes,' answered the child.

'Then come on in.'

'No.'

'Why "no"?'

'I don't want to.'

'You don't want to eat pancakes?'

'No.'

'That means there is more for us.' Senior Sergeant Frederico interrupted the banter as he walked past the child and back into the kitchen, dressed in what looked like a robe covering his pyjamas.

'I want to eat pancakes.' The child raised her voice and showed her face for a moment before realising her vulnerability and moving back to hugging the wall in the hallway.

'This is Biljana.' Yovanka flipped another pancake, the smell and sound made Raj's mouth water. 'She is our sweet little girl who suddenly doesn't like pancakes anymore.'

'I do like pancakes, Mama,' Biljana pleaded.

'Well.' Yovanka poured another ladle. 'We can't eat in the hallway.'

The little girl was a little lost for words with that argument. She remained silent for a few moments as the crackling and spitting sound of the pancake mixture filled the air. Raj could see Biljana staring at the two foreigners from the jamb to the kitchen but was a little lost for words himself.

'Come on, peanut,' Frederico insisted, with open arms he called for her to join him at the table. 'These boys won't bite. Come and meet our guests.'

Biljana dashed from the entry and ran straight into her doting father's arms. He lifted her up onto his lap and faced Tomo and Raj. She immediately shoved her face into her father's torso as if to disappear.

'Hello, Biljana,' Raj began. 'My name is Raj. And this is Tomo.'

The girl just grunted from her father's grasp.

'Now, now, peanut.' The sergeant spoke. 'There is no need to be rude.'

He followed this with some Italian which Raj didn't understand, but Yovanka clearly did, as she added her two-cents to that particular conversation.

'Nice to meet you,' Biljana turned and said in a soft voice.

'Cute kid,' was all Tomo offered, and Biljana gazed at him warily.

The group of five said a prayer of thanks before beginning their meal. The pancakes were closer to crepes, as they were paper thin, but rather large and plentiful. Raj thought they were delicious with a slight crunch to the edges. Honey, ricotta cheese, prosciutto and tomatoes were also offered on the side, with a big jug of fresh, cold milk to wash it all down.

'Delicious,' Tomo announced, after he put his fork down. 'Thank you very much. We haven't eaten this well since home.'

'You're welcome,' Yovanka responded. 'And exactly where is home?'

'Hercegovina,' answered Tomo. 'Not far from Mostar.'

Yovanka shared a glance at her husband before continuing. 'Catholic?'

'Yes, ma'am.' Raj put his fork down too now.

'From what I have heard' – Frederico now joined the conversation – 'you guys are getting smashed by the commies?'

'Indeed,' Raj answered. 'That's why we are here.'

'Do you drink?' asked Yovanka surprisingly.

'It's a bit early.' Tomo smiled. 'But I could take a nip.'

'Well, then stop.' Yovanka's tone hardened. 'The first thing that lets all of you down is your thirst for Rakija.'

Raj and Tomo looked at each other but Raj spoke first. 'We are not quite that fond of the drink, Yovanka.'

'You might not be.' Yovanka stood and grabbed a few plates as she began clearing the table. 'But he is.'

Tomo's head moved back.

'Wait a second,' he began. 'I thank you for the meal, but that doesn't give you the right to hurl abuse.'

'Go and wash up, dearest,' Yovanka said calmly to her daughter. 'I don't think you should eat anymore.'

'Yes, Mama.' Biljana looked up at her mother with huge eyes and a full mouth. Her face was a delicious mess and her hands were covered in sticky honey and crumbs of cheese.

Raj thought about his father in that brief moment; he remembered Mirko always warning about the perils of alcohol. Raj was much like his father; he didn't mind a drink, if the occasion was right, but generally milk and water would suffice as a beverage.

'We had a runaway come through a few weeks ago,' Frederico began once his daughter was out of earshot. 'He was brave and seemed smart.'

'What was his name?' asked Raj, his thoughts now moving to his brother Krizan.

'Slavko,' answered the Sergeant. 'He was from Dalmatia.'

'And he was a drunkard and fool, in the end.' Yovanka completed the story as she grabbed the last of the dishes from the table. 'He got caught pissing on with the Udba and is probably rotting in a jail right now.'

Silence fell across the room. Raj knew the Yugoslav secret police was active within Yugoslavia but had no idea about their presence across borders.

'You look surprised, Raj,' Yovanka stated. 'You do know of the Udba?'

'Yes,' Raj answered, 'but I have never met them.'

'That is your first mistake,' Frederico chimed in. 'You assume that you would know if you met them. Most of the time you will only learn of their presence once they have you under lock and key.'

'You can stop looking so sour,' Yovanka told Tomo. 'I'm not meaning to insult you, nor am I calling you an alcoholic. But rather, I'm trying to protect you. If you are willing to take a drink with a strange family straight after breakfast, what would you do when a pretty spider spreads her legs before you?'

'Sure, sure,' Tomo said uncomfortably. 'I understand.' But to Raj, it just sounded like insult was added to injury.

Raj's family warned him about Tomo. They all knew his kin to be risk takers and self-centred, and now, over a simple meal, this Italian family had worked him out with ease. Raj knew Tomo was the best choice at the time, but after so much effort to cross the border, he now wondered whether he should let Tomo go, for his own safety. There had been multiple times where his companion made sporadic decisions that led to danger and anxiety, but there were also times where Tomo had saved the day with his irrational instincts and bravado.

'What are your plans?' asked Frederico.

Raj spoke honestly. 'We just wanted to get out of Yugoslavia. We heard Italy was the easiest.' Raj's father's advice suddenly came to mind. 'Then onto Germany.'

'What is it with the Slavs and Germany?' Frederico looked at his wife, who rolled her eyes and kept stacking dirty plates.

'We heard they were looking for workers,' Raj added.

'They are,' Frederico answered. 'But only if you have a visa.'

Raj looked despondently at Tomo.

'Germany can't help you,' the sergeant concluded. 'And if you are not careful, Italy won't help you either.'

'What?' Tomo came to life at those words.

'Did you think you could just waltz in and the red carpet would be rolled out for you?' Frederico poured himself some more milk and added a dab of honey.

'You will seek political asylum.' Yovanka broke the slight tension the men were feeling. 'Through Social Services.'

'How do we do that?' Raj inquired, looking away from the sergeant.

'My sister has a contact there,' Yovanka stated proudly. 'We've been using her for years.'

'Thank you,' Raj said, but Tomo remained silent.

'Don't thank us yet,' Frederico insisted. 'Nothing is guaranteed.'

'You should start thinking of a contingency too,' Yovanka added. 'Just in case.'

'If everything goes well, we won't see each other again,' Sergeant Falzone stated as he drained his cup, then stood from the table and moved toward his wife. 'It's been a long night. Thank you for breakfast, love, I'm off to bed.' He kissed Yovanka on the cheek and continued down the hall and toward the staircase.

'So.' Yovanka put her hands on her hips and smiled at the two foreigners. 'Who wants coffee and cake?'

CHAPTER 15

It was late in the day, and Raj and Tomo spent most of their time just waiting for Yovanka's sister, Lisa, to complete reams of paperwork at the Social Services building in the centre of Trieste. Once the hours had passed and the papers were all signed and stamped, the two men were herded onto a small bus with a motley crew of other migrants. The vehicle was full of dirty twenty-something-year-old men who for the most part smelled as poorly as they looked. Sitting two by two and all facing forward, there were twenty-four migrants, plus baggage, packed into the cabin. The mini-bus seemed to struggle under all the weight, particularly when riding uphill, but still somehow chugged along the cobblestones of Trieste and wove its way back towards San Sabba.

In the late afternoon the bus made its final turn; passed the timber fencing and through the entrance to the San Sabba Detention Centre. All eyes within the cabin faced out to see their new accommodations, and the whispered voices that kept to themselves for most of the trip, now became a little louder, growing in confidence with the arrival at their destination.

'What is this place?' asked Tomo, to no one in particular.

Raj kept silent, as he really had no answer, apart from the obvious sight before them. Bordering the wide driveway were two low laying industrial buildings running for at least half a kilometre on each side of the gated and guarded entrance. The grey timber warehouses looked well-worn and were lined with windows and doors at different intervals, but Raj couldn't see what was held within them. There were other vehicles parked along the driveway, which was wide enough for ten mini buses side by side. The scope of the detention centre was large indeed and seemed to stretch endlessly before the small bus.

In the distance, more buildings rose, taller than the warehouses they currently passed, but their purpose was just as unclear. The din within the encampment rose the further they drove, and Raj saw men milling around while chatting and smoking, while others carried goods and looked to be working. Raj also noted a slight military presence, both with the number of army green vehicles parked to the side and the personnel attired in the same colour. There was no real tension anywhere though, and Raj felt a sense of merriment among the strangers that sojourned in the large quad that made up the thoroughfare.

'It's an old military complex,' a Croatian voice answered from behind them.

Raj turned to see a man of similar age smiling back at him.

'Military?' Tomo inquired without turning.

'Yes,' answered the stranger, looking out the window again. 'Both forces used it during the war. It's a great location.'

'How do you know that?' asked Raj, not sure why he would believe the man.

'My brother wrote us last year,' answered the stranger. 'He had been here.'

'You have a brother here?' Raj's interest perked up, his caution slowly dropping away.

'No,' the man stated. 'This was the first stop. He wrote from Bari.'

Raj had never heard of Bari. Nor had he heard of San Sabba either until yesterday, now this stranger's information placed his own brother's whereabouts in a new light and possibly within the same area. Perhaps Krizan had been here too and moved on. Maybe he was in Bari at the moment and was trying to correspond with his parents. This reminded Raj of the need to write a letter home. His mother, in particular, would be worried and, as much as five days of travelling felt like a lifetime abroad for Raj, it probably felt even greater to his folks.

'You boys Croat?' the stranger asked, breaking Raj's reverie.

'Yeah,' Raj answered and turned to see a hand presenting itself, he grabbed it and shook. 'I'm Raj Krizic, this Tomo.'

'Cheers,' said the chatty man, now grabbing Tomo's hand over the seat. 'I'm Branomir Veslic. Call me Bran. This is Denis Gerobac.' He pointed to his seating partner. 'He doesn't talk much.'

'You talk enough for us both,' Denis stated without looking at Bran.

'Did your brother tell you what happens next?' asked Raj excitedly.

'Not in detail,' Bran replied.

'We'll be processed,' Denis said. 'Again.'

'Great,' Tomo joined in sarcastically. 'Just what we need – more paperwork.'

All four men laughed out loud causing the others on the bus to turn toward them briefly.

'Looks like we are heading toward the taller buildings up at the end,' Raj stated.

'Yeah,' Bran agreed.

'I can't wait to get off this fucking bus,' Tomo said frustratingly.

'Better than walking here,' Bran offered before he sighed.

'We understand that all too well,' Raj concurred.

'Where are you boys from?' Bran took sudden interest, leaning forward.

'We came from Siroki Brijeg,' Tomo answered, this time looking back. 'In Hercegovina.'

'Ah.' Bran sat back once more. 'Then your feet will be aching even more than mine.'

'Where are you from?' Tomo asked in return.

'Dalmatia. Not that far from the border. But I got in a couple of days ago. I have an aunty here in town.'

'Lucky you,' Tomo responded, just as the bus began to slow.

'Have your papers ready,' the driver called out in a big voice then changed gear before bringing the bus to a swinging stop. 'And don't leave anything behind.'

Raj, Tomo, Bran and Denis stepped off the bus amidst the throng of other young men looking for a new life. The fresh Italian air was a relief from the heat and body odour that was becoming oppressive within the bus cabin. Raj was excited that there were still a few hours of daylight left to explore their new surroundings. He stretched his arms out wide and arched his back before following Tomo and the mob into a white building with some strange Italian words on the brick walls.

The processing was everything Raj had expected; standing around and waiting for his name to be called, then standing around some more as the clerk behind the glass barrier sifted through the papers before once more standing around until his name was called again.

'I need a drink,' Tomo announced after returning from the window. 'I wonder if there is a bar somewhere on the campus.'

'If there is a Slav present,' Bran joked. 'Then there will be a bar present.'

The three men laughed but were all tiring now. Denis was one of the first to be called and so had already left the waiting area while the three companions had all been up to the counter and now waited their turn.

'And a woman,' Tomo added. 'I could really do with a lady tonight.'

'Good luck there,' Raj noted. 'I have yet to see a female in the camp.'

'Come to think of it' - Tomo seemed perplexed while looking around - 'you're right, neither have I.'

'Nor any children,' Bran mentioned as he too surveyed the scene.

'There's not a family in sight,' Raj concluded. 'Surely there are women and children also looking to enter Italy?'

'I say.' Tomo turned toward a guard standing by the door. 'Where are all the women?'

Maybe every man in the room was eavesdropping at that precise moment, or the mere mention of the opposite sex was enough to catch the primal attention of these tired and horny boys. Either way, a pin could be heard dropping at that particular point in time as all fell silent in anticipation of the guard's answer.

'Women and children are kept in different areas,' the man stated matter-of-factly. 'Families can congregate once a day. But for safety, the men are kept away from the women and children.'

All shoulders simultaneously dropped at that answer and a disappointing sigh echoed throughout the room. Then the murmurs once again began and the wait continued.

'A drink it is, then,' Bran said. 'Maybe Denis has found something.'

'How long have you known Denis for?' asked Raj.

'Since this morning,' answered Bran. 'We met at the government services centre.'

'I don't know if we'll see Denis again,' Raj stated. 'It's a big place and he didn't seem too social if you asked me.'

'Well, whatever happens,' Bran continued, 'can you boys wait outside for me? I don't know anyone here and you two seem decent.'

Raj thought about their new friend and felt comfortable around him. They were of a similar age with a similar background and Raj was happy to have a different person to converse with.

'Branomir Veslic,' a male voice called near the glass window. 'Branomir Veslic!'

'I guess I'll be waiting for you.'

It wasn't a long wait as ten minutes later Raj was called and soon after, so too was Tomo. Raj suddenly felt like a free man as the three travellers walked out into the open space and cooling afternoon air. They made their way across the tarmac and into one of the long warehouses they had passed earlier. Two more guards greeted them at the entry to their dormitory, checking their papers one more time before allowing them in.

Once inside, the air exploded with sound. Raj quickly estimated that at least a hundred men milled around the massive rectangular space in that moment. Numbered beds lined the central part of the room in four rows stretching from the windows at the far wall. At either long end of the room, there was space for tables and lounges and activity in general, with both sides having large, panelled doors dividing the warehouse into partitions. Music was heard from multiple stations as laughter, chatter and cigarette smoke filtered through the air. The smell of food also permeated the space, but Raj couldn't see a kitchen or dining facility anywhere.

'This is more like it.' Tomo smiled as he strode his way in.

Raj looked at his papers and found his bed number. Fortunately, he, Bran and Tomo all had mattresses next to one another near the windows at the far side. Raj also spotted Denis only a couple of beds closer to the centre and well within earshot of the trio. The general din leant heavily toward the Slavic tongues of Yugoslavia, but upon further concentration, Raj did notice some languages that were completely foreign to him.

'Look at this.' Tomo fell back on his bed as he spoke. 'We finally made it, Raj. We did it!'

Raj could tell Tomo was genuinely happy at their situation, and he was glad for his friend. But for Raj, this was just one more battle in the overall war. He was still determined to find his brother and somehow bring the rest of the family away from the insidious Communist regime that penetrated every aspect of their lives.

Raj sat at the edge of his bed, took a deep breath and gave his environment another look; most of the men kept their packs beneath their beds as no furniture, apart from the beds, was provided. The beds themselves were bolted to the timber floor, as were the tables in the communal area. Up above, the curved ceiling was dirty and dusty, with cobwebs interlacing the pendant lights that hung at regular intervals across the room. The migrant men mostly congregated in groups of threes and fours around tables and beds to socialise, with the occasional loner keeping to himself whilst reading a book or magazine.

The common theme among all the men was their haircut; shaved as close to the scalp as possible. In fact, it made Raj and his newly arrived companions really stand out in the room, it also made all the refugees look tough and hard. Mixed with the odd scribbling tattoo and rowdy noise bursting above the din, Raj made a mental note to always hold his money on his person, even when sleeping for the night, as he suspected many of his fellow inhabitants had chequered pasts.

Suddenly a bell rang.

Almost at once, anyone sitting or lying down in the room arose. Every last man turned toward one of the long ends of the room where two security guards pushed aside the large square timber panels in opposite directions. Raj could now see metal tracks carved into the floor and ceiling, that made sliding such large doors effortless. The smell of food gushed unhindered into the dwelling now and really made Raj's appetite rise. Beyond the sliding doors, an industrial kitchen revealed itself; steel and porcelain clattered as men and women, wearing long white hats and aprons, rushed about beyond the glass counter that now separated the rooms. Steam rose from many points in the kitchen, accompanied by sizzles and pops and words being yelled in Italian in a flurry resembling anything but order. Yet all the refugees marched to one side of the bain-maries and respectfully grabbed their plates to wait their turn.

'Looks like chow time,' said Bran as he and Tomo walked past Raj.

The meal was satisfactory: a small slice of pork, mash potatoes, creamy pasta and a dinner roll. Raj and his friends ate on their beds as no tables remained available and now they understood the hurry to get served first. Once their meals were complete, they placed their plates on trolleys found at the end of each row of beds which were then promptly taken away before the sliding panels closed once more, obscuring the kitchen. Within the hour, dinner was served, eaten and taken away with professional expediency.

'How are you gentlemen holding up?' A new face appeared to Raj's left. It belonged to an older man, well into his thirties, quite tall with some alarming scars on his face. It had been thirty or so minutes while Raj and his compatriots lounged around on their beds chatting about their old homes when the stranger appeared.

Raj looked at him, but Tomo spoke first, quite sarcastically. 'We are good, my fine sir. And how are you?'

'Well I am fine, sir,' the strange man moved past Raj and stood before Bran's bed, which was the middle of the three.

'What can we do for you, my friend?' asked Raj cautiously.

'Well,' began the stranger, 'firstly let me introduce myself; my name is Lubomir Asamovic. Your friend over there pointed out that you boys might fit in well with my crew.'

'It's Denis.' Bran acknowledged his travelling acquaintance, as all three looked past Lubomir. Denis gave a slight wave to them before continuing to talk to someone a few rows ahead of them.

'I'm quite tired.' Raj tried to sound polite. 'It's been a long trip. I'm sure you understand.'

'Oh yes, indeed,' answered Lubomir. 'Our towns are only a few miles apart. You're from Siroki, yes?'

'Yes, I am.' Raj's caution perked up once more, sounding not so polite this time. 'What about you?'

'Take it easy, pal.' Lubomir tried to defuse the direction of the conversation. 'I'm from Grude. Denis told me about you boys.'

Raj thought back to the conversation they had on the bus, and although Denis hadn't really said much, he must have heard everything.

'But it's okay,' Lubomir continued. 'I get it. This is all new to you and you want to find your bearings. I was the same. But if you ever want to hang out for a game, or some drinks, we are usually by the corner at the far end.'

'Nice to meet you, Lubomir.' Tomo rose and reached for the man's hand just as Lubomir took a step away. 'I'm Tomo. Don't let this old grandma turn you off, I'm quite thirsty myself, and would love a drink.'

'Of course.' Lubomir smiled and shook Tomo's hand. 'Please, call me Lubo. You're all welcome.' He looked at Raj and Bran. 'It would be good to chat with some more fellow Hercegs.'

Tomo walked off without even looking back. Raj wasn't completely surprised, as he knew Tomo's penchants for socialising

'What do you think?' Bran asked. 'It couldn't hurt?'

'Feel free.' Raj wasn't in the mood. 'Maybe tomorrow for me.'

'Fair enough,' Bran agreed. 'I'll give it a miss too.'

It wasn't long before the lights in the grand hall overtook the power of the sun and only black could be seen beyond the windows at the edge of the room. Little by little the after-dinner excitement wore off and one by one Raj's fellow refugees started lying down for the night.

As Raj dozed, he kept thinking about Krizan, his brother, and the chance that perhaps he was in Bari at that moment. He would also need to find out how to send mail from this place, to get in touch with his parents back home.

'Hey, Raj.' Tomo's whispering voice interjected Raj's plans. 'You should join us tomorrow.'

The smell of Rakija was the first shock that led to Raj opening his eyes. The second shock was Tomo's face staring at him only a few inches away from his own. Raj was startled and shifted a little in his lying position.

'I'm serious,' Tomo continued. 'You'd like these guys. Even Denis. He is okay.'

'Sure, sure.' Raj dismissed his friend. 'Tomorrow. I want to sleep now.'

'They're patriots, Raj.' Tomo looked around, still keeping his voice low and ignoring his friend's subtle hint. 'I mean real patriots. Not some pretenders.'

'I'm sure they are,' Raj answered. 'But please, Tomo, let's leave it for tomorrow.'

'It was good, Raj.' Tomo must have had quite a few drinks, as he persisted. 'They'll have our backs. I can tell.'

'I'm sure they will.' Raj turned to his side and away from Tomo's stinking breath.

'Okay, okay.' Tomo staggered away, finally getting the hint. 'You too, Bran. You'll like these guys. They're cool.'

Before Bran could respond a bell began to ring piercing any chatter that remained in the room. Slowly, one by one, the huge pendant lights began to flicker and fade and every man loitering found their way back to their beds quickly lest they be lurking in the dark. Raj checked that his purse was tucked away inside his pyjama shirt before he closed his eyes. His thoughts now drifted away from his brother and parents, and toward Tomo and what fresh trouble awaited him in the morning.

CHAPTER 16

Raj was already awake when the bell sounded again. His sleep had been light and oft interrupted by snoring, movement and the occasional thump as a sleeping body fell out of bed. The mattresses were not particularly comfortable, nor large, so Raj imagined some of the taller men would be struggling to sleep at all, hence all the movement. The quietude of the night was strange as well in that size of room, as the large vicinity still managed to create a slight reverberation with every noise, no matter how small, causing a creepy, ethereal effect.

The morning sunlight had only started to penetrate the room, so the atmosphere was still quite dark, but Raj pulled himself out of bed and joined the other early birds that were stretching and dressing themselves for the day ahead.

Raj made his way quickly to the guards at the door and inquired about a pen and postal services. They were pleasant enough, but made it be known there were other priorities for the newcomers before correspondence would be allowed.

'Like what?' asked Raj.

'A haircut and bath,' answered one of the two guards stationed at the entry, who spoke broken Croatian well enough to communicate.

'Okay, but after that?'

'Of course,' the guard continued. 'You are not in prison. We have mail services leaving once a week. You'll have everything you need.'

'Any luck?' asked Bran, who had arisen while Raj spoke to the guards. Tomo still snored heavily.

'Yes,' Raj replied. 'But after we get cleaned up.'

Breakfast was as efficient as the previous night's dinner: one egg, a slice of ham, a piece of bread and a small cup of milk. And again, within an hour there was no trace of any meal to be seen. A couple of hours passed before the guards rounded up all the travellers who arrived the day before and escorted them out of the dorm, across the tarmac and into the baths. All the men left the hygiene vicinity with shaved heads and clean bodies, ready for further processing.

Upon returning, Raj noticed the dormitory was at least half empty, so the noise was much lower, and a calmer atmosphere surrounded the room in general. He couldn't stop from running his fingers across his scalp and feeling the spiky hairs that now poked out of his head.

'Come meet the guys,' Tomo insisted for the fifth time.

'Okay.' Raj eventually broke and after they ate lunch he and Bran followed Tomo to the tables in the corner of the room.

'Welcome, brothers.' The pocked face of Lubo was all smiles when he saw the trio arriving. 'Grab a seat.' He gave Raj his own chair.

'Thanks,' answered Raj timidly as he sat down, not really knowing what to expect.

'Are they cool?' asked one of the men sitting at the long table.

'Yeah,' answered Tomo confidently. 'They're with me.'

'And me,' added Denis, who stood at the far side of the table.

'Okay.' The stranger smirked, looking at Lubo. 'But they only got here yesterday.'

'And you only got here the day before,' another man said and the table erupted in laughter.

Even Raj laughed at the joke, dropping his initial caution and getting into the spirit of things.

'It's okay, boys,' Lubo began once the merriment subsided. 'We are all brothers here; all with a common purpose and a common enemy. These new chaps are Raj and Bran. They are from the heart of the homeland. Where the kings of old lived and reigned. Their blood is more Croat than most of these vagabonds surrounding us. Let's have a toast to welcome them!'

Many of the men around the table nodded in agreement while looking at Raj and Bran. Lubo seemed to be the clear leader here as no one questioned his position on the matter, and they poured the newcomers a couple of glasses of Rakija and everyone knocked back the shot.

'Like I was saying,' the first man resumed, 'the movement is getting stronger. I reckon within three months. Six months tops. At least before next winter. Guaranteed.'

'You're talking shit, Smiljan,' another man replied. He was smoking and sitting near Denis at the end.

'Fuck off, I know I'm right,' answered Smiljan.

Raj started keeping tabs on the names of his countrymen.

'So.' The smoking man puffed in between words. 'You are fucking guaranteeing it within three months; then six months, then by winter. Remind me not to buy anything from you in the future.'

The men all laughed once more.

'You want another Raj? Bran?' Lubo grabbed a bottle of the clear liquid and nodded toward his new acquaintances.

'No thanks,' Raj said. 'A bit early for me.'

'Me neither,' Bran added. 'That shit is rocket fuel.'

'I understand.' Lubo smiled and poured himself another small glass instead.

'Give me one more, brother.' Tomo walked around the table with his glass in hand.

'I'm telling you,' Smiljan insisted, 'it's rising. And it's not just here. It's around the world.'

'I'm sure it is.' Another man joined in. 'But I still don't see it happening. As long as they have Soviet backing, I don't think even America will touch them.'

'Sorry to butt in, guys,' Raj interrupted, 'but what are you talking about?'

'They are talking about the overthrow of the Yugoslav government,' Lubo responded, pulling up another chair for himself. 'They are talking about the fall of the demon Tito and the Communist dogs that are suppressing our families as we speak.'

Tomo smiled. 'See, Raj, I told you they are cool.'

Raj was a bit shocked at the fact this little group of young men, that were stuck hiding in an immigration centre so close to the border of Yugoslavia, could so openly discuss revolution amid such large numbers of people.

'You look doubtful, Raj,' Lubo inquired. 'Do you feel like Martin here, that it's all just talk?'

The whole table looked at Raj, awaiting his response.

'Well,' he began, 'it is all talk. It's just great to hear it talked aloud with pride in your voices.'

'Here, here.' Lubo raised his glass once again as the whole table smiled and approved of Raj's sentiment.

'But what can we actually do from here?' Denis asked frustrated after the triumphant toast was had. 'Raj is right, it's all talk unless we act.' He moved side to side with angst. 'And we are stuck here after fleeing from the problems at home.'

'It's all about how you see it, isn't it?' Lubo began cryptically.

'What do you mean?' asked Bran.

'Well, what are we doing with our time?' Lubo asked rhetorically as no one replied. 'We can sit around like the gypsies and wait for handouts, or we can get organised.'

'What do you mean?' Raj asked only to realise he had echoed Bran's words verbatim.

Lubo smiled. 'I mean we stand up for ourselves and our brothers back home!'

'Great.' The critical smoker near Denis piped up once more. 'Now you sound like Smiljan. Do you also have some guarantees for us, Lubo?'

The men smiled, as did Lubo.

'I can guarantee this, Papac: Smiljan is correct about the global effort against these monsters. I have heard directly.'

'Directly from who?' asked Papac, the humour now gone from his tone.

'I have a cousin in Argentina,' Lubo said. 'I received correspondence only a week before crossing the border.'

'Argentina?' Papac laughed. 'Do you know where the fuck Argentina is? I hope your cousin has a boat... and a fucking navy.'

The table burst out laughing once again, but Raj saw the looks on the men's faces and he was certain many of them really had no idea where Argentina was located.

'Do you know where Argentina is, Raj?' Lubo smiled as he posed the question, seemingly not taking offence at Papac's taunt.

'I know very well,' Raj offered confidently without giving the exact location. 'There are rumours that many a patriot fled there after the war.'

Mentioning the war settled the table down and made for a slightly less jovial mood.

'Indeed,' Lubo stated. 'But those rumours are based on fact.'

'Still,' Raj countered, 'Papac is right. You have to cross the ocean to get there.'

'True as well.' Lubo adjusted his seating position and poured himself another drink. 'But what if I was to tell you many of our brothers in South America have already crossed.'

The men around the table gasped and then looked at each other, chattering in excitement about the possibilities of Lubo's tale.

'And not just South America,' Lubo continued. 'North America as well. Australia too.'

'Australia?' Raj had heard of the country but knew very little about it.

'All over Europe too.' Lubo sounded prouder than ever in that moment. 'We are legion, brothers. But we are nothing without organisation.'

'So.' Papac wasn't giving up that easily. 'Where are they? Where are all these freedom fighters? Where are the prodigal sons returned? I certainly saw none as I dodged bullets getting out of that fucking shithole.'

At the sound of Papac's story, it made Raj realise some of his tribulations might appear meagre when compared to other runaways. Still, he and Tomo had some hair-raising incidents of their own and were also lucky to be alive.

'Slowly, Papac,' Lubo confided. 'Slowly at first, then when all is in place, we strike quickly and without remorse.'

'Yeah, I don't know.' Papac stood. 'I need to relieve myself. If the revolution gets any slower, I'll end up shitting myself here at the table.'

Everyone laughed yet again as Papac moved away only for Denis to take his seat. As if an unspoken ritual had occurred, the prior conversation magically ended and playing cards were brought out and dealt among the men at the far end.

'You boys in?' Martin asked as he passed the cards out.

'No thanks,' said Raj, as did most of the men around his side of the table, but Bran did move over and join the game. Cigarettes were alight and Rakija was poured and other things were spoken of: home, women and tales of their journeys.

'But seriously, Raj,' Lubo began in a quiet voice, moving closer, 'we are getting organised. It will happen, it just takes some time.'

'I hope it does,' Raj conceded, not certain what angle Lubo had with him in particular.

'Papac is a good man. And I'm sure he will be in the trenches with us, when the time is right,' Lubo continued. 'We'll need everyman we can get, if you catch my drift?'

Raj then knew Lubo was on some kind of recruiting drive and he had no real issue with it. In fact, he encouraged it and was glad to see his brethren were not all spineless in the face of their adversaries. But he also understood Papac's stance and the logistical nightmare that raising a revolution would be, particularly from abroad.

'Look.' Raj tried to be gentle. 'I commend your spirit, Lubo, I really do. But I got here only yesterday and before I become a crusader for the homeland, I'd like to at the least write a letter to the homeland before we commence.'

'Of course, of course.' Lubo backed off a little. 'I apologise. Sometimes I get a little carried away. It's easy to get excited when I meet young bloods like yourselves fresh from the escape.'

'I understand.' Raj reached for a glass. 'I might have that second drink now.'

'A letter home, you say?' Lubo spoke while he poured Raj a drink. 'They usually move the mail weekly around here. But I have a contact at the postal section. He can get it out quicker if you need.'

'That would be great.' Raj was pleased, but then began to wonder. 'How long have you been here, Lubo?'

'It's been over two months, for me,' Lubo confessed. 'So I've gotten to know people.'

'Is that normal?'

'No, no.' Lubo laughed. 'A month is considered average here; less is better for the centre. They want us in and out. They probably get paid more that way. I don't know. Someone fucked up my papers and so they kept me here. I don't mind for now. I'm meeting contacts and newcomers like you, which helps the cause. Like I said, I'm doing what I can from here. I'll never give up.'

Raj had finally managed to get paper and pen and complete his letter home. He kept the story simple, as he knew the correspondence might be pried upon. He mainly let his parents know that he was safe and well and had arrived across the border. He never mentioned which border he crossed, or where he was staying. He also let them know Tomo was fine too, as his friend seemed in no hurry to get in touch with home.

Lubo was kind enough to walk with Raj into the afternoon air toward the post office. It was located on the same side as their dorm, but all the way near the entrance of the detention centre. People milled all about the outside area. Men could be seen moving boxes, using trolleys and repairing parts of the building, while others were just hanging out and assessing the scene. Many men moved in and out of the postal office as Raj and Lubo approached but no documentation was required to enter.

'I'm still getting used to it,' Raj stated as they entered.

'What?' asked Lubo.

'Not looking over my shoulder all the time.'

'That's what a normal life should be.' Lubo sounded irritated suddenly. 'Not this shit we've been putting up with.'

'Indeed.' Raj walked up to the counter where an older man stood, wearing round spectacles and sporting a grey moustache.

'Giovanni,' Lubo began, changing to a more jovial mood as the two men chattered quite quickly in Italian.

Raj was surprised how promptly the moment came and went. Without any effort, he passed the envelope to Giovanni and the old man nodded at him and turned to put it away.

'Grazie.' Raj had picked up a few words while in Italy and realised that pleasing manners were the cheapest way to get far in life.

'Prego,' Giovanni responded with a kind smile.

'So, you are fluent?' Lubo mocked Raj.

'No, you just heard most of my repertoire,' Raj responded and both men chuckled as they walked toward the door.

'What does that say?' Raj asked, pointing to a piece of paper with Italian writing and dollar signs stuck to the window by the post office door.

'You see dollar signs and so you're interested?' Lubo smiled. 'They are looking for workers. Something about pipes, or drains. My Italian is good, but I speak far better than I read.' He turned to Giovanni once more and inquired about the sign.

'What did he say?'

'He says the sign was put up an hour or so ago. If I understand correctly, some mob is running pipes around the centre and is looking for some strong hands to help.'

'Can we work off site?' asked Raj.

'Yes, yes, I know a guy. He'll give you special papers this soon since your arrival,' answered Lubo. 'But after a week or so, you will be approved to come and go within certain hours.'

Raj wasn't sure how much money he could make in a week, but even if the wage was a pittance, it could well come in handy as his journey unfolded.

'Where do I sign up?' Raj was excited by the prospect.

'Aren't you going to ask how much you get paid?'

'Whatever the pay, it's got to be more than I'm making at the moment,' Raj replied and both men laughed again.

'Okay. Okay, if you are that eager.' Lubo talked again with Giovanni, who then left his little stall and accompanied the two men outside, pointing across the tarmac to a couple of fellows who stood talking and smoking with a military guard.

Raj was pleased to find out that the company offering work was run by a local of Slovene ancestry. The work was simple, manual labour; digging trenches to run new sewerage pipes from the detention centre out to the sea. The work would start the next day as nearly all the positions were filled, so Raj knew he had to get Lubo to pull some strings with his contact.

'Don't worry,' Lubo said confidently. 'My friend is solid. You will have your papers by the morning.'

CHAPTER 17

Lubo was correct, again. Raj's papers were complete by that evening which allowed him off the premises and onto the fields in the morning. Most of the dorm was snoozing lightly as Raj made his way to work. There were a few other men that arose with Raj, each nodding courteously to one another as they walked out into the grey morning light.

'Raj? Isn't it?' asked a familiar voice.

'Yes.' Raj was just outside the dorm when he turned in surprise. 'Papac. Good morning.'

'Please, call me Ivo. Papac is my last name.'

'Sure,' Raj acquiesced. 'You off to work as well, Ivo?'

'Yeah,' Ivo Papac replied. 'Some trench digging thing. I thought it's better than sitting and listening to all those armchair freedom fighters in there.'

'How about that.' Raj was now even more surprised. 'Looks like we'll be working together today.'

'Oh, really?'

'Yeah, Lubo hooked me up with the papers to get out there before my probation was up. He even helped me translate the advertisement on the flyer at the post office.'

'That Lubo sure is a generous one,' Ivo commented with a smile and a nod.

'What do you mean?' Raj noted a hint of sarcasm in Ivo's voice.

'He was the one who told me about the work,' Ivo admitted. 'I signed up late yesterday afternoon. I filled the last position.'

'Lucky you,' Raj noted, not giving too much thought to the matter. 'How long have you been here?'

'This is my second week,' Ivo said as they walked to the front gate. 'I thought I should get out a bit. I'm finding it a bit stuffy cooped up in that room all day and night.'

'Fair enough,' Raj agreed.

Apart from his journey over the last six days, Raj spent his entire life digging, chopping or ploughing around the farm in one way or another, so he was used to both the shovel and the earth, thus the job outside the detention centre recalled muscle memories that were ready and willing.

The work was both tiresome and invigorating, but moreover, nostalgic in so many ways that even Raj didn't realise until the labour began. The smell of the earth was the first sense to come rushing back; a slight wet odour, neither sweet nor foul, that was so common in his life thus far that he hardly noticed it. Now, he not only noticed, but was aware how much he missed the scent.

The sound of the work was another surprise to Raj. The crunching of every blade of grass and root beneath as the sharp blade of the shovel sliced into the ground, sang to him of home and family. As the day grew longer, the breeze caressed his sweaty brow, cooling him and reminding him again, of the long days spent tending tediously in the late winter planting periods back home; preparation that was so necessary in order to harvest at the right time later in the year. And as the day finally ended, even the stink from the sweat of his underarms, from eight hours of pure toil, was somehow relieving. A smelly statement from his body that he still had the ability to work and, just like on the farm back home, as long as he put in the work, then he knew he would be rewarded.

Raj slept well that first night and, in fact, slept well for the rest of the week. His muscles were a little tired, and rightfully so. He had worked hard and remained working while many other men came and went; some because their time was up and were being moved on, while others just could not take the physical demands of digging all day. Raj mostly kept to himself, but did notice the high turnover of employees, so he was comfortable in his job security and knew he didn't have to over exert himself. He was also happy because a whole week had passed, which meant it was pay day.

'I guess it's our turn to spring for Rakija back at the dorm,' said Ivo, who persisted just as Raj did and was holding an envelope with Italian lire placed in it.

'I guess it is,' Raj agreed, but only patronisingly, as he could think of many better things to spend money on.

But he did chip in for a bottle from one of Lubo's contacts. Half a litre of the good stuff that was smuggled straight out of Hercegovina now sat atop their table ready for a taste.

'Well done boys,' Lubo announced and lifted his glass. 'To hard work!'

'To hard work,' came the chorus and then everyone drained their glasses and went for a refill.

'I have to talk to you, Raj,' Lubo approached, as the festivities really got swinging.

'Yes.' Raj allowed himself to relax a little. He felt that was the least he had earned on this trip.

'Well, you know how passionate I am about our homeland,' Lubo began. 'I'll do my utmost to help our people back home.'

'Of course,' Raj concurred.

'I'll help anywhere,' Lubo continued. 'When it comes to my people, I treat us all like family.'

'That's why everyone respects you, Lubo. You are a good man.'

'Have you received anything in the mail yet, Raj?' Lubo asked.

'Not yet,' Raj responded. 'But thanks for that. And thanks for helping me get the job. It's been great to get out there and do some real work.' He raised his glass again toward his friend.

Lubo raised his drink in return and took a swig.

'Like I said, I'm trying to help as many as I can, in any way that I can.' He paused for a moment and refilled his glass. 'But sometimes I need help too, you know. I can't do everything myself.'

Raj looked at him more sternly.

'Name it, my friend, and if I can help, then I will help.'

'Well, there is one thing,' Lubo said. 'It's nothing urgent, but I'm putting the feelers out there, and you know me,' he laughed, 'I'm all about the long game and being prepared.'

'What is it?'

'I've gotten more word over the last week,' Lubo opened up a little more.

'Word?' Raj was interested. 'From who? About what?'

'We are counting numbers.' Lubo dropped his voice a little. It was the first time Raj heard him take a cautious approach. 'You know, finding out who is all talk and who is ready for action.'

'What kind of action?' Raj's interest turned to concern.

'Nothing to worry about.' Lubo relaxed, perhaps sensing Raj's mood.

'Just a head count. We need to know who can be counted on. I mean really counted on. When the time is right.'

'You can count on me, Lubo,' Raj explained. 'But I need to know details before I can commit to anything serious. Do you know how long it took me to plan my escape from Yugoslavia? I must have read that map a thousand times.'

Both men laughed.

'That's a good thing,' Lubo approved. 'You're a man after my own heart.'

'So, what are you getting at, Lubo?' Raj persisted, now feeling more drunk than he had in a while and quite a bit more confident. 'What's the real deal?'

'We are committing to it,' Lubo revealed. 'A club. Official. Members. Numbers. Identities. Organisation. All the things that we can build on and use when the time comes to burn those commie fuckers to the ground.'

Raj sat back and looked at his new friend. It was an interesting idea, but in reality, the same problem existed as a week earlier; they were stuck over the border with little to no resources. *What could they really accomplish from here?* Raj thought. But then again, all ideas have to start somewhere and perhaps Raj and his generation were the perfect candidates for the job.

'I know what you're thinking,' Lubo continued. 'What could we do from here? But it's not just us, Raj.' An excitement entered his voice. 'Like I said before, we are legion. Thousands of us around the world ready to reclaim our homeland. Plus, thousands within the homeland ready to burst forth. Besides, we also have some money behind us. I'm getting word that a few of our American brothers are preparing funds for the cause.'

'Really?' Raj never really thought about the funding side of combat.

'Oh yeah,' Lubo reflected. 'There's no chance of liberty without money. You'd have to be pretty naïve to think freedom is paid in blood alone.'

'Fair enough, I just never really thought about it that much,' Raj admitted. 'I was always too busy trying to get out.'

'As we all were, Raj,' Lubo conceded. 'But I believe now that we are out, we have an obligation to do something for all those that never could escape. I don't want to abandon our people like the Germans, English and Italians all did after the war.'

The irony was not lost on Raj; sitting comfortably in an Italian detention centre yet complaining about the deceptions of World War

Two seemed a little rich. Raj had heard many stories of wartime betrayals met upon his countrymen, and the insidious political manoeuvrings after the war where Croats were sold out by former allies. Borders were the obvious compensation as maps were often redrawn without any concessions given to the local people, who somehow always seemed to pay the highest price in the end. There were also horror stories of prisoners of war that were promised salvation once the fighting ceased, yet ended up facing atrocities well after the Allies secured victory. Lubo's heart certainly was in the right place and he had proved it beyond a doubt with the many times he helped Raj since his arrival.

'What do you need me to do?' asked Raj, still a little uncertain of the pact being formed.

'You don't have to do anything,' Lubo answered. 'Just put your name down. We need to show our financiers over the Atlantic that we are serious and have the numbers to back the funds. You'll get some papers proving you're in, which will also allow us to trust others on the path forward. As I said, this isn't some small cell. I'm talking to others who are doing the exact same thing around the world. So, wherever you are, you know who to trust by the membership of our club.'

'Wow,' Raj exclaimed. 'Sounds like you thought this through really well.'

'And that's what I want you to do,' Lubo said solemnly. 'Think about it. You can join and then just fuck off to wherever you are planning, but I'd rather we have all our boys on this continent and within striking distance. That way when the time comes, none of us are too far away from the action. So, let me know over the next few days, okay?' Lubo winked at Raj and moved toward Bran and a few others playing cards on another table.

In the morning he and Ivo strolled to work as they had done all week. The air was still crisp, but the light was stronger a little earlier each day as the summer slowly approached. Raj couldn't help thinking about his previous night's conversation with Lubo. The whole idea seemed like some kind of fantasy whereby he and all the other renegades returned home together to liberate their people and bestow freedom upon the land. As whimsical as it was, Lubo seemed to be quite intent in his mission, with talk of funding and organisation. *Perhaps it was not as fanciful as it seemed,* Raj thought, and maybe there was a real chance of having his family returning together to enjoy life in peace.

'You seem to have something on your mind,' Ivo mentioned before they reached the front gate.

'Oh, it's nothing. Just something Lubo mentioned last night.'

'Lubo?' Ivo questioned as he pulled out an apple for himself and threw a second one to Raj.

'Yeah.' Raj crunched into the green delight. 'I don't know what to think about it all.'

'Is he asking you to join his little club?' Ivo talked with his mouth full. Raj nodded as he chewed.

'The only thing to think about is what you'll spend your hard-earned money on.' Ivo smiled and took another bite.

'What?' Raj was a little shocked by his companion's advice. 'What do you mean?'

'Oh, come on, Raj,' Ivo continued. 'You can't take him too seriously. Don't get me wrong. He is a lovely chap who has helped me much of the time. He helped you too. He helps everyone. He just doesn't help himself very well.'

Raj was confused. 'I still don't get what you're talking about.'

'Did he tell you why he has been here for so long?' Ivo asked, this time a little more sternly.

'Yes, he said someone screwed his papers up.'

'He is a connected guy.' Ivo stated the obvious. 'That's how he can help so many. But that's how he can also keep himself here for longer than most us would want to stay.'

'He said he's been here a couple of months,' Raj replied, now perplexed once more by the situation at hand.

'Who would know?' Ivo said. 'But he isn't the only connected guy here. Rumour has it he's been hanging around for quite some time. Think about it; free food, free accommodation and sporadic work if you want it. There's also plenty of freedom to come and go as you wish between the curfew hours. It's a perfect place to live the patriot dream without actually having to pull a trigger. It also gives you the chance to fuel your desires with fresh ears coming in weekly to join the constant recruitment drive.'

'Really?' Raj wasn't sure if he could believe Ivo's tale. 'Sounds a bit farfetched.'

'Maybe.' Ivo sounded like he didn't really care. 'Look, there is no doubt that Lubo is a patriot, of that I'm sure. But if I had a dinar for every time some freedom fighter made a call to arms, I would be a rich man. Or a dead one.'

Raj could relate to Ivo's last words. Many a time back home his young friends would talk brave and denounce their overlords, but at the sniff of police or some kind of official presence, they would run quicker than anyone else. The next day, those same brave souls would just start again with the hyperbole and wishful thinking, as if no one saw them cower the day before.

'It's all talk, Raj, trust me.'

Raj wasn't sure who to trust. Ivo definitely put a new spin on Lubo's perceived patriotism, but then Ivo was just as much a stranger to Raj as was Lubo. Lubo's ideals were grand indeed, and spoke to the devastation his people felt for a few decades. The years of history lessons his father had told him regarding the kings of old all seemed to be washed away with the current war and politics. The power of faith and the spirit of Christianity were being suppressed more and more each day, with traditions that spanned centuries now eroding unnaturally, via edict and fear. Rights and laws enjoyed by other free states around the world were just a dream to Raj only a week earlier. He had experienced it himself now, the liberty of walking around and speaking freely without needing to watch his back nor mind each word he spoke. Seeing his family with such freedom would be a wonderful gift, a gift Lubo insisted was the responsibility of each refugee.

But Ivo had a point too. Was Raj going to jump at every chance that sprang his way on his journey abroad? And what exactly was Lubo's plan? As far as Raj could tell, all that was on offer was the retaliation against the Yugoslavian state, but that was hardly a plan. As fantastic as the tales were: the mysterious funding from overseas, worldwide networks of Croats co-ordinating for the common good and foiling a professional army, they were still just that – simple tales. Raj liked the ideas, as most expatriate Croatians would, but he had to be careful to not put at risk all the things he had worked so hard for up to that point. If Lubo's opaque machinations proved to fail, then Raj would be worse off than when he had left a week earlier. Raj's father's voice rang through his head that day, and many others after – *'Don't let them pull you around by the nose.'*

Another week passed without incident. A whole new group of immigrants entered, but only a few would stay in Raj's dorm as it was already quite full. As far as Raj knew, no one had left the centre from that particular room, but he hoped he would soon be due. His thoughts bounced around from Lubo's well intentioned plans, to the potential of running into his brother in Bari, though the latter idea lost impetus as each day passed. Still, there might be word of Krizan at the next port of call, so Raj held on to that. There was still no correspondence from home, but Lubo assured Raj that letters from Yugoslavia could sometimes take a month to arrive. Lubo left Raj alone for the most part; he did occasionally refer to their conversation, but always respectfully without a hint of coercion, which Raj appreciated.

At the end of the third week of Raj's stay, a letter arrived from his parents. He felt a joy and warmth that was difficult to describe. His elder sister penned the letter, as his parents only knew how to sign their names, and she sent love and best wishes to him. All was well back home and nothing had really changed in the month. They were worried for Raj and were so very glad when they received his letter. They insisted he keep writing and let them know of his travels. Raj read and re-read the words until tears filled his eyes. The letter revealed the depth of sorrow he had inside himself at the absence of his family, a void that must have been camouflaged by the rush of the adventure to escape, a survival mechanism to keep focused and alive. Now that he was safe and settled, the emotions could stream forth and a mourning felt deep in his heart could be embraced.

'Check it out.' Tomo was beaming with pride on the evening of their fourth week at the camp.

Raj had been working all day and was tired but played along anyway, 'What is it, Tomo?'

'Have a look.' Tomo handed a small piece of paper to Raj.

Raj unfolded it and saw the Croatian coat of arms at the top of the page. Below, in bold lettering the words 'Croatian Liberation Army' were imprinted, followed by Tomo's name, his signature and the date of the transcription.

'What do you think?' Tomo still smiled.

Raj felt a distance had grown between them during their month sojourn. Perhaps it was fatigue born from spending a week on the road together, or perhaps the two of them simply had different personalities and their need for each other was now over and each man was going his separate ways.

'Looks good.' Raj turned the page over to see if there was any more information on the back. 'What is it?'

'Lubo asked me to become a member,' Tomo answered. 'He's got some great plans, Raj, I'm sure he'll ask you soon too. It's the beginning of something great.'

With that, Tomo grabbed his sheet and walked away. Raj was surprised how long it took for Tomo to be invited. It was clear Lubo was a little more discerning than Ivo gave him credit for, even if Raj did say so himself.

'He's already asked you, hasn't he?' Bran asked once Tomo was out of earshot.

'Yes.' Raj lay back on his bed. 'A couple of weeks back. How about you?'

'Same, one night at the table.'

'Did you sign up?' inquired Raj.

'Sure did.' Bran pulled out his sheet and waved it at Raj. 'What's holding you back?'

'I'm not sure.' Raj was honest. 'It might be all as expected, but then again, it all might just be bullshit that bites me on my arse in a few years' time. Why did you sign up?'

'To protect the homeland, of course.' Both men laughed out loud at Bran's sarcastic answer.

'You really think Lubo is onto something?' asked Raj.

'I don't know,' Bran responded. 'But it's a bit of fun and at least you get to know who you can trust at the centre.'

'Fair enough.'

'I mean, you do hate the commies, don't you?' Bran asked light-heartedly, but Raj sensed an undertow, as if his new friend was just making sure they were on the same political page.

'Hell yeah.' Raj played along. 'More than most. I just don't know Lubo well enough to sign my life away, that's all.'

The bell rang and dinner was served. The men followed their usual routines and ate and talked and drank and smoked. When it was nearly time to wind up the night, Lubo approached Raj once again. 'So have you had a think about my proposal?'

'A little,' answered Raj. 'But I'm still not sure. It all seems a little out of my league. I'm just a simple farmer trying to get a better life. Rebelling against dictators is for heroes, not the likes of me.'

'History will account for the heroes, Raj,' Lubo said. 'Many a champion rose from nothing.'

'That's true, Lubo,' Raj acknowledged. 'But I still don't know.'

'It's okay, my friend,' Lubo reminded Raj. 'There's no pressure. Let me know when you change your mind.'

The fourth week began like every other week, as did the entire following month. Two months spent working in an Italian town was just the remedy Raj needed to lift his spirits. He wore his cross with pride once again and felt a freedom he could never remember enjoying back home. He only wrote home once more; a simple letter assuring his kin that he was safe and well, but he never really expected another reply. All the achievements were immense and Raj was grateful, but they paled in comparison to the true freedom awaiting him once he left the camp and attained a new citizenship. There were rumours spreading that his employer was offering working visas to those digging in the team, although no one had yet approached Raj with an offer.

The trench was winding its way towards the sea while the plumbers and pipe fitters brought up the rear, laying grand cement piping through the dirt and mud. Raj was told they would soon have a few days off, then when they returned they would begin covering the channel. Raj was content with the work. It was quite menial and intensive, but it gave him something to do and something to look forward to. It also allowed him to save enough coin to buy some new clothes and keep some aside for the next leg of his journey. At this stage, he no longer expected Tomo to continue with him. They had grown more and more distant as the days passed. Raj respected him and was grateful for his company, but he could see that their goals were different, as were their personalities. Tomo coveted attention and could not wait for the group to get together for drinks and chat. Raj didn't care that much for the group, although, they were nice enough people; he just didn't get too attached as he knew they would go their separate ways eventually.

'Tomorrow's off,' Ivo announced as they walked back to their belongings at the end of another day. 'The boss reckons three days, maybe the rest of the week, until the other crew lay that piping.'

'Hopefully we are gone by then,' Raj said.

'Maybe.' Then Ivo asked, 'What's your plan after all this? I know you said you want to find your brother, but have you thought about what to do if you don't find him?'

'I don't know,' Raj responded. 'Get a job somewhere. Get citizenship. Maybe try for America.'

'Yeah, that's where I'm heading.' Ivo threw his sack over his shoulder and the duo began their walk back. 'I've heard it has the best opportunities.'

'I suppose we have to wait and see where they send us next,' Raj said. 'And when.'

'It will happen soon, I'm sure,' Ivo insisted. 'Unless we get called up by the freedom fighters!'

It was a running joke the two shared and it never failed to get a laugh.

'Even if I get the call and it's all real,' Ivo continued. 'I'll be so far away the boats from Argentina will have to pick me up.'

Raj laughed, but then a thought popped into his head. 'What do you mean "if" you get the call?' he asked.

'It's not going to happen, Raj, we both know that. I just signed to get Lubo off my back,' Ivo admitted. 'Has he been pestering you still?'

Raj was a bit surprised at his colleague.

'Yeah, he's been asking, but he's not being too pushy about it.'

The next morning Raj lazed in bed longer than usual as there was no work that day. He had some breakfast, read a Slovenian paper as best he could and just let his body rest in the dorm throughout the day. It was after lunch Lubo noticed him and came over.

'A day off for the hardworking man?' Lubo asked.

'Yeah, well needed too.' Raj was not lying, as much as he loved to work; he was really enjoying the rest that day.

'Have you seen Papac around?' Lubo asked, innocently pulling out a small sheet. 'I have his I.D. papers.'

'I think he said he was heading into town,' Raj replied. 'Something about a hot Italian bird.'

Lubo laughed out loud. 'I'm sure he's not going out for Italian roast chicken.'

This time Raj laughed out loud, then looked at Lubo, with the paper in his hand, and felt a sense of pity for the man. Here was Raj and all the other escapees, looking out for themselves and their families, while Lubo relentlessly campaigned for the freedom of all. His ideals were lofty, and perhaps deluded, but his heart seemed true and his actions proved it. In fact, Lubo was the one man that helped Raj more than any other in the camp. There was never going to be a rebellion launched from the San Sabba Detention Centre, of that Raj was quite certain, and he suspected Lubo knew it too. What would happen after they all left was a mystery as well, and if there was ever a need to return for a fight, then Raj could cross that bridge when it arrived. In the meanwhile, there was no real harm in supporting a fellow patriot.

'Lubo,' Raj conceded, proud to help a friend. 'Where do I sign?'

CHAPTER 18

It was Friday morning on the ninth week of Raj's stay at the detention centre. It was also another day off; three in a row and he was getting a little antsy. Word had come through that the boss would require them to return at the start of the next week to begin covering the channel and finishing up on that section of the track. There was also word that more work awaited around Trieste and the company was sincerely offering sponsorship to migrants that were interested in taking up employment. Raj would broach the subject when he returned; a matter that excited him greatly.

Then, surprisingly, between breakfast and lunch, the dormitory bell rang. Raj popped up out of bed to see an official make the announcement many of the men had awaited so desperately. The small man spoke as loudly as he could, but it was all in Italian. After a few short sentences, he pointed to a fellow official that was pinning up a large poster near the entrance to the room. Raj looked around and saw many of the migrants huddling around anyone who could best translate the man's words.

'We apologise for some... delays in our processes.' Raj and a few others made their way closer to Lubo, who translated. 'Our issues have cleared, and we will be getting back to our previous... efficiencies... the list is on the board... check your number... next week many shall... be processed. Enjoy your weekend. Thank you.'

The two officials barely left the room when the flood of stateless men crowded around the bulletin board. Raj realised quickly he was not going to get anywhere near the signage so waited for a while until it cleared. The bustle in the room increased exponentially over the next half hour, as many migrants realised their fate was now clear. Tomo came rushing back from the crowd toward Raj, Lubo, Bran and the others with a smile beaming across his face.

'You're looking happy, neighbour.' Raj spoke first.

'I'm out.' Tomo grabbed Raj by the hands and danced around him in joyful celebration, finishing with a kiss on each of his friend's cheeks. 'Thank you, thank you, thank you!'

'Great news, my friend,' Raj answered, as did all the compatriots that had gathered around. A few of the others returned as well, with smiles on their faces too. The joy was palpable and the drinks started to flow immediately.

Raj made his way to the sign, finding a space between the late comers. The page was filled with numbers, all in numeric order, which made things much easier. At the top was the vehicle number and below were the numbers of the migrants. It didn't take long for Raj to find his number tucked near the bottom of the fourth column.

'You on there?' asked Bran, who stood right behind Raj.

'Yeah.' Raj pointed to his number.

Bran then pointed his own, right above Raj's.

'So we are on the same bus.' Bran confirmed and then pointed to a number just above his. 'I'm pretty sure that is Tomo's number as well.'

'Just like our bed locations,' Raj noticed.

In fact, it appeared most of the Croatian group that socialised together made it onto the same bus. It was a blessing for the young men, as they were quite comfortable with each other, and disagreements were few and far between. Fortunately, any quarrels between the men had been minor, and only began after a few drinks and were also quickly resolved after a few more drinks. But there were no disagreements that evening, from anyone at the centre. The upbeat murmur within the large room remained well into the night; all chatter revolved around the move away from the centre and onto bigger and better things.

'Are you on the list, Lubo?' asked Ivo Papac as he placed a matchstick down on the table. The men often used matchsticks as chips when they played cards, a gentlemen's agreement within the group as many of them had little funds with which to gamble.

'No, no,' Lubo announced. 'It seems I'm stuck here for a little longer.'

Raj and Ivo exchanged glances.

'If you stay much longer, I reckon you'll be running this place soon.' The table burst out laughing at Ivo's jibe.

'Yes, yes, well done.' Lubo was smiling. 'I've heard all those jokes before.'

'Any idea of where our bus is taking us?' asked Denis, who folded his cards after seeing Ivo's hand. 'I hear the next stop is a guarantee of freedom.'

'Not sure,' Lubo answered as he poured a drink. 'I'm not running the place just yet.'

The table laughed again. There was a real positive mood that evening and Raj felt like a collective burden had really been lifted.

'But what I am sure of' – Lubo looked at Raj – 'is that we can officially welcome our newest member, Raj Krizic. Here you go.'

Raj took the piece of paper off Lubo as those around the table cheered. It was his certified identity paper as part of the fledgling Croatian Liberation Army.

'All you need to do is sign.' Lubo handed Raj a pen.

'You do know how to write your name, don't you?' Ivo was in a particularly jovial mood.

The laughter suddenly stopped, then the men started tapping the table with their palms; at first softly, then with a crescendo as Raj put his name onto the page, cumulating in another cheer, even bigger than the first.

'You better check the spelling,' said Raj, joining in the merriment.

Lubo grabbed the document and shook Raj's hand firmly. 'We will make those commies burn,' he said aggressively.

Raj raised his glass. 'I sure hope we do.'

The weekend passed without incident and what was generally a messy common area seemed to be clearing up around the edges. Clothes that might have been left on the floor or under a bed, were now placed away, newspapers and magazines, spread across beds and tables, were removed and bundles of blankets or pillows that were once strewn haphazardly, were folded, sorted and put away.

It seemed like no one could sleep on Sunday night; the amount of movement in the beds in the darkness was unprecedented and even Raj felt anxious as he laid awaiting sleep. He couldn't help but think about the prospects of freedom, a true freedom this time with the possibility of citizenship in a safe and democratic state. He thought of how he could bring his parents and siblings over too and finally even reconnect with his elder brother Krizan. Raj would bring his whole town away from the Communists if he could. Then he thought about the work he already had and the opportunity cost of moving away from a sure thing. He truly enjoyed the job, and it seemed plentiful, but Raj knew that the further he moved from the border, the better his chances were at achieving a genuine break from the past. Besides, as much as it seemed like a sure thing, nothing was certain at the moment. Escape was still the predominant thought that ran through Raj's head and he knew it would be so until his future was absolutely guaranteed.

Eventually sleep came and went as Raj opened his eyes and stretched out wide while still lying in his bed. The sound of mid-summer rain smashed the tin roof that Monday morning, making the bustle of preparation unnaturally hushed, while ironically forcing the men to talk louder amongst themselves, due to the volume of the battering deluge. Raj hopped out of bed and saw Tomo already packed and waiting.

'That's the first time you've been up so early since the farm in Pivka.' Raj smiled at his friend.

'Then I was scared.' Tomo smiled back. 'Now I'm excited.'

Like most men in the room, Raj had packed much of his gear the night before. He had thrown out some of his old garments and replaced them once he had saved enough from his job. Raj was quite good at saving; in the two months he had been working, he had managed to save a few thousand lira, buy some new clothes, drinks and tobacco. Of course, Raj was not much of a drinker or smoker, but he understood the value of a currency; at the street level, alcohol and tobacco were more often used in exchange for goods and services than was gold.

'Don't forget your papers.' Lubo came up to Raj after breakfast, offering a firm hand shake. 'And your bus number.'

Raj double checked that everything was in order then reached out his hand.

'Thanks, Lubo. I wish you could come with us. It seems unfair that you are stuck here yet again.'

'It's all good, Raj.' Lubo winked as he spoke coolly. 'I'll go when the time is right.'

The group of friends suddenly congregated around Lubo, giving him hugs and scuffing his hair playfully.

'We'll miss you, old man,' said Ivo Papac, ever the joker.

'Thanks for everything,' Tomo stated, almost in tears. 'Don't worry, we'll take it back soon, brother. We'll be in touch.'

'Take it easy.' Denis shook Lubo's hand. 'And thanks for everything.'

'All the best,' Bran stated respectfully as he strode away.

Finally, Raj shook Lubo's hand once more.

'Thanks friend,' he said. 'Hopefully we see each other again soon.'

'Cover yourselves.' Lubo was the eternal father figure. 'It's pissing down out there.'

Slowly the room emptied as the double doors funnelled three men at a time into the sodden outside world. Raj took one last look back as he passed an official standing at the door. He could see Lubo idly watching the exodus, along with a few others who were not chosen on this round of processing. There was a bitter sweet sense to the ending of his sojourn; Raj had met some wonderful lads in that room and had forged his way into the local workforce which brought him a greater sense of financial wealth and independence. Yet he knew it was always going to be just a stepping stone on his journey to absolute freedom. He was glad for the experience and the lovely memories he had made, and he was also glad that, at the least, Lubo wasn't left absolutely alone in that large dorm.

As one space emptied another burst with activity; the tarmac that separated the buildings was now abuzz with action. People were walking, talking, laughing and shouting everywhere. Buses were waiting and arriving and honking, as umbrella wielding stewards tried to prevent any accidents while guiding the myriad of soaked migrants toward their shuttles. It was the first time Raj saw women and children on the tarmac since his time at the detention centre. Families were finally reunited; children jumped in puddles while fathers hugged their wives, all their tears hidden by the rain. A sense of rapture engulfed the area, juxtaposed against the downpour that dampened everything except the human spirit. All the while, a loud speaker droned through the din in an Italian voice barking orders of one kind or another that Raj couldn't comprehend.

It was all quite overwhelming. The pelting rain created a grey haze of migrants moving in random ways around the car park, alongside the arbitrary sounds of diesel engines and shouting voices, echoing into each other to create a cacophony of human and machine noise. The atmosphere was thick with heat too; Raj wasn't sure if it was the weather that alone brought the humidity, or the amount of bodies and buses loitering so close together. It was all so messy and unorganised that Raj just stopped for a moment when he realised he had lost Bran and Tomo in the melee. He looked left and right hoping to see Ivo or Denis too, but it was all hazy and moving too fast. He checked his papers for the bus number he had written down earlier but couldn't see it on any of the buses before him, so he strode further away from the dormitory and deeper into the rain. There were more buses on the other side of the tarmac, facing away from him so their numbers were not apparent, although, at that distance, he was sure he wouldn't have seen the numbers through the rain anyway.

He walked on, now soaking through his clothes, then stepped it up and ran toward the buses. He avoided two buses that were already full and making their way toward the exit and safely made it to an undercover bay on the far side of the car park. It was there he spotted Tomo.

'Tomo,' Raj called in relief.

'Raj.' Tomo turned and saw his friend. He pointed to a bus out in the open, parked a distance away from the rest of the fleet, almost randomly sitting in the rain. 'That one over there, that's ours.'

Raj nodded and took a few quick steps, while dodging those around him, just to try to catch up, but Tomo was just as excited and was also moving quickly toward their shuttle. He saw Ivo and Denis then too, but there was no sign of Bran. His friends had already left the sheltered area and were moving in the rain toward their bus. By the time Raj caught up to them, everyone was drenched to the core.

'Why the fuck did they put us out here?' fumed Denis. 'There's plenty of space back there?'

'Why haven't they opened?' Raj asked, not seeing clearly into the cabin.

'Driver's not in,' yelled Ivo, who was only a few metres away but still had to shout through the rain and chatter of the other displeased men.

The murmur from the waiting men grew and grew but no one was about to leave the area as this bus was their road to freedom and they had all been waiting so long already. Suddenly the door opened and an older, hardened looking man popped his head out. Raj thought he saw a slight grin on his weathered face.

'Hey,' a stranger in the group shouted. 'Where did you come from? Didn't you notice, it's fucking pouring out here?'

A crack of thunder suddenly roared all around and the silent bus driver stepped back to allow the men onto his bus. The weather was loudly announcing a change of atmosphere and Raj couldn't help but feel the analogy within the movement of the lives of the men boarding the bus. In single file the soaked migrants poured into the long vehicle and found a dry sanctuary beneath the metal roof. Two by two those who entered first found seats after stowing their luggage in the open compartments above. As he entered, Raj stopped for a moment at the door and looked quickly behind him to see if Bran had caught up, but the glance didn't prove fruitful and he didn't linger lest his fellow travellers turned their wet ire toward him.

'Have you seen Bran?' he asked Ivo as they found their way to some empty seats.

'No,' Ivo sounded perplexed. 'I can't say that I have. But I did see him when we left the dorm. We were all together. Then we lost you. And him too, by the look of it.'

'I hope he makes it.' Raj was a little concerned for his friend.

'He's probably soaking at the back of the queue.' Denis poked his head from the seats behind them. 'I still can't believe this idiot couldn't bring the bus in closer.'

'Hey,' came the cries from outside the door. 'Let us in!'

The door to the bus squeezed closed just then, nearly cutting off the arm of the last man on.

'Wrong bus,' the bus driver stated remorselessly, not waiting for a reply before ticking over the motor.

Raj could see a few more men still waiting at the door, some even starting to whack their hands against the panelling. But the driver seemed to be right; the bus was full and the last man sat down just as the vehicle started to roll.

'Tough nut, that one,' Raj said to nobody in particular.

'Yeah,' Ivo responded. 'Reminds me of the commie driver that used to take us to school.'

The fixed windows that surrounded them were both foggy from the inside, and wet from the outside, making visibility for the passengers very poor. Raj rubbed at the glass, still trying to see if Bran was loitering anywhere on the yard, but that was nigh on impossible now. More buses had started moving out, while others were still coming in, just adding to the difficulty. Raj thought his friend could have mistakenly boarded the wrong bus in the confusion of the morning, which might not have been such a bad end to the entire process. Then it suddenly dawned on him that this bus was full, so even If Bran was here, there would be nowhere for him to sit.

'You still looking for Bran?' asked Ivo.

'I have a soft spot for him,' answered Raj. 'He is a bit younger and we met on the bus that brought us here.'

'You might have to let it go,' Ivo added. 'If he's stuck at the centre, then Lubo will look after him. If he is on one of these other buses, then he'll be fine and there's nothing much you can do for him anyway.'

Raj knew Ivo was right, but it would still have been nice to have the whole crew together for the next leg of their journey.

'I'm sure he had the same bus number as ours.' Raj was a little confused by the proceedings.

'I hope we are off to Bari.' Denis spoke from the seats behind, ignoring Raj's confusion.

'Why Bari?' asked Ivo.

'I don't know,' responded Denis. 'I just heard good things about it. I heard if you get to Bari, then you are guaranteed to be safe.'

The bus approached the exit to the centre, joining the line of other buses all slowing at the gates to be checked out by the guards. One after another, the vehicular giants slowly rolled out of the driveway and turned left toward the open road.

'So many police cars,' Ivo noted.

Raj followed his friends gaze toward the front of the bus and was surprised at the view. Now that it was their turn, the street beyond the centre could be seen and the bus driver's windscreen was the clearest of all the windows within the transport. Beyond the grounds there were several small, three door, Italian built police vehicles parked on the street near the entrance. None of the vehicles seemed to be running and no flashing lights could be seen.

'Maybe acting as security for the day?' offered Raj.

'Why would they need security on a day where everyone is set free?' inquired Ivo.

The whole bus quietened down now and looked perplexed at the sight before them. Surprisingly, unlike the others, this bus turned right onto the road through Trieste. The bus driver turned on some music just then which seemed to settle the migrants, and after a minute or so, they all began to talk again. Raj relaxed a little too, but noticed Ivo's eyes were darting back and forth, his head checking the rear as often as the fore, unsettled in his seat and even tenser than before.

'What's up, Ivo?' Raj talked quietly but wasn't sure why.

'I don't like it,' Ivo answered.

'What don't you like?' Raj smiled, trying to ease the mood.

'I don't like any of it.'

'What do you mean?'

'Answer me this: why are we turning right, while everyone else turned left?' asked Ivo.

Raj thought for a moment. 'Maybe we are off to a different site. Maybe the other centres aren't as big as this one.'

'I don't know, Raj.' Ivo wasn't sounding convinced.

'I'm thinking they are sending the bachelors to a different district, as I don't see any families on our bus.' Raj was proud of this newest argument and awaited a response.

'Why the police cars, then?'

'I don't think they're for us.' Raj looked around, but with the rain still falling and the men still breathing, the visibility remained poor. 'And I don't see any following us.'

Ivo took a moment and settled in his seat.

'You're paranoid, Ivo.' Raj tried to further comfort his colleague. 'But there is nothing to worry about. We are home free.'

'Then tell me, Raj, why is the bus driver playing traditional Serbian music?'

Raj hadn't even noticed the language of the song. Suddenly, Tomo sang out quite loudly in chorus with the particular tune, creating a cascading effect as one by one other fellow travellers joined in until the whole bus resonated in song, prompting the driver to turn up the volume. Yugoslav music was a mish-mash of many traditions born from centuries of folklore that now melded Croat, Serb and Macedonian tunes, but rarely was anything but Croatian music played in Raj's home town. Raj was perplexed though. *Why would an Italian bus driver be blasting Yugo-ethnic tunes for the drive?*

'Maybe he knows we miss home?' Raj contemplated. 'You know, makes us comfortable for the trip.'

Ivo shook his head dismissively and moved closer to Raj, then whispered, 'Like lambs to the slaughter, and these fools celebrate along the way.'

Raj looked out the window and noticed the blur of a small white car driving alongside them. He wiped at the fog and saw the police lights atop the vehicle.

'Still think I'm paranoid?' Ivo was looking out the window too.

'I'm sure it's nothing.' Raj wasn't convinced though.

The bus drove on for a few more minutes, but the accompanying police car maintained its position. The men aboard the bus had broken out the Rakija by now and were singing along to every tune blasting from the radio. A sense of merriment spread quickly around the cabin, and as the heated breath and vocal volume increased, the windows of the vehicle became opaque to the point of obscurity. All the while, Raj kept wiping at the glass every few seconds in the hope that the car beside them disappeared and with it his looming sense of dread.

'We are still travelling east, Raj,' Ivo mentioned.

'I noticed,' Raj responded, getting more and more nervous.

'Travelling east from the eastern most city in Italy is not a good sign.' Ivo stated the obvious. 'I'm sure we should have turned by now.'

Raj took a deep breath and kept checking outside his window again, and every time he checked, the police car was still there, although the lights and sirens were still turned off. The rain had subsided into a lighter shower, which made the outside world clearer but did nothing to clean the inside of the glass and had even less effect on Raj's nerves as the bus rolled on.

'Come on, you two.' Tomo stood and reached over the bench seats to grab Raj and Ivo by the shoulders. 'Join in the song. It reminds me of the folk songs from school.'

Ivo just shook his head and Raj smiled. Tomo looked surprised by the two then sat back and resumed his singing.

'Idiot,' Ivo whispered. 'I don't know where you found him, Raj, but that one could be substituted for an oxen without any loss to our conversation.'

The bus merged onto a highway and continued driving for a few more minutes with music blaring and alcohol flowing, before exiting the multi-lane road and stopping at a large public car park at the edge of a lush, forested area. The singing men hardly noticed the stop, as most of them kept their song alive with only a few of them focusing on the outside world. The driver killed the radio and rose from his chair, looked back toward his passengers and took a long drag on a cigarette while smiling silently before leaving the bus.

'What's this?' Tomo apparently had noticed the bus stop.

His question was echoed by the mob whose tipsy frivolity only a moment earlier gave way to a sober shock at the sight before them. The bent arms of all those who sat near the windows rubbed furiously at the glass in order to expose the sight before them.

'I told you this was not good, Raj.' Ivo sounded more fearful than ever. 'Do you still think I'm paranoid?'

CHAPTER 19

'Everybody off!'

A middle-aged Yugoslav soldier gave the command in a strange Slavic dialect, with enough authority in his tone to leave no doubt about the order. Raj looked at Ivo and around the bus as a nervous murmur grew through the cabin. Slowly, each man stood and grabbed their packs and headed toward the front. The soldier in charge had already exited, leaving a younger underling near the driver's seat to ensure a steady egress.

'Come, on, come on,' the young officer suddenly shouted. 'We haven't got all fucking day you turncoat cowards!'

Those words prompted an increase in the speed of the withdrawal but there was still a natural limitation to the amount of people that could leave a bus at once. Raj had risen and grabbed his bag. He waited for Ivo, who waited for another young man to pass. Raj didn't know the man ahead of Ivo, but the tears in the youngster's eyes told a tale that many shared in that frightful moment.

'What do you think?' Tomo asked surreptitiously from the seats behind Raj.

'I think we're fucked,' answered Ivo candidly.

Raj just looked at his friend and shrugged his shoulders as a reply. He knew they were on their own now. There would be no more words of wisdom from Raj and no more daring escape plans from Tomo. All the successful schemes to leave Yugoslavia had now been somehow undermined by a mysterious betrayal across the border, leaving Raj with no idea as to who was behind the treachery. His mind raced. Could it be Lubo? Was it the policeman in Trieste? What was his name? Falzone? Or his wife? Or her sister? Was it the boss at Raj's workplace? Was it Ivo? Tomo?

Raj was panting as his thoughts turned to the next phase in his journey; would they send him to the military? Or worse, maybe even prison? Or even worse – death! There were plenty of stories of escapees being tried for treason and executed. Many dissidents were simply disappeared by the state, without trial or fuss, leaving families forever wondering what happened to their loved ones. Then Raj's thoughts moved to his parents and the abuse they would now have to endure just because of Raj's selfishness.

'Take it easy, Raj.' Ivo spoke gently. 'Catch your breath. You'll pass out.'

Raj hadn't even realised they were off the bus already as he looked outward, gratefully replacing his dark reverie with the dark clouds in the sky.

'Thanks, Ivo,' said Raj.

'No worries,' Ivo stated. 'Have you seen our old friend over there?' He nodded his head toward their right side and took a bite out of an apple.

'I can't believe you have an appetite.' Raj was surprised at his companion.

'I don't.' Ivo winked. 'But you're still looking at me.'

Raj looked around properly for the first time; he counted six Italian police cars parked equilaterally around the boundary of the large, public opening. There were also two large military buses, complete with red stars painted on the sides, plus the civilian bus that had transported them to that locale. Three khaki jeeps with outsized wheels also waited in the car park and dispersed among all of them were a variety of officers, both Italian and Yugoslav, military and civilian.

The police cars lights flashed, but the sirens were muted, giving the feeling that the crisis was under control but not completely over. The migrants milled around in no particular order but were casually contained within the parameters of the cordon. As Raj scanned the rainy scene toward his right, he noticed a familiar face near one of the jeeps, talking and smoking with the commander who first appeared on their bus. It was none other than Bran.

'I guess we now know where he disappeared to.' Ivo spat on the ground in disdain.

'Attention!'

Raj looked to see the same smug, younger officer from the bus now standing before the men.

'Single file, to the bus.' The soldier pointed toward one of the military buses. 'Stop at the door for inspection. Now!'

One of the younger migrants must have cracked a joke beneath his breath as Raj couldn't hear the words, but he did hear the blow across the man's head after the officer back handed him in response.

'Your holiday is over, pigs,' announced the commander after seeing the incident, who now strode purposefully toward the joking man. 'When an officer gives an order, you listen.' He followed the words with a surgical blow to the man's solar-plexus, winding him instantaneously.

The young migrant's knees bent slowly and he clutched at his abdomen, struggling to breathe. He gently sat on his back side, wheezing lightly in a puddle of water, the entire mob stepping back in apprehension of the violence. Raj and Ivo stood toward the rear of the group but now could clearly see the situation.

'Now!' the first officer yelled again, causing the migrants to gasp in simultaneous surprise.

The detainees slowly walked around the winded man, avoiding any semblance of association and made their way dejectedly toward the new bus. Ivo put his hand against Raj's chest and shuffled sideways in an appearance of movement but without really going anywhere.

'Let's not be first for this one.' He justified his actions and Raj just nodded.

The rain picked up a little at that moment, as did the wind. It was still far from cold, but a sense of misery ensued among the men, nevertheless. The progression in the queue was taking a while and the weather certainly didn't help. The stone beneath their feet absorbed none of the rain, leaving puddles everywhere that drenched the men from below, just as the rain saturated their clothes from above.

Raj was three quarters of the way to the officers in charge of administering the changeover when he noticed why the process was taking so long; the soldiers were conducting full bag and clothing checks, allowing the elements to penetrate the migrant's dry apparel as well as their provisions. Raj also noticed some of the men being escorted to the second bus a few metres away, while others were simply allowed onto the bus before them.

'I wonder why we are being separated?' Raj quietly asked no one in particular.

'This is what's going on.' Ivo swallowed a piece of bread he had been chewing and quietly removed his Croatian Liberation Army certificate. He ripped it quickly and dropped the small fragments of paper as covertly as he could, then stomped on them with his feet, rubbing them into the stone as he looked left and right in case he was seen.

'You think?' Raj wasn't so sure. 'That's just some harmless fun.'

'I don't know, Raj.' Ivo sounded intense. 'But we are in a moment where I don't want to give these commies any extra ammunition. We are fucked right now. I know Bran fucked us. I don't know if Lubo did. Or if someone back home did. But the last thing I want is to be caught with this piece of paper, with my signature on it, that swears my allegiance against the people that are about to incarcerate us!'

'I see a few from our group being taken over,' Raj said quizzically. 'But there are a few that I don't recognise.'

'Like I said.' Ivo was adamant. 'It's not a risk I'm willing to take. Besides, I don't know what other conspiracies are going on around here.'

'Okay, okay,' Raj agreed defensively, seeing Ivo's point. He immediately withdrew his certificate and followed his friend's example by destroying it as quickly and covertly as possible.

'And eat, for God's sake,' Ivo added, sounding quite parental. 'With these fuckers, you don't know when your next meal will be.'

By the time Raj faced the officers at the door to the bus, the rain had settled into a light shower and the wind had calmed down too. The atmosphere looked brighter as the clouds thinned into the late morning, hinting at the possibility of sunshine toward the end of the day. Raj was still wet, but now his belly was full after he had scoffed all the food in his pack. Even though he had overeaten, he was glad he did; beyond the administrating officers, there was a pile of soaked contraband destined to become garbage, among which plenty of confiscated food laid soggy in the summer rain.

The closest soldier took Raj's watch and wallet then ripped the cross from his neck, putting the jewellery and cash in his pockets before beginning the pat down, while the other soldier rummaged clumsily through his bag, taking the cigarettes and a small bottle of hooch Raj had been saving. In that dejected moment he was still thankful to Ivo, though, for discarding the paperwork regarding their little rebellion established at San Sabba. After answering a few basic questions regarding identification, Raj was allowed onto the bus nearest to him where he sat gratefully in the dry surrounds and waited nervously for the rest of the men to be processed.

After an hour or so, the bus was three quarters full and the engine roared to life. Ivo sat next to Raj once again, but both were solemnly silent as were the rest of the men. The sense that transitory migration had turned into indefinite detention was palpable within the cabin, hence the silence that engulfed the space. That, and the fact the armed soldiers ordered everyone to keep silent, also ensured quietude. Even the driver and accompanying soldiers said little, with radio silence only being broken by an occasional communiqué over the airwaves.

The official Yugoslavian/Italian border didn't take long to cross. There was no stopping at the customs station for the military escort, in fact, there a was a special lane off to the side of one of the control rooms, with boom gate open and patrolling guards awaiting the convoy to pass. They could have driven straight through the main causeway because there was no one trying to enter Yugoslavia at that particular time. Raj wondered if anyone ever wanted to enter the dismal country and only wished it had been this easy to leave the Communist state in the first place.

It was suddenly becoming even more emotional; the journey that took him and Tomo nearly a week full of struggles and misadventures was all nullified within moments once the bus had moved over the borderline. Raj felt small and insignificant, merely a pawn in some greater game once more, with all his hard work simply erased by the powers that be. Behind him, the second bus chugged along too, complete with all those that Raj thought might be deemed a greater security risk to the state, including Tomo and a few others that associated with the Croat group at the migration centre.

'How are you holding up?' asked Ivo after a while.

'Quiet back there,' was the immediate response from the supervising officer.

'I'm fine,' answered Raj in a hushed voice, after waiting a while. 'Just nervous.'

'Me too,' replied Ivo, in a manner far from his usually stoic tone.

A few hours must have passed, and the sun had moved considerably closer to the west and appeared much lower than Raj had expected now the clouds had dissipated. The bus then stopped at what looked like a small military establishment a mile or so off a main road that only contained two small buildings and a handful of troops. The surrounding area was flat and quite sparse, with small trees and brush scattered sporadically around the grassy boundary, but with no other establishments neighbouring close by. A short, wire fence could be seen in the distance but only proved that nothing important was being held at this locale. Raj thought that it might be a testing ground of some kind, for training or bombings. The men were allowed off the bus to use the toilets and stretch their legs for a few minutes but were kept huddled together not far from the buses, and were always under armed guard, even though the security detail wasn't on full alert.

'What's going on?' asked Tomo, sounding anxious as he talked quickly with his reunited friends. 'Where do you think we are headed? Why are you guys on different buses?'

'No idea,' Ivo answered curtly.

'What do you think, Raj?' Tomo nervously continued, scratching at his neck. 'You reckon they'll notice if I jump in with you?'

'They'll notice, Tomo.' Raj consoled his friend. 'Relax. Take a breath. You sound nervous.'

'I'm okay, I'm okay,' Tomo answered as his eyes darted from side to side. 'So you reckon they'll notice if I jump on your bus?'

Raj felt for Tomo; he could see the anguish on his companion's face but didn't know if any words would comfort him.

'They'll do a roll call before we get back on.' Ivo showed some mercy. 'You have no chance.'

Just then one of the detainees broke ranks and ran away from the group. Everyone turned to see the young man as he bolted toward the boundary fence. He was a stranger to Raj and was on Tomo's bus for the journey. Raj hoped the man had the speed to outrun the soldiers who were taken by surprise and so were slow to take up the chase.

'Halt!' the soldiers cried as two of the younger officers started running.

Murmurings of a full-scale escape quickly started circulating among the clustered men, with brave words being exchanged beneath their breath while their feet shuffled, subtly expanding the huddle. But then a shot rang out with a depth of tone and strength in volume that caused everyone to cover their ears and squat slightly in shock. Raj looked toward the running man who was now lying still on the ground, most probably dead.

'Is he alive?' the commander yelled, pointing his rifle down after completing the successful shot, smoke gently disappearing from the barrel.

'Yes,' the soldier that arrived first shouted back.

'Finish him.' The commander gave the order and the merciless soldier put two more bullets into the fallen escapee without saying another word.

With that action, all talk of escape ended abruptly, and the captured men returned to their dejected postures, bringing the circle in tight once more. Raj now wondered whether this army encampment was left so vacant as to allow space to dispose of all the bodies the Communists had killed. He pondered about how many other men might be buried out here.

'Let this be a lesson for you,' the commander said as he casually walked past the group and handed his rifle to another soldier.

The troops then took out provisions and ate and drank around the vehicles while Raj and his hungry compatriots looked on. Containers were brought out and the buses were refilled with fuel, oil levels and tyre pressures were also checked, and a few bags were brought out and placed within the vehicles.

'Looks like there is still a way to go,' Ivo said quietly.

'We'll be driving into the night,' Raj added.

'Into the night?' Tomo sounded even more anxious than before, but no longer mentioned changing buses.

'Definitely,' Ivo agreed. 'Another hour or so and it will be dark. They wouldn't be stopping and refilling if we were close.'

Once all the checks were complete and the soldiers were satiated, the men were ushered back onto the buses to be moving again. Tomo gave a despondent look toward his friends and waved slightly as he stepped onto his bus.

'I bet you are glad you ate now,' Ivo whispered with a tight smile once they were inside. He gave Raj the window seat.

'Indeed,' Raj responded. 'And thanks.'

'If we are driving into the night,' Ivo continued, 'we could be heading anywhere.'

'I reckon our direction is south east, so I doubt we are heading toward Zagreb,' Raj postulated.

'Thank God for that,' Ivo added. 'That would be a hornet's nest.'

Just then the officer at the front of the bus stood up and walked toward the rear with a disgruntled look on his face. He stopped at Raj and Ivo's position and grabbed Ivo by the ear then violently dragged him toward the front of the bus. Raj thought his friend's ear was being ripped off as Ivo yelped at surprise from the pain, looking like a child being punished by an angry parent. Without a word, the soldier let everyone know that any chatter among the men would not be tolerated. Now Raj sat alone by the window, watching the countryside move by as the shadows of the day became longer and dusk cast an orange hue across the rocky landscape that was his birthplace.

Several more hours passed as the daylight finally dwindled and night took hold. The rain had gone, taking the sunshine with it, but the constant drone of the diesel engine remained. Raj could see very little of the outside world now, although he knew they had passed his home village a while ago, as well the larger town of Mostar, because there were enough lights in the populated areas to see signs and landmarks to guide his way. They must have gone the longer way around because the mountains had kept their distance during the entire trip. Perhaps the roads were better down south, or they were trying to torture the passengers. It didn't matter either way, as there was no arguing with the soldiers carrying the guns.

CHAPTER 20

Sarajevo was the largest and most populace town in Bosnia. It had been the capital city for hundreds of years, but its beginnings were humble indeed. Sarajevo's central, inland location was not a favourite destination during the Roman Empire and was only really taken off the Illyrians for tactical control, hosting a small colony and some military garrisons. For a few centuries after the Roman schism, the Goths held control of the area, followed by the Slavs. As a specific geographic locale, it was hardly more than a few villages scattered closely about the valley and river in the region. Its unassuming beginnings only grew due to commerce and the emergence of a marketplace that drew together different folks from around the area.

Eventually, a century or so after the time of Christ, the kings of Hungary held sway over much of central Europe, spreading toward Bosnia in direct competition to the Byzantine Empire, Rome and the various autonomous principalities on both sides of the Adriatic Sea. The population, in what would eventually come to be known as Sarajevo, continued to grow, and the greater area became important enough for churches, forts and citadels to be built and fought over. Bosnia became its own independent kingdom in the twelfth century, albeit still under the watchful eye of the Hungarians. It acted as a self-governing vassal state stuck between the Catholic and Orthodox ideologies as it fought to find its own identity in the high Middle Ages.

This all changed when the Ottoman Empire arrived in the thirteenth century. The Muslim conquest brought much cultural change to the area and an impetus that really gave birth to Sarajevo, both in name and as an important capital city to the region. The first Islamic governor of the town immediately got to work with infrastructure builds such as a mosque, public baths, a bridge and a hostel. The work brought people, and the people brought money, which in turn brought more people. The marketplace was so favoured by the Islamic leader that it was covered and extended to promote more commerce, while keeping the traders free from the influence of the outside elements.

As time passed, the city grew into an Islamic powerhouse. By the sixteenth century, Sarajevo was a jewel in the Ottoman Empire and would be remembered as a golden age for the city, comparable to Istanbul itself. Schools, mosques, churches and even synagogues were all built as migrants were invited to help expand the town. An independent water system was created, as was a clock tower, advancing Sarajevo's technological status, while libraries and schools flourished during this time, increasing the quality of education to many who inhabited the city.

But no kingdom lasts forever and the decline of the Ottoman Empire took a heavy toll on Sarajevo. Being on the periphery of the realm meant it was one of the first to fall when the tides of war turned. By the middle of the nineteenth century, inner political and religious turmoil placed much pressure on Bosnian leadership, while externally the great powers of Europe arose, aided by advancements in the mechanics of war and the desire for expansion within the continent. Sarajevo was eventually taken over by the Austro-Hungarians, with the blessings of the main authorities in Europe, and with little more than local resistance as the Ottoman's control in the area waned.

Industrialisation came to Bosnia, and Sarajevo was the first city in southern Europe to have a tramway. The architecture, politics and educational systems were all overhauled during the late nineteenth century, as the Austro-Hungarians looked to distance their principalities from the Ottoman's systems of governance. The population of Sarajevo declined though, as the damage done after the tumultuous takeover left many dead, much structural damage and forced a steady exodus toward parts of Bosnia that were ethnically divided.

Unfortunately, Sarajevo's greatest claim to fame came on the 28th of June, 1914, when the Archduke of Austria and his wife, the Duchess of Hohenberg, were assassinated while driving through the streets of the town as part of an official visit. This moment was one of the most pivotal in modern history, leading to World War One and an upheaval of politics across both the continent and the globe.

The Kingdom of Yugoslavia was born after the First World War, but

Sarajevo was not really treated with any great significance during this time. It was only after the Second World War, once the Communists took hold, that the city was again built up with heavy investments in restructuring and industry.

Raj guessed it was around midnight when they arrived at the outskirts of Sarajevo. In the darkness they approached an area fenced off with barbed wire, spotlights and patrolling guards. Two buildings towered in front of the large gates ahead of them; they were multi-storied, square concrete boxes that could fit a few hundred people during working hours but only showed a few lights to be on at that moment. The cascade slowed only for a short period, and after the front car quickly sorted their entry requirements, they passed into the fortified area, driving along a narrow road between the two buildings, into a new kind of darkness.

It could have been any suburb in the world, Raj thought, but the red stars painted on every surface that surrounded them left no doubt that they were in a Yugoslav town. A large amount of military vehicles also confirmed this wasn't simply a civic locale, but one of high security and strategic importance. They drove slowly past a few more buildings before pulling up to another gate with even more guards and more fencing. Within, there was a large lot for vehicles and another four-storey dwelling beyond the car park. This one had slits for windows and Raj saw human silhouettes on the roof. It was quiet at that time of night, the clouds were gone, and the stars shone above, while the only sound came from the engines that idled and the footfall of the men that were marched off the buses. A few spotlights, held on high poles, lit the way down toward the building and, aided by armed guards stationed in pairs along the way, the prisoners walked slowly toward their new home.

One by one the dissidents were led into the concrete structure. A small antechamber awaited them, well-lit with two more armed guards at the ready, while another guard was located in a smaller administrative room to the left, secured by a door and a service window that had steel bars running across them. There was also a stairwell to the right that ascended and descended into darkness and looked decidedly ominous. Behind the armed guards, the main wall to the foyer looked like a continuation of the concrete that surrounded the building, with another iron barred door in the middle, securing any further access past the lobby. Every word the guards spoke echoed in the space, making the small area seem unnaturally bigger than it was. Raj took it all in as he was patted down once more upon entry; his details were quickly recorded and his travel bag thrown in with the pile that sat heaped in front of the door to the service room.

Once the administrative detailing was complete, Raj was escorted up two flights of stairs and into a corridor lined with prison cells on either side. Yet more guards kept watch at the entry to the level and took over the transition of the inmates to their particular cells. Raj counted ten compartments on each side as he walked to the very last one in the space. He was alone in the cell and took a moment to absorb the environment; straight black steel bars dropped from the ceiling to the floor throughout the room, dividing the space into square cubicles of caged isolation. The lighting was terrible, with only three flickering bulbs down the hallway to illuminate the entire dorm. The smell was far worse though; a mixture of human waste and body odour emanated in the air as each cell was entrusted with a steel bucket for a toilet and Raj wasn't sure exactly how often the guards cleaned the facilities.

Each cell had at least one man in it, some had two. Raj did a quick calculation and realised the number of prisoners was too great to have all been brought in from Italy. This heightened his awareness through his fatigue and made him glad he was alone in the cell for the time being. There were no beds or chairs in the cells, so some men slept on the floor while others sat or stood and talked amongst themselves. Raj took a seat on the cold, concrete floor with his back to the cold, concrete wall and stared silently into the darkness around him. He realised this might be the first place the Communists got right. In fact, if Raj was to design a prison for his worst enemies, he thought that this would probably be it. Comfort and hygiene were not on offer in this miserable place, and hope was truly lost in the myriad of metal bars and the disgusting stench of inhuman accommodation.

Raj must have nodded off for a while as he awoke with a jolt to the sound of a cell door creaking open and the call of a man's name.

'Mehmet Isdabeg!' Two guards stood at an open cage door down the hall.

The cell was three cubicles away and Raj could see two men were held in there. One man stood while the other lay on the floor, sleeping.

'Mehmet,' the conscious inmate called to the sleeping man. 'Get up.'

Before Mehmet was allowed to fully wake, one guard swiftly kicked the man in the legs which led him to jump up in fright. The guard grabbed him aggressively by the back of the neck and pushed him out of the cell, meanwhile the other guard threw in a dishevelled man they had brought back with them.

Feeling stiff and sore from the discomfort of his seated sleeping position, Raj arose gingerly and moved closer to the bars that surrounded him in the hope to discover what else was going on. It was early morning now, the light streamed through the small windows around the prison to reveal the dull grey motif that was usually found in Communist design. He looked through the cages and saw yet more prisoners being escorted up near the entry to the level, the clanging, creaking sound of metal doors opening and closing accompanied the movement of the men, with some light banter from the guards, and some complaining from the prisoners, all echoed around the room making it sound like a greater flurry of activity.

'Friends of yours?' asked Raj's neighbouring cellmate, who stood before his pissing bucket and relieved himself.

'No,' answered Raj, without looking directly at the man. 'No one I know is on this level.'

'Doesn't matter anyway,' the man said. 'What can we do? This place is a fucking fortress.' He finished his business and pulled up his pants, wiped his hands on his shirt and came closer to Raj.

Two more guards entered the space at that moment and made their way to Raj's chamber. They threw in a new prisoner to share the cell, an older gentleman with a fully grey beard reaching up to his ears where the rest of his hair still maintained its darker brown colour. His face was cut, with a small amount of blood dripping from the corner of his left brow, while black soot and bruising adorned the rest of his face.

'Hey,' the new cellmate announced, touching the side of his forehead where the blood trickled.

'Hey,' Raj responded. 'You okay?'

'Yeah,' the older man answered. 'Just a cut.'

'Looks like they worked you over nicely.' The man from the neighbouring cell joined the conversation.

'Nah,' responded the new entrant. 'This is nothing. The last guy I shared a room with came back with missing fingers. There was fucking blood all over the place.'

Raj was taken aback; just when he thought he was as scared as he could get, a new level of fear entered his mind right then. He looked down and thought he could make out some brownish stains blotched randomly over the filthy floor, but in the morning light it was hard to tell and so he dismissed it as paranoia.

'Name's Djuro.' The bleeding newcomer reached out his hand to Raj. 'Djuro Loric.'

'Raj Krizic.' Raj shook the man's hand.

'I'm Pavao Sinac,' the adjoining prisoner shouted out. 'And that's Vuk Burilic.'

'Hi.' A prisoner across the corridor spoke for the first time, hands hanging between the cross bars while facing Raj's cell, a big bruise covering his left eye. 'Welcome to the Hotel Yugoslavia.'

All four men laughed aloud at the joke.

'How long have you boys been in?' Raj inquired.

'I got in yesterday,' answered Djuro.

'Same here,' Pavao added.

'Did you guys come together?' asked Raj, just as a two more guards returned another inmate into a cell a couple of doors down.

'I don't know about these two.' Djuro spoke first. 'But I came in with a few others, none that I can see on this floor. Although, they do keep chopping and changing things.'

'You're right,' Pavao continued. 'Vuk and I came in together yesterday morning. And it was only last night that they brought him into that cell.'

'They do it on purpose.' Vuk stepped back from the bars.

'What do you mean?' Raj asked.

'Well you're just full of questions,' Pavao interrupted. 'Aren't you?'

'Leave him, Pav,' Vuk consoled. 'He's young.'

'You're lucky you're young,' Djuro interjected. 'At my age, this might be my last stop.'

'Now, now.' Vuk sounded serious. 'Pav over there is no spring chicken.'

Again the men laughed out loud which relieved Raj as he was feeling a little green and vulnerable after spewing all those questions to these strange men in a prison.

'By the look of that eye' – Djuro broke the silence – 'looks like you were taken downstairs for a while too, Vuk.'

'Yeah, before they moved me here,' Vuk confirmed. 'Apparently I left a lot of unanswered questions.'

'There were a few questions I couldn't answer correctly, too.' Djuro smiled. 'And you know what happens when you answer incorrectly?'

'What were they asking you?' Raj couldn't contain himself.

'Usual stuff.' Djuro looked around. 'Who are you? Who do you know? Who knows you? Where are you going? Where have you been? You know... usual stuff.'

'You sound like you've been here before?' Vuk asked, which piqued Raj's interest.

'I've seen a few things, but I've been lucky,' Djuro continued. 'Most of mine have been minor discretions. But not this time, I think this time it will be the end of the line for me.'

Raj thought about the three men for a moment; he knew none of them and had no reason to trust them. He knew he had to be careful, but also wanted knowledge regarding the process and the expectations within the prison.

'Where are you from?' Raj inquired of Djuro.

'I'm from the north,' he said indifferently.

'Were you trying to get to Austria?' Raj continued as casually as he could.

'No,' Djuro answered. 'I'm from the north, near Banja Luka. But we got caught down south, trying to get into Greece.'

'Greece, huh?' Raj never really thought of Greece as an option.

'How about you, Raj?' Vuk asked. 'Where did you get caught?'

'A few of us were in Italy, in Trieste.'

'Been there, done that,' Pavao responded. 'Remember, Vuk?'

'Yep,' Vuk agreed. 'That whole town is a nest of spies and double-crossing fuckers.'

'Were you at San Sabba?' asked Raj, a little too eagerly.

'No,' Pavao responded. 'I can't remember the name exactly. Gesuilli or Gesuiti, or something. It was downtown. A real shithole too. Reminds me a bit of this place but without the bars.'

Raj looked toward the doors at the entrance to the floor and saw the rotation of prisoners continue with those returning looking worse for wear than those leaving, and it reminded him of Vuk's earlier comment.

'Why did you say they rotate the prisoners on purpose before, Vuk?' asked Raj.

'Pavao Sinac,' a guard suddenly called out as he and his comrade approached the cells while carrying a man beneath the arms, dragging his feet as they walked.

'Looks like it's my turn,' Pavao said despondently.

The guards tossed the injured prisoner into Pavao's cell and accompanied their newest victim away from the stench and darkness of the second floor.

'Where were you boys caught?' asked Djuro once the guards and Pavao disappeared.

'We weren't fleeing,' answered Vuk. 'Not this time. We got caught on a tobacco run near Konjic. I'm not sure why they brought us here, though; maybe it was just the closest joint.'

Memories came rushing back for Raj right then; planting, cutting, bundling and drying tobacco with his father and brothers, season after season, was a family tradition for as far back as he could remember. The overpowering smell of the sheds that kept the plants dry, to the stained yellow hands after working the shrub, all came flooding back to him. Even the crunch of the dry leaf had a peculiar sound that stuck with Raj. His father smoked a pipe his whole life, and Raj would even pack his dad's pipe when he was a little boy. Tobacco was a hot commodity and the black market was rife with customers who were happy to bypass the official Communist channels and avoid the taxation that was enforced upon the public.

'Off to Dalmatia?' Raj asked.

'Yeah, they pay well near the sea.'

Raj and Vuk both smiled knowingly.

'You both said you had been to Italy?' Djuro changed the subject.

'It was a couple years ago for us,' Vuk responded. 'I'm not in a hurry to go back.'

'Trieste, was it, Raj?' Djuro continued, turning his back to Vuk.

'Yes.' Raj moved to sit down again, he still felt tired and the adrenaline of the morning action was wearing away.

'I've never been,' Djuro prodded. 'Tell me about it.'

Raj looked over to Vuk and noticed the man nodded ever slightly in a negative manner. Raj wasn't sure if he saw correctly as it was still quite dark in the prison even with the morning light growing stronger.

'Not much to tell, really.' Raj played it cool and chose his words carefully. 'What do you want to know?'

'Oh, I don't know.' Djuro walked over to the pissing bucket and undid his pants. 'We have time. Tell me about Italy.'

'It was nice,' Raj began, trying to be as aloof as possible. 'I was in the town for a night then got picked up and sent to the detention centre in San Sabba.'

'Nice,' Djuro said. 'The weather must have been lovely?'

'Indeed, it was. I just wish we had time for a swim and time at the beach.'

'So, you weren't alone?'

'No.' Raj was feeling a little uncomfortable now, as the questions started flowing quite liberally. 'A friend was with me.'

'Is your friend okay? Did he make it out?'

'Yes, yes,' Raj added. 'Well, at least he was fine the last time I saw him. He's in here somewhere.'

'So, you said you stayed at the tavern in Trieste?' Djuro pulled up his pants and walked to front of the cell again.

'Now look who's asking a thousand questions,' Vuk interrupted.

'Just passing time, friend,' Djuro stated, with his back to Raj now. 'If you don't want to talk, then that's fine with me too, Raj.'

'It's okay.' Raj didn't want to seem to secretive either. 'I'm just tired. I haven't slept properly for a few days.'

'I understand,' Djuro said. 'It's just that if I ever do get out of here, Italy might be the place to try next. Maybe you can give me a few pointers.'

'Sure,' Raj said. 'But we got lucky, too.'

'Of course,' Djuro agreed. 'Luck always plays a great part.'

'You don't know the half of it,' Raj stated, remembering the misadventures he and Tomo shared.

'So did you go by boat or land?' Djuro continued his inquiry.

'A bit of both, actually.' Raj smiled.

'Really?'

'When I left home,' Raj declared, 'I said I would make it out by any means necessary and that's what it took.'

'That sounds very courageous for one so young,' Djuro admitted. 'Did you take off from Split?'

'Yes.' Raj yawned, the fatigue creeping up on him. 'We boarded a speed boat, and paid top dollar. We got dropped off a few miles north of Rijeka and snuck our way inland.'

'Do you remember the speed boat operator?' Djuro asked.

'He didn't give his name.' Raj was lying but kept cool while speaking. 'But the boat was called the Red Whore. The name was what drew us to it.'

A couple of guards entered the room in that moment and Djuro immediately called out to them, 'This bucket is disgusting. Come and change it or I'll pour it all over you.'

Without a word, the two guards walked up to the cell and opened the door, then slapped Djuro across the face before taking him by the neck and dragging him off towards the exit. They left the bucket behind.

'You talk too much,' Vuk said once a few moments passed.

'Relax.' Raj was still seated. 'I didn't say anything.'

'Earlier, you asked why they rotate prisoners on purpose,' Vuk reminded Raj. 'It's like a shell game. They can move their spies among us and find out far more than they could through violence. And I think you just got played.'

'I knew he was playing me,' Raj announced, then stood up and walked toward the cell door to face Vuk.

'Did you?'

'Yeah,' Raj continued. 'He said something about a tavern and I knew he was fishing because I mentioned nothing about the place we stayed. All the talk about the speed boat was bullshit. I just wasn't sure if you and Pavao were planted as well. When you sent me that little signal, I made up my mind.'

'Great.' Vuk sounded relieved. 'You saw that. I was trying to be discreet. I was pretty sure you weren't in with them.'

'What makes you so sure?' asked Raj.

'You're far too green to be a spy for the commies.' Vuk smiled.

Once more, the door to the level opened and a couple of guards came walking in with another prisoner. This one wasn't beaten up too badly but was limping and struggling to keep up with the marching guards. The three men walked the whole block and made their way to Raj's cell at the far end of the room.

'Raj Krizic,' the guards announced as the cell door was opened.

CHAPTER 21

With one guard ahead and one guard behind, Raj was marched down to the lower levels of the prison. The concrete stairs became even colder after the ground floor was passed, with the moisture in the air growing and adding to the chill. The lighting was as sparse as the upper decks and the ever-present darkness continued, but now, without any windows at all, this part of the prison made the time of day impossible to deduce. *At least the dank atmosphere smelled better than the toilet buckets upstairs,* Raj thought, a small price to pay for the drop in temperature.

On the second floor below ground, the guards turned into another poorly lit, but wider, hallway that was painted grey and had four closed doors on each side with bench seats between them. Another door was present at the far wall that ended the corridor, with two more armed soldiers standing watch. Above them, a picture of Marshall Tito hung on the wall, as did the Yugoslav flag. Raj was moved to the first door on the right and led in. Inside the windowless room, the grey motif continued, and all that was located within were two wooden chairs and a steel table, all of which were bolted to the floor. Across the table, a thin steel beam was welded, with handcuffs already placed in wait. Once Raj had sat down, the guards affixed his left wrist to the cuff and told him to wait.

A few moments later, a man entered the room dressed in simple military greens without the bulk or armament of the previous guards that Raj had dealt with. This man was wiry, balding slightly at the forehead and wore small round spectacles that barely covered his eyes. He walked with a straight posture and a purposeful gait and looked well-presented and serious about his work. In his hands he carried a portfolio and a pen that he placed on the table before sitting down. He then opened his folder and read from a piece of paper before looking directly into Raj's eyes and smiling.

'Raj?' the man asked.

'Yes, sir.' Raj had no idea what to expect next.

'It's an Orthodox name, isn't it?'

Raj had sometimes been teased by his school friends for his name. He knew it wasn't a popular given name and he also knew the Christians of the Orthodox faith had used it far more often than the Catholics, but his father explained they had a great uncle in the family with that name and so it was the name his parents had selected.

'Yes, sir.' Raj thought it best to say little and agree a lot.

'Are you Serbian Orthodox?'

'No, sir.'

'Macedonian Orthodox?'

'No, sir.' Raj now felt like he was leading his interrogator on, so he cut to the chase. 'I'm Roman Catholic.'

'Perhaps your parents were confused.' A little smiled crept across the stern officer's face. 'It says you're from near Mostar. Is that correct?'

'Yes, sir.'

'Why would they take the name of their sworn enemies? That would be a vile thing to do to a child.'

'I don't know, sir,' Raj said to buy some time then quickly added a lie, 'My father mentioned something about a friendly Serb that helped our family after the Great War, during the time of a plague... or something. He said he was forever indebted to him. It was before my time, sir.'

This caused the man a moment to pause; he put his papers down and looked at Raj with steely eyes, reading every aspect of his face. Raj looked back curtly but then looked away like he saw many animals do that feared predators in the wild.

'Your father sounds like an honourable man,' the officer began again, relaxing in his seat.

'Yes, sir,' Raj replied.

'My job here in the army is a difficult one. Do you know what my job is, Raj?'

Torturer? Tormentor? Violent Abuser? were the first three that came to Raj's mind, but he instead just honestly asked, 'Interrogator?'

'Ha.' The man laughed out loud. 'I do like you, Raj, I do. And I like your father even more.'

'Yes, sir.'

'My job can be given many names, but at the heart of it, my job is to find out if people are telling the truth, Raj, and in all my considerable time in the army, I have yet to meet a Croat Catholic to admit taking a Serb Orthodox name just out of a sense of honour.'

'Yes, sir.'

'In fact, I have beaten people to a pulpy mess.' He shook his fist animatedly. 'And I mean, really inflicted bodily harm on them, did some brutal things...' His mind seemed to drift off in a moment of darkness, then returned. '...And yet these people wouldn't allow their family names to be spoiled. Even when I knew what the truth was, and even when *they* knew that I knew, they still would not admit to a particular scandal or infamy committed.'

Raj took a deep breath. He knew now he faced a real psychopath and was worried that the happy demeanour presented by the man was simply the calm before the storm.

'Yet, here you are,' the interrogator continued playfully, 'readily confessing to a family betraying its culture because of a deed done close to a generation ago.'

'Yes, sir.'

'I know Croats that would rather die than take the name of a Serb. And I know Serbs that would rather die than be seen in the presence of a Croat.'

'Me too,' Raj added cautiously.

'Ha.' The officer laughed again. 'I should make you my court jester, that's how much you made me laugh today.'

'Yes, sir.'

'So, I think you are telling me the truth, Raj. And I think you are an honourable man, as is your father.'

'Thank you, sir.' Raj felt a little relief, even though he had probably just told the biggest lie in his short life.

'The only question now is.' The officer paused as he took his glasses off and reached for a handkerchief to clean them. 'Is your brother Krizan also an honourable man?'

Raj took a deep breath in that moment of surprise, his blood started pumping quickly, making his heart pound hard in his chest as he tried to hide the nerves that felt like they were strangling him.

'You see,' the officer continued ever so casually, 'your last name shows up in my papers far more often than your first. Now... I get it. You ran to avoid the draft. Fair enough. If we killed every youngster that fled the call of duty we'd have a population full of women, children and retards. I know the military isn't for everyone and most leave after their minimum service.'

Raj kept silent and just listened, trying to settle himself internally.

'So, we can fix that. You'll do your time in the army, maybe a bit longer, or some time in the pen, or a shitty post on top of a freezing mountain for a year... whatever. That's beyond my rank.' He tapped the portfolio before him. 'But your brother is a different proposition. Do you follow?'

'I'm not sure, sir.' Raj tried to sound timid but spoke the truth this time. 'I haven't seen Kriz in over a year.'

'Really? Are you absolutely sure?'

'Yes, I'm sure.'

'Remember, young man.' The officer gave a warning. 'Until now I have believed everything you have said.'

'I swear it.' Raj stood his ground. 'I haven't seen my brother in ages.'

'So, this report that states he helped you cross the border is false?'

'Report?' Raj was genuinely perplexed. 'What report?'

'I have two reports actually.' The man sat forward again and pulled out two pieces of paper, holding one in each hand before Raj's face. 'One says that your brother met you along the coast near Rijeka and smuggled you to the west. The other one says you paid for a speed boat called...' He put his glasses back on to read the printed word. '"The Red Whore", which took you north toward Trieste.'

Raj knew where the second report came from, that part was easy. But why was Krizan implicated in his movement to Italy when they never even crossed paths? Raj knew the Communists kept detailed files on everyone, particularly those in the priesthood, so information regarding his brother would have been easily accessed. But the movement of information around the country was still quite slow and the fact that Raj had only arrived the night previously meant someone who knew about his brother talked, or his brother's file was on hand because he had been a captive himself at this particular base. Raj decided to play dumb and deny all the accusations.

'I haven't lied to you yet,' Raj lied once more. 'and I'm not going to lie to you now. Both of those reports are false.'

'Both? Really?' There was a sarcasm growing in the interrogator's tone.

'Yes,' Raj clarified. 'I haven't seen my brother, like I said, a few times already. And where would I get the money to pay for a speed boat?'

'Indeed,' the officer agreed with a smile. 'We really need to train our moles better. Djuro gets spotted more often than not these days, but he is persistent. Maybe he's just getting old.'

Raj said nothing for a moment and just watched the officer looking over the paper work.

'Djuro, I get,' the man continued. 'You feed him some bullshit, which gets to me and you just waste my time. But why would Tomo lie?'

Raj went cold. It seemed the officer was playing with a full deck and calling Raj's bluffs. What had Tomo been saying? What crazy ideas were spewing from that idiot's mouth under the pressure of interrogation? The only reason Tomo would involve Kriz was to save his own backside, of that Raj was sure. Then Raj thought that perhaps it was the officer himself that was bluffing; sure, he knew that Tomo was delivered in the same group from Italy, and maybe he even talked to Tomo and dropped a few names to get a reaction, but maybe Tomo mentioned nothing about Kriz and the officer was just prodding in the hope of getting lucky without resorting to violence.

'Tomo?' Raj decided to call the bluff. 'Tomo would lie to his own mother if it was to save himself. Just look at his academic record. Look at his employment record. Hell, I reckon he might even have a criminal record.'

'So you deny travelling with Tomo?'

'No.' Raj had to tread carefully between the truth and the lies lest he forget where his feet stepped. 'I travelled with Tomo, that's true. I'll even admit looking for Kriz. Like I said, it's been a long time and I love my brother. But I never found him. My last hope was in Trieste, but nothing came of it. I wish I had found him. I could let my parents know he was safe. My poor mother always worries about him. As far as I know, he might even be dead.'

Raj looked down for dramatic effect, but the tears that rolled down his eyes were heartfelt and as real as could be. The thought that Kriz had left the earth was a real possibility; alone and away from those that cared for him. Raj felt saddened in that moment of truth regardless of what the officer before him thought of his story.

'Let me give you some advice, Raj,' the officer began again.

'Yes, sir.'

'You are going to come across some people worse than me,' he stated. 'Much worse. They will ask things and state things and expect things. The best thing you can say is "I don't know". Understand?'

'Yes, sir.'

'Not "yes, sir", but...' The officer raised an eyebrow awaiting Raj to finish his sentence.

'I don't know,' Raj complied.

'That's better.' He winked at Raj. 'You'll be fine. Nothing to worry about.'

'What happens from here?' Raj wiped his eyes with his free hand. 'Do I get to go home?'

'Ha!' The interrogator seemed to be having a great time in that room. 'You are really making me laugh now.'

'What do you mean?'

'You fled the country, young man. Do you think that will simply be forgotten because you spoke well?' The officer stood and straightened his paperwork. 'No, you will be dealt with shortly. This is just preliminary. You'll be sent to a panel shortly.'

'A panel?'

'Yes.' The official organised his papers as he spoke. 'To be sentenced. This place isn't a long-term refuge, but more of a remand centre. You'll spend some time locked up somewhere more established, I imagine, but again, beyond my rank and interest. Good day to you.'

With that, the interrogator walked out of the room. The guards returned and took Raj out into the corridor again and sat him on a bench. Hours passed before the door at the end of the hall finally opened and another inmate was led out. A despondent look covered the man's face as he made eye contact with Raj. After a few more minutes, an older officer appeared and called Raj into the chamber.

The soldiers brought Raj into a meagre court room with one long table at the end, one small table to the side and another a few feet away from the entry. A tall bookshelf and cabinet also stood in the far corner next to a second door to the room. Three men sat at the long table, dressed in army greens complete with badges of honour on their lapels and shoulders. A female officer sat to their side at the smaller table, with pencil and paper in hand. Yugoslav regalia covered the walls and cabinet and the lighting in the room was better than any he had seen elsewhere in the building.

'Raj Krizic,' the officer in the centre of the three asked.

'Yes, sir,' answered Raj, still standing and handcuffed by the small table.

'Sit,' the man ordered, his Croatian tone clear and concise. 'You come to us from Italy where we found you escaping not only your country but your duty. Do you deny this?'

Raj thought about his earlier interview, but decided to answer truthfully. 'No.'

'Let it be known' – the officer looked to the stenographer – 'that what you say in this room will determine not only your fate, but the fate of others too. Do you understand?'

'I don't know.' This time Raj thought it might be useful to play the ignorant card.

'It's pretty clear,' the lead attendant continued, 'you have friends and family that are just as culpable as you. If you comply, you can be certain of a just trial.'

Raj kept quiet, not wanting to agitate his accuser.

'You are a poor farm boy from near Mostar,' the man continued quite condescendingly. 'Yet you made it all the way to Italy. We are of the opinion you had others aiding you in your quest and this trial will determine the exact people involved.'

Raj remained silent but had a feeling where this conversation was heading.

'We have undeniable proof that your brother, one Krizan Krizic, was not only involved with your preparation to escape, but with the execution.'

Raj still remained quiet, as there was no real question being posed.

'Young man.' The officer to the left of the table spoke for the first time; his tone was not as assertive as the accuser in the middle. 'What say you to these accusations?'

'I don't know,' Raj answered, trying to sound as innocent as possible.

'You don't know what?' the man in the middle asked frustratingly.

'I don't know about anything about my brother,' Raj proclaimed. 'I went to Italy on my own and met others there. Apart from that, I don't know anything else, sir.'

'Remember,' the officer on the right chimed in this time. He was relatively younger than the other two at the table and sounded cocksure as he spoke. 'We know exactly what happened. You can't lie to us. Our files are complete and we really don't need anything from you.'

He looked to his brethren behind the table. 'In fact, this process is pointless as we have enough on you to throw you in jail for a long time. I call that we adjourn and move on to the next perpetrator.'

'Now, now, captain,' the man on the left interjected. 'Let it not be said that Tito's justice system is unreasonable. This young man should be given a chance to explain himself. We all make mistakes when we are younger and now there is an opportunity to make some corrections. What say you, Raj, do you think you can find redemption for your crimes?'

'I don't know.'

The man on the left smiled gently then added, 'It might be better to put it this way; do you *want* redemption for your crimes?'

'I understand,' Raj answered. 'I will do the prison time assigned to me. I am sorry for fleeing the country and promise not to do it ever again.'

The man on the left sat back in his chair and looked a little disappointed.

'You can save yourself some prison time,' the brusque officer in the middle spoke again. 'But not only that, you can save your accomplices and your family some heartache too. All you need to do is speak freely about the role your brother played in your movement across the country. Can you give us some details of your brother's whereabouts?'

'I don't know where my brother is,' Raj answered. 'I haven't seen him in months.'

'You don't seem to know much of anything,' the captain said.

Then the three officers took a minute to confer quietly with each other before the middle man gave their verdict.

'Stand up,' he announced. 'Raj Krizic, you are found guilty of fleeing Yugoslavia and abandoning your responsibilities to your country by avoiding military service. On the charge of aiding a suspected traitor within the border of Yugoslavia, you are also found guilty. On the charge of influencing accomplices and conspiracy to commit treason, you are also found guilty.'

Raj was a little shocked at the last two charges, as nothing was mentioned regarding espionage and conspiracies throughout this mock trial. It seemed the officers were just throwing anything at Raj in the hope to scare him into confessing against his brother.

'You are convicted to three years in prison,' the officer continued, 'after which you will serve two years of your military service in the Yugoslavian Army. Take him away.'

Three years? Raj thought as the soldiers delivered him out of the court room. It seemed like an eternity ahead of him. He would be in his mid-twenties by the time he finished his jail time and military training and that's only if everything went well. His anger grew as he walked, and he gained a new level of understanding as to why his father hated the Communists so much; their blatant disregard for the truth affected all who stood in the way of their ideologies, and with the army under their command, there was no way for any independent thinkers to offer alternative opinions to life without being brutally punished for it.

The soldiers marched Raj back upstairs, but this time to the first floor and a different cell. The smell was still the same as was the lighting, although the mid-morning sun shone through the slits in the walls, so the floor seemed a little brighter and the stains a little worse. Raj was placed alone in a cell near the far end of the level. All sides around him held prisoners and they all perked up at the newcomer in their presence.

'Hey.' Raj's neighbour to the right spoke first.

'Hey,' Raj responded courteously but was in no mood for a conversation.

'You just get in?'

'No,' Raj continued. 'Came in late last night.'

'So, where have you been?' The neighbour to the left suddenly joined the discussion. The man's face was damaged, beaten all over with multiple cuts creating a scary mess to look at.

'Downstairs,' Raj answered, trying not to stare.

'Downstairs?' At first the beat-up man sounded surprised, his tone then turned angry. 'Then why doesn't your fucking face look like mine?'

'He's a stooge,' the inmate across the way announced, who himself had a few blemishes to show. 'No fucking way anyone comes from downstairs looking like that. No fucking way!'

'Yeah, I agree, Sim,' the man to the right chimed in again. 'Fucking commies.'

'I'm not a fucking stooge,' Raj bit back, his emotions turning even more sour at the accusation. 'Fuck you. Maybe you're the fucking stooge.'

'Ooh,' the beat-up inmate retorted ironically. 'You hear that, Ivan? Maybe you're the stooge.'

'My old man died fighting these pricks,' Ivan responded. 'No one calls me a fucking stooge.'

'Yeah,' the beat-up man continued. 'This youngster's got some balls. But so did the last spy that came in.'

Raj knew the cage kept him safe and wasn't in the mood for a hazing. He also knew if he didn't stand up for himself initially, these creeps would walk all over him while he was surrounded by them. It was one thing to be lambasted by the kangaroo court, but Raj was not going to take abuse from these common thugs.

'Maybe you're the stooge?' He now accused the beat-up man.

'Look at my face, dickhead. Do I look like a stooge to you?'

'You look like an ugly son of a bitch.' Raj let loose. 'Maybe you're dumb enough to let them beat you up as part of the plan.'

The inmate smashed his hands against the bars that separated him and Raj, causing a ringing echo throughout the block. The other two neighbours burst out laughing at Raj's comment but then restrained themselves when they saw how upset their beaten companion was.

'I'm going to fuck your pretty little face up too,' the inmate said. 'You hear me?'

'I hear you, Ugly,' Raj answered, then dropped his pants and relieved himself while the surrounding inmates all cursed and jeered at him.

Suddenly, two new guards appeared with another prisoner. This man held onto his right side while wincing with every step. The block went quiet and watched the men pass until they reached Raj's cell. Before the sentries strode off, the beaten inmate called to one of them and the two spoke at a whisper between the bars, quickly exchanging words in a cordial, yet devious, manner.

'How are you going?' Raj asked his new cell mate as the chatter within the cell block returned.

'I'm fine,' the newcomer stated. 'But my fucking ribs are killing me.'

'I'm Raj.'

'Stevo,' said the man and they shook hands. 'What was all that about?'

'Not sure,' Raj answered. 'But I reckon ugly over there has some friends in high places.'

'You should watch your fucking mouth.' Raj's neighbour could hear everything. 'I fucked up the last stooge in here.'

'Your face tells a different story.' Raj couldn't help himself, and smiled at the man enraging him yet further.

'You'll fucking see.' The threat was venomous.

'Tell me this,' Raj asked very loudly for the whole floor to hear. 'How is it that you can chat so easily with the guards? Do you have their ear?'

This caused the entire block to hush immediately and a sense of anticipation overwhelmed the space. Raj knew he needed to create doubt in the other inmates which would enhance division, and he had to stand his ground by showing no fear, regardless of the inmate's connections. Raj hoped his words would at least keep the other prisoners off his back and allow him to work out his differences with the injured man alone. He also knew his new nemesis was wounded quite badly, so if there was any kind of confrontation, the odds were slightly in Raj's favour.

'Don't worry, stooge,' the beaten convict asserted. 'You'll see.'

Another hour or so passed before a couple more heavily armed soldiers entered the space and announced lunch. One by one, each compartment was opened, and each inmate was ordered to remain at the rear of their cells. A third soldier then entered the corridor with a trolley of food and dropped a plate of slop at the base of every door.

'I don't know what's worse,' Raj said while carrying Stevo's plate toward him. 'The food or the toilet bucket.'

'Don't make me laugh.' Stevo sat and still held his side and even found breathing quite difficult, but his anguished chuckle stopped when he saw the contents of his plate. 'Do they actually consider this food?'

'Shut it.' The soldiers remained within the block while the prisoners ate. One of them reprimanded Raj and Stevo. 'You have five minutes to eat.'

Raj ate a little but couldn't really stomach much of the gruel. He offered his leftovers to Stevo who politely declined. They left their plates at the foot of the door and the soldiers reversed their process, collected the plates and left the room. Strangely though, even the usual guards at the entry followed the kitchen regiment. More strangely still, the doors to the cells remained open allowing the prisoners free reign within the cell block. Raj thought this oversight was quite odd as up till now the soldiers within the base were extremely efficient and attentive. Then he remembered the earlier whispered conversation between his neighbouring inmate and the guard, and so he immediately headed toward the steel bucket in the corner of his cell.

'Move to the other corner,' Raj instructed Stevo.

'What's going on?' asked Stevo as he shuffled over.

'Come on, boys.' The battered man now stood at Raj's door, smiling for a change. 'Let's teach this stooge some fucking manners.'

Raj took a moment and quickly looked around. The prisoners Sim and Ivan started making their way toward their friend, but the rest of the inmates just looked on sheepishly from their opened cells. Raj noticed for the first time that Ivan limped as he approached, and also remembered what his interrogator had said earlier regarding this base being a short-term facility. This meant that the injuries that most of these inmates suffered must have been fresh and probably still hurt just as much as poor Stevo's ribs.

'Take it easy boys.' Raj brought time as his left foot felt for the toilet bucket beneath him. 'I'm no fucking stooge.'

'I don't give a fuck.' The battered man had made up his mind and aggressively lurched forward to attack.

Raj immediately grabbed the steel bucket and threw it at his adversary. The surprise pitch caught the aggressor off-guard which gave him little time to move. The bucket flew straight at the man's face, smashing him in the left cheek as he attempted to duck to the right. In that moment Raj was grateful the guards didn't clean out the toilets very often as there was a bit of weight to the metal container. The attacking man fell from both the blow and the surprise, as the bucket ricocheted beyond him and toward his allies. Sim was first to the door and ducked a little, but the bucket's trajectory had changed after hitting the first man and now crashed against the bars that made up the cell door's frame, which in turn shook most of the putrid contents from within, causing a brown spray that made many of the by standing inmates move back from their vantage points.

Sim and Ivan were drenched in piss and faeces and tried to wipe away the filth before continuing the attack. Raj wasted no more time and launched a counter attack by stepping up to the downed assailant and kicking him as hard as he could into the guts. The man beneath him groaned at the blow, then turned but found himself rolling in the contents of the portable latrine, which in turn caused him to roll back in disgust and opened him up to another kick from Raj. The man groaned again, but this time he pulled his arms and legs in as a defensive mechanism rather than slipping back into the filth that covered the entrance to the cell. Raj kicked one more time before Sim approached, although, he was closer than Raj had presumed and when the inmate's fist hit Raj's face, the surprise punch was harder than Raj expected. Raj then jumped at Sim and in the process pushed him into Ivan who had just entered the cell too. All three men slipped and tumbled into the faecal covered floor when a gunshot suddenly rang out.

'Up!' came the cry. 'All of you. Up! Now!'

A soldier stood before them and two more behind him. All three had their pistols out and looked ominous in camouflage green with weapons at the ready. Raj stood up first and felt a hand grab him from the top of the head, ripping at his hair as a method of dragging him from the cell block. Raj struggled to keep up with the soldier who seemed determined to scalp him without a blade. They passed a couple more soldiers who were hurrying up the stairs as they moved down and straight past the foyer into the sunlit afternoon. There, the soldier utilised some kind of Judo move to flip Raj over effortlessly, while still holding firmly onto his hair, bringing him down onto his back into the gravel and rock that made up the walkway to the front of the jail.

Raj squinted at the daylight and put a hand slowly to the top of his head where he felt a wet and sticky substance that stung as he touched it. His head bled from where the soldier tore away chunks of hair while the rest of him was covered in filth from the bucket and the floor. His right eye was sore too; the punch Sim delivered now left a sensitive spot around the socket that drew blood to it and a deep, fast pounding that mirrored his heartbeat. The throw caused a little vertigo too, so he tried to get up to a seating position when a kick smashed him in the chest and returned him to his back. He lay there staring at the sky, took a deep breath and simply accepted his fate.

Raj knew he had gotten lucky with his interrogator earlier on, leaving the meeting without so much as a scratch while everyone else had returned busted in some way or another. In fact, the whole movement to Italy seemed like a lucky dream in that moment on the ground, but now, his luck had clearly run out and with the next five years of his life accounted for, he hoped his anger hadn't just added extra time to his sentence. It also seemed the luck of his assailants had run out too, as a moment later they were violently dropped right beside him. The four of them lay helplessly staring up at the blue sky, smelling like excrement and caressing their injuries while waiting for their reprimand.

CHAPTER 22

It wasn't long before a higher-ranking officer appeared.

'Get them cleaned up,' he shouted. 'They're not getting in my bus smelling like that.'

The four men were marched away from the prison and into an open area that looked to be a training vicinity. A large quadrangle space awaited them beyond the prison car park and outlying buildings. It was mostly just flat dirt, rock and grass with a few manmade structures placed around it. A very high, wooden steeple was located in one corner, complete with ropes on both sides. Barbed wire littered another area, with muddy trenches beneath and large tyres surrounding. There were rope ladders attached to the roofs and windows of the buildings at the boundary and a couple of dummy vehicles parked near the walls. A small, above ground pool was also located on another side of the yard, with a tiled wall of shower heads and taps beyond it.

Raj felt a sense of relief when the four of them were marched toward the showers. His last wash and shave had been at Trieste a couple of days earlier, so he knew he was overdue for a good cleanse and, although under normal circumstances he could probably last another day, the stench of the toilet sludge really propelled his need to bathe. He had showered in front of others before, so there was no shame in that, and he was pretty sure the armed soldiers that corralled them would not allow fighting to break out. He just hoped they had soap and warm water but knew that might be stretching his expectations a little far. All Raj's hopes were dashed once a smiling soldier appeared carrying a hose that looked like a giant, red python.

'Strip off,' the commander ordered once the four men stood at the showers. 'Lieutenant, begin the clean!'

Without waiting, the soldier obeyed the order, braced himself and released the liquid. As Raj scrambled to remove his shirt he was hit flush in the chest with a force that knocked him backward beneath the showers. He ignored the buttons and ripped off the fabric, aware that this would be the last time he wore that particular top. He managed to lose his pants, socks and shoes while the hose was focused on the other inmates. When the soldier pointed his way again, he was ready. This time it hit him in the face, so he turned to try to actually get a wash and not just a pummelling. As he turned, a part of the spray touched the top of his head which made him wince at the pain. Across his shoulder, the water was stained red as his wounded scalp had not yet congealed.

The water stopped unexpectedly, and two new soldiers appeared wearing plastic overalls, gloves and masks. They held canisters in their hands and proceeded to douse the inmates with some kind of white powder. Raj coughed and rubbed at his stinging eyes, as did the other prisoners, when the hose suddenly came flooding back once more. Raj imagined the powder had something to do with mites, but he also knew it must have been a powerful chemical for the soldiers to be so well covered when applying it. He really tried to wash all of it off before they ended the clean. The hose was then turned to Raj's initial assailant, who covered his broken face and testicles from the force and looked quite dismayed at the whole process. Blood and powder covered the man's naked body making his appearance look like a dishevelled and undignified mess. Raj felt a little sorry for the man just then and wondered whether much of this was his own fault for having a smart mouth and misreading the situation within the prison.

Within ten minutes the unruly saturation was over. The soldiers marched the naked and drenched prisoners away from the wet area and gave them towels and clean overalls and a minute to prepare. They then moved quickly between the buildings, marching handcuffed and bare footed toward the entrance to the base, where a bus, from the night before, waited. The bus's motor was running, and a few other men were already seated when the four freshly cleaned convicts boarded.

Raj sat alone near the back of the bus, while his three attackers were spread around the vehicle. Sim was closest to him, but they never spoke nor even made eye contact. Everyone's hands were bound and only two soldiers secured the vehicle, which was plenty because there were only ten convicts seated for the journey. As far as Raj could tell, they headed north as the sun moved overhead. They left the main road after about half an hour and traversed mainly rocky farm roads for the remainder of the trip. It all felt uphill in terms of terrain, with the big diesel motor always revving on high, disturbing the otherwise serene landscape that surrounded them. It became cooler too as they ascended, and Raj noticed that the mountains in the distance were getting a little bit closer.

It wasn't much longer before they came to a corner clearing, where a barbed wired fence secured one side of empty grassland that looked to span roughly half a mile. Beyond the grass, a wooded area emerged, but it was in the distance and Raj couldn't really make out much of the detail. As the bus continued to chug along, Raj saw crude brick battlements casting shadows every hundred metres along the barbed barrier, each with an armed guard at the top, silently watching over the grassland and forest within.

They continued along the rocky road, following the fence line for a few more kilometres until finally, they stopped at a patrolled gate with a large steel sign that read "Yugoslav Labour Camp Number 23", complete with Marshall Tito's face next to the customary red star. Raj's heart sank in that moment as he had now reached a new low. If his parents knew of his predicament, they would be both ashamed and afraid, and his neighbours would undoubtedly whisper rumours regarding his unsuccessful antics and cast blame on him for bringing the watchful eye of the authorities upon them. The bus idled a while as the paper work was checked and the prison guards even boarded the bus to do a head count. A few minutes later, the gate opened and let them into the compound.

Once they passed the grassland, they entered the shady woodland which continued for an extra kilometre or so. Raj could see tree stumps and felled logs within the woods. Another gated fence appeared after the forested area thinned out, and more guards boarded the bus and checked the paperwork once more. The sun was lowering in the western sky by the time Raj had stepped off the bus and his stomach started to growl. His hunger had grown over the journey and he just hoped for a better meal than the last one he had.

Like most hopes within Yugoslavia, the wish for a decent meal disappeared when he saw his new surroundings; the centrepiece was a dirty looking concrete dwelling that clearly held the majority of the prisoners because it was very large and there were bars on the small windows that dotted the walls. It was surrounded by yet another fence and yet more security guards, this time with leashed dogs as an accompaniment. There were a few other smaller dwellings dotted around the compound, also made of concrete and also well-guarded. The khaki and camouflage greens were replaced by black uniforms and there seemed to be more guards than inmates at this facility. It was clear to Raj that they were being handed over to a different department as this was no longer a military establishment; what wasn't yet clear was whether this place was better or worse.

'My name is Franjo Ludovski,' said the short man, in what Raj estimated to be a mix of Macedonian and Serbian. He stood in front of the handcuffed newcomers with a pipe that kept moving from his hand to his mouth as he spoke and smoked at the same time. 'I am the warden at Number Twenty-Three. Some of you are here for shorter and some for longer. If you want to stay even longer, we can arrange that.' He smiled and puffed between sentences. 'We have been authorised by Marshall Tito himself to shoot onsite, so, please, feel free to attempt escape.'

A few of the guards chuckled with the warden, and as the bus drove away with the soldiers aboard, a sinister look crept across most of the faces of the armed men that now held responsibility over the prisoners.

'You will learn your roster,' the warden continued, 'and you will work where required. Those who work, eat well, those who make trouble, don't. Any questions?' And without waiting for a response the short man turned away in a puff of smoke.

A subordinate stepped up with a folder in his hands and started calling names and directing the process. Most of the captives were sorted and led off to the large prison, but Raj and two other young men were led to a different area, away from the main jail and closer to the boundary of the complex.

'Why aren't we going with them?' one of the prisoners asked, but the answer given came from the butt of a guard's rifle that smashed into the side of the inmate's head, causing him to fall.

'Get up!' the lead sentry called, but the convict struggled to his feet.

Raj thought about helping the rising man but disregarded the compassion and steeled himself in an attempt to get used to his new life and perhaps minimise his time spent in the camp.

'Doric!' the lead guard called and one of the prison officers at the rear of their little column came forth holding tight the reins of a german shepherd that growled at the prospect of sinking its teeth into a prisoner.

'Okay, okay.' The downed man suddenly found inspiration and stood back in line, rubbing at the side of his cranium.

The prisoners reached another gate with more guards and more dogs that secured a long white building beyond them. It was a single storey dwelling, built relatively low, with no windows on the side that Raj faced. Once beyond the fence, the men were stopped before a small wooden entry door set to the right of the façade that led inside the rectangular structure.

'A special place for special men,' the leading officer stated, tapping his folder as his accompanying guards giggled. 'You asked why you are being taken away from the rest, and that is the reason. You're special. You will spend some time on your own, just to help you remember your love of Yugoslavia and to curtail your treasonous desires for foreign lands.'

The wooden door opened and Raj was marched into the prison first. It was very dark within and much cooler than on the outside. There was no artificial light in the dwelling and Raj knew it would be close to pitch black once the entry was closed. It felt like the building was made of stone because, not only did the temperature drop, but the sound was suddenly different. All external noises disappeared upon entry and Raj noticed his breathing and footsteps sounding far louder than before. The right side of the interior was the windowless wall that Raj had seen from the outside and the left was also a wall but broken up by solid doors every few metres. His eyes adjusted as he walked on and he noticed some light passing through small open slits in the doors to his left. Raj was taken to the very last door and one guard opened it while the other unbound his hands and pushed him into his new home.

'What's with the fucking buckets?' Raj asked himself once the cell door was closed. He could see that the military and civic prisons both liked the same type of waste management system, but Raj was thankful that at least this bucket was empty so the smell in the cubicle wasn't that bad. In fact, the cell looked very clean indeed, not that there was much that could be dirty in such a sparse environment. Still, there were no marks on the floor, no stains on the wall and as far as Raj could see, not even a speck of dust in the air. He did notice the source of light in the room was a small slit in the stone wall opposite the door, which was better than absolute darkness, he thought.

There was no bed in the space, nor tap or sink, but he did find an old blanket scrunched in the corner. Unlike the cell itself, it looked and smelled as though it hadn't been cleaned in a long while. The faint sound of the other cell doors closing could be heard in the next few moments, but apart from that, not much else was making a sound in the building. The light was fading too, as now the sun was well and truly on its way down and Raj was quite sure that starlight alone would not be enough to penetrate the small slit in the wall to illuminate the evening.

It cooled quickly and considerably once the sun had completely vanished for the day. All Raj could do was sit on the black stone floor in the black stone cell and ponder his fate. How long would he be in solitary confinement? What other punishments could be waiting? What kind of labour was done here? All the questions bounced around in his head as he stared with heavy eyes into the darkness and gradually became more tired. As time passed he became colder and hungrier but there was no sign of dinner and sleep just would not come. Summer was ending, but at this altitude, and with these walls, the coastal warmth he experienced for the past few weeks was already long gone.

Raj couldn't do much about his hunger, but he could at least try to keep warm, so, in desperation, he reached for the dirty blanket. It smelled like an old sick dog, but it offered him an extra layer which was all that mattered at that moment. He tucked his left arm under his head and threw the torn woollen cover over himself and waited uncomfortably for sleep.

The clicking of the door lock woke Raj from an already broken and rough slumber. He lifted his head and saw two guards standing in the morning light but quickly laid back as a muscle in his neck felt strained from his sleeping position.

'Breakfast,' one of the guards said brusquely before turning away.

Raj tenderly sat upright with his back to the wall and turned his head gently from right to left trying to stretch his neck a little before rising fully. The light from the outside world was a pleasant distraction from the pitch darkness of the night before as was the slight rise in temperature. Raj finally stood and made his way to the wooden plate and cup left at the foot of the door.

'Is this it?' Raj asked himself as he picked up a solitary roll of dark bread from the plate.

He stood to eat. The bread was hard, yet chewy, and lacked as much salt as it did sugar. Raj had definitively tasted better, but he was starving, and this was all that was on offer so he ate it as quickly as he could. The other consideration was the timing of the meals; for all he knew, this could be the only meal of the day, or for a few days, or even possibly his last meal! The small cup had fresh water in it which tasted fine and allowed Raj to wash away the bland taste of the prison bread. A few minutes later the guards returned and took away the plate and cup and brought with them a different bucket, filled with water and a large rag inside.

'The warden likes a clean house,' the prison officer stated. 'Make sure the floor is clean before I return with your lavatory. Then clean yourself too.'

Raj was a little shocked. He now knew why everything was so clean; the prisoners themselves kept the cells in check. Raj grabbed the bucket and started in the far corner. His knees didn't appreciate the chores and the water in the bucket was ice cold, but at least the toilet got cleaned out. After he scrubbed the floor, he quickly stripped down and washed himself as best as he could. Within ten minutes the guard had returned and Raj was once again left alone in his spotless cell.

Every day the routine was the same; a hard breakfast roll, followed by the cleaning, then a solitary walk outside for half an hour or so before isolation for hours on end. There were no other meals for the day, nor was any more water brought. There was no interaction with other inmates either and the outside walk was done under armed guard in a fenced off area. The detrimental side to the cleanliness started becoming clear too and Raj realised that it was a particularly nasty punishment; the floor was always a little wet and cold. With such little circulation in the room, the stone beneath Raj's feet never really dried properly making sleeping an unhealthy practice to say the least. It was a clandestine form of torture, of that Raj was now sure, but how long he could take it was a different question. Within a few days he had started using minimal water in the cleaning practice and even tried leaving an area untouched. The guards checked, however, and watched Raj clean for the next few days, ensuring the entire floor was soaked. All Raj could do was move from covering himself with the old blanket, to covering the floor beneath him while he slept.

'How long are you keeping me in here?' Raj asked his guard as he walked back from his exercise at the end of the first week. The isolation had started to take a toll as did the cold, hard floor.

'We'll check and let you know when we come back tomorrow. Is that okay, Krizic?' the guard answered with a gentle smile.

The next morning the usual guards brought his bread and water in the morning and Raj questioned them once again.

'I asked yesterday,' Raj said, 'did you find out about my release?'

'Oh, sorry,' one of the guards responded. 'My fault totally. I forgot. I'll find out when we come back for your plate. Okay?'

Raj grew a little in confidence at the answer and thought that they surely couldn't hold him in solitary confinement for three years. But when the guards returned, they were no longer smiling, nor were they gentle in their manner and, instead of two sentries, this time four big brutes entered the cell, making it feel extremely crowded and incredibly dangerous.

'So, we heard you were asking about your release?' asked the first man to enter. 'Is that right?'

Raj didn't answer for he knew that anything he did in that moment would only make the upcoming beating worse. As the guards set upon him, Raj fell to the floor in a foetal position and to the best of his abilities covered his face, kidneys and testicles. This wasn't some inmate brawl; this was a beat down, a show of force to teach Raj some respect and remind him of who was in charge, and any retaliation would have just made them hit harder, longer and possibly return more often.

'Did that answer your question, traitor?' spat the last guard before leaving the cell.

The next morning there was no breakfast and no water, and the guards who brought the cleaning bucket simply emptied it across the floor. Raj stood crying when they were gone; he was hungry, sore and demoralised. He had bruising around his ribs and thighs, while his left shoulder continued to ache due to his sleeping position. He said a hopeful prayer in silence and thought about his family. He said a prayer for them too, particularly his parents who would now be worried sick about the disappearance of a second son.

Raj counted the days, as it was all he could do. He was bored and scared and felt weak from malnourishment. Most nights he cried himself to sleep while sitting, but by the morning he had somehow laid down again and spent the night on the cold stone. His neck was always sore and his back was stiff. When he paced the room, his movements reminded him of his father and grandfather before him, always needing to stretch his arms and spine as if his bones would otherwise fuse together. He was scared for the long term because he knew he was aging unnaturally in that dark cell and there were more years in prison ahead of him than behind.

Two months had passed and the days were definitely getting colder. Summer was now a memory and those delightful Italian days were a pleasant dream that left a bitter taste. Raj was contemplating his situation again, hoping that at least the solitary confinement would soon end, when a different officer opened the door at a far earlier hour than usual.

'Let's go, Krizic,' he announced, and Raj followed as quickly as his body would allow.

The two men made their way out to a grumbling brown Volkswagen combi van in the cool darkness of the autumn morning. Raj hopped in gingerly to join three other inmates in the back. Another guard sat behind the wheel ready to drive, while the guard that brought Raj, sat at the front as a passenger.

'Do we need to handcuff you guys?' he asked.

'No.' Raj looked at the other two inmates who also shook their heads.

'Remember,' the front guard said in a light tone, 'if you behave, this can all be so easy. Besides, we have the guns.'

'Where are we going?' asked Raj once the van passed the first gate out of the jail.

'Work,' the front guard said, then remained silent until they passed the second gate and moved onto the public road.

'Okay, this is the deal.' The passenger guard started speaking after lighting a cigarette and putting his feet up on the dashboard. 'We have a job that needs a few more hands. They're building a training facility close by.'

'What kind of training?' one of the other prisoners asked.

The first guard looked over his shoulder in surprise then laughed, filling the compartment with smoke.

'What's so funny?' asked the inquisitive inmate.

'I don't know what kind of facility.' The guard was jovial. 'Do you see any stripes on my fucking shoulders? Any stars on my chest? Jesus... maybe it's a facility to house your mother... you know... when she comes around and offers us her services.'

'Don't ask too many questions,' the driver chimed in, now smoking as well. 'Just go and do what you're fucking told. Trust me, this is better than digging in the fucking mines.'

They drove for fifteen minutes or so toward the mountains in the distance. It was a beautiful rural setting with no houses or towns in sight. The trees were bare and the ground was covered in frost but the sky was still clear and it seemed the morning chill would soon give way to sunshine and some autumn warmth. Raj cynically assumed it was all government land that was probably stolen from the humble farmers that toiled the earth here for generations. In the distance, a small smoke stack became visible, and as the van drove closer, a few other vehicles appeared, as did a formative structure worked on by a few men who busily went about their chores.

'Okay,' the passenger guard announced once they had all left the vehicle, then pointed to a large, heavy set man that barked orders. 'Go see Voitek. He'll sort you.'

Raj walked to the rear of the column and stretched his neck and back continuously. Around the camp, Raj saw four other guards spread out at the perimeter, each holding a shot gun while watching the workers. Ten men in prison greys toiled around the facility doing various jobs and another three men also worked but they wore dark blue overalls and were clearly not part of the prison crew.

'Are you sending me cripples, now, Rob?' Voitek asked with a wide grin and a booming voice. 'I can take 'em back if you like,' the guard responded, and both men laughed as they approached each other to shake hands.

Voitek looked over the newcomers indifferently.

'They'll do,' he stated. 'But give them some fucking boots.'

The job was menial: mixing concrete, shovelling concrete and moving wheelbarrows full of concrete. The structure was at its early stages with pegs still in the dug-up ground connected by colourful strings that outlined the footings of what would become quite a large building by the look of it. Raj struggled for a few hours but pushed himself well until the sun was high and his legs were sore. The smoke stack that appeared earlier came from a fire that cooked meat slowly all morning and permeated the worksite, driving Raj's stomach into spasms.

'Lunch,' came the cry and the working men split into two; one group remained working while the other ate, then they swapped, ensuring any of the cement that was being prepared didn't dry out during the lunch break.

Raj ate with the second group so pushed on for half an hour longer. When he finally sat with his meal, he felt so fatigued he could hardly lift the meat to his lips.

'Who sent you here, boy?' asked Voitek, standing above him with his own plate in hand, showing no visible fatigue apart from a little sweat on his brow.

'The guards just came in the morning,' Raj replied between mouthfuls of spit roasted lamb. The flavour was so appetising that he struggled to focus on Voitek.

'You should be in a fucking hospital, not a worksite,' the foreman continued. 'You've been struggling all day; you can't turn your head, you can hardly bend down and you're sweating like a pig going to slaughter.'

Raj breathed deeply between chews then swallowed, not saying a word.

'Looks like you need a good meal too.' Voitek's voice became a little softer and more concerned than when he began.

The day ended with the footing of the structure complete. Every square metre or so, a small pillar of grey concrete now arose from the ground, giving a clear outline of the building that was to come. The string lines still stretched across the form and were left in place while the men packed their gear and prepared to leave. It was a long and arduous day, but Raj felt relief from being in the sun for so long and for being around other men. He also had a full belly and felt he had achieved something with his time at the construction, even if it just was simple manual labour. He washed his hands and face before joining the other men on their march back to the volkswagen.

'Hey.' A cry reached Raj's ears. 'Aren't you forgetting something?'

Raj and the three other prisoners turned and saw Voitek standing before them. They all looked down at themselves and then at each other in surprise.

'What did we forget?' asked Raj.

'Your fucking boots,' Voitek answered. 'I'm not a charity. Take 'em off. You can put them back on tomorrow. Maybe get that fucking tightarse Warden Ludovski to give you some fucking shoes, too.'

'Fat chance of that.' One of Raj's guards joined the conversation. 'We struggle to get our clothes mended let alone the prisoners. Quickly now, guys, we have to get back.'

Raj slept deeply that night. His body was sorer than it had ever been, both from the work and from the sleeping position, but neither of those ailments stopped him from passing out across the dirty blanket on the stone floor.

'What's wrong with him?' a man asked at the door to Raj's cell.

Raj was disoriented for a moment as he awoke and looked at the strange man with glasses and small hat on his head.

'Voitek reckons he's pretty broken,' answered the guard that brought him to the work on the previous day.

'Broken?' the strange man asked.

'Yeah,' the guard responded. Both men now stood in the cell and looked down at Raj, who was struggling to sit up again.

'What's he in for?' the stranger asked.

'He fled,' the guard answered. 'Across the border somewhere.'

'Oh.' The stranger hardened his tone and removed his glasses ironically. 'Well in that case, he looks fine to me. I give him a clean bill of health. Good day.'

Raj managed to get to his feet just as the door closed and the clicking sound of the lock echoed around his cell. The dim light of early morning crept into the room and Raj felt like he had only shut his eyes for a minute before being disturbed by the officials.

CHAPTER 23

It was the third week of continuous work at the building site and the structure was still in its infancy. Sand and steel had been placed within the initial footing and more concrete was poured. Timber and brick were delivered to the site by big trucks just as dirt and rock were being taken away. The process was all quite foreign to Raj, but he really enjoyed it. He loved getting his hands dirty and feeling the strength in his body awaken with the physical labour. He also loved the rich foods that were satisfying his belly every day alongside the fresh country air that filled his lungs. There was a hustle and bustle around the workplace that made him feel alive and part of something greater, as well. His body still ached though, but he made a conscious effort to look at ease when he passed any officials, particularly Voitek, even though at times it was quite difficult.

'My bet is, you boys won't be here too long.' Voitek began talking around the lunch feast one day.

Raj's interest immediately piqued and despaired at the news while not obviously showing it, he rather inconspicuously listened and kept eating while those in charge continued the discussion.

'Weather permitting, I reckon there's at least a year's worth of work left here, Voitek,' another guard retorted as he looked to the heavens. 'You wouldn't get rid of free labour so easily, would you?'

'They'll bring the professionals in from the army to do this,' continued Voitek, smiling with the rest of the men at the cheap joke at his expense. 'So don't worry, the labour will still be free, but they will also do a better fucking job. And in half the time.'

The men all laughed once more, reinforcing the feeling of camaraderie that had really taken hold among the group. Raj sensed many of the prison guards were just making ends meet and cared little for the politics involved in the country and were happy to sit and eat next to the artisans and the prisoners alike.

'Why do you say we'll move on?' another guard asked as he chewed his barbecued beef. 'Ludovski hasn't mentioned anything to us.'

'Ludovski is an idiot,' Voitek replied. 'It's the reason he oversees a labour camp in the middle of nowhere. The powers that be wouldn't trust that prick with anything of real importance. His old man is probably somewhere up high, so they had to give him a position.'

'I think it's his uncle,' a third guard interjected. 'Secret police or something. Or so I heard.'

'There you go.' Voitek wiped his hands after licking his fingers. 'Regardless, my sources reckon there are bigger games going on at the moment. International shit between the US and the Soviets. And our armies need bolstering.'

The group went quiet at Voitek's last comment, all chatter and jibes ceasing in a reverent silence as the well-respected foreman bestowed his knowledge on the group.

'They reckon something is brewing in Latin America,' Voitek continued as he checked his watch. 'Just starting, they said. And the new president in the States is the first Catholic. So the Communists are worried.'

'What's that got to do with us?' the first guard asked. 'I don't even know where Latin America is.'

They all laughed once again and the mood eased up. Raj knew where Latin America was, but did not know anything about the presidents of the United States and the politics involved with the American continents.

'It doesn't matter.' Voitek stood and stretched. 'All you have to know is how to point and shoot at Capitalists.'

They laughed again before rising to get back to work.

Another week passed and Voitek's prophecy suddenly rang true. Two guards picked up Raj from his cell early one morning and ushered him to the outside common area where at least fifty other men, none older than Raj, had been corralled in the bleak autumn morning. Most of the prisoners stood in singlets and shorts, many were barefoot with arms folded and shivering in the cold. Ludovski stood before the men; a large jacket covered most of his body, adding an unspoken insult to the scene. He was smoking a cigarette and looking clearly outranked by the military personnel that stood alongside him. Two green buses, complete with red stars, chugged and spat as they idled near the main entrance gate, their tailpipes pushed grey smoke consistently into the crisp morning air. More soldiers loitered near the buses and the military entourage that now pervaded the campus was well equipped with machine guns in hand and pistols at their sides.

'Right,' the warden began, 'this is Sergeant Becel. He has some important news for you.'

'Thank you, Warden,' the sergeant said, looking at Ludovski, then turning to face the uneasy crowd. 'Attention!'

The sergeant's voice blasted across the space and immediately settled any murmurs and whispers among the waiting convicts. Raj looked to see that even the guards and their dogs took notice to the announcement about to be made.

'By the approval of the Yugoslavian Justice System,' the sergeant hollered, 'the Yugoslavian Defence Forces and the Communist Party of Yugoslavia, and by decree from the great Marshall Tito himself, you men that stand before me will have your prison sentences mercifully revoked forthwith and begin your obligatory two-year period in the Yugoslavian National Army immediately. Once your name is called, you will make your way to the gate and occupy the buses waiting to transport you to the barracks.'

'Fuck me,' Raj said, a little too loudly, causing a few of the other prisoners close enough to him to smile.

'You will do so quickly and quietly,' the sergeant continued a little louder, as many of the youngsters listening were taken by surprise and began to whisper amongst each other. 'So as the warden can have his prison back to normal. Corporal, you may begin.'

The corporal next to the sergeant started calling names immediately and, one by one, the young men who went to bed the night before as criminals, now woke up to become instant soldiers.

'Voitek was right,' a quiet voice behind Raj stated.

'He sure was,' another answered. 'I told you that guy was connected.'

Raj looked over his shoulder and recognised two fellow labourers from the countryside work place. He didn't know their names but did agree with them regarding Voitek's prediction and connections. Raj wasn't sure about all of this though; on one hand, the government had just lessened his sentence by nearly three years, but on the other hand, Raj had no idea what to expect in the military. Either way, he admitted to himself that it seemed he was destined to serve in the Yugoslav Army one way or another and so, perhaps it was simply better to get it over with sooner than later. Then another thought dawned upon him; if Voitek's forecast was true, then perhaps there really was a new major global conflict brewing in the Americas and he and his fellow prisoners were simply being moved from the frying pan and into the fire.

As the sun rose in the morning, so too did the clouds gather, and before a third of the new recruits had been processed, the rain began to fall. Raj stood without shoes and watched the dirt around his feet turn to mud while the cold crept up his legs and the dignity left his heart. The surnames being called were in alphabetical order, so he didn't have too long to wait before he made his way to the soldiers near the buses.

'Krizic? Raj Krizic?' the first beret wearing soldier asked.

'Yes.'

'On to the first bus,' was the command followed by the flick of a pen on a page behind a folder.

Raj found a seat near the back of the vehicle and was grateful to be out of the rain. The bus held ten or so miserable looking men by that time, all who sat silently and kept to themselves. Raj too was mindful as he looked out onto the muddy prison ground and rubbed at the left side of his neck; as much as his upcoming military sojourn was a mystery yet to be experienced, he remained absolutely certain he would not miss his horrible time here at the labour camp. He crossed himself and gave thanks to God for the early release and chose to believe some of his prayers had finally been answered. It was not long before the remainder of the men, and the commandeering soldiers, were aboard the bus driving away from jail.

Once beyond the gates, the senior officer stood up front and engaged the reluctant recruits.

'Listen up, we are on our way to Mostar,' he announced. 'We should be there just before evening. We'll sort you out and get you ready for the first day tomorrow. Be alert, we don't like to tell you things twice. So focus and follow the directions. Understand?'

A feeble response in the affirmative hardly created an echo within the cylindrical steel chamber of the bus, with only about half of the occupants bothering to raise their voices in reply at all.

'Understand?' the officer sounded, and looked, instantly enraged, with his voice booming louder than the combined effort of the seated men.

'Yes, yes... Fine, sure... Okay, okay...' The reaction was hardly united, but at least most of the men made a noise.

'The correct answer' - the officer still was not happy and he began a slow walk down the aisle of the bus - 'you flea ridden, sons of fascist whores is "Yes, sir", and you'd better start getting used to saying those two fucking words.' The man's ire grew as he spoke, and Raj witnessed everybody seated in front of him adjust their postures in response to the vitriolic barrage being spat out in that moment. 'In fact, when you say your little fucking prayers at night, and think of your bastard fathers and cunting mothers, I want you to repeat to yourself, "Yes, sir, yes, sir", a thousand fucking times so that instead of counting the fucking sheep on your filthy peasant farms, you count the two magic words over and over and over again. "Yes, sir, yes, sir, yes fucking sir". Do you fucking understand now?'

'Yes, sir.' The chorus of voices was loud and tight.

'I can't fucking hear you.'

'YES, SIR.'

The bus instantly fell into silence after that little interaction and Raj's earlier thoughts about the grass being greener on the military side were already beginning to look suspect. He sensed the same mood being shared by the other young men, but none would dare speak out loud now, even just to make small talk.

They travelled on in solemn silence for a few hours. The views in the distance were breathtaking with the outlying mountains already being well covered in snow while the surrounding flora sparkled green from the drenching given by the clouds above. An occasional herd of cows or sheep could be seen, but at the sight of the sheep, all Raj could think of were the two little words that the officer had just drilled into them. The cold was bearable in the bus, as the bodies combined with the heat of the engine at the rear, all lifted the climate enough to be comfortable, but Raj still wished he had a pair of shoes on, as his feet were sore and cold. He looked at the way the soldiers at the front of the bus were dressed and found a little hope in the next stage of his journey. He knew the army would clothe and feed him well, and that alone would be an improvement over the months of solitary confinement, but how hard the training would be, and how difficult his superiors would be, could make all the food and clothing in the world feel redundant.

They started their descent into Mostar, one of the oldest and most populace towns in the Hercegovina region. It was roughly twenty kilometres from Raj's village and he felt glad for the return to familiar territory. Mostar was named after the old arched bridge that connected the town for nearly half a century and allowed the east and west to cross safely over the Neretva River. The military convoy never went that far into the town but rather skimmed the edges of the river to the north and made its way to the foot of one of the many ranges that surrounded the city. There the military paraphernalia was clear for all to see; giant signs on barbed wire fences warned any intruders of the dangers that lay within the compound, paired with the troops that patrolled both the ground and battlements above the perimeter, leaving no doubt about the importance of the area beyond the barbed wired gates.

The sun was fading, and the rain still fell lightly as they left the bus to be herded into a common area within a large, steel shed. A long, white table acted as a counter between the entry and the storage shelves at the rear of the room that contained the apparel the men would soon be wearing. Once again, the young men's names were called but this time they stepped forward two by two to receive their fittings.

'Don't put it on yet,' the lead officer yelled. 'Are you an idiot?'

'No, sir,' the young recruit said. 'Sorry, sir.'

Raj felt for the man who attempted to get dressed there and then. Like Raj, the man had nothing on his feet, his pants were torn and his singlet was filthy. He looked much younger, though, and Raj wasn't certain if he was of a legal age to be joining the army.

'You need to wash up first,' the officer reprimanded him again. 'Didn't your mother teach you anything?'

'My mother died when I was a baby, sir,' the man answered innocently, looking a little lost in his stare.

'Maybe because she knew what a fucking disappointment you'd become,' the officer yelled mercilessly. 'Now get over there and wait for the fucking rest.'

Next, they made their way to the barracks where every man was assigned a bed and a storage locker. The place was large, but nowhere near the size of the dorm in San Sabba. Still, Raj felt good to be in the company of others, even if they were all ex-convicts and here against their will. They stood before their beds as they were ordered to and awaited their cruel master's next instruction.

'This is your space.' The officer walked down the aisle between the standing men. 'As it is now, is how it will always be. Do you understand?'

'Yes, sir,' the men responded quickly and with purpose.

'The showers are beyond that wall – he pointed in the direction he was standing – 'eight men can shower. You will all shower before you rest your heads on those pillows tonight. Lights are out at 10 p.m. We rise at 6 a.m. There will be one call to rise. If one of you is late, all of you will pay. Understand?'

'Yes, sir.'

'Assume that this is now your home,' the officer continued. 'You respect your home, don't you?'

'Yes, sir.'

'And now we all share this home, like a family. I don't want to live in a pigsty.' He looked at the hapless youngster that tried to put on his uniform earlier. 'And if your mothers didn't teach you correctly, be sure that I will. So, take a good look at your beds, if one corner of one bed is not folded correctly after you awake, you will all pay. If there is any rubbish found around your house, you will all pay. If there is a stain inside your toilet bowel, you will all pay. Understand?'

'Yes, sir.'

'Assume your family is dead.' The officer continued to walk and talk, turning near the end and making his way back. 'The person next to you is now your brother. You will learn that the only person you can rely on is your brother, because when the war *does* come, your family *will* be dead and the only thing that will keep *you* alive is the trust you place in your brother. And on the battlefield, if one of you is not trustworthy, then you will *all* pay. Understand?'

'Yes, sir.'

'Now.' The officer looked at his wrist. 'According to my watch, you each have a minute to shower and prepare for bed. If one of you isn't clean in time, you will all pay. Understand?'

'Yes, sir.'

Thankfully every man was clean and in bed when the lights went out. A strange silence fell over the barracks as Raj's eyes adjusted to the darkened space. There was no murmur and no whisper, nor did any of the men cough or sneeze in those quiet moments, there was just silence within the room and a small amount of background noise from the beyond the walls. The rain still fell outside and the effect on the tin roof was bittersweet for Raj. The sound itself was quite soothing in its monotony, but it didn't take long for him to remember the last time he had heard such rainfall on a roof; his final day in Italy before his hard-earned freedoms were snatched away by the very people he now served.

The morning bell was a short blast in a shrill frequency that could have woken the dead. Raj jumped to his feet, still remembering the officer's warnings regarding tardiness and cleanliness. He was dressed in his fresh pressed greens and shiny new boots within minutes; he then made his bed and double checked that everything was in place.

Raj was surprised at just how good this all felt. He had a reason to rise, a need to get ready and a self-determination that involved responsibilities toward his fellow soldiers. There was also a clean bed and bathing facilities available and now all that was left was a decent meal. It shamed him to think it, but it reminded him of his home and the duties required around the farm. As he waited patiently for his bunkmates to prepare, he wondered if all these new emotions would be the same if a real call to arms was made and he had to actually point a gun at another human. He tempered his feelings in that moment, promising to always remember that this was not his family and the comforts he now appreciated were born by the blood and sweat of incarcerated men that were, more often than not, forced to be here.

A few minutes passed as Raj pondered his situation when suddenly the door burst open and two men marched in.

'Attention,' the officer from the previous day began. 'This is Drill Sergeant Vudomir Vabric. Your life is now in his capable hands. He will report to me regarding your development. Drill Sergeant.' The two men saluted, and the superior officer left the barracks.

'Right,' the new drill sergeant began. 'Kindergarten is over!'

CHAPTER 24

Each day began the same; get prepared, followed by some vigorous exercise then a light breakfast. The sun was now barely visible in the cool winter mornings and some days Raj felt like he was jogging in the dark. The cold hadn't quite fully taken control just yet, but it wouldn't be long until snow and mud became the soldiers' training ground and the icy wind once more penetrated the flesh and chilled the bone. After breakfast, a brief interlude was given to the soldiers in order to digest their meals before yet more training began. They never left the base and were not allowed beyond a certain perimeter. A two hour nap followed lunch then some more training before an early dinner, shower and bedtime to bring an end to the day.

The initial daily program lasted three cold months and ensured the rookies were fit and strong both physically and mentally. The middle of winter was particularly hard and many of the softer men struggled. Some cried at night while rocking to sleep, while others struggled to get out of bed in the mornings. But the drill sergeant showed no remorse, forcing the weakest links into submission through fear, intimidation and punishment. In the end, the training simply became easier than the reprimand, so all the men fell into line if only to avoid the sergeant's wrath. Raj noticed his body shape become leaner and more sculpted over the time while other men that were rotund when they arrived, now looked far thinner and muscular. Raj also felt stronger; the whites of his eyes seemed brighter too and he was no longer as tired when he lay to rest at night.

On a Sunday afternoon in early spring, the men were brought into a forum that was hosted by a senior officer who stood on a small stage at the end of a large room in which the men had never been in before. Foldable metal chairs were placed around the space awaiting the young soldiers to be seated for the presentation. The air outside was fresh and cool, but the winter chill had lost its bite and the wind that blew had a touch of warmth to it now. The clouds that had brought rain and snow over the last season were becoming thinner and more sporadic, inviting the twinkling of the stars to show their sparkle to human eyes once more. Inside, most of the men wore t-shirts as all the bodies in the building acted like a heater, generating plenty of warmth to keep everybody comfortable.

'Settle down,' the drill sergeant announced. 'This is Corporal Arstevski. You will give him your attention.'

'Welcome.' The corporal began with a joke to ease the mood. 'It's good to see all your faces. I hope the sergeant here wasn't too soft on you.'

A few men laughed ironically, but the drill sergeant's face held no humour.

'It's alright,' the corporal continued. 'You can be at ease now. We are here to talk about the future. Your basic training is now complete and soon you will be placed in different divisions that specialise in all aspects of warfare.'

A murmur grew among the young men at that moment and Raj sensed in them feelings of excitement arise. He felt it too. For a brutally cold season, he and his fellows had watched tanks roll by, heard machine guns fire and bombs explode, while they marched in rows and did push ups and squats for hours on end. Anything would seem like fun after the boring rigours that this crew had been put through.

'You will also be paid monthly, including back pay for the last three months. Some of you might choose to send some money home and we can facilitate that. Others might want a savings account with the army and may consider the option of a long-term career in the Yugoslav Military.'

Now the murmur grew until the drill sergeant stepped in to settle the lads.

'It's okay, Vabric,' the corporal resumed. 'I understand the excitement. Everyone likes to get paid for their hard work, and the drill sergeant here tells me you are one of his hardest working groups ever.'

Raj's instincts awakened at that moment and the corporal before him took on a new aura. He seemed to have turned from a simple announcer into a salesman of some kind, because Drill Sergeant Vabric had just spent three months berating this group of men about how they were the worse examples of humanity that he had ever trained. The only thing Raj wasn't quite sure of was exactly what the corporal was selling.

'I know many of you did not come here by choice, but let me guarantee you that a career in the Yugolsav Army is a very wise option,' the corporeal continued. 'You will have opportunities available here that many in the civilian world will never experience.'

Just got to sell your soul and get your head blown off in the process, Raj thought to himself as he now understood the corporal's recruitment angle.

'You will get to see the world, learn other tongues and become educated in whichever field you desire. You will have access to the latest technologies, the most powerful weapons and represent your people in the highest way possible. And let's face it.' He smiled as he paused, 'Women love a man in uniform.'

The men burst out laughing and the excitement became even greater as jokes flew around and sexual posturing soon followed, which just made the immature minds of the men laugh even louder. Raj took it all in but wasn't falling for it; a season ago he was held captive by the same people who now made promises of a better life but without ever mentioning the price that needed to be paid.

'Okay, okay.' The corporal settled the crowd himself this time. 'Any questions?'

'Yeah,' one of the men said, 'when do we get paid?'

The men burst out laughing once more and the room felt like a party had now started. The mood was jovial and light and a welcome change to the demanding physical work the rookies had just experienced. Just then a door to the left of the corporal opened and two men walked in.

'Attention!' the drill sergeant announced.

Within a second, the room fell silent and all the soldiers stood with their right hands to their foreheads.

'At ease,' the oldest man of the two entrants ordered as he made his way toward the corporeal. 'Looks like you've trained them well, sergeant.'

'Thank you, sir,' the drill sergeant replied.

'I was wondering what all the ruckus was about,' the older man said, 'so I thought I'd see for myself. Please continue, gentlemen.'

'Thank you, sir,' the corporal said. 'You can sit down again, men. We are indeed fortunate to be graced by the highest serving officer on camp. This is Colonel Jozo Mrvac.'

The old man smiled as he looked upon the young recruits.

'Now, we are actually at the end of our presentation, sir,' the corporal stated. 'We were just taking some questions. I believe pay was the first question...'

A lesser murmur began among the men as the earlier excitement became tempered with a high ranking official now watching over them.

'Tomorrow you will receive your payment,' the corporal announced. 'And you will also be placed into your prospective units to learn the skills needed to enhance our defence force. You will be moved away from your current barracks and into a new home. Some of you will even move to different bases around the country. This night might be the last time many of you see each other.'

Raj noticed the corporal's change in tone. He suddenly seemed less jovial and more pragmatic.

'Just so you know,' the corporal concluded, 'leave is granted, but only after a full year of service and only if your behaviour is deemed worthy. You can, however, write and receive correspondence from your families on a monthly basis. Sergeant Vabric, is there anything you would like to add?'

'Yes, sir,' the drill sergeant answered then stepped forward. 'Remember, men, you are now soldiers in the Yugoslav Army. You may be of the lowest rank, but you still represent the defence force of our great nation. You represent us whether you are on base or off. You also represent me; I am the one who trained you here first, so I will take it personally if I hear problems about your behaviour. Do I make myself clear?'

'Yes, sir,' the men strongly voiced their response in unison.

'Very good,' the old colonel added with another smile.

The next morning dawned and for the first time the soldiers didn't start the day with their usual routine. Rather, the men grabbed their packs and made their way to the administrative building where pink envelopes stuffed with Yugoslav dinars awaited the troops. Once the cash was dispersed, each man lined up outside and awaited his call for further instruction. Before long, the group was divided into smaller units that focused on particular utilities within the army.

'Raj Krizic,' the drill sergeant called. 'Artillery.'

Raj made his way to a new officer; of whose rank he was yet uncertain. Four others had already assembled near the man and quietly waited for any further calls. By the end of the morning, six men formed part of the artillery unit which was the smallest section, with standard infantry forming the largest.

'Follow me,' said the new commanding officer and brusquely walked away toward a green pick-up truck with oversized wheels. 'Get in the tray.'

The six rookies sat in the back of the truck and, to Raj's surprise, the new commander joined them too.

'Let's go, Haim, but not too fast.' The officer slapped the side of the vehicle and the driver revved the engine before taking off.

'Now,' the commander addressed his new company, 'my name is Captain Ivan Madzic. You boys are going to learn to blow shit up,' a broad smile spread across his face as he reached for a fat, brown cigar, 'but before you blow shit up I thought I'd give you a tour of the base. I'm pretty sure Vabric didn't show you around?'

'No, sir,' one of the seated men answered.

'Just as I thought,' the captain continued as he puffed away. 'Now, to the left here, you know the mess and the admin area we just left. Up to the right is the armoury, although I don't think they have given you guns yet. The giant hangar behind the armoury houses most of the vehicles on the base, including tanks, and can hold small aircraft if we ever need.'

They passed the buildings as described and there were soldiers milling around; some training while others looked to be running errands. The ground was covered by a greyish-white crushed rock surface that acted as excellent drainage and allowed both pedestrians and vehicles easy movement around the base. The sun shone down as lunch time approached and Raj was pleased that the coldest time of the year was well and truly over.

'To the left now,' the captain continued, 'we have a medical facility; you can tell because of the giant red cross on it,' the men laughed comfortably in their leader's presence, 'that one doesn't go down well with the hardcore commies.'

The comfort instantly disappeared and the seated men all looked in different directions trying to avoid the topic of Christian crosses versus Communist ideologies. Raj wasn't sure if the captain was joking, serious or simply testing the men, but either way, Raj didn't intend to break the silence.

'Next to that there are some more training facilities,' the captain continued as if nothing happened, 'including an indoor shooting range, which is handy. The buildings to the right are more dorms and behind them is the library and learning centre, for you intellectual types.'

Raj immediately took a mental note of the building just mentioned and would check out what services it provided when he had some free time. Now that the troops had finished basic training, they were no longer confined to the earlier area and would be free to explore the wider base.

'Alright.' The car pulled to a stop before a double storey concrete building. 'Here we are.'

The men jumped out of the tray and lined up awaiting their commanding officer. The sun was high and shone down upon a large grass field that stretched for a few kilometres toward the range of mountains in the distance beyond the building before them. A cyclone fence acted as a border between the large dwelling and the grassland beyond, with a double gate allowing access for both larger vehicles and foot soldiers. Men came and went from the dwelling, mostly moving to and from the field. There were boxed out stations every few metres where the field began and soldiers busied themselves with setting up the area for whatever military exercises were planned for the day.

Bang, bang, bang...

Suddenly several explosions were heard, and the rookies instinctively ducked their heads. In the distance, dirt and smoke burst from the ground as mortars were launched from the boxed areas at the entry to the field. Raj felt a little excitement at the prospect of that kind of power in his hands and he could see, by the smiles on the faces of his small company, that the other men were feeling the same.

'This way,' the captain ordered and walked into the double storey dwelling.

The men marched into a vast indoor area that had floor to ceiling windows overlooking the outside bombardment grassed area. There was a grand table in the middle of the room with a large, printed map upon it and several older officers milling about it. There were doors across on the far wall, some were open and looked to be offices where soldiers went about their work. A staircase ran along the back wall and led upstairs which was beyond view from the ground storey. The large space was a hive of military activity; many men watched through binoculars and analysed the explosive demonstrations through the windows, others walked about studying papers in their hands as they headed to meetings in the satellite rooms, while others appeared and disappeared along the staircase as they headed toward their destinations.

'This is Artillery HQ,' Captain Madzic explained, then pointed out the windows. 'But out there is where you will really learn your craft. There are offices around the edge of the room and even more upstairs. Some are for meetings, others are repositories and some will be used for training purposes, but we will get to that.'

Raj saw more bombs exploding in the distance but was surprised that very little could be heard within the building.

'About face,' the captain ordered, then marched the men outside where the sounds of explosions could be heard again.

They walked past the headquarters to another building which was longer with only a single storey. It had an arched roof and reminded Raj of an umbrella. There was a soldier awaiting them as they approached.

'This is your home,' the captain announced, 'and this is Sergeant Barkov. He will show you the ropes and get you settled. Training starts tomorrow and we will see how many of you keep your fingers by the end of the month.'

'Attention,' Sergeant Barkov yelled and the rookies fell in line. They followed the eager young sergeant into the barracks and settled down in their designated areas.

'These are your accommodations,' Sergeant Barkov yelled again. 'Keep them neat and tidy. I don't want any mess. I will inspect daily and will punish accordingly. You are now soldiers, so start acting like soldiers. You have an hour to sort yourselves, get to know the space or take a rest.'

Raj organised his clothing and placed his bag in the tall locker that each man was assigned. He looked around and saw at least twenty other sleeping stations up the line that were clearly already taken by men not present. He then sat on his bed and counted his money.

'They give us nothing.' Raj looked around and saw a fellow soldier doing the same thing. 'Three hundred dinars?' the man continued. 'Is that what everyone got?'

'Yes,' Raj answered as he looked at the cash in his hand. Others chimed in too, each echoing Raj's answer as they eagerly studied their funds.

'And what's that going to buy us?' the disgruntled man continued. 'A pack of cigarettes?'

'A pack of shit cigarettes,' another man answered, and the room burst out laughing.

They were right, Raj thought. The Yugoslav currency was still in its infancy as was the nation itself. International trust in the dinar was non-existent so the exchange rates meant that any purchasing power was only found within the nation's borders.

'What did you expect?' a newcomer entered the room, followed by an entourage of camouflage. 'You want to get rich serving in the army?'

Raj looked over at the newcomers. They were seasoned and dirty, with hands and faces covered in soot. They laughed as they passed the rookies with many making toward the bathrooms at the end of the room.

'Besides,' added the alpha male, now standing in the middle of the rookies surrounded by his own posse, 'you haven't even paid rent yet.'

'Rent?' one of Raj's younger companions responded.

'Of course,' the soldier continued, his words now dripping in sarcasm. 'Nothing is free. Especially protection.'

'Protection from what?' the greenhorn continued, although Raj quietly had hoped that the youngster desisted.

'From this...' And with those words, the gang of thugs descended upon the recruit with fists and feet violently pummelling the man as he lay on his bed. Raj and the other novices simply looked away lest the gang's focus turned to them.

The senior recruits stopped beating the youngster after a while, grabbed a handful of his cash and quickly shuffled about the room in preparation for their down time. Within a minute the room was calm and all the men relaxed on their beds silently.

Raj couldn't sleep and so just kept silently to himself and thought about his situation. On his next pay day he would inform the administration of his desire to send most of his measly wage home. He was sure there would be some fee to that scenario, but he would rather give the money back to the state than these bullies that now surrounded him. Besides, how much could he spend in a place where the food, lodging and clothing were all taken care of by the army.

'Arise.' Barkov was back. 'Quickly.'

Raj must have dozed off as he couldn't recall hearing the sergeant enter the room. Within minutes the men waited outside in formation, ready for their orders.

'Rookies,' Barkov yelled, 'to the gate. Corporal Antonic will guide you to your duties.'

'This is the blasting field.' Corporal Antonic had his arm outstretched pointing to the grassy field beyond the gated fence the men had seen earlier that day. 'I'm going to pretend you all aren't idiots and know what goes on here.'

Raj looked around and saw a rather peaceful scene with empty artillery stations and a silent horizon. No more explosives rocked the earth in the distance and no men scurried around the place.

'Practice is finished for the day,' the pragmatic corporal continued while walking past the entry. 'And so clean up must begin. The most important lesson you must learn now is that when this gate is closed, shelling is no longer allowed. Do you understand?'

'Yes, sir.'

'The gate is the safety mechanism.' The corporal hammered home his point as he closed the gate now that all the rookies were beyond the boundary. 'It tells us all that there are friendlies on the field. See that red flag now being raised above the HQ?'

Raj looked up and indeed saw a red flag slowly making its way toward the sky.

'That's the other sign. It also means be careful when you are out here if the gate is open. This isn't something you fuck with. This is life and death.' The corporal's tone increased in volume and an anger spawned beneath his tone. 'Do you understand?'

'Yes, sir,' the rookies stated aggressively in response to the seriousness of the situation.

The corporal relaxed his tone then, satisfied with the newcomers' response and changed his focus to the distant land that was shelled all day.

'Being the new kids here,' he announced, 'you get the shit jobs.'

Raj looked around, as did the others, but saw nothing about them that indicated work duties.

'All day we smash the grass in the distance,' the corporal elaborated as he walked to a nearby artillery station. 'And as you can see, it leaves quite the mess. Your first duty in the artillery regiment is to clean up the mess.'

One by one the men formed small groups and placed the cartridges and discharged cases into barrows that then were wheeled off to the dumpster area. The steel was black and filthy, and a myriad of shards of timber and metal were spread about needing to be collected and disposed of. The afternoon dragged with the menial work and concluded once the sun began to fall.

'I hope it's not like this for weeks,' one of Raj's compatriots mentioned. 'I'd rather do push ups all day.'

'We've got to start somewhere Zeljk,' another man answered, both men's dialects sounded northern, perhaps closer to Zagreb. 'Did you think they'd give us rocket launchers as soon as we arrived?'

'No, Pavo,' Zeljk continued as he dropped some more burned out steel into the barrow. 'But after the prison camp, I was hoping for a little more action. Honestly, I didn't mind all the training in boot camp.'

'You're scaring me, Zeljk,' Pavo added quietly. 'You sound like you might want a career with these fucking commies.'

'You're the one who is fantasising, Pavo,' Zeljk responded. 'Do you honestly think there is a better future out there than in here?'

Raj kept working. He listened to the arguments from both men and it reminded him of himself and his brother Vlad. He had seen the two recruits before, in boot camp, and knew their names but had rarely spoken to them, or anyone else for that matter.

'There is no future here,' Pavo stated then looked at Raj. 'Or out there. You agree?'

Raj was a little taken aback that he was asked to join the conversation.

'That's why we ran, isn't it?' Raj still didn't trust anyone here but was quite certain that every man in his squad was paying a price for some kind of criminality, so he just assumed these two soldiers had also fled the nation.

'I didn't flee,' Zeljk replied.

'I did.' Pavo smiled as he turned the wheelbarrow away. 'Twice.'

'Then why are you here?' Raj enquired.

'Because I trusted that idiot.' This time Zeljk smiled as he pointed to Pavo.

'Let's wrap it up,' Corporal Antonic announced and the men stopped talking and moved in double time to finish what was left. 'I'm starving.'

'Join us, Raj,' Pavo said, as the men made their way into the mess hall.

'Sure, thanks.'

Raj rarely socialised with anyone during basic training and had felt quite isolated the whole time. He didn't mind mostly, as much of the talk shared among the other rookies seemed vain or downright stupid. The feeling of segregation wasn't healthy though, and Raj sensed his negativity growing with every brooding thought about his current situation; a situation that would not change for the next two years, regardless of his mood. He was ready to let his guard down a little, but only with those that had also been forced into serving the state.

The dining area was loud and warm, as the soldiers were allowed some freedom whilst enjoying their meals. Long rows of timber tables filled the mess with an open kitchen on the far end, divided by a steel counter and bain-marie. It was one of the few times Raj heard outbursts of laughter echoing around the camp. It was a mixed group that ate together; seasoned veterans could be seen, along with the rookies. Even the fare was better than boot camp, with fresher vegetables and better cuts of meat and larger portions too. The aroma was inviting and the atmosphere was comforting, so Raj relaxed and started on his mashed potatoes.

'What's your story, Raj?' asked Zeljk whilst chewing.

'I got caught in Italy,' Raj responded then kept eating in the hope that his answer was enough.

'Italy?' Pavo sounded surprised. 'Most try for Germany. That's what I tried.'

'Yeah,' Raj conceded, 'but it looks like we both came up short.'

'Indeed.' Pavo nodded.

'How about you, Zeljk?'

'I got caught banging some council man's daughter, back in Zagreb, so it was prison before the army.'

'I told you not to do her,' Pavo interceded.

'You told me that you'd keep watch,' Zeljk shot back. 'Next thing I'm staring at some old man watching me go doggy style on his next of kin on his bed.'

'You were taking too long,' Pavo defended himself.

'Anyway,' Zeljk surrendered. 'That's how it goes when you have the worst cousin in the world.'

The men laughed and kept eating and talking and Raj felt safe, although the irony wasn't lost on him; all this time fleeing to avoid the system, yet here, amidst the enemy, he no longer felt threatened and insecure, but rather warm, cosy and replenished.

'What did you think of the spiel the corporal gave yesterday?' asked Zeljk in a quieter tone.

'Sounded good,' Raj replied. 'On the surface.'

'See,' Pavo interjected, 'Raj has some brains. Don't get fooled, Zeljk. You get stuck here, there goes your life.'

'And what do you think our life will be when we leave here in a couple of years? Do you think we have work waiting? Do you think there is a pot of gold given to each of us when we get home?' Zeljk sounded terse and Raj imagined this argument was rehashed between the two cousins over and again.

'Do you think there is a pot of gold waiting for you here?' Pavo retorted.

'I've told you before.' Zeljk sounded a touch frustrated. 'I think it's the better of two evils.'

'It's still evil, though,' said Raj, and both men looked at him as if it was the first time someone else had bothered joining their discussion.

The mess was starting to be cleared and some of the tables had already become empty. A loud bell was then rung by a young cook that walked about the large room flicking his wrist to make the wordless announcement that dinner time was done.

Raj and his two new friends quietly made their way toward their dorm and a well-earned slumber. The night was still and fresh and Raj felt exhausted. It had been a long day, with many new circumstances unfolding, and the next few days were sure to be much the same. But Raj's view hadn't deviated, nor would it. His family had a proud heritage of faith and culture and all the temptations offered by the powers that be would not be enough to entice him into changing his mind. He was stuck here, of that he was certain, but he was also certain that two long years of service would pass. In that time, he knew, he would give the military his body for whatever cause they required, but it didn't mean that he had to give them his mind. He would take one day at a time, knowing that every new day brought him one step closer to the final day of his service.

CHAPTER 25

'There is nothing to be ashamed of, son,' Mirko stated. 'You tried. It's all you could do. Now learn from it and let it go. We're just glad that you are safe and well and back home.'

It had been a long two years of constant training, and for all of Raj's indignation, the time wasn't totally wasted and was often quite enjoyable. During his military sojourn, Raj managed to complete his primary school education at the chagrin of certain officers. He learned about weapons and explosives and managed to see much of Yugoslavia on patrol throughout the country. His fitness and health were also in peak form and he made a few good friends during the time. He sent most of his meagre wage back home to help his family, of which he was proud, as the situation at home was not any easier. Fortunately, there was no war declared during his service of which Raj was especially thankful for, as were his parents.

'I know, Dad,' Raj answered. 'But I keep thinking how I could have done it differently.'

'Could have, should have, would have...' Kata mocked. 'Let it go, darling. Move on.'

'I know, I know...'

Raj would let it go, eventually, but he needed to analyse the last two and a half years first, and he was yet to tell his parents of his new plans. Ever since he returned to the farm he had a sense of yearning, a sense of loss and missed opportunities. There was also a hint of failure in his mind, not only of letting down himself, but also his elder brother Krizan.

'Here.' His mother smiled and gave him a basket full of spuds. 'Peel these. It should help take your mind of things.'

'You also need to think about work,' his father added while stuffing tobacco into his pipe. 'Maybe there is something going at the mines.'

'The pay is shit, Dad,' Raj cussed and his mother's look said more than words.

'I know, son, but it's better than nothing. And there's not much to do around here for all of us.'

The spring harvest would be upon them soon, as the planting had already been done before Raj's return. His father and brother Vlad could handle the maintenance of the farm easily enough, as they had done since Raj had been gone. Many of the larger animals were already at the communal area up north, with cousins and neighbours all chipping in to help, and Raj's sisters were now bigger and stronger and could also do more. Raj simply wasn't needed as much as he used to be.

'There's no hurry,' Kata stated as if reading her returned son's mind. 'You just got home. Take your time. There's plenty to do around here. Like helping me in the kitchen.'

Raj's mother's smile was sweet, as were her words, but ultimately, he knew his father was right. He had returned home two weeks earlier and was welcomed warmly and was glad to reconnect with his family. But time was moving on now and work needed to be found, not only for Raj's own sanity but also to contribute to the household. Amidst his sense of yearning, he also missed the feeling of independence and responsibility the last two years had brought. Although he had been stuck in the military, he still needed to make day to day decisions that affected others and himself. There was no safety net on his journeys to escape the nation, nor were there in his service, as any mistakes were swiftly punished by his superiors. Raj felt he had grown into his manhood somewhat over the time and understood some things better than before. His return home also reminded him why he had left in the first place; the need to make a life for himself with the hope of helping his family too, and perhaps creating a family of his own.

The following months brought odd jobs in limited industries. Working in the Bosnian coal mines was tough and dirty and extremely dangerous, and paid enough simply to live and eat on site. Working as manual labour on state run farms rewarded even less and the industry was sporadic and corrupt. Illegal tobacco runs paid quite well, but the competition was fierce and the risk was high. Of course, if Raj had succumbed to the Communist cause and joined the party, his job opportunities would have been far greater, as would his wage, but that was never going to happen.

Raj knew his prospects in Yugoslavia were just as grim as they were before he fled. There was no future for a dissident in the land, even if he wasn't politically active. The only option was abroad and that meant leaving once again. His decision was still quite challenging; he no longer had to worry about dodging conscription, but now he had a permanent black mark against his name, so he might already be under observation. He also would face a greater punishment if he got caught fleeing a second time. On the positive side, he was now older and experienced, and felt far more resilient after two years in the army. He would go alone too, no longer feeling the need for support on his quest. Besides, he still didn't know exactly what had occurred with Tomo and all his attempts at reaching out, since his return, fell on deaf ears.

'Good news, son,' Raj's father announced one sunny afternoon while they sat outside enjoying the day. Mirko was puffing on his bone pipe that had been handed down from his grandfather.

'What's that?'

'Your plans to leave might be easier than you imagined.' Mirko's voice was filtered through the smoke, sounding thicker than usual.

'How did you know of my plans?' Raj asked but really should have known all along.

'Come on.' Mirko smiled. 'I know you better than you know yourself, son.'

Raj loved his father. He hoped one day he could be as wise and honourable as his dad. He hoped he could look after a family just as well as his father had and that he could help all those that lived close to him too.

'So? What is it?'

'Looks like the commies are being screwed,' Mirko announced. 'There are rumours that movement around the continent might become easier for us.'

Kata then made her way from the kitchen holding a tray that contained slices of cheese, cold meat and coffee.

'What do you mean "easier"?' Raj was immediately interested.

'I was chatting with the townsfolk earlier and they reckon the government is passing laws to allow travel for work. I don't fully understand it, but there's something about the expense Yugoslavia has to pay to the UN.'

Raj got excited. He rose and was about to leave and seek evidence about his father's information when his mum placed the tray on the outdoor table.

'You're not going anywhere right now,' Kata announced as she sat and poured the coffee. 'I didn't prepare this snack just for me and your father.'

'What else did you hear?' Raj sat down and tried to stay calm.

'Thanks, love.' Mirko grabbed the cup of coffee and brought it closer to himself. 'Nothing much. You know it's hard for us old timers. I can't read. Neither can any of the other elders. So, we go by radio talk and rumours. From what I can tell, it's costing the Yugoslav government every time a migrant gets rehabilitated in a foreign land. I'm not sure of the details, but I think there's a political game being played, and the Communists just lost.'

'Interesting.'

Early the next day, Raj made his way to town and picked up a newspaper. There was a flurry around the public area and an energy among the townsfolk that Raj couldn't remember seeing before. It felt like people were speaking louder and faster than usual and even their movements seemed rushed and purposeful.

The only newspapers available were strictly controlled by the state but Raj knew the Communists couldn't hide any major European developments and would be forced to spin the words to make themselves seem in control. The front page confirmed Raj's suspicions. The heading was 'Spreading Yugo Culture To The Continent,' and the caption was atop a large picture of Tito on the podium at the United Nations. Raj continued to read:

> The Yugoslavian Government, under the auspicious leadership of Marshall Tito, has decreed a new Intercontinental Travel Law. In the interest of Greater Europe, and our western neighbours' desperate need for the might of the glorious Slavic labour force, passports for travel will be issued with new national standards. Travel papers will be processed quicker than ever before as the dwindling Capitalist economies desperately struggle to find precious workers to fill positions in all industries. Movement between borders will be eased in the hope that we can lead our brothers and sisters in Europe out of their dark and depressive struggle...

With the stroke of a pen, the government just overturned years of draconian migration laws and set Yugoslavia onto a new international path. Raj thought of all the poor souls that lost their lives attempting to escape this rotten system and how many of them unknowingly played a part in the development of this new national policy.

'Great news,' a familiar voice to Raj's left called.

'Bero.' Raj hadn't seen his older cousin in years and ran up to him and gave him a great hug. 'When did you get back?'

'We arrived this morning,' Bero answered. 'But more importantly, when did you get back?'

'It's been a few months already.' Raj had heard his cousin had been off to work on the coast but knew that was simply a cover story. 'It's good to see you.'

'You too, cousin.' Bero smiled and waved the newspaper in his hand. 'What about this?'

'I know. I never thought I'd see it.'

'I don't know if I can trust it.'

'What do you think it's all about?' asked Raj.

'The same thing its always about.' Bero smiled and put a hand around Raj's shoulders as they walked toward a cafe. 'Money!'

The two cousins sat and enjoyed Turkish coffee in the town's square. Raj told Bero of his adventures and time spent in the army. Bero let Raj know a little about his recent smuggling operation off the Dalmatian coast. It was a pleasant morning that felt like the dawning a new stage in Raj's life.

'And what of Krizan? Any news?' asked Bero as he drained his cup.

'Nothing recently,' Raj stated. 'But my parents did hear from him about a year ago.'

'Really? Well, that's good.'

'Yeah, apparently he his, or was, making his way to France.'

'France?' Bero sounded surprised. 'I don't think I know anyone in France.'

'Well you do now.' Raj laughed.

'Will you join him?' Bero tried to read the coffee remnants like the older women did.

'I don't know,' Raj had thought about it, 'I think my dad was right in the beginning; Germany is the way to go. How about you?'

'Not sure yet. I've got to see how my mother will handle another child leaving. Besides, my parents are little older and I'm scared they might not be able to maintain the land without me.'

'Fair enough,' Raj agreed. 'My parents are lucky to have Vlad. And the girls.'

'Vlad? Lucky?' Bero laughed this time. 'You serious?'

'I know the score, Bero. The eldest gets the farm, but Krizan is as good as gone. Vlad will get it even if he fucks everything up. Unless I want to be taking orders from him my whole life, I have to find my own way.'

'I understand,' Bero concurred.

'So, what do you really think is behind this whole change of rules from the commies?' Raj looked around as he asked to make sure no one was eavesdropping.

'Like I said, money. From what I heard, the UN is starting to charge the Yugos a fee for each refugee that is settled in a foreign land. And an ongoing tax until they take citizenship. You can imagine how much the commies are losing. But this way, there are no refugees, just working visas. So, it seems the commies are playing their own games to circumvent the west.'

'But why would they pay?' Raj asked. 'They don't seem to listen to anyone else, why the U.N. all of a sudden?'

'I'm sure there are trade deals, financial debt and who knows what other kind of sanctions that the west can enforce. Besides, how much money are the commies losing at the moment, just chasing all the people trying to escape? There would be tax issues too for many of these countries; how many of ours are dodging taxes over there and sending cash home at the expense of the locals? Besides, I'm sure the Russians are also playing a part in the push. There's not much the Red Army doesn't touch and who knows how many more spies can be sent via Yugoslavia if the laws change? I don't know what games are really being played in the corridors of power, but it seems they want more people moving around Europe again.'

'Well, I'm going to make a move soon just in case they change their minds,' Raj asserted. 'It kills me to say, but I don't think there's much left for me here.'

'In your shoes, I would do the same.'

They said their farewells and Raj wasn't sure when, or if, he would see his cousin again. It was well before midday when Raj arrived home. His mother greeted him with a big hug and kiss. And a letter.

'Who's this from?' asked Raj in surprise.

'Your oldest brother.' Kata had a tear in her eye and turned away as if ashamed that her son would see her cry.

'From Kriz?' Raj became excited and tore open the envelope.

Dear Raj,

I hear you have been on an adventure.

I hope you are doing well, brother. According to my calculations, you should have finished your military time by now and if everything is going to plan, then you should be preparing for your next adventure.

I have made my way to Lyon, in southern France. All is well here and I'm settling in slowly. There is plenty of work as the town continues to grow. There is a great sense of freedom here, far more than back home, and the people are very open minded. I am not going to state my exact address but if you are clever, and interested, one day you will be able to find me. If things remain as they are, I will never be able to return home. I'm receiving mail at the post office, so please write and stay in touch. I know Mum and Dad can't write without help but I know that you can, and I would love to hear from you regularly.

Don't let Vlad make any important decisions and don't let your heart bleed for him too much, he has a mean streak that is selfish at the best of times. I fear his future will not bode well and he will take everyone near him down too.

Be careful. Look after yourself, little brother, and continue your own adventure. Don't let anyone stop you. I hope we meet again someday soon.

With love,

Kriz

Raj wiped the tear away from his eye. It was a nice feeling to know that Kriz was well and had successfully escaped the clutches of the Communists, but after all this time, Raj would have liked to know more details; was Kriz really ever in Italy? Did Kriz complete his training into the priesthood? Was Raj even close to catching him on his travels? Raj understood the need for secrecy in the letter but still, he thought that this correspondence might offer some closure to the mystery of his brother's journey.

'Why are you crying for, you little girl?' Vlad teased as he walked into the living room.

'Stop it,' their mother admonished. 'It's from Krizan.'

'Oh,' Vlad continued unapologetically. 'The prodigal son has written, has he? When will he return? Will he bring all his riches with him?'

'Watch your mouth.' Their mother looked up from her chair, a little more seriously this time. 'He is your family, whether he is here or not. Show some respect.'

'Sure, sure.' Vlad backed off a bit. 'But where is his respect for us? He just disappears and expects us to hold down the farm on our own.'

'It's nice to hear from him, after all this time.' Raj wasn't looking for an argument. 'I do miss him.'

'We all do, dear,' his mother consoled.

'I missed him this morning when I was digging that channel for the pigs,' Vlad said cheekily. 'He would have been a great help.'

'You dug up a metre then complained how tired you were.' Raj's father walked in at that moment to set the record straight. 'I finished the rest while you disappeared.'

'Are you boys hungry?' Kata stood up and changed the subject. 'I'll put some eggs on.'

'Thank, Mum,' Raj answered.

'So, what does Kriz have to say?' Mirko inquired.

'He is in France and seems happy. He says there is greater freedom there. He is working, but he didn't mention specifics.'

'I thought you would be happier after hearing from him?' Raj's dad asked.

'I'm happy for him, but I was hoping for a few more details in the letter, that's all.'

'You will catch up again, I'm sure,' Mirko added hopefully. 'Then you can pick his brain all you like.'

'I'll have to go to him.' Raj understood his mother's sadness now.

'I know, son.'

'Why?' Vlad interjected, in his usual brusque style.

'He didn't spell it out, but he can't come back,' Raj answered, suddenly becoming aware that Kriz never wrote to Vlad directly.

'Meh' was all Vlad offered as he turned and walked out of the room.

Early the next day, Raj made his way to the town centre once more and joined the line of young men and women seeking exodus from the place they called home. A sadness grew within him at the spectacle; there was a sense of doom for the small town, as if the future of the place was being robbed by the new freedoms the government allowed. Raj knew he was as much to blame but what other options did the younger generation have in a place like this? Unless you were part of the system, there was no proper work available, no real education and no chance of prosperity. Even the most senior members of the Communist Party sent their children abroad to study, and rumour had it that much of the investments in the nation were pilfered to bank accounts in foreign nations. The greatest talent also went missing, either escaping with help from the west, or just being made to disappear by the government for standing out in a system that demands mediocrity. The small town of Siroki Brijeg now shared the same fate as many small towns in the country, Raj thought, and if the exodus continued, then the whole nation would surely share the same fate eventually.

It took three weeks for the migration papers to arrive and now all that held him back were the admittance papers from the German side. Others around town had already received all their documents, and the rumour was Germany was desperate for labour, so Raj was confident of his chances. Raj was in no hurry as it was well into winter now and the Christmas snows had fallen and continued to fall. Raj postponed his move until the spring of the following year not only due to the weather, but he also wanted to spend one more Christmas at home with his family. He had asked Vlad if he wanted to join him on his travels, but his older brother just showed disdain for the idea and a further separation seemed to grow between them at any mention of the matter.

Raj spent as much time as he could talking with both his mother and father. He didn't know what awaited him and, if like Kriz, he never got the chance to return, then he wanted to embed as much of his parents into his memory as he could. He knew they had the same feeling, and after losing one son to a foreign land, they probably felt the pain even more than Raj. He also spent time with his sisters too, but not so much with his brother. Vlad was often out socialising even in the most bitter weather, and when he was home, he was in a sour mood with no real inclination for chatter.

Once the snows abated, Raj felt his time was at hand. He methodically prepared his things over a few days in mid-February. The cold was breaking and he thought it would be a perfect time to make his way. The German temperature was even cooler than in southern Europe, so by the time he got to Munich, their cold should have started to ease, making employment opportunities greater as well.

His parents joined him at Sarajevo station on a cool but sunny morning. It was the first time his mother had seen a railway station in her life, but her eyes were solely fixed on Raj. The platform had others waiting too; a soldier, dressed in khaki green, carried his pack over one shoulder, a younger couple stood further away, hand in hand with their suitcases next to them and a younger man sat and smoked while reading a newspaper on a bench. Two inspectors, dressed in their dark uniforms, complete with officers' caps, ambled along the tarmac eyeing everyone around them. Raj thought about his previous adventure and was relieved that this time he no longer needed to look over his shoulder along the way, but he still fingered the paperwork in the pocket of his coat.

'I love you, son,' Kata said, and gave Raj a big hug and kissed him multiple times on both cheeks as the train moved into the station.

'I love you too, Mum,' Raj said, squeezing his mother close himself as she kissed him.

'You take care, son,' Mirko said and moved in to join the group hug. 'We will miss you. Be careful.'

'Thanks, Dad.' Raj kissed his father on the cheek. 'I'll write as soon as I arrive.'

The sun shone through the cabin windows as Raj waved to his parents. The train slowly began its movement north, through Bosnia, toward Croatia and beyond the once forbidden boundaries of the Communist nation. Raj was still nervous, a sense of disbelief remained within him, and probably would until he arrived at his destination. He was also far more excited than the last time he boarded a train because his travel was now mandated by the state. His destination was still foreign, but at least the Germans had a reputation of hard work and diligence, which was exactly what Raj was looking for in his life.

The future was finally promising, so Raj let himself relax into, and got comfortable for the journey. He looked to the mountains and forests in the distance and said a silent prayer; a prayer to keep himself and all his loved ones safe, wherever they were and whatever challenges they faced. He knew his parents still had the more difficult future under this regime, but with the rules for international travel becoming lax, Raj hoped it was the first step to many more freedoms for the combined Slavic people of Yugoslavia.

Shawline Publishing Group Pty Ltd
www.shawlinepublishing.com.au

SHAWLINE
PUBLISHING
GROUP

Printed in the USA
CPSIA information can be obtained
at www.ICGtesting.com
CBHW011458270624
10772CB00010B/115

9 781923 17